THE WHITEST WALL

A NOVEL

BOOTLEG BROTHERS TRILOGY - BOOK ONE

BY JODEE KULP

BETTER ENDINGS NEW BEGINNINGS

Published by:

Better Endings New Beginnings

Minneapolis, MN

763-531-9548 • www.betterendings.org

FIRST PRINTING – SEPTEMBER 2008

08 09 10 11 12 ~ DP/DD ~ 12 11 10 9 8 7 6 5 4 3 2

Printed in United States of America

ISBN   978-0-9637072-6-0

Library of Congress   2006901771

RIDDLES AND RIPPLES

IN THE BOOTLEG BROTHER'S TRILOGY
AN INVISIBLE SERIAL KILLER
RAVAGES THE MINDS,
HEARTS AND SPIRITS
OF THE INNOCENT AND
MORE THAN ONE KIND OF
DEATH IS REVEALED.

WHEN CARING PEOPLE
BECOME MINDFUL
HOPEFULLY THEY DO NOT TURN AWAY.

WHO IS AFFECTED?
IT MAY BE A SON OR DAUGHTER
A FATHER OR MOTHER
A BROTHER OR SISTER
YOUR FRIEND?

IT MAY BE YOU.

Better Endings New Beginnings
Selections

By Liz Kulp

Best I Can Be

By Jodee Kulp

Journey To Life

Families at Risk

Our FAScinating Journey

FASD Support Workbooks

Heartbreak

Bear In Mind

The Bootleg Brothers Trilogy

Book One - The Whitest Wall

Book Two - Tiger Butterfly — Sept 2009

Book Three - Different Beats — Sept 2010

By Stephen Neafcy

The Long Way to Simple

By Ann Yurcek

Tiny Titan

Dedicated to

Ivory — Emmy Lou Darling Horner Gallagher

1924-2003

Ebony — Mary Frances Rivera

1924- still going strong!

Finishing the race of life.

TABLE OF CONTENTS

Some people spend a lifetime sidestepping

the beauty of individuality and difference.

Others wrap their arms around diversity and

intimately embrace the sensitivity of spirit.

The sounds and characteristics of a culture, of a person and of a community are not a singular voice. Solidarity builds through the tapestry of individuality and difference. It is a process built through struggle, birthed in pain, tendered with care, and acknowledged with shouts of deference.

In the element of light, white is the addition of all colors. In the element of pigment, black is the element of all colors. In a multidimensional world the variations of additive and subtractive make us whole and our indifference grows when we cannot see. To break through the whitest wall, the screams of each character must expose their invisibilities.

We can no longer whisper.

INTRODUCING THE CAST

JOHNSON FAMILY

Emmett 'Doc' and Sally Johnson — (husband and wife) and Michael 'Mike',
    age seventeen. Doc is the local town chiropractor; Sally is an ER
    nurse. Cocker spaniel named Happy.

O'RILEY / KELLY FAMILY

Sam and Deb O'Riley — (husband and wife). Sam owns O'Riley Garage, Deb
    is an RN, Shaun (son) died two years ago at age twenty-nine.
    German shepherd named Sergeant Reg.

Sheriff Larry Kelly — County Sheriff, brother of Deb O'Riley.

HUNTER / PALMQUIST FAMILY

Jared and Alison 'Ali' Hunter — (husband and wife) Jared is a local farmer
    and Ali is the county social worker, their two daughters are in col-
    lege out of state. They live on the old family homestead with Gunner
    and Lucille Hunter (Jared's parents).

Gunner and Lucille 'Ma Lu' Hunter — Parents of Jared and Annie, Called
    'Bumpa' and 'Bobby Lu' by granddaughter Kissy. Old border collie
    named Kultz.

Hans Palmquist — Widower, father of Trapper. Called 'Bobpy P' by granddaughter
    Kissy.

Doug 'Trapper' and Annie Palmquist — (husband and wife) Trapper is a local
    bricklayer; Annie is a clerk at Hans Hardware (sister of Jared Hunter).
    They have one daughter April 'Kissy,' age four. Yellow Labrador named
    Lucy.

JONES FAMILY

Margie Jones — Single mother of Tasha, age sixteen, Quintell 'Q', age thirteen.

ABBOTT FAMILY

Kevin Abbott — Transient, age twenty-one.

John and Lydia Abbott — (husband and wife) Kevin's parents.

WATKINS FAMILY

LaMar and Tamara Watkins — (husband and wife) LaMar is a forensic psychologist, Tamara is a Montessori teacher, Shayna, age four, and Johnny, age one. Chocolate standard poodle named Harry.

Reginolt 'Reggae' and Tina Watkins— (husband and wife) Reggae owns a recording studio in Minneapolis, Tina is a paralegal for a large legal firm, They are the parents of LaMar and the grandparents of Shayna and Johnny who refer to them as Granddaddy 'Bups' and 'Granny T.' German shepherd named Corporal S, also referred to as Chorus.

COMMUNITY MEMBERS

Eddie Schultz — Local beloved middle-aged gentleman who works at Hans Hardware and has a rescued mongrel named Blue.

CLERGY

Pastor Wilson — Lutheran Church of Peace
Father Flanagan — Riverdale Catholic Church
Reverend Anderson — Riverdale Methodist Church

FOREWORD

What you don't know won't hurt you is a lie.

...a big lie.

Knowledge is still power, and the power found in these pages is undeniable. When Jodee Kulp began to explain the insidiousness of Fetal Alcohol Spectrum Disorders (FASD) I did not get it. I could not sympathize. It was too much like an out of control virus that was taking over the world. But when I began reading the life stories of the characters in this book I became educated vicariously, without knowing it. The strength of story could not be better illustrated than within these pages. Full, rich, deep personalities walk through your imagination close to your family while this epic-like volume clings to your heart.

You will want to pick up the phone and call each one to say, "I'm right here, and I understand, or watch out." The identity of these characters becomes so personal you just know you are reading their memoirs.

Fiction, as C.S. Lewis stated so well, 'adds to reality, not just describes it. It enriches daily life and irrigates the deserts of our lives.' I found *"Whitest Wall"* so compelling I wanted to jump to the end, but I'm so glad I didn't.

Life is complex and lives are intertwined to a greater degree than we think. We tend to be myopic, critical, judgmental, and basically self-absorbed, or is that just me? Jodee Kulp is so adept at casting the players in *Whitest Wall* and so passionate a story teller you will look at your neighbor through different eyes. I believe there are many books in this book and I trust at least there are many more books coming from Jodee.

Mac McConnell

LET'S BEGIN . . .

He screamed

projecting full power.

This was different.

The whiteness had no escape.

Emerald green terror filled his gaze darting from floor to bed, wall to ceiling. His eyes saw nothing though he knew he was not blind. He had been here before. His demon – the whitest wall – had returned for a face-off. He screamed powerfully to escape. The door, locked for safe-keeping, imprisoned the whiteness.

Isolated.

He shrieked hoping to unlock his sleep.

Abandoned.

His father was lost, his dog dead.

He burst through the whitest wall into the light.

"Yes! Light!"

"But, the whiteness stays?"

"Alone."

There was one difference.

▼

His sleeves were orange.

1

THE LAST HAND

Second by second a droning quietness filled the halls of the Riverdale Hospital. The eleven to seven was a hard shift when you weren't used to it and as hard as Sally Johnson tried to stay alert, by 5:30 A.M. she was dragging. Her ICU patients slept peacefully. Monitors displayed vitals. The trauma gowns hung untouched and the ambulance sat in the garage under the dim emergency sign. She rubbed her face and then poured another cup. Easy shifts were the hardest. Too bad, the excitement of a baby insisting to be born at some ungodly hour never arrived. Small town weeknights were always quiet, too quiet, and though she graciously changed hours with best friend Deb O'Riley, she preferred her busy dayshifts. They'd met twenty years earlier in nursing school and through Deb's husband Sam, she was introduced to her future handsome husband Emmett Gunnert Johnson, called Doc.

Deb and Sam's decade plus of marriage already had an eleven-year-old red-headed pixie who was more than a dickens filled with endearing charm and spontaneous charge. Initially, Sally thought it was poor parenting, but as they grew together as couples she understood the creative skill Deb and Sam used to parent him. Something inside the child seemed short circuited. Her son, Mike, fourteen years younger claimed Shaun as his best friend and Shaun protectively watched over her little guy.

Then one day, despite the years separating the boys, she noticed Mike caretaking adult Shaun and that very day life spun out of control. The accident took Shaun's life, but spared Mike and their previously unflawed friendship suffered.

Sally drew in a deep breath imagining a wisp of air sneaking through the secured hospital window. She visualized Doc bustling in the kitchen sharing bites of peanut butter toast with Happy, their cocker spaniel. Seventeen-year-old Mike would be in school, and if Doc didn't have an early appointment, his embrace would linger. Her tired body anticipated his strong arms, warm hands, and encouraging voice. Doc's hands were his profession, and as the town's chiropractor, he knew exactly how to soothe her tired muscles and release her pressure points. She hoped to arrive before he left for the clinic. But if not, then she planned to curl up with Happy under the down comforter to sleep late into the day.

"Oh sweet sleep."

Doc's colonial blue eyes still had that devilish twinkle, and his lips curled into a smile every time she entered a room. He built her a Courier & Ives dream home with a riverstone fireplace and they enjoyed this new life season of long walks by the ravine with Happy and simple times cuddled by their blazing fire in silence. Their burning romance, lit that first night, remained bright and needed little to flame up.

▼

Sally hummed turning her red Escort up the winding tree-lined path. A row of blackbirds, perched like clothespins on the telephone wire, seemed to await a clean wash over Happy slinging her tail to greet her. But instead of the normal jump on Mom, the dog twisted and turned two tight circles in front of the brillant sumac, country living in autumn was breathtaking.

"Happy, what kind of greeting is that?" Sally bent down to rustle the soft fur. "Come on girl. You ready for bed?"

She stopped. Mike's work boots were set on the porch. "Funny, I put those in the house and he was in bed when I left for work." She shook her head, making a mental note and closed the door.

"Head to bed, Happy. Coast is clear. "

Happy pawed at the front door.

"You were just out. Come on."

The dog sat super-glued to the floor.

"Happy, come! I'm tired. "

The dog whimpered.

"What's wrong? You leave a rabbit outside? I can't let you out alone, you'll do naughty dog stuff."

Happy tried digging a hole under the door!

"What's wrong girl? You got a dog idea? My, you're silly."

The cocker sat on Sally's feet.

"Ok, show me, but let me change first."

The mutt was antsy. Up, down. Whimper. Whimper.

Sally put on her sweats as the dog ran downstairs barking and then poked her calf with his nose. She pocketed her cell phone.

Happy crashed through the door and loped towards the woods, returning to tug on her pants. "Ok, ok, I'm coming, so much for bed."

▼ SAM

"It's 7:45 Riverdale! Looks like it's a nice fall day folks. You're listening to KYCR River Country Radio." The morning coolness was departing.

Sam O'Riley removed his headset, flipping his red embroidered cap to the ground. He'd been waiting forty-five minutes! At last night's card game Doc said 7:00 A.M. Doc was never late and Sam hated waiting. He rubbed his leg. Seven was seven and for the last thirty odd years Doc's reliability was as sound as Sam's new credit card guzzling gas pumps where day and night people inserted plastic cards to buy gas. Still, he liked personal touches and hiring Kevin Abbott was a good idea. The kid needed work and since no one knew much about him, no one wanted to hire him. Most people saw a rough city gangsta' with a cocked hat attitude.

Sam didn't.

"Hi! My name's Kevin. I need a job. I can do anything."

Sam was struck by the way Kevin walked without picking up his feet. His son Shaun had the same shuffle. No matter what Sam tried, his son's feet refused to leave earth's gravity.

"Can you work the counter, kid?"

"Sure. I'm really good with customers. Had a lot of customers in my city job." Spontaneously Kevin ran out the door to greet Mrs. Carlson. "Good morning, may I help you? Let me fill your tank. You look pretty today. Nice dress. Can I get your windshield." Kevin filled the tank, washed her windows, and followed her to the counter.

"Nice energetic fellow you got Sam. Reminds me of Shaun, Lord bless his soul." Old Mrs. Carlson gulped as if she let the cat out of the bag, paid her bill and quickly drove away. A memory chill ran down Sam's back, was God giving him a second chance? He and Deb were too old to start another family, and Shaun's death, well . . .

"Kevin, is that your name?"

"Yes sir."

"Hmm, I'll see what you can do. One day at a time. How's six bucks an hour to get started?" Sam watched.

Kevin smiled, "Can I start today?"

"Looks like you already have." Strange? Shaun would have said the same thing. "Here, wear these," Sam hesitated and pulled out Shaun's small-sized O'Riley Garage jumpsuit and red hat, lovingly holding it's brim.

"No way, man, I ain't wearing that. It will mess my style."

"My way or the highway little buddy," Sam wasn't playing.

Kevin pulled on the jumpsuit, donned the red hat, cocked it to the left and ran to the pumps, "Hi! Yo, my name's Kevin. Can I fill your tank? Clean your windshield? Need a soda? How 'bout diet?" his smile was infectious and he made small talk until the rain started.

"Hey, Sam I can't work when it's raining?"

"What you say, boy?"

"I can't work. It's wet outside."

Sam laughed, "It's six bucks an hour rain, snow, or shine. Take it or leave now." He offered an ugly plaid umbrella.

Kevin learned to answer the phone when Sam was under a car, ferry shop tools, and keep the garage clean. He was nice to have around, hyperactive, but did just as you told him. Sam liked that. He tried teaching him the simple mechanics of changing a tire, but Kevin cussed like Hollywood every time something didn't go as expected. It seemed for Kevin, like his son Shaun, many things didn't go right. No sense asking him to check the oil; dipsticks changed places in every car, and neither kid had a chance in heaven to find it. Some things were easier to do yourself; besides Sam knew every vehicle in Riverdale and each customer by face.

Sam's vehicle repair reputation was renowned and since Kevin arrived, every vehicle was clean and vacuumed before the customer paid the bill. He liked that about Kevin, after you showed him a few times how to do it, there were no surprises as long as Sam kept everything clear and simple. In some ways Kevin was easier than Shaun because whatever silly, obnoxious behavior Kevin exhibited, Sam didn't take it personal since he wasn't his father.

"I can't believe God created two of the same kind of goofballs every thought in their heads flies out their mouths."

Sam glanced at his watch. "Time for work, got a grease job regardless if Doc's got a time problem." He snatched up his hat to walk across the street and call Doc's cell. Maybe someday he'd get a cell phone.

Sam rustled through the mail and circulars, and then dialed Doc. No answer. He left a message, "Hey buddy, where are you? Thought we had a meeting. You still mad I won the last hand?"

Doc promised Sam he'd be available whenever Sam needed him and set a Sam-only ringtone. He respected Doc for keeping the secret. The last thing he needed was Sally figuring out something was going on and telling Deb. On most days the men's stealthiness ran like clockwork. Sally left for her hospital day shift at 6:30 A.M. and Doc and Sam met at the clinic around 7:00 A.M. before Deb arrived home at 7:30 A.M. to sleep. Since the clinic opened at 10:00 A.M., no one seemed wiser to the . . . Sam dialed Johnson Chiropractic clinic. Closed.

Then he dialed Doc's home.

Ring . . . At 8:30 A.M. there was still no Kevin.

Ring . . . It was one of those days.

Ring . . . He didn't leave a message.

▼

Sally heard a familiar ringtone following Happy to the ravine. She stopped. Happy vanished into the brush. Her eyes searched for the dog.

"Oh my God," her hand clasp her mouth, "Could it be a heart attack?" She saw the familiar red and black wool lumberjack shirt Doc wore to walk Happy. She ran hoping to help the love of her life.

Happy licked Doc's face.

As an emergency RN, there were few in Harris County better than Sally. If not too much time had passed, and not too much damage, there was a chance she could save him. He was strong and healthy except for German high blood pressure.

Doc lay in a fetal position. She dropped to her knees to take his pulse . . . his right hand gone! This was no hunting accident, three points of entry and departure showed on what remained of his wrist. It was obvious a large amount of blood was lost; his skin was pale. Cool. She unbuttoned his shirt; the area over his heart was flooded with cold blood, a clean bullet wound in perfect position pierced his heart.

The daily strength she rallied for medical crises evaporated into heartbreak as she brushed back her hair. Denial separated reality into a madness that poured like an icy ache into the hole growing within her. She took the phone clutched in Doc's left hand and pressed send to return the missed call. Happy lay next to his master whimpering. Sally crumpled.

▼

Sam banged his head on the car hood as he ran to get the phone. "O'Riley's Garage. We Service Better."

"No! No God. No!" It was Sally.

The caller ID said M, Doc's code. Something seemed very wrong.

"Sally can you hear me? Are you all right? Where's Doc?"

Sam heard Happy whine.

Sally gasped, "Oh Lord, no!"

"Hang on Sally, I'm coming!" Sam hurriedly locked the garage and high-tailed out of town in his tow truck. Shoot! Why didn't he have a cell phone? What if someone was hurt? Stupid . . . stupid . . . stupid! What if his penny pinching self cost another life?

Sally's car was parked in the drive. The house door was open. Sam slammed on the brakes and ran onto the porch.

"Doc! Sally! Happy?" he bellowed.

In the distance Happy barked. Sam ran toward the alert. Conflicted he ran back in the house and called emergency.

"911. May I help you?" Jill Jenson was a fixture at Harris County dispatch and it was good to hear her voice.

"Jill, something's happened out at Doc Johnson's. I need help. Sally called but couldn't talk. She was crying. His dog's barking up a storm in the woods. Send Larry. We might need an ambulance."

Sam hung up and ran to the dog. "Happy, good girl," the furry face was bloody. "Where's Dad? Where's Mom?"

Frantic, the dog twisted down the deer path.

"Sally!" Sam raised his voice, "Sally, it's Sam!"

Sally lay across a fallen figure. She raised her death-stained face, her hair wet with tears, her sweatshirt soaked in blood.

Sam felt a weight heavier than a car hoist fall upon his shoulders. "Oh, oh no! Sally are you alright?"

She nodded.

He knelt beside her, "I've called 911."

She fell into his arms, "He's been shot. He's gone," she lacked words and fought for air. Sally tightened her arms around Sam, "I can't save him!"

Once again Sam's life was surrounded by horror, and pain. "We'll find who did this Sally. He will pay." A flashback of Shaun's head broken against the maple triggered wretched memories.

Sally's vacant eyes startled him. His worn hands gently wiped her bloodied cheeks. The sound of large vehicles rumbled up the drive.

Sally's head fell to his shoulder. He held his best friend's widow securely. Doc dead? He trusted her expertise. Her large pupils reflected the dark eyes of Sergeant Reg calling him to duty. Doc's hand lay a distance from his body. Sam's skills returned as he penetrated and scanned the forest . . . transfixed in a hundred yard stare, watching . . . listening . . . sucking details. Haunting questions of past fused into present. He squinted to get a better look at the wounds. Senseless.

It was a long time ago, but he had been in such a place before, huddled together . . . waiting for the Sheriff, the paramedics . . . and Sgt. Reg held him waiting for the Huey . . . and the investigators . . . the medics.

Something snapped. His left leg fallen asleep . . . a million army ants running, crawling, eating . . . his leg hot and cold. His heart tortured.

Happy ran to see who was coming.

Festering anger and flashes of utter cruelty . . . a rainstorm of blood, soldiers and children, women and old, slaughtered. Death was ugly.

Happy returned and rested his bloody head on Doc.

Blurred, Sam walked with Sheriff 'Larry' Kelly to the house. "Got any ideas, Sam?"

"Nope."

"You know if Doc hurt someone in his practice?"

"Doc's hands were his profession. Deals sealed with handshakes."

"Doc break a deal?"

Sam didn't answer.

"Tell me about last night Sam."

"Sally worked the late shift to cover for your sister. Doc invited me up to play cards so I wasn't alone. His kid, Mike, got in sometime after nine, ate our pizza and went to study in his room. Said he was going to school early to pump iron. I left around ten. Sally was getting ready for work."

"What did you drink Sam?"

"You insinuating we were drinking Larry. Hell, I haven't had a drink in thirty years!" Sam stopped. "Sodas damn it, we drank sodas!"

"How do Mike and Doc get along?"

"Fine Larry, just like any other dad and soon-to-be-emancipated teen son. I don't have any more to say to you." Sam nodded toward Sally, slumped on the kitchen chair. Ali Hunter, the social worker, was helping her clean up.

"Don't worry, Sam, I'll take care of it."

Sam watched the paramedics jump out of the ambulance. Men in uniforms ran tape to cordon through the woods and across the drive. Last time Sam saw that yellow tape Doc busted it placing first in the Riverdale Marathon forty plus category. He stared numbly as the forensic team donned disposable suits and latex gloves.

The Johnson yard soon filled with every squad car in the county, the ambulance, the photographer's truck, Ali and Jared's minivan, Pastor Wilson's Beetle, Sally's Escort and why not a firetruck. Larry sent an armed guard to the end of the drive, registering whom, why, where, and how, anyone was to be let in. It was dizzying.

"Hey Sam, I'll drive you and your truck home?" It was Ali's husband Jared making the offer.

"Good idea," Larry agreed.

Sam climbed into his tow truck. Silent.

Jared wound down the drive, past Porter Potts' scrap yard, between Hunter cornfields and over the bridge. Gleason's hearse passed.

"The coroner will declare Doc deceased," Jared offered a feeble statement.

"Everyone knows that," Sam mumbled.

"Turn the investigation over to the police as an official homicide."

"It's official. The Johnson sanctuary is a forensic circus." Sam's unsolved past rose like waves against a rocky shore, smashing memories against his skull. He needed a drink and the sheriff opened a closed . . .

"You okay Sam?"

The small talk was as irritating as a mosquito buzzing around your head. "Jared, I'm fine. Leave me alone!"

Jared shut up.

Sam scanned the boulevard of prisoner elm trees thirsting for release. Their gray tentacle fingers screamed against the injustice of the day. Golden leaves fell like bottle caps against neon orange deathring shackles. As Jared turned into his drive, Deb's healthy orange maple heckled and Sam mentally chopped it down. Deb loved that tree filled with O'Riley history, his story he wanted silenced. To Deb, fall triggered jumping off tire swings into leaf piles and memories of Shaun's happy childhood. To Sam, autumn smelled of jungle defoliation showers in Agent Orange and getting drunk.

The truck stopped. Sam cleared his throat, took a deep breath and got out. He stood as tall as his prosthesis allowed to offer a proper handshake. He knew Jared missed his devastation signals. "The crime tape banned you Jared. You were too young for 'Nam. You can't understand without seeing?"

Sam held back. His soul staggered, "I'm the one covered in blood."

Sam stepped up his porch steps with a limp.

▼

Behind the radial saw in the basement woodshop sat a dusty brown paper bag. "Almost thirty years," he purred. The two brown bottles had waited. Sam carried them upstairs. He set the radio to pre-game. The glass glistened on the oak kitchen table. The blood on his face, from Sally's hair, waved dark red on the curves. Each silver label paved a ticket to his past. Sam smirked in the reflection.

Reg the Third, his German shepherd offered calming signals licking his lips. The dog's eyes convicted him.

Sam grabbed both bottles.

"One life lost, another lost life," he sneered.

Reg puppy bowed to divert the dangerous situation. It didn't work.

Sam leaned against the refrigerator slowly sliding to the floor.

Deb, his wife, was in the city.

Doc, his best friend, was dead.

Shaun, his only child, was dead.

His dog. What does a dog know?

Alone. He was alone.

Reg yawned sorrowfully.

Sam mechanically peeled back the foil paper and with each shred ripped away the protection of sobriety. He snarled and caressed the cap.

The naked spirit in the bottle taunted to twist open demons on a path of difficult return. His hand trembled as he turned the golden cover.

Released! He flicked it high and it spun back hard won seasons. Silent, it hit the trashcan.

Reg placed a pleading paw on Sam's leg. The dog sighed.

The brandy's heavenly scent rose like a genie from a bottle and floated into the locked memories of his middle brain, bypassing logic and promises.

"You son of a bitch, you got the last hand." Doc's last words echoed, hand . . . hand . . . hand.

Sam lifted the bottle to his lips, "To Doc!"

Fire blazed down his parched throat.

It had been years since he'd had a drink and he drank both pints.

2

THE LAST HURRAH

News travels small town fast, and Michael Johnson didn't need to hear of his father's murder in the high school locker room. "Slow is fast, Larry. Take it slow," Pastor Wilson sermoned Larry before he fetched Mike from Riverdale high school. "Everything comes in due time."

"Yeah, guess so," the sheriff replied, feeling about as slow as a racehorse at the starting gate. "Speed isn't going to resuscitate him. Doc's father's 1974 case is still unsolved."

Once again, an officer found what looked like the slug of a .44. The bullet wounds appeared deliberate and precise, a .44 punches a big hole. Hans from the hardware said Doc and Mike held Minnesota small game licenses and Doc owned a .44 Remington Magnum rifle. It was a quick handling rifle for a whitetail, but it wasn't deer season. A local early morning hunter would have used a shotgun to shoot a grouse he'd kicked up. There was no reason for a .44 to be anywhere but on the gun range.

"Take your time," Wilson patted Larry's shoulder, "Slow down, use that new Palm Pilot." Pastor turned and walked toward the school.

Larry had served as county sheriff for fifteen years, knew everyone and everyone knew him. He was a fair man to the average Joe and one look in his eyes expressed the man before the uniform. He remembered what it was like to be a teen, to be poor, to be drunk, to be angry. He stood as the proud admiral of the oldest jail in the state of Minnesota. Small. So small, filled, it held only sixteen prisoners.

Larry and his boys tolerated a bit of liquor with the kids, but no drugs. He ran a clean county and no underage drinker wanted a ride home from a party with the sheriff listening to his 'why you shouldn't do what you were doing' speech and 'I oughta knock on your door and wake up your parents' which he often did. Larry relished private talks with the youth to gain missing links to unsolved cases. He christened himself premier designated driver and while no one called it campaigning by all rights it did the same thing and no one got hurt. Larry never wasted his money on printing ink. Rumor was, even if he didn't run next election, he'd get enough write-ins to keep his job.

Lucky for Larry, the commissioners were required to approve the budget and figure out how to follow state and federal mandates, but had little say in how he ran his office. If the County Board didn't like the way he did things, "They could take their politics."

▼

"Nice rig for a sixteenth birthday present from a dad," Larry sauntered over to Mike's truck. "Too bad, the kid's such a hot head." More than once a squad pulled Mike over with warnings to take it easy and his recklessness had increased after the four-wheeler accident with Shaun, but Larry's boys knew how to handle local ruffians.

Larry opened the truck cab taking a cursory look for contraband finding a few Marlboro butts, a green chamois cloth, a virgin Newport, some empty Pepsi One cans, a couple tennis balls, and the metal screw-in piece of a light bulb. He didn't find any beer cans. 'Strange, usually Mike keeps the inside of his truck spiffy.

"An empty condom wrapper?" Larry had expected Mike to sow oats, but without Doc to ride his back, he decided a few alpha dog to puppy chats were in order by the sheriff. Rumor had it Mike had the hots for Amber Carlson, but neither kid needed to be shanghied by a baby.

The hay filled truck bed looked in order for the Apple Fest parade, except . . . a city-slicker tennis shoe stuck out between two bales. Larry kept an eagle eye on his town and shoes were important. Larry grabbed the shoe. The only person he knew who wore those shoes was that goofy kid who worked for Sam. Larry took pride in minutia.

"Shit dawg, don't wake me up. It's too early! You on white man's time?" Under the top row of hay bales and between the two neat rows smelling of vomit and beer, was a very hung over, but alive, Kevin Abbott.

"Get out here now!" Larry bellowed. "What the hell you sleeping there for?" He slammed down the tailgate and pulled Kevin from the truck. "Get up! Arms in the air!" He wasn't sure if he had a good reason to detain Kevin.

Kevin's arrogance vanished, "Oh, officer. I'm sorry, officer, Sir, Sheriff, Sir, I musta' fallen asleep last night. Mom told me I should never, never, ever never drink," he slurred.

"What time was that?" Larry took out his Palm and selected the notepad he already kept on the kid. The file was at the tip of his stylus.

"Huh?" Kevin whispered, "It was dark."

"Where were you?"

"I dunno, some woods."

"Who were you with?"

"I dunno, Mike and a mess of kids."

"What were you doing?"

"They like my dancing," Kevin beamed.

"How many kids?"

"Lots."

"How many?"

"I dunno."

"Got ID?"

Kevin handed the sheriff an old student ID card.

He looked fourteen. He was twenty-one. "Got any other ID?"

He handed the sheriff a shabby social security card and wallet.

Larry took the wallet finding a ten-dollar bill, a stress mood card, a photo of Margie's daughter Tasha, a picture of an unknown adult woman with a small boy on her lap, an old family photo of two adults with a younger Kevin sitting between them, and a half-smoked flattened Newport cigarette.

"That's Mom and Dad," Kevin smiled pointing to the family photo.

"Got names?"

"Uh, Lydia and John Abbott. I lost them."

"I got to pat you down, make sure you don't have any weapons," Larry checked for unusual rips and blood. The kid flinched when touched which ignited Larry's mind with questions. Stay calm Larry. "Kevin, I might want you to come down to my office and talk later. I don't want you going nowhere."

Kevin teetered.

"I said get out of here!"

"No you didn't."

"Out! Go! You hear me!" Larry growled. "Skedaddle!"

He pushed Kevin.

"Cops can't hit people!" Kevin rocked toward Larry.

"Oh for cryin' out loud, go!" The sheriff puffed his chest and placed his hand on his sidearm. Kevin ran.

Larry patted his PDA, the nifty contraption offered reassurance when his middle-age brain had holes. He added a note hoping he hadn't let a prime suspect go, but to detain or question him could start a kangaroo court and Doc didn't deserve that.

▼ KEVIN

Kevin shuffled toward town in a bad mood. His head hurt, his feet felt buzzy, and when his feet went buzzy he wanted to fight. "Margie said, no cussing in Riverdale. Sure feel like cussing." People thought it funny when he reorganized his swears. He kicked the dirt, "Can't cuss, can't cuss. Sam's the boss. Sam said I wasn't a sailor, so no cussing."

He did two unbalanced jumping jacks and slapped the side of this head. "Oh flipping jack rabbits."

"I was sleeping in puke? How come I was in Mike's truck? Mike probably took care of me." They had been friends now for a week. "I hate when I black out. Lucky for me I met Mike. It was lucky when Mike's truck came into O'Riley's Garage for brakes. Doc wanted Mike safe. Told me to spiff it up parade special. Spiff it up I did. Spiff. Spiffy, spiff I did." Kevin danced as though buffing a car. "Made it shine."

"Doc's an asshole," he covered his mouth with his hand. "Can't swear. Can't swear! I mean DANCE HALL!" He shouted. "Doc's a dance hall!" and shuddered, "Doc wanted to hit me. I know it. Sam didn't see the low-low truth. Told me to quit grumbling. Grumble I did. I will teach him a lesson. Grumble grumbling! Grumble, mumble, fumble. DUMB BELL! I only put a rag on Mike's hood."

Kevin spun, "How can cloth hurt paint? Man, Mike's my friend. He'll throw me some good candy. Gotta be nice. Gotta be nice to him. Mike's a someone, class president, quarterback. Smart. Looks good with Amber Carlson. Amber and her girls. . . . oh eee . . . bouncing and throwing candy. Gonna sit next to Tasha and catch me goodies."

The stones created a moving picture of Mike and Amber, two big white stones. He walked carefully around them. Twice.

"Breasts!" Kevin waltzed. "Amber's got big ones. Saw 'em waiting for submarine races. Mike and Amber came too, only they were watching each other," he giggled. "I waited. They was squirrels. Drank a beer and stayed hidden. Watching," he chuckled again. "Can't swear. Flocking. They was squirrel flocking. Flocking squirrels they was."

His feet slid, "Fight the Sheriff. Revenge isn't fighting. Revenge is revenge. Pinky promised Tasha I'd stop fighting."

Kevin tripped on his pant leg switching his brain to a new channel.

"Found the burner under the seat. Mike hid it, but I found it. Thick pretty green chamois cloth under the seat." He anxiously butterfly flapped his hands near his head. "Mike told me open it. He called it Blackhawk, said it was a dandy hunting handgun. Clean, accurate kills at a hundred yards."

"Wonder how you shoot a hundred yards? That's a lot of houses," Kevin pointed his index finger, thumb up toward an old fence post. "Shot a hundred beer cans. I did. I did. Dirty Harry!" He danced. "Pow, ca-pow, pow, pow!" He shot the sky.

"Mike has mad respect. Pow, ca-pow! A hot boy .44!" Kevin shook his arm remembering the recoil buzz. "Smoke and gravel, kickin' up the hill. Shot the gun twice. Cool black shooting gloves. Mike said 'Hey little buddy, want to party down at the kegger.'"

Kevin shook his phantom tingles. "So, I said, a chocolate caker? I hate people laughing at me. Mike said 'It's okay little buddy, you remind me of Shaun,' that's what Sam says too." He kicked the street hoping his toes turned on his brain.

"Called me dance bandit. Someone said that when I juked. Puked. Musta drank too much brewski from the metal can Mike called the kegger. I traded my smokes for beers. Never found the cake. Sure like chocolate, don't do drugs."

"Chief ordered his send away boyz to stay away from drugs. Mike poured a white powder from a tennis ball into the broken glass bowls. Friends can trick you. Chief said that!"

Kevin patted himself on the back, "I said, no thank you, Mike."

His foot kicked the curb and he fell on his face in front of two big boots.

"Going somewhere?" It was Larry.

3

THREE STRIKES

Alcohol's sensuous spirit wrapped its arms around Sam and sometime before the last inning of the World Series, he passed out. He dreamed of riding a Harley out of Riverdale and never looking back. Motorcycles were out of the question, at twenty-one he didn't care about anything, though he tried to fake it for Mom.

"Deb? Beautiful?" Sam watched Deb Kelly bounce onto his front porch. It appeared the neighbor girl gained womanhood while his life detoured.

"Sam, Deb's here with a plate of cookies. Do you care if she comes in?" Mom was happy he was alive.

"Don't care," he mumbled.

Deb, sassy as ever, stood in front of his pathetic wheelchair holding his favorite, still warm, chocolate chip cookies. Sam looked up.

"I made cookies. I remember you liked them. Can I come and visit you sometimes? I am glad you're home." She exhaled four well-rehearsed lines.

He wished he joined his buddies in heaven or hell, rather than exist in the limbo of Riverdale. Sam closed his eyes mustering a somber, "Thanks." Home? He felt guilty to be alive. A purple heart didn't fill the black hole in his chest.

"See you around," Deb set the cookies on the end table, and skipped out the door. She knew Sam would heal. In her imagination they'd marry, raise a family and live happily ever after. She persistently brought him fresh-baked treats and encouraged him to talk about a war he refused to share. She wrote jokes and hid them under his coffee cup on the windowsill. She wrote poetry and stuck pictures in his mailbox.

She clung to her fantasy as tightly as Sam held on to his secret – to walk and ride out of Riverdale on a Harley to look for pieces he left blown up in the steaming jungles of 'Nam.

No matter what amount of combat despondence waged against him, the darkness of his heart was no match for Deb's sparkling blue eyes, sandy brown hair and flirting smile. Sam buried the screams and deathly silence that ricocheted in his head. He refused to disclose the atrocities of humans against humans. He damned the 'special' behavior modification training that made it easy to pull the trigger. His achievement of 90% shoot to kill was nothing to be proud of when he sat in a wheelchair. He wished he had shot overhead, then he'd be dead, but he wouldn't be cursed. Two worlds ago he left Riverdale High a lettered athlete, now he wasn't even sure if he was still a man. On the field his skills provided safety, back home he questioned the insanity of war.

Deb's unconditional love eroded his armor and bit-by-bit she weaseled into his life. Then one day she boldly planted herself on his lap, grabbed his cheeks softly in her hands, and attacked him with a passionate kiss. He surrendered. Feelings and abilities he believed exploded in the steamy tropics arose. Could the passion he felt for the dark haired rice paddy beauty be transferred to Deb? Deb was pure innocence.

▼

Reg the Third barked.

▼

Sam watched the delivery man carry a holey box to his porch.

"What on earth are we going to do with this?" His mother smiled curiously as she placed the panting package on his lap.

A short yelp jolted the ringing in his ears. He reached into the bag attached to the arm of his chair carefully avoiding the plastic resemblance of a foot to get his pocketknife. Cautiously he undid the strapping. The box exploded in jumping fur. A brown and black tail wagged so hard the furball almost fell to the floor.

Sam smiled for the first time since he had come home. The most beautiful German shepherd puppy he had ever seen licked his face. He rubbed the puppy's ears as hot urine soaked his shirt. "I should call you Pisser."

His mother scowled and handed him the *DOD Working Dog Program Trainers Manual*. Sam read the note stapled to the flyleaf.

Good Morning Corporal.

My name is Reg; carefully bred from a long line of field working dogs. My great, great, great, great grandfather carried medical supplies and water in saddlebags for the Red Cross in World War I. He searched and dragged wounded men to safety or carried an item from the soldier in his mouth to signal he had found someone injured. He led rescue teams to survivors. An uncle was trained to parachute and scout the front lines for land mines as a detector K-9. He fearlessly searched the tunnels, and was trained to attack. He guarded the camp and carried messages through enemy fire in Vietnam. He was among the ranks of 4,000 mighty Dog Scouts.

My world is significantly different from yours. I have been bred for my keen sense of smell, endurance, speed, strength, courage, intel;-ligence, and adaptability in almost any climactic condition. My vision is inferior to yours, yet I can detect movement, however slight, at greater distances. I depend on my superior senses of hearing and smell.

My working dog training begins by establishing the handler - dog relationship through constant close association — feeding, groom-ing, exercise and play. This develops my natural instinct for compan-ionship. Once this relationship has begun to develop, basic obedience training is introduced and must never stop. Patience, firmness, repeti-tion, reward, and correction will always be a part of our life together. Of these factors, patience is the most important.

You, Corporal O'Riley, the handler, must never lose your patience and become irritated, or Reg will become confused and hard to handle. He does not understand right and wrong according to human stan-dards. The dog is never allowed to suspect that there is any correct response except total obedience. In return, Reg will remain a loyal, devoted guardian to you and your family.

Department of Defense Military
Working Dog Program, Reg.

No name was attached, perhaps the name Reg held a clue — Sergeant Reg, the man who saved his pitiful life, one of 9,000 military dog handlers.

▼

The puppy pulled on everything — his sock, his wheels and his heart. Alligator teeth attacked his safe corner, chewed his leather boot and charmed Deb who came each day to pet the ragamuffin. Sam moved his chair from a dark corner to the sunny porch and on a particularly beautiful day he accepted Deb's invitation to push him to the park while Reg puppy-strutted alongside to the top of the panoramic riverbank. Then, in a moment of spontaneity, Deb jumped onto his lap and accidentally released the brake. It was a swift amusement park ride over the edge and the two of them shot down the hill crashing into a heap on the mossy bank near the rustling Dale River. Reg frolicked with jumps and dives, and licks and wiggles. Sam embraced Deb enjoying the moment, her blouse unbuttoned exposing a firm breast. His disability no longer mattered. He caressed her face, smelled her hair and in the moss softness their unexpected union created new life. Shaun was conceived and Sam rebirthed. He offered Deb a drink from his flask to celebrate a life commitment. And then, in the healing waters of the Dale River, they swam naked.

That summer Sam and Deb spent beloved hours in their moss-laden hovel, loving and laughing, kissing and drinking. Sam's heart began healing and the loud memories quieted, taunting him only in the wee night hours with chopper sounds, grenades and mortar fire. Sam stood in the safety of Deb's non-judgmental eyes and encouraging smile. Reg braced to steady him. Sam faltered and then walked to her outstretched arms. Deb held him lovingly. Throughout the summer, they drank cheap brandy to celebrate each success. They laughed and toasted each fall.

By autumn, Sam walked with a cane and Deb began feeling ill. Her worried mother sent her to the doctor. The news, a day later, was a surprise. Deb and Sam were going to be parents. Sam gave up his wheelchair and his dream for a Harley. They married that fall before her belly made a birth announcement, but their marriage in Deb's senior year of high school was a walking billboard that a new life was on its way. Sam began working at Riverdale Garage and training in auto mechanics. The threesome rented a room on top of Dee's Café, and though the stairs were tough to climb, Sam was determined to overcome hardships and place happy anniversary dates over memories of body bags and the airlift.

Some days he wondered if life was worth it, until he looked at Deb's rounding belly wrapping a Christmas gift of new life. Deb celebrated the

upcoming holiday festively drinking while Sam drank to numb memories
of lying on a dirty laundry bag, feeling the warmth of the previous day rising from the damp earth, waiting for the VC to bring on some smoke after
the truce, watching the clock tick . . . tick . . . tick . . . until the artillery
resumed. He drank to forget Walter Wonderful hospital, gray plastic trays
filled with lime green gelatin and apple juice resembling urine samples. It
was 1971 and alcohol was their drug of choice.

Sam introduced Deb to drinking and she was hooked. With the help
of the VA program, on Christmas Eve, six months pregnant; they toasted
one final drink to sobriety and Sam secretly placed his two remaining bottles of brandy in the #10 can.

▼

Reg the Third, grandson to International Champion Reg the First,
yawned to a down position and put his head on Sam. Furry eyebrows
raised above soulful brown eyes.

▼

The blast erupted into Edgar Allen Poe ear ringing as Russ and Joe,
and Wally and Fred, beckoned from a pit of hell. Night loneliness left him
exhausted and ashamed as the ice in his mind melted and the dead rose in
nightmares of mind-blowing terror. Survival anger stirred into the scent
of blood mixed sweat with explosions and fire.

Sam argued with his civilian self while wounded enemies popped up
and down like a carnival game. In combat, the adrenaline pumped through
his veins and he'd just kept on doing what he had to do – hyper-alert, vig-
ilant, energized and focused on the task at hand. War was no time for
melancholia. The enemy was dehumanized.

Back home the Vietnamese of his dreams became sons and daughters,
sisters and brothers. Children who fought for what they didn't understand
. . . dying . . . crying . . . struggling to breathe . . . to live. The little
Vietnamese restaurant was now his favorite besides Dee's Café.

There were moments he desired finding a comrade to process all
he'd seen, and the trauma and pain he caused to others, but there was no
one in Riverdale except his dog who seemed to understand his despair.
The two men who fathered him when he lost his dad as a teen were expe-
riencing their own reality, Gunner's son, Joe, was now a number in the
58,000 young Americans killed. Hans son, Russell, was MIA. The old
men's wounds were too raw to mentor his membership in the more than

300,000 wounded in action club. He hoped to God that Russ was missing, and not a prisoner of war. His hope had lasted for thirty years.

▼

Reg, the dog, licked Sam's face and pawed him.

▼

Sam felt the soft licks of an Army dog's wet tongue and the throbbing pressure of blood loss held fast by a human Sergeant Reg. Sergeant Reg put Black Power to the test and his life on the line when all hell broke lose. In the heat of battle, color, rank, and religion no longer mattered; it was how you gave your mind and body to another person. Surrounded by grenades, claymores, and automatic weapons, Sam heard Reg sing softly 'It is well, with my soul.' His baritone serenaded chopper sounds landing in the paddy past the Agent Orange defoliated trees. 'It is well, it is well, with my soul.'

Reg's kind brown eyes were the last thing of 'Nam he remembered before blackness. The battleground wasn't like the movies; someday he would look Sgt. Reg up and thank him.

▼

The metal trashcan fell sounding a tambourine.

▼

And on mainland USA, Riverdale's longhaired flower power youth marched to denounce a war he didn't understand and had almost given his life. Sam wasn't about to discuss anything with protesters. The sight of disabled Sam reminded them of their angst and the passive Riverdale folk stepped carefully around with polite silence.

Sam walked on. His memories had to depart. He had no choice if he and Deb were going to be a part of the community. He pushed his thoughts away to an outward quietness, but like the Dale River in winter months the deep frigid water continued to transverse the veins of his human landscape.

▼

Reg made a low guttural growl and tugged on Sam's shirt. He circled and lay next to his master. Sam snuggled close, tugging on fur. The dog sounded a high pitch yowl.

▼

Shaun Samuel O'Riley arrived with a piercing cry, red, wrinkled, and angry. The infant loudly proclaimed the sentiments of his father towards the world and Sam's anger broke free as his son screamed with life. While baby Shaun struggled to sleep and suck experienced local mothers offered advice that never worked. Deb felt inadequate and leaned on Sam for security while Sam leaned on a teeny boy howling forth his release of emotional expression Sam refused to yield to. He didn't care that Shaun was demanding. He understood and he poured his heart into his son who magically melted his despair. Sam joked that God sent a spindly leprechaun to save his soul. His child's thin lips broke into a smile so wide it almost reached the tiny points tipping each ear. Irish green wide-set eyes sparkled with mischief above an upturned nose. Shaun's antics and tall tales were as unmanageable as his Einstein strawberry hair. The child overflowed Sam's life with joy, and confusion, as he grew.

Eventually the town gossip of premarital sex and early pregnancy moved on to the next high school senior class. Sam bought the garage and it flourished. Deb got her nursing degree. They bought a little white house on Maple Street that was lined with elm trees and Deb laughingly planted a maple seedling in honor of their new home. Now huge, it spewed a torrent of beige helicopters each spring. The tree set their yard ablaze in orange each fall. Then every leaf dropped. Deathly.

Deb's bratty little brother Larry became county Sheriff.

They were happy in cozy town life until . . .

Crash!

Shaun was dead. Killed.

▼

Sam awoke on the kitchen floor surrounded by garbage. His head hurt. Reg the Third had dumped the trash and was busy chewing something that looked nasty.

What had he done?

Reg's dish was empty. There was a yellow puddle under the table. The dog needed out.

What time was it?

K evin wasn't sure what the Sheriff meant about going nowhere, but he knew he meant business. He ambled over to O'Riley's Garage finding it closed. He peeked in the window of Dee's Café and waved to Margie.

She didn't wave back.

He returned to the quiet townhouse to call Sam. The phone said, "please leave a message after the beep."

So he did as he was told. "Sorry I was late. How come you're closed? Where are you Sam?" Then he went to bed.

Just as he fell asleep, the answering machine blared, "You're fired, you lazy bum!" It was Sam.

Kevin called back.

"O'Riley Garage"

"How come?"

Click.

Kevin redialed.

Bzzz. Bzzz.

Kevin tried again, "You can't fire me Sam. I want to work. It's not fair! The garage was locked." He showered, pulled on a clean pair of boxers, an oversize knee-grazing jersey, and jeans big enough for two. He tightened his belt around his thighs insuring his pants could ride low and remain on.

"I gotta talk to Sam. Don't need no more trouble." Just in case he held his crotch as he walked back to town. "Sam's mad about something."

▼

A tall blue-haired woman pointed a finger toward him. "There, there he is! I bet he did it. I bet he killed Doc Johnson."

"Lord, rest his soul," crooned old lady Carlson, "Doc was such a dear sweet gentleman."

Kevin approached and addressed them loudly "Who ya'll talking to?"

The women scurried into Thompson Drug and Kevin followed, "What you mean Doc Johnson's dead? I only hated him. I didn't kill him."

The barrel chested bald druggist glared from the high counter.

The ladies hid in women's hygiene.

"Ya'll a bunch of white folks don't know nothin'," Kevin cleared his throat and spat on the floor, wiping it with his shoe.

The women jolted into the main aisle, their mouths frowning so deeply you could walk under them. "I'd say that family's cursed," said one.

"This murder is almost like his father before him," said the other.

"Sam said people don't curse in Riverdale. Margie did too." Kevin turned to the pharmacist. "Hey baldy, what are they talking about?"

"It's time to go. You're not welcome here." The druggist took Kevin by the back of his jersey. "It's time to leave, son."

"I ain't your son, I have a mom and dad. You can kick me out for magazines, but not for nothing"

"Do I need to call the police?"

"No, sir. Not the police, sir."

Kevin evacuated. "Where to go? Where to go? Library. Yes, no, yes nowhere. Nobody goes there. Maybe Tasha will show." The library had been their hiding place in the city. He ducked into the back corner of the library and melted into the chair. His uncontrolled mind raced around nuero-tracks wiping out in chaos. "Don't know nothing about no murder," he mumbled. "What to do now? Chief will kill me if I go back to the city." He picked up a Hot Rod magazine, "Old baldy kicked me out!"

"Young man!" whined the librarian. "Quiet please."

Thinking of Tasha quieted his mind, she was an electric plug to his brain. He'd spent his lifetime avoiding books because he didn't read well, but Tasha did and he liked listening to her voice. "I love you Chipster. I love your chocolate chips on golden cookie skin. They ain't freckles you can lick off. God, Bring Tasha to the library. She'll help me think. Oh yeah, and Amen"

▼ TASHA

Tasha held the yellow sticky note from her teacher, 'Come straight home. Mama.' Mama never sent messages to school and if Mama took time to call school there was no room to disobey. The library beckoned, but she looked the other way and peddled faster.

"Thank God for the bike. I hate busses - metro busses - school busses. The line of economics runs along the bus line, and I'm not moulding my life to it." She stopped to watch a young girl and her neighbor on the park swings. A scrawny mutt in a blue sweater was curled up to a yellow lab.

"I'm going to touch clouds with my toes," laughed the girl.

"I'm bigger, I can go higher," smiled the man, his upward slanting eyes squinted into the sun.

"Two more swings and we go back to work," blonde pigtails flew.

"Don't want your grandpa mad," he held his thick tongue between his teeth, his face flat. "Back to work for us," he laughed. "You wanna jump?"

"One, two, three jump!" Both adult and child landed in a heap, the two dogs danced around them. Young, old and different had jobs in Riverdale and most teens drove cars. Riverdale sure wasn't the city!

Mama's sista Auntie Polly transformed her life with a better job and a car. A vehicle offered freedom to live wherever and visit who, where, and when you want. With driver's license in hand she flashed Mama a know-it-all smile and moved out of the city boasting about shopping circular deals and avoiding the 'inconvenience' store. No one could bully her and she bragged she hadn't missed a parent-teacher conference the whole year. Mama had shrugged. With her a Welfare-to-Work job, she was too tired to attend any meeting.

Mama didn't have Auntie Polly's brains, but she still set high standards for her kids. In Mama's house, "Education's free and soap's cheap. I'll keep you clean. You get educated. Do your dreams to get rich and care for me."

Tasha dreamed of a fancy job in a tall glass skyscraper and university classes with thick manicured grass. Her quick mind examined intricacies others didn't attend to and she planned to learn the rules known by the suits and New York City high heels. But, having a brain filled with questions was a liability to city girl friendship where it was safer to appear dumb than be stigmatized for acting more white. At her old school, integration meant bumping shoulders, books, and bodies trying to beat the bell for class. Teens hung out in familiar alliances, divided up in self-determined neighborhoods to discuss magazines they flipped, songs they sang, idols they imitated and sport plays. The lighter side predominately offensive in a controlled aggression. The darker side playing defense, performing reflexive maneuvers without counting the cost. It remained offense versus defense and offensive behavior usually triggered defensive reactions. The male ethnic playing field rarely switched and being female gave her a stratified hand up. A hand she planned to use to her advantage.

When Tasha sat at the table of white students in the lunchroom to discuss Advanced Biology her neighborhood friends called her on it. The laughter at the next table overrode her discussion of parasites and symbiotic relationships. "Oh you mean 'white' Tasha, she's an Oreo, black on the outside, inside she's a snowflake. Ain't right she likes white boys. Girl should stick to her race." Was the human race good enough? Her spirit burned. Venter said, 'human beings are 99 percent identical genetically.'

But, that was city and this was Riverdale where Mama obliviously soaked up small town life. According to Mama "Riverdale is heaven on earth, our home, and the best we ever had." Tasha wasn't so sure. When a local boy asked her to a dance it didn't matter to the boy's father that she had a white daddy, all the father saw was brown. For the first time, she felt this corrosive untruth as a free time organizing factor. She was so much more than 'that cute little black girl.' In Riverdale it seemed that the beauty of skin tone variations were invisible.

On her lighter skin side, Nana Johnquist had called her "little dark one." Then after Daddy died she couldn't remember seeing Nana again. Mama said they didn't want anything to do with her. She didn't know why. She was a perfectly nice little girl.

On her darker skin side, Granny Jones declared "You sure are lucky to be paper sack brown." When Tasha asked Mama what that meant Mama told her, "its opportunity to be a black elite."

In school, she was considered by some an Oreo and Kevin qualified by others as a whigger. She figured they went together as good as a peanut butter on Wonder bread. "Wonder what he's doing?" Tasha glided downhill. "At least, my beau lives here now."

Before Riverdale, Mama had worry enough keeping herself under the radar of her man that little brother Q referred to as BadOne. Q planned to kill BadOne, but thankfully Mama had enough of having enough before he did and social services offered her family a hush house in Riverdale. She'd promised Mama she wouldn't tell Auntie Polly where they were going, but she didn't say anything about Kevin. He'd surprised them saying he had trouble in the city. Mama furrowed her brow, placed one hand dramatically on her hip and the other in the air preparing for a lecture. Then Kevin offered $225 for rent. End of discussion.

He was starting over too at the new vinyl sided yellow townhouse with orange marigolds, sparse grass and skinny trees where everyone slept off the floor. Where they had a phone was in the house and not at the corner store and where the television didn't flicker with a mind of its own. Between Mama, Kevin and free school lunches, there was just enough money for food and even Kevin had a lightly used sofa to sleep on.

▼

Historically, local residents cared for family and Eden Valley was far removed from the traditional 'rural infill projects' on homesteads where garage apartments or small cottages provided intermittent care. Then, two years ago, the Protestant clergy agreed with Father Flanagan to the idea of Eden Valley Center. And even though Father Flanagan thought it up, the protestant's liked it! Ali wrote the grant, Jared donated two acres of farmland, the Lion's Club provided decorating funds, and members of all three churches joined forces to paint and wallpaper. In state meetings and on paperwork the project appeared perfect – every i dotted, every t crossed.

It was a grand experiment for semi-assisted independent living, and the state department provided subsidy so tenants contributed only 30 percent of adjusted annual income for rent and utilities. Out of the starting gates it seemed win-win. Two neat rows of one and two story town homes grew from Hunter cornfields. Accessibility ramps filled with friends and family hauling possessions for six senior units and two accessibility units. Everyone agreed it was a perfect opportunity for the young man who worked a bit at Hans Hardware. Eddie and his mongrel Blue were precious to town folk. For ten years he had voiced his dreams of his own place and finally the town listened.

Within months, no one agreed how to handle the three families chosen to live in the designated units and soon there was talk among the locals of NIMBY, meaning 'not in my back yard' with opinions intertwined like grass in a hay bale.

The mission field the church members humbly planted began filling
with briars as the three spiritual leaders divided responsibilities to quell a
social storm. Father Flanagan took responsibility for a Hispanic family and
Reverend Anderson took another. Pastor Wilson and his congregation
adopted Margie. Wilson believed the Jones' family was just the wake up
Riverdale needed. Margie was hard working, warm hearted and determined for her life to progress well.

▼

Tasha and Q followed Mama's orders and came straight home after
school. Mama brought home leftovers from Dee's for dinner and
announced, "Tasha, now what we gonna do about 'THAT'!" her fisted hands
planted firmly on her hips. "That meaning, you know who!" she pointed to
the sofa.

THAT was not good, Kevin's status had deteriorated. Then Mama
went into a thinking and when Mama thought, nobody talked. Lights
clicked out and she went to bed shutting her door with a slam.

Tasha and Q quietly went to their rooms.

Tasha pulled on an over shirt, "Lord, I know Kevin didn't do it, please
send an angel to help us. Amen."

Struggling, she rolled over and turned out her light. 8:55 P.M. 'That'
was Kevin, her beloved. 'That' she picked up free at the Save Even More
store where restaurants shipped overages and suburban vendors recycled
post-dated products. She dozed.

In Mama's house, "nothing in a store was for sale, unless it was on
sale" and everything was on sale at Save-Even-More. Some things were
even free. For very little Mama got a lot with her, 'anything free you took,
anything cheap you used' mantra. She cuddled her pillow.

Kevin was one of the 'free products' she picked up at Save-Even-
More with the line, "what elegant green eyes you have." Mama always said
'where there's a will there's a way' and when she met Kevin she felt a great
big will rise up from the tip of her toes to the top of her head.

"Yo, Shorty, the better to see you with. What's yo' numbers?" The
streaks on his apron from peeling brown lettuce vanished.

"Name, rank, serial number. What digits yo' mean bro?"

"Hey, Boo? That's a start," his eyes, jadeite, bedazzled her.

"Tasha," she had stammered. "How old are you?" She strutted and
postured herself as available.

"Nineteen. Sorry jailbait," he laughed. "Name's Kevin."

Tasha handed him a crumbled paper reserved only for 'dime' pieces. "Call me. Gotta bounce." Black curls jiggled as she skipped to the check-out. She watched him cheese up and salute. It was all there – name, rank and serial number. Tasha Jones, 1285 14th St. N #202. He was cute with his red hair and freckles. White on brown. Brown on brown. They combined into a motley pair and catching him as a boyfriend qualified as a great summer project, but she needed money and finding a job at not quite sixteen was scarce. Thankfully, she had a ready and needed commodity that with the right marketing scheme would cost only paper cups, tin foil and water. Depending on desperation for a clear drug test, she sold one fresh cup of urine for two to five dollars and her business flourished. Mama never caught on, or perhaps she didn't care. To Mama, money was the means to the end that was needed. But, Mama's life experience kept her holding tight reigns on Tasha, "Girl, you're not dating 'til your sixteen. I don't want you run over, drunk, drugged or shot. I don't need no grand-babies. I don't want no pimps using my baby girl."

So, to keep on the good side of Mama, Tasha snuck around obeying the double negatives. It was Kevin's idea to become best friends with Q. The threesome spent lazy summer days shooting hoops at the park and keeping their relationship under the radar by creeping to the library for free movies, free music, free Internet, free access to the world. The library was a refuge to avoid her click of 'gurlz' who flashed their fake Id's proud-ly to bootie dance at the club, but wouldn't be caught dead showing a library card.

▼

Kevin walked home when the library closed. The dark house was sti-fling and he lay down on the sofa. The spring he usually wiggled around poked his back. The rainbow crochet blanket refused to cover his feet. The pillow didn't cooperate with his head. His sock seams irritated him. He took off his t-shirt and turned it outside-in to avoid the tag. His feet burned and he stuffed his socks under the sofa to join his other dirty clothes. Finally, he got up to pee, making a detour into Tasha's bedroom.

"Yo, Chipster. Come on gurlfriend talk to me." Kevin sat at the edge of her bed whispering. "I need you gurl, talk to me."

Tasha feigned sleep. "Go to bed Kevin, Mama will kill us."

"Whispering can't get us in trouble. Yo' Mama won't know."

Tasha placed her hand in Kevin's trying to listen.

"I need to talk. Talking won't hurt none," and Kevin's random thoughts merged sweet as honey soothing her ears. He wasn't like Mama's boyfriends. He was funny 'and' loveable. He never wanted to do things wrong, his temper only rose when he was hurt, scared or confused and Tasha knew how to dip and dive when there was dipping and diving to do. She discounted words said in anger. Kevin turned down the covers and spooned behind her.

Tasha snuggled, "Sleep sweet Kevin, tomorrow may be different." And it was, as one miniscule egg said hello to a very determined sperm.

▼

Anxiety. Rising. Building. Kevin's heart raced with a zinger and when that happened his hands flipped up like a mechanical toy and it took shaking to pull them back down. He didn't want to wake Tasha. He slid quietly off her bed, pulled on his boxers and returned to the miserable sofa.

He was scared and when he was scared he felt angry, and when he felt angry he paced. He promised Tasha he wouldn't! Then he did it. With Tasha, not Doc. It was Tasha's fault. She gave him the Riverdale address. He bit the jailbait. This would not be happening if he had stayed away. He didn't do it!

▼

According to police data Kevin Abbott attacked an innocent eight-year-old female in a park while she was playing and then hid from the police. He landed in 'JD', the juvenile detention center, doing ninety days at age seventeen for aggravated assault.

Larry watched the clock — midnight, one-fifteen, two-thirty . . . Kevin was a public threat. All he needed was hard evidence or a confession and the case would be solved. It was going to be a very long night. Tomorrow he'd carry Doc to his grave and then work to clean up the Riverdale slime.

It was high time somebody hauled the kid off to jail.

D eath was an accepted life passage, but not like this. Once again murder drew the rural community together, tearing off the scab with a quiet sadness and unspoken fear. Nearly everyone from Riverdale turned out to pay respect to Doc Johnson and to comfort Sally and Michael. Clients, old friends, and the simply curious offered condolences for hours.

Many lives had changed with one death, as each season harvested Doc a new patient crop. The hard work of rural living stretched and pulled muscles that put undue pressure on well-used joints. Snow shoveling turned into plowing, and plowing into summer projects, and summer projects grew into harvesting. Doc had massaged the tightness from Ali Hunter's shoulder the afternoon before he was murdered. Larry had stopped by his office during his coffee break to have Doc work on his lower back, and rumor had it Sam O'Riley was having some kind of secret treatment before clinic hours.

It didn't take long for the conversation to ease over and center on Sam. Ya know talk about Sam seemed safer than to reflect on Johnson murders. Rumors and gossip spread fast.

"Saw Sam leaving Doc's the other morning?"

"Again?"

"Yep. Ya know, Sam and Doc were best friends."

"Yep."

"Started when Grandpa O'Riley died in Germany in World War I"

"Then ya know Sam's dad died in that harvesting accident at the

Hunter's right after World War II."

"Not to mention, well, ya know, he lost his leg in 'Nam. Never believed in that war, did you?"

"Got little Deb Kelly pregnant while she was still in high school, ya know, and then, well, ya know Shaun . . . "

"Shaun was the last Riverdale tragedy. And, in that same woods. Can you believe it?"

"And, ya know, he was only twenty-nine."

Sam wanted to puke. He tried to move away from words buzzing like flies around summer picnic leftovers. The sickening sweet overdone flowers gagged him. He wished he had a hearing aid he could flick off.

"Lucky Doc raised such a fine young man."

"Ya know, he's talented. Saw him play football the other night."

"Ya, he scored four touchdowns in interdistrict skirmishes."

"Two more in district games."

"Ya know, Doc would have been proud."

"He sure is a handsome protector for his mother."

"Guess she'll need him more than ever now, ya know."

No one ever talked of Shaun with glory. Sam escaped to stand with the men chosen as pallbearers. Pastor Wilson, Sheriff Kelly, and Hans Palmquist stood in the opposite corner with Jared and Gunner Hunter working out funeral logistics.

▼

"What a wonderful, dear man," Ali Hunter sighed as a warm tear pooled and then caressed down her cheek. She wiped her face and bit her lip forcing herself to look and pay respect. Proper respect. Mortician John Gleason, was an artist and his casketing was perfect. Doc's blue-white skin was returned to his natural ruddy glow, the embalming fluid and cosmetics had created a look of peace. He wore his best Sunday suit and a red tie neatly hid the fatal wound to his chest. There was no indication that Doc's right hand was dismembered. His left hand was gently placed on top of his right arm. His knuckles were artistically blushed. Ali wrapped her arms around Sally. "I'm so sorry," she whispered, "I am so sad for you."

Sally pursed her lips to prevent another flood of tears. Despite her sorrow, she looked beautiful alongside the elegant oak casket surrounded by lavish bouquets. In a choked voice, she replied, "Oh Ali, I planned on growing old with him. We had such a happy life." She wore the black birthday dress Doc gave her and the Christmas pearls. Ali remembered the sweet coffee moments at Dee's Café when Sally showed off her new gifts. Ali held the cream memorial card with Psalm 23. Their eyes met.

"It was his favorite verse," Sally's voice trailed as she reached out to hug the next person in line.

Ali flipped the card – Dr. Emmett Johnson survived by his wife Sally Ann Johnson and son Michael Samuel Johnson, preceded in death by his father Emil Ludwig Schulzt Johnson and his mother Helen Ann Johnson.

Such a tragedy - father and son, both murdered. She hadn't remembered the name Schultz. The scent of Sally's perfume lingered on Ali's cheek as she departed for home to organize the potluck and prepare food for the coming day.

▼

Mike's school friends congregated in a far off corner by the pall bearers. "Whose paying for our spring jerseys?"

"No one!" Sam snarled. "You can't reposition the DVD or push restart for game two. Murder is murder, done, gone, finished." He spread his hands.

"Things will work out kids, they always do," sermoned Wilson.

"Gonna be a lot of people at the funeral tomorrow," Sam observed. "I could ask Father Flanagan if we can use the Riverdale Catholic Church's BINGO hall for the luncheon."

"Ya gotta be crazy Sam, Doc's a Lutheran. We've had enough wars," Hans interjected. "Besides, Church of Peace is the Johnson's church for three generations. Wouldn't be proper to eat where Doc wasn't baptized; confirmed and married."

Sam huffed and shrugged, "Crazy protestants, mark my words."

▼

The day's weather worked to their favor and Sam was right, the church overflowed. "We could open the main doors, and provide outdoor seating," he offered. "I can get the Riverdale Lion's to fetch chairs and speakers from the highschool."

"I can hook them up on the church steps," offered Hans.

Reverend Anderson, "I'll get our folding tables."

"We've got extra chairs in the BINGO hall," offered Father Flanagan.

"I knew we'd be using the BINGO hall," Sam ribbed the Father.

Wilson admired the work of the Lions as they set up their seating with fly-in pancake breakfast efficiency, a local event visited by over 100 private airplanes that fed the county. The funeral was interdenominational. People sat at the Methodist's folding tables on the Catholic beige chairs. The school speakers broadcast the service across the Lutheran lawn.

It had taken over a hundred years for the Catholics, Methodists, and Lutherans to grow accustomed to each other and into mixtures of Irish, German, Russian, Norwegian, and Swedish grandchildren. Fifty years ago within each holy huddle these intercultural marriages were considered uneven yokings.

Town ladies busied themselves with hotdishes and Jell-O in the church basement. Deb O'Riley shared her bread and butter pickles, Gunner's wife Ma Lu sent a crock of baked beans along with Ali Hunter's famous double chocolate brownies, Dee's Café sent over two Honey Crisp apple pies, Gunner's daughter Annie Palmquist made tuna salad with macaroni rings and canned peas, and one of Riverdale's new arrivals, Margie Jones, shared her spicy corn bread. Most people brought a dish to pass and those who didn't were fed any way – there was always enough to go around.

Pastor Wilson admired Margie working with the kitchen women. He liked her spunk and unstoppable spirit of determination to fit in regardless of what people said or did. Nothing seemed to get her down. Wilson liked that, and so did Larry.

Margie smiled. Her round face, hardened by years of stress and poverty, was framed in black curly hair that glistened in the sun. She placed a piece of warmed cornbread on Sheriff Larry's paper plate. He was quite a handsome fellow out of uniform and it had been a long time since she'd looked into the eyes of a man. She was a warrior and as soon as she finished serving she saddled up alongside.

"Hello, Sheriff. Mind if I sit a bit?"

"Nice day in Riverdale, Margie," Larry offered, she was a pretty little woman with a dynamic personality. The rich mixture of Native American and African American features was startlingly attractive. Her cinnamon skin was set off by a golden front tooth hiding a silver ball tongue piercing.

"Fall air is better than spring air. That spring air is filled with things polite people don't talk about."

"How you doing in Riverdale, Margie?" Larry hoped to prolong conversation.

"I have enough experience to do well here, Sheriff. I do my best thinking after I have experience. I've slept outside so I know how come I need to keep a roof over my head. Riverdale's nice. Don't need to negotiate affections for chump change. No alley gunfights to walk through. No hood rats in jailin' jeans and cheap white tees flipping for a quick buck. Knock downs, knock outs and hard knocks. I rather ring door bells and shop garage sales."

"Good corn bread. You make it?"

She glistened, "Sure did Sheriff, I'll get you another."

"That's okay, how's work?" He hoped she'd stay.

"Working for Dee is good. Working at Smitty's is playtime." Rumor had it no one had ever danced like Margie. "Money meets my needs. No more hiding in abandoned buildings and unlocked cars for this girl. Don't need to dumpster dive for vittles or wait for handouts at the back of a restaurant at closing time. Dee sends me home with fresh care packages if we're lacking."

"You miss the city?"

"City life ain't easy Sheriff. It's the 'same-o, same-o' of public transportation, no pay jobs and set aside housing for those of us who don't have enough," she paused, "enough money, enough brains, enough anything. Who'd imagine I'd live life like the Cosby's in Riverdale?"

"Nice church service, eh Margie?" The woman's life had more action than a movie, and she housed Kevin.

"Pastor Wilson couldn't tame a lion with his ministry. Now, Brotha Smith, that's a fire and brimstone preacher. Gets fancy folk to give miracles of bikes and toys that work til they're stolen. He fetches up unstained and washed clothing. Has a place to sleep twenty," she paused, "fifty on a cold night. Clean sheets any night you're throw'd out. People and folks, lay down differences to fellowship when the cupboards are bare. Brotha words you up to feed your spirit. Brotha feeds your belly last three days of the month and passes out bags of groceries on the fifteenth. He's a keepin' on brotha. He don't do good, he does God. He fills up the gaps between the haves and have nots with his storefront Find the Way church."

"Sounds like a fine man, Margie," Larry pressed his belly on the table edge and chewed the corn muffin. Somehow this woman had found sanc-

tuary from a culture that cannibalized itself and survived surrounded by a
preacher with a parapet of vigilance. "Church of Peace is tame by comparison. Nice cornbread, Margie. I'm glad you found the Way church."

"Find the Way," she corrected. "I'll get you another," in Riverdale she
felt normal, but single motherhood was lonely. A longing for laughing
times knocked in the middle of her nights. Could she cut the cord of teen
pregnancies and meaningless sex? Her old life was fueled by the unfairness
of life jumping out of the bushes. Was it wrong to say "Hello" once she had
found a safe harbor for her family.

6

APPREHENDED

The morning darkness made waking difficult and it didn't help that she heard Kevin snoring. Tasha was startled by her strong feelings. She wanted romance and had persevered defiantly against premarital sex. Doing it with Kevin felt like she'd betrayed herself. She stood in the hot shower wishing she could wash it off. The water cooled to cold. She wanted to hide. She didn't like even her pearly whites when she checked her teeth in the mirror. How could God let someone have freckles and be black? Why couldn't she have a clear face of any brown tone. Chocolate milk would be better than this. She was stuck with the curliest 'bad' hair of all her friends plus the humiliation of 'ice folk' freckles. Why did she have to live with the bane of both?

Mama challenged her to walk outside the color line, but Mama was mixed with respectable ethnicity. Her DNA salad was not mixed with a white father. Tasha felt like flotsam in the chasms of cultures – each chiding her. Why did race matter?

Mama said, "Life will be different in Riverdale. It will be a safe place to be accepted." It was different, all right. In pristine Riverdale the cackling continued and now she expected things to get worse. If she knew what was good for her she'd get on that bus and beat the bell for first class instead of lolligagging on the bike like yesterday.

She passed Kevin, still sawing logs. She loudly huffed as she grabbed her backpack and stomped out to catch the bus.

▼

Tasha confidently walked into Riverdale High wearing her 'Blue Light Special' t-shirt and faded jeans. The long row of grey lockers supported gangly white teens who glanced away without hello. She felt like a black and blue thumb among the student population. Tasha read the body language of pointing fingers and cupped hands to ears. Instead of street talk her new acquaintances scorned her with small town cattiness, camouflaged in nice.

Amber smiled, shaking her straight, shiny hair. "That's Tasha! Those Whoopi braids are fake. I heard they're glued in."

"I heard she doesn't have hair," the laugh was sinister.

To protect her soul, Tasha frosted the girls into faceless statues. Glossed lips glittered like fireflies in front of the hollow of a dark cave. She mirrored back a smile, kindling her anger with a hurricane of teen emotions. She was a finisher, and no one here knew her street reputation. In the city it would have meant get down to business with tightly tied scarves over kinky hair. All piercings and pullable jewelry vanished and fingers were bedecked with gaudy rings. It wasn't her style to lose a fist-t' cuffs and the hood knew not to get her started.

"You'd think her mom would buy different clothes," they cooed.

Tasha batted her curly non-mascara eyelashes. "With what? Is that a right of passage at Riverdale High?" she countered.

Six 'mean mugging' students departed apparently ignorant that they held the power to diplomatically shut up cheerleading Amber and her crony Alyssa. Were they afraid the 'in crowd' would bully them too? Teasing was fun and no one got hurt. This was deliberate targeting and the barbed words stung. The girls upped the ante. Their bullying was no longer the subtleties of exclusion with rumors and gossip behind her back, it was in her face sucking the oxygen from the hallway. Her stomach tightened.

"Think upside down girl," Tasha raised her head high, and pulled back her shoulders. She filed her anger knowing the right time always came. She donned a sweet hello, "Hi, My name is Tasha. I am in your English Class."

Coyly, flashing cheerleading facials, Amber replied. "Nice to meet you Tasha. You must be the NEW girl."

Tasha wanted to scream. She'd been noticed since she arrived in town. She bit her tongue. They used contrived politeness to hide their cruelty. It was a war void of tanks and guns, but fully loaded with two-faced snide comments. Very political.

"I'm Amber and this is Alyssa. We were BORN here. I'm a cheerleader and Alyssa plays soccer. She's REALLY good. We're both in the school play. It's Annie this year. You know Orphan Annie. Too bad YOU CAN'T try out." Amber's lithe body morphed back to life as she turned on the heel of her sport shoe. Looking back, she added. "Aren't YOU Kevin's girlfriend? You know the one who murdered Doc Johnson? That WAS my boyfriend's father! Hope they pick up your boyfriend and haul him off to jail."

"We gotta go." Alyssa shook her pretty head. "Can't be late for class. Nice meeting you."

Tasha wanted to grab her and throw her against the locker. Sticky sweet voices pranced off to class, ponytails swinging. Alyssa's insecure laughter ricocheted off the lockers filling the hall and Tasha wished for a can of anti-asshole aerosol.

The hall emptied as students entered classrooms. Room 202 was around the corner, down two flights, and past the lunchroom. She needed to hurry. Run! Running was against school rules. There was no way to be on time. Once again she would . . . BR R R R R R G G G G . . . be late. She slowed her roll and plodded to class.

"Tasha Jones, you're late for the third time in two weeks."

You're late ping ponged between her ears. She swallowed hard answering in somber surrender, "I'm sorry," she offered.

Tasha scanned the rows of desks with thirty-five light skinned students lined up like headstones in a cemetery. Among the faceless tombs there was no blonde hair, freckle-free Lisa. Once in fourth grade she opened her desk to find new smelly markers, paper, pencils, and crayons. No one admitted doing it, but in her heart she knew it was Lisa. All year, she had borrowed Lisa's stuff and Lisa's eyes sparkled with anticipation when she found the treasures. Lisa invited her to sleep over and no one had ever done that!

On one memorable weekend, they snuck into the kitchen and pricked their fingers holding them in a blood covenant of friendship. They shared impossible dreams. They snuggled in Lisa's soft bed with a big yellow cat that danced on their bellies before settling into a furball. They dressed up in Lisa's mother's suits and high heels and fantasized wealth and fame. When Tasha and her family moved to a shelter, Lisa's mom picked her up for weekends and never once commented about the big brick building with twenty other families. Lisa's mom hugged Mama for real and at bedtime she prayed for the protection and favor of the Jones' family.

Days later the case manager found the Jones family another living place and Mama washed her jeans and melted Lisa's phone number into a gooey mess, but not her memory.

Tasha looked attentively at her teacher . . . The difference between rational and irrational thought is that rational thought is based on facts and will move you forward in life . . .

▼

. . . Insanity is doing the same dumb thing over, and over, and over again, expecting a different outcome . . . Kevin stayed in the town home going 'no where' to obey the Sheriff, but by the third day he felt crazy. Tasha didn't talk to him and he didn't know what to say to her. Margie avoided him and referred to him as 'that' problem.

"Maybe if I get my job back things will change. Gonna go see Sam," he put on his O'Riley uniform, cocked his red hat and walked to town. "By now Sam must really need me. Bet his customers miss me too."

▼

Sam's legs stuck out from under Ali's minivan.

"Hey Sam, I'm back did ya miss me?" Kevin grinned, peering under the car. His green eyes reflected the trouble light clamped to the fender.

Sam rolled out on the dolly and cleared his throat, "What are you doing here? I fired you. Think I changed my mind?"

"I thought you missed me. Who's cleaning the cars?"

"No one."

"This car is dirty. I got work to do," Kevin ran his finger through the dust on Ali's car making a wiggle-squiggle."

"Go right ahead. Clean it up Kevin," Sam smirked as he walked to the office to call Larry and let him know whom the cat drug in.

▼

Two calls came into Larry's office simultaneously. Jill answered line one from a frantic high school student reporting a black gun handle in a hay bale. She advised the girl to leave it and dispatched a squad. Line two was Sam tipping off Larry that Kevin was at the garage and he would keep him occupied. Larry was busy, but she assured Sam he'd call back. Meanwhile the police crew uncovered a Smith & Wesson .44 Magnum with four fired cases. Two hollow point bullets remained in the cylinder and the safety was on. It appeared to have been discharged since it was last cleaned

The two slugs, one from Doc's spine and another found in a nearby tree trunk didn't match. The rifling pattern, although very similar, seemed to raise the question of two firearms or two perpetrators - both .44's.

At the scene, there were no known witnesses besides the dog. The problem in this whodunit was that Kevin was the obvious 'acceptable' suspect, but not necessarily the 'only' suspect. From the statement taken at the crime scene from Sam O'Riley, Kevin Abbott had a problem with Doc. In fact, old Mrs. Carlson said she overhead him threatening to kill him.

There appeared to be no signs of an altercation. Doc may have known the murderer and waved to him, taking the first shots in his hand, or he may have taken the first shot in his chest and then raised his hand toward the shooter. Being right handed Larry figured Doc probably used his right hand to cover his heart if that was the initial penetration. Sole prints from the woodland so far matched Sam, Michael, Doc and Sally, but it had rained twice in two days and the area was now also filled with footprints from the coroner, police, paramedics and Larry.

Unlike the movies, a gun barrel is a lousy surface and it was fortunate that the detective secured two prints from the many smeared ones. Whoever handled the gun was gripping it tightly with sufficient perspiration to leave imprints. Two prints appeared to have similar ridges and loops that matched those on file of Kevin Abbott. From the hand residue and matching fingerprints the crime lab determined that Kevin had fired the pistol recently, and since there was no other residue he remained the primary suspect.

On the night of the murder it was clear that Kevin was intoxicated, but Larry never determined the blood alcohol level and that could knock a charge down from First Degree to Second Degree Murder in a plea bargain. It would save the county the expense of a trial, but it would provide the opportunity to let Kevin go free.

The file thickened with reams of paperwork and hours of writing. Crime scene logs, autopsy reports, lab reports, scene photographs, pieces of clothing, plaster tracks of shoe soles, and the suspected weapon accumulated to provide forensic evidence. The hunch quickly progressed to articulable suspicion as clues pointed to the transient. Finally, the County Prosecutor determined there was sufficient preliminary evidence to charge Kevin Abbott with murder.

Making charges would settle the score. Doc was a long-standing friend. If Kevin did it, Larry hoped for a life sentence, Riverdale didn't need riff-raff.

Larry called Sam back to get Kevin's fresh fingerprints off the glass counter and was surprised when Kevin answered.

"O-Riley Garage, we service you better."

"Sam there?"

Kevin handed the phone to Sam and watched the conversation as he leaned on the counter marching the sweaty print of his thumb in a circle. Sam was happy he was back. He even winked at Kevin when he hung up,

"Don't worry Larry, I already have it taken care of!"

"I'll be right over."

Minutes later, Kevin greeted Larry, "Hey Sheriff, you need a fill?"

"Yeah, I need a fill all right, I need you to fill me in on Doc Johnson. I need you to come down to the station and fill me and the boys in."

"No problemo officer, anything you say," Kevin smiled.

"I need you to hop in the car."

"Can I sit in the front? Run the sirens? Flash the lights?"

Larry glared. This was no joke. "Get over here, I need to pat you down before you get in. I've got no time for funny business. I've got work to do."

The sheriff frisked Kevin, who flinched with each pat. Noticing his reaction, the sheriff remained careful to retain the boundaries of law, and feeling no hard object resembling a gun he went no further than an out-side pat down. He was curious however about a pocket. "Take it out and show me." Larry asked gruffly.

Kevin put his hand into his pocket, feeling the small switchblade Chief gave him as a gift for radical sales. He threw it as far as he could. The sudden movement startled Larry and he grabbed Kevin's hand instinctive-ly slapping on a cuff.

Kevin fought to run, "What the hell?"

"Watch the language, boy!" Larry tightened his grip, grabbed Kevin's left hand and clamped down hard.

"You got 'em too tight. They are too bucking tight."

"I said cut the cussing!" surprised at the escalating tirade.

"You oinking pig." Kevin knew from experience that police don't play, but in the drama of the moment, it no longer mattered, he felt like an animal and he kicked the squad car hard enough to dent the fender.

"There will be no cussing." A small crowd gathered and Larry tried to maintain some semblance of professionalism.

"Don't grab me, you pig!" Kevin oinked.

"Shut up!"

Kevin's strength surprised Larry. Without the hand cuffs, it would have felt like he was handling an octopus. The tiny kid didn't even come up to his shoulders and probably weighed less than one hundred pounds soaking wet. It took all the energy Larry could muster. Kevin was indomitable.

"You have the right to remain silent. If you give up the right to remain silent, anything you say can and will be used against you in a court of law. . ."

Kevin cleared his throat and 'hocked a lugie' missing Larry's shoe.

"You have the right to an attorney. If you desire an attorney and cannot afford one . . ." Larry pushed Kevin into the squad car, "an attorney will be obtained for you before police questioning," and slammed the door, "Shut up if you know what's good for you!"

Larry wasn't one for police brutality, but if Kevin landed a blow, he would gladly swing back and Kevin's repertoire of offenses would escalate to assault of an officer after resisting arrest. Kevin was in police custody and the tables turned. Now the guys with the white hats had the opportunity to discover the truth. Funny how, questioning and possible detention often led to arrest.

The three-block ride to the station was too short for Kevin to settle down. He kicked the police cage and Larry's seat back while he threatened to kill the son-of-bitch who arrested him and blow up the squad car. His statements qualified as terrorism, but in the heat of arrest Larry let it go. Words were words, and he'd heard all of them before. Larry had given him the Miranda Warning though he doubted Kevin paid attention to a word he said. Sam and a number of others in town who were drawn into the spectacle heard him state it, but he'd have the booking agent repeat it to be safe.

By the time Larry reached the station, Kevin realized he might be in trouble; he quit kicking the seat.

Larry sat silently. He refused to haul Kevin into the booking area kicking and screaming so they remained in the parking space listening to the afternoon news. Larry drank the dregs of a cold coffee and picked on a dried donut waiting for the obscenities to subside.

"What are we doing Sheriff?"

"Listening to the news."

"For how long?"

"Until you're ready to go in like a man."

"For how long?"

Larry didn't answer, he was content to listen to the radio talk show.

"Okay, I'm ready, Sheriff, sir."

"Well, it's about time."

▼

Larry learned long ago that once he delegated something, regardless of how much 'he' wanted to do it, he had to step back and remain in leadership to retain his position as county sheriff. This time stepping back was hard. He wanted to do the whole show — but the interrogation belonged to Officer Tim Turner, the investigator who had no real experience interrogating a person accused of murder. Larry wished he had signed up to be part of that newfangled city pilot program, the Criminal Teleport Conferencing System. The Sheriff's Conference had offered it to eight select counties in greater Minnesota and the conferencing gizzie was as if the person sat in your office. With the CTCS he could have accessed a virtual skilled interrogator from the cities, in addition to watching it in 3D himself. He declined the offer, Harris County rarely saw trouble.

▼

Sam resumed working, but his thoughts kept nagging him. Each time someone had hauled his son Shaun's butt out of something, he had a fit like Kevin. When Shaun broke a window with a ball in fourth grade, he broke one 'for real' with his fist in the principal's office to prove that was how a person broke a window. Shaun had kicked, cussed, and broken the baptismal font when Father Flanagan caught him smoking a cigar in the confessional.

Only if Sam remained in control did Shaun remain in control. It worked like a grounding wire and regulated the deregulation.

Something about arresting Kevin wasn't right.

▼

"Turner," Larry didn't want Kevin's statements rendered useless, "Throw new batteries in the recorder and start with the Miranda warning." Larry preferred to hear a live confession of Kevin admittance, but a law required audio tape would do.

Ten years ago, Turner had done his college senior thesis on murder interview techniques so he knew what to do. He'd provide friendly listening and appear to be an ally by asking simple questions. If Kevin made a clear and unambiguous request for counsel he'd honor the request and quit the questioning. He hoped he only stated, "maybe I should talk to a lawyer," that was ambiguous and if the interview was going well, he could ignore it and legally continue. Or if he ceased questioning Kevin, and the kid initiated further conversation, any incriminating future statements were valuable.

"Hello Kevin, my name is Officer Turner and I am here to help you. I need to ask you a few questions. I will be taping this interview to protect you. Do you understand?"

"Sure, Hi," Kevin wasn't sure if he should answer, but the man in front of him had a nice smile and he wanted to go home.

Turner pressed record, "Are you Kevin James Abbott?"

"Yes."

Turner recited the Miranda warning, "Do you understand?"

"Yes."

"Can you sign this paper that says I have read you your rights?"

"Sure," Kevin liked signing his name on lines.

"Do you want to talk to me?"

"Yes," Kevin knew he was innocent, he might have hated Doc Johnson, but hating someone was no good reason to kill him, he'd tell the truth for a 'stay out of jail' pass. He was a good talker and had bamboozled his way out of police situations before. What was that word they told him to use – no contesto, no commento, he remembered using that word to save his butt before. He learned it from a public defender in the city. Kevin fixated on a small black fly as it walked across the table.

"Kevin, do you know why you're here?"

"I killed Doc Johnson," Kevin put no questioning inflection in his voice and Turner was surprised the confession came so easily.

"Did you have an altercation with him?"

"Huh?"

"Tell me when Doc Johnson made you mad?" Turner sat back with his arms behind his head; appearing open and relaxed for conversation.

Kevin's eyes rolled up scanning from left to right. He was quiet.

Turner waited and smiled.

"Last time I saw him I was at Sam's working on Mike's truck. Doc came in and tried to hit me when I put a rag on the truck."

Turner rubbed his hand along his chin; he couldn't imagine gentle Doc striking Kevin or anyone else for that matter.

Kevin pretended to write and then shook his writing hand waving it at Turner, "He raised his right hand at me. I don't let people do that. He's a no good son-of-a-b.b.b." he stuttered, "stitch. I didn't let him hit me. I ain't no punk."

Turner took out the 44 and lay it on the table.

"How did you get that?" Kevin shouted. "That's my gun!"

"Have you ever used this gun, Kevin?"

"Sure, Mike let me shoot it. Did you get to shoot it too?"

"Where did you shoot it Kevin?"

"Down in Mike's woods. Where did you get that gun?"

"In Mike's truck."

"Oh yeah."

"Did you shoot Doc Johnson?"

Kevin laughed, "No, are you stupid? The gun shot him."

"Did you kill Doc Johnson with this gun, Kevin?"

"Oh yeah, I killed Doc Johnson," Kevin scrunched up his face. There was no remorse. The kid smiled and shook his head.

This confession was too easy. "Are you guilty, Kevin?"

"Guilty," Kevin raised one nostril and then was silent as if in deep thought. Kevin liked to talk and he sang like a bird, too bad he never said the magic words. A lawyer would have protected him from his statements.

My lucky day, a not guilty plea could be changed in the future; but not this, Kevin had provided enough information to help the prosecution build a complete case against him. The confession was as solid as the batteries.

"Can I go home? I answered your questions," Kevin asked.

Turner was dumfounded, "No, you are under arrest."

Kevin pushed the table forward against the wall and tipped the chair, "What do you mean asshole, I didn't do it! Are you calling me a liar?"

Turner requested Kevin be sent to booking and placed with the permanent prisoners. It wasn't unusual for a suspect to recant a statement.

The jailer handed him a fresh prison outfit.

"I don't like orange, you got a different color?"

"Shut up or I'll dress you myself."

Kevin emptied his pockets and took off his shoes.

Kevin didn't want the big guy dressing him so he zipped his lips and laboriously put on the ugly pants, granny slipper socks and flashy neon orange shirt.

"Man you guys have bad taste," Kevin sucked his recently inked finger. "How do I get this ink off?"

The booking agent handed him an acetone wet wipe and directed him to put his slippered feet on the black footprints.

"Hey let me see my picture. I can smile better, I want another one."

"Sit down."

"That picture is no good."

"You're the one who's no good and this is no photo studio."

Larry stopped the nonsense and ordered the jailer to place Kevin in a holding cell. Kevin threw up his middle finger shouting, "I shut up. You promised to get me out of here. I talked. I'll talk more if you take me home. What do you want me to say? I didn't do nothing."

Sheriff Larry noted the double negative.

There was sufficient evidence to put together a viable case and though a conviction could not be obtained solely based on a confession, there was probably enough admissible evidence to charge him with murder. It was looking like the guys with the white hats had more points. With the confession, things could move fast and felony charges for murder would be filed.

Larry wished the 'good old days' were back, there would have been a street hanging over this felony, but the law remained on Kevin's side, innocent until proven guilty. Accusation of murder was serious; and a life sentence in prison was a damn expensive solution. Free loading in trade for freedom. It was a cheap trick of a sensitive society. In trade for Doc, a reputable, tax-paying citizen, a transient would pay his debt by losing his freedom and gaining a lifetime of government support. Kevin had probably never paid a dime of taxes in his life.

Turner was concerned that a fair jury of his peers would be tough to find. And, Kevin never asked for an attorney and without a lawyer present his confession may have violated his Sixth Amendment right to Counsel leading to it being thrown out of court. The kid needed to get lawyered up quick. Questionable confessions or limited circumstantial evidence to a grand jury could mean dismissal of murder charges. An attorney would probably try to cop a plea bargain and wave the cost of indictment, trial and appeals in exchange for a reduced sentence. Then he'd be shipped off to the state prison, out of Harris County and off their watch. Meanwhile, Kevin could live in the Harris County Jail permanent section and Sheriff Larry would do his best to play by the real rules.

Jail simplified Kevin's life. He wasn't expected to think. He had a warm place to sleep. Clothing choices were a cinch and someone gave him a clean folded pile of new stuff before the old got dirty. He sported the jailin' style, sagged his pants and no one reminded him to wear a belt. They even had a rule against belts! No one cared if he always ran around in socks because they didn't allow shoes. Meals came at the same time every day on a plastic platter that he didn't have to wash. Actually, it wouldn't be a bad place if he could get past the gatekeeper and leave to see friends. He tried to make friends with his cell-mated, but they were jerks.

"Hey, the tall skinny guy with eyes closed," Kevin had rambled for two hours because talking made life easier, even if no one talked back. The other cellmates were fisting to fight.

"I sure miss Margie's family and cookies. Cookies!" He hadn't thought of Mom forever, "Wish Mom would visit. She'd bring cookies," Kevin mumbled increasing his tone to a shout. "Homemade cookies!"

"I'll home make cookie you," shouted back a cellmate.

Shagrinned, Kevin shared, "My Mom sends cartoons and cards in pretty envelopes. They'll bring cookies, wait and see. You'd like me if I shared my cartoons and cookies." He needed a friend-making machine. He didn't like checkers, hated cards and didn't know how to play cribbage.

"Hey, ya wanna see me juke. Everyone will like that!" The idea popped into his mind like a jack-in-the-box. Street music didn't need instruments and the cell picnic table was 'perfecto-mundo.'

Kevin tapped his fingers on the metal, listening for differences in tone. He tilted his head toward the sound and moved his free hand along the aluminum to change pitch. He added tempo with his feet rhythmically moving from his toes to his heels. He closed his eyes and shook his head like a bobble head doll. The motions mesmerized his cellmates as they tried to figure out how he did it. He opened his mouth spurting ticks and tocks, and whirs and horse knickers. He stood, jumped, and twisted.

Even Trapper, the tall skinny guy looked up.

In the city he'd provided rhythmic 'beat box' training to higher level gang members wanting to look 'fly.' His beats gained him the status he needed to be jumped into the Rangers. He was too small to fight well.

Kevin bounced from floor to tabletop. Checkers flew across the room like miniature flying saucers. A slide on his belly across the table evacuated the deck of playing cards like jet fighters off a carrier; it also evacuated two cellmates. Kevin paid no mind. The more he moved, the more noise he was capable of. The angry men folded their arms across barrel chests and growled about killing him for space invasion.

Kevin didn't notice.

It was quite a show and no one was getting hurt.

A police officer and the jailer watched, thankful Trapper had recently moved in with the permanents. He was a good man to stand in the gap and if needed could quell the ensuing storm manifesting itself as a tornado spinning out of control in the common area.

▼ TRAPPER

The tall, skinny guy, Doug 'Trapper' Palmquist like most of the local folk acquired his nickname through life experiences. As a teen he ran the Palmquist trap line with his grandfather down by the slews of the Dale River and off the banks of Clear Lake. Up until the last two decades the skins of the critters bought the extras the family needed to make wholesale pre-holiday inventory purchases at Hans Hardware just in time for local Christmas shoppers. For three generations the Palmquist family had owned and operated the hardware store and it was expected that each son would take over the store for the next generation. Trapper, however, independent and strong-willed chose masonry.

Outside jail, Trapper's life was filled with outdoor adventure that he unwrapped like yarn while he downed beers and told tales to bar patrons in good ol' country fun. He had the uncanny ability to eloquently smooth over the discrepancies when voices heated up trying to correct the details of an event. He was an editor's editor, and the best newscaster this side of the Dale River. He was a fun guy to have around, got along with the most difficult person, and mostly kept his nose clean. He was the kind of guy you called when you needed help, patient to a fault, and willing to work straight through if a job needed doing.

Born and raised in Riverdale he was well respected in the community until he picked up that first beer. It didn't matter that in forty years he had spent a cumulative seven behind Larry's bars and less than a hundredth of that time drinking. Somehow he always seemed to find a good reason to stop at Smitty's Pool Hall and have a cold one – a good day, a bad day, a hot day, a cold day, feeling really good, or not feeling well at all. Smitty's comforted him. He liked the camaraderie and quick fix of a dollar pull-tab.

He should have figured it out. The equation was simple – as long as he avoided sitting on a stool in Smitty's he didn't sleep on a bunk at Larry's. Jail house sleeping should have been incentive enough – small unventilated basement airspace filled with smelly men who farted, sweated, snored, and belched. His last beer won him the the daily double plus a go to jail card. Larry charged $20.00 a day for the opportunity to live in 'his' jail and the DWI fine was higher than property taxes. He lost his license, increased his insurance rates and his wife Annie became his chauffeur. Not driving for five years seemed like eternity, but to his sweet daughter, ninety days without Daddy 'was' eternity. Puckered lips through wired glass and two-way jail phone talks stunk. Now punishment for breaking work release banished him from church services with the other jailbirds. He was sitting fast with no opportunity to wink 'I love you' to Annie during hymns. Embarrassing Larry was obviously a big mistake.

To save professional face, it didn't matter that Larry was his shirttail relative, friend and customer. Too bad the sheriff from the next county was having lunch with him, regional reputation won out and his coveted twelve hours a day on work release flushed down the crapper.

Trapper opened one eye scouting Kevin. The kid's creative sounds were a pleasant sound track invoking freeze-frame memories. Annie's offer for venison chili and hot cheese biscuits was a no brainer, but the consequence of a moment's passion over lunchtime wasn't worth the cost. Two days ago Larry caught him coming out of his house buckling up his jeans. Annie warmed his heart, and he felt a strong desire to warm his hands and his . . . Ever since he got hauled off to jail Annie rallied her support. Before lockdown and their noon randevous, she had waited each morning outside the jailhouse with Kissy while he switched from prison wear into work clothes, picked up his pocket change, and walked semi-free past the aged doors of Harris County Courthouse. They greeted him with kisses and hugs, a thermos of strong freshly ground coffee and a black metal lunch pail filled with his favorite – white soft bread with mustard, salami, lettuce and mayo. Annie filled his lunch box with the same kindness and special treats with which she filled his life.

Annie was a good woman from hearty German stock who believed she could conquer anything if she had to. They made a good team. She could skin furs, stretch a pelt, and filet fish as well as he. Not many women left like Annie, except his baby girl, who already showed a propensity for hunting, fishing and trapping.

Trapper closed his eyes to block out Kevin's antics. This kid's behavior reminded him of Sam and Deb's Shaun. Deb said it was her drinking that caused him trouble and if that was true Deb's drinking with Shaun saved his daughter Kissy's brain. Nothing could sweep the damage Shaun lived with under the rug, his reality was permanent. Almost five years ago his wife Annie filled his life with Kissy and went on a wellbriety rampage. She stopped cold turkey as soon as they begin trying to conceive.

Then came Kissy, his sweet, sweet, baby girl. Trapper laughed remembering her kissing a painted turtle that retaliated by locking onto her perky lip. Kissy loved the turtles at his dad's hardware store. She spent her days with Annie helping Dad and Eddie. She played with Eddie's mongrel Blue and his pup Lucy. Kissy had been surrounded by adults since birth and had an uncanny mix of child and adult-like expressions and behaviors. To unsuspecting adults she could be irritating, but she endeared herself to Trapper and the community. She empowered her woodsy Daddy, elevating his gentleness and encouraging playfulness.

▼

Kevin quacked.

Trapper thought on.

His sun up moments with Kissy created a deeply bonded relationship. He loved listening to her embellish daily events, tossing her in the air to hear giggles, and holding her close. He loved reading Bible stories and holding her tiny hand in his to pray. She insisted he leave an empty chair at the supper table for Jesus. She placed a pillow on the floor in case Jesus got tired watching over her while she slept. Her prayers were real.

He imagined her head upon his leg as he squatted by the morning fireside stirring wood ashes to build up the fire. She'd nuzzle his beard and tap his shoulder, "Don't use oak daddy, that's night wood." His little monkeyshine in pink footie jammies didn't miss a beat. She picked up things quickly and was growing up way too fast. He loved wrapping her in his arms and stroking the sleep softness of her cheeks.

▼

Trapper felt the wind of Kevin's performance. The kid's words jumbled together. Kevin put two fingers to his lips and blew.

▼

The teakettle whistled loudly and Trapper poured two mugs of hot chocolate while Kissy added pink and yellow marshmallows for herself, and orange and green for Daddy. They sipped cocoa and dunked pieces of hot buttered toast, sprinkled with sugar cinnamon. Kissy magically turned her toast droppings into minnows and licked them up.

She delighted in running his trap lines and after the house warmed he helped her dress, putting purple hand knit socks over jammies. She zipped her snowsuit. He tied her rabbit fur hood. She wrapped her candy-striped Bobe Lu scarf around her neck and twirled, "I'm snug as a bug in a rug. Oops Daddy! Where are my boots?" and off she'd run coming back carrying garage sale boots so small they fit inside his matching pair.

They were the Palmquist team. Kissy rode with her boots on his shoulders as a forest princess along the Dale River deer trails. They watched great horned owl babies grow from roly-poly cotton balls into majestic hunters. Along the cliffs, near beaver houses, they watched eagles soar. They hunted Tiger butterflies and they planted milkweed seeds to feed Monarch caterpillars. They crouched behind fallen logs to watch wiley fox games and baby ducks ride on mother's back. At almost five, Kissy valued life and respected death. She could already smell the forest and read the details of creation.

Trapper laughed as he remembered trying to remove two brown boots sticking out from the heavy comforter. "No!" she had shouted. "I've got orders from Bumpa! Gotta keep my boots on in times of trouble. I'm muckin' up my nightmare monster tonight."

Childhood innocence amazed him. Her life was clearly black and white, yes and no. The fog of sometimes, and maybes, and mostlies had not settled in. Her world was fresh and exciting. He missed the scent of white ginger on Annie and the baby shampoo smell of Kissy.

▼

Kevin honked.

The noise transported Trapper into his pickup with his pup, a pure-bred yellow lab. Perfect structure, a great temperament and more dog than he ever hoped to own and he was missing important field training time. He missed the yap, yap, how are you and Kissy's blonde hair flying behind her as she ran to say welcome home. He longed to swoop her up and swirl her high above the ground spinning around mud caked hands from mixing sand and water into pretend concrete. He would lay down his life for his baby, why couldn't he lay off the bottle?

The last time he talked to Kissy through the jail phone, she told him she wanted him to be a good boy on earth so he'd get out of jail and go to heaven. Trapper hoped there was a pause in that order. He didn't plan to screw up again. He was going home for the last time and some other Joe could have his jail bunk.

Trapper wiggled his toes in his prison slippers. Things sure could go from bad to worse quickly. Two days ago he whined about changing into prison gear when he came back from work release. Sixty-two days ago he complained about family responsibilities. Now he would give anything to have either of those opportunities back. The slipper seams ate into his big toe. He wanted to pet his dog and make love to his wife.

▼

"Get out of here! Move!" shouted a cellmate.

"Who do you think you are?" exclaimed another.

"Shut up or I'll beat you!" roared a third.

The angry voices burst into Trapper's imagination. Out of his ninety-day sentence, he had twenty-eight days left and this 'Free Ride To Jail Pass' was going to be his last. He would keep his promise to his family even if he had trouble keeping it to himself.

Kevin might be a weirdo; but maybe if I protect him and gain trust, I can score information for early release.

8
SQUARE DEAL

Jail felt claustrophobic and Kevin faced a communication jam. People talked. He misunderstood. He talked. No one listened. It was obvious impressing his cellmates got him into trouble. Every time he tried, loud angry words pelted him.

"What? I speak a different language?" he yelled.

"Whomp. People talked at me," he whispered. "I know what you're saying. You liars change your words. I hear good. The ear doctor said so." He picked a booger, ate it, and wiped his finger on his pants.

"I can hear things you don't." He walked up the Trapper, "Yo, you mad doggin' me? Wanna fight?"

Trapper rubbed his beard, "Mad dog? Pets aren't welcome here."

"You need a blankie Kevin?" a cellmate teased.

"Ya'll playa haters" He threw down flat palms, the derisive gang sign for f'you. His strong gesture exploded invisibly among rural cellmates.

"Ya'll blind dumb asses," he screamed. "Don't you know English!"

Two cellmates distanced themselves.

"Treat me like I'm stupid, you get what you get. Don't need attitude from a white honky," Kevin mumbled and sat cross-legged in front of Trapper. "Yo, ya gotta square?"

"Square? You can't bring tools in here."

"What are ya stupid? Square, like let me go 'n blaze a square? Like share a short? OK, OK like do ya have a cigarette dawg?"

"Square? Dog? Hell no my dog Lucy's at home." Trapper replied wryly. "Sheriff's got a no smoking rule. Why? You got a cigarette?"

"This ain't the first of the month. Nigga you crazy?" Kevin slapped his knees, the bearded guy was straighter than Dad. Even the unwritten law of smoker friendship was failing and he never liked being jonesed. Kevin tried laying out another face card. "Ya know, when what you see, isn't what ya'll see, and what is real is different from what is?"

Trapper tilted his head, cocked his eyebrow and lifted his right lip. Introspectively he acknowledged, "Maybe."

"Touchdown," Kevin moved in. "I 'gots' a block from Diplomat. They call him D. He's on top of Chief and Chief is on top of me," Kevin didn't wait for an answer. "Thursday the street is full of color. Veggies. Fruit. Noise. Makes blowin' a kiss to the suits easy. They leave the money buildings to get their gurlz flowers for the weekend. A safe place to hide my candy." Kevin pretended tokin' a reefer, "No one sees what's real."

"Yep," Farmer's Markets obviously sold more than vegetables. Trapper decided to 'let us see' more. He was tired of TV.

"I'm like secret agent style. I recruit teens at bus stops needing a friend." Kevin tried to look tough, "I fit in like a regular kid between the city layers. One layer you see, and the other is right in front of your eyes making deals, and you don't see it." Kevin tried to Alpha Dog Trapper, but was no match.

"Guess you need the right glasses," Trapper offered. It didn't all make sense, but there was time to sort the details and ask questions later. Patience prepared you to understand the life of your victim and trapping was a covert art form. He remained careful. He'd bait the line with a look of interest in hopes of landing a get out of jail early pass.

"My best day is market day. People think I am with the market. See my red hair and freckles." Kevin pointed repeatedly to his cheeks. "D says I look like a nice white farm boy what comes in with the farmers. They sell tomatoes and peppers. I sell green."

"Like lettuce?" Trapper trolled.

"Hell, no. I hustle out of the QPs on the street," Kevin lowered his voice to a delicate whisper, "weed, marijuana, quarter pounds. D takes text cell messages and Internet orders. Then we deliver like morning paperboys. We add pizzazz to the news. When you know how to do it you never get caught. Pizazzz delivery at your service," Kevin took a bow. "You an old G?"

"Maybe," Trapper figured he meant geezer not gangster.

"I gots friends in the city, I'm a," Kevin mouthed the words, "a Mo in the Black Stone Rangers. No tears." Would he continue? "Teardrop tatoos come with kills. Killing will get me a teardrop. Chief has two. Calls them scout badges.

"Ain't pillow talk when I tell ya. I ain't no shorty. Two stars." Kevin slapped Trapper's knee. "I got rank, know how?" Kevin took the bait. "D wanted a brand new black Monte Carlo, and I done did it. I ain't got no license so the other guy drove. My heart pounded so loud I thought we'd get caught driving round that parking ramp rolling in that whip on those great dubs. Leather seats. Black Star War dash. D told me I was a gangsta. It was coo' and I got me a star when I delivered."

"Star two?"

"That was star two, star one was . . . well, every thinks it's real? See this little girl was flying a kite and I ran to cut the string to joke her, only I tripped and my knife stuck in her leg. She was the little sister of the gang we'd been fighting. Guys juiced up the story to build my rank for Chief to want me in." Kevin was silent. He shivered. His hands flapped by his head. Ever since he was small, dramatic moments energized him, and once his hands went up they were hard to get back down. He reminded Trapper of a juvenile beaver excited over an unwanted intruder.

Kevin rambled, "Chief's a hot boy with two burners, one in his boxers and one in his socks. He uses his gurlz cell for deals and scrubs cops clean." He chuckled, "They think hot boy is their friend. Ha! He'd call his church-going daddy and tell him how much he loved him, then he'd hang up and 'blow off a nigga.' I saw him shoot a guy who flashed down."

Kevin's green eyes grew wide. Trapper noted the enlarging pupils.

"Chief is one coo' dude. I got Ranger rank, ain't no wannabee. I got jumped when I wasn't looking. Right hand signalled go! They took it easy. I was no longer a send away. Chief set his watch for only sixty seconds. Kicks and punches!" Kevin reenacted the Roman holiday fight of brutality, gore, and initiation entertainment.

"Then it was over," Kevin lay on the ground, his hands outstretched, beaten. Trapper put his fatherly hand on Kevin who sprang back to life, "Chief put his arm around me and the guys gave me fives. Don't tell. Chief told me never to tell." He smiled when he didn't know what else to do.

"Secret's safe with me Kevin."

"Ghost, call me ghost. I stayed at Chief's main gurlz crib for two weeks. They were surprised I was so beat up. Chief's gurl is light skin so she knows about colors. Chief showed me the white lines on his dark skin from his mama's belt. He told me never saw no rainbow person before. No one he knew ever went from red, to blue, to green, to yellow. Homies came to check out my colors. When the yellow left Chief helped me catch the bus to Mom and Dad's. But we weren't family. His gurl got me a mattress and blanket. She's nice to everyone and makes us food. When Chief grubs he calls her names. That's mean."

"Seems like it to me, Ghost."

"She works. For real. It's her crib, you know, apartment and she pays for everything. She put a cool cloth to my head and touched me nice when Chief went out. I like her. I took blankets and food from home to share with the Rangers what was my family. They protect my life." Kevin switched gears. "Stabbing the girl gave me 'cool points. When the police caught me, I copped a plea — that was a good idea, huh?"

"Ya, Ghost."

"Chief said getting jumped out is ten times worse. You might die. He showed me the black metal chair with the nose poked in the steel from the boy who tried. The boy died bleeding bad." Kevin followed the rules of the street — he held his honor, took the rap and accepted the star. No one but the members, and now Trapper, knew the reality of where he was, or why he disappeared. Trapper bet his parents thought he ran away and to Trapper it seemed a heartless baptism a vulnerable person could never escape — the unlawful plea, a beating that qualified as initiation into the law of the pack, a new name to a white boy in a tough black gang.

"My homeboys didn't visit, but every Saturday Mom and Dad brought cookies. When I got out they kept me on lockdown. Chief said they would. Mom and Dad hate me, made me go to church and always asked stupid questions. Chief said I was the dawg he needed. Mom and Dad didn't need me. They didn't want me. So I went night crawling."

"Uh um," just the kind of unsure-footed critter Trapper liked.

"I got skills to teach the boyz to 'pop' and 'grind' with their gurlz, his body language demonstrated dancing. They invited me to parties when they 'hit a lick.' I'd just kick back. Sip some ju. Smoke a blunt."

"Uh um." Trapper tarried on translating street talk.

"You a rapper?"

"Usually, I let Annie wrap the presents. My fingers fumble with the paper and my thumbs stick to the tape."

"You been drinking? Dad said only have one drink so I get the biggest glass and fill it to the top." Kevin licked his lips. " I drink lick straight. No one holds it as good as me. Smooth as milk and puts me out at bedtime," Kevin yawned. "I don't sleep much and I get tired of watchin' the boyz juice their gurlz." Kevin's body inkled mating.

"Uh um."

"Mom and Dad disappeared, but I don't miss 'em. I slept at Chief's gurlz place. I hope Mom didn't get hurt, she used to tease me about being a used car salesman, said I could weasel my way out of trouble. Mom and Chief call me smooth. Chief said I didn't need my old man holding me down. Parents don't know nothing. Chief said they're a business liability. I was free. Rangers had my back. Ghost, cool name huh? Sometimes Chief called me Eerie-dance-int. I miss my dawg."

"I miss my dog, too. Welcome to jail, Ghost."

"Yah Dawg, Ghost, cool huh," Kevin's head bobbled. "Chief lined me up with my own block. I ain't no 'punk.' My light skin and curly red hair makes me a good hustler to push G's to 'ice folk.' I blend into the market, selling dimes and nicks and bricks. I'm a produce professional and I look respectable at the Save-Even-More Store. I really am really black, I ain't no cracker." He continued to crow out details of naughty things he'd done.

"Uh huh."

"That's where I met Tasha, ooh-eee, she's a fine woman."

"I bet she is, Ghost," Trapper felt like spanking him.

The kid blew up like an M-80, "No respect! You're a hater!"

"I tried to protect you," Trapper shrugged. Larry didn't need another murder, it was time to send Kevin away. "Hey Ghost, you really want a square?" the jaws of the trap opened.

"You for real?" Kevin sauntered.

"Ceiling panel above the crapper," Trapper cocked his brow toward the back corner. Kevin rolled his eyes and licked his lips. "Wait til' just before you are locked in your room and you hear the guards take a break."

"Tobacco, tobacco, tobacco," Kevin swooned, holding himself back from charging. "Mission toe-back-how," he paced between Trapper and the corner. Up, down, turn around and sit down, ad nauseum.

Trapper stopped him midtrack and held on, "Tell you what Ghost, I'll keep the guys busy, you get the stuff. You only get one cigarette and one match. Take more, I'll kill you."

""I'm off to see the wizard," he sang and continued "I gotta piss like a racehorse and take me a big dookie."

Eyes rolled as he continuing singing.

Dramatic grunts and groans mixed with expletives broadcast from the toileting area. His cellmates struggled to concentrate on a poker game wagering Sunday's bacon.

The red cigarette pack was faintly visible and he was almost tall enough. He stood on tiptoe on the toilet edge. "Trying. Trying to," he groaned. "It's no use! I use one foot and stretch. Yes!" Kevin cheered. "It worked!" He caught the pack falling toward the john. Kerplunk! His foot landed in the water.

"Thought he ate the same stuff we did," a cellmate snorted.

"Sure sounded happy to get that piece out."

"I'll wager you a strip."

Taking one match and one cigarette from the pack Kevin put them into the waist of his jail pants. "One more," taking a match and another cigarette from the pack. "One more," Kevin slapped his hand hard to stop taking. Now that his slipper was wet the throne was slippery. He hopped on his dry foot grunting in feigned constipation.

"You idiot! Do I need to shut you up myself?" Trapper shouted.

Kevin scored. In celebration, he clicked his heels and landed both feet kersploosh in the toilet water.

"It sounds like he fell in."

"Do you think we should pull him out?"

"Let him sink. I thought he was taking a dump not a bath."

Puddles followed each footstep, but Kevin came out smiling.

"You decide to go for a swim, boy?"

"Showers are in the morning."

"Next time use hot water, not toilet water?"

"Go on and tease me," Kevin challenged. The jingle of the jail keys startled him to hide behind Trapper.

"You're in first kid," the gruff guard ordered.

"Good night sir," Kevin politely replied. "Quiet. Tonight I'll stay quiet, no games," he mumbled. Going to sleep gave him fits and a game of payback was always fun. Only one simple rule. Make just enough noise to wake the cellmates.

He stroked the bedraggled cigarettes, "Slow and easy," placing the square between his lips, he struck the match on the concrete. The sulfur tickled his nose. "Ah Choo!" saliva sprayed the match like a fire hose. He held his breath and lit the next match. He rested his head on the cool wall. "I'll be famous someday, rappin' and dancin' is my way."

"The pleasure to measure, no shizzle be dizzle no gurlz in the middle, no room at all, way too small, like a long hall, sitting on the bed, rather be dead, than in this cell, sell no dubs, just bars, no whip, no car."

He took a drag, the smoke curled to the ceiling. "Rusty, rusty. Mah' freestyle game is lame, not the same, in the tank, where I sank, in a cell, not pastel, you see, for me, no key." Warm smoke flowed into his chest, he exhaled trying to blow a smoke ring, "Smiley, wiley, Sam O'Riley, how does your garden grow? With gasoline and kerosene and pretty pumps all in a row. People go, Doc is dead, ah laid him low." He was finally calm.

"Stupid no smoking rules. Health? Smellth. Who believes in wealth? Cancer sticks are my pick," he connected the white stick to the red tip of the first. "A square for each hand, the life of O'Riley. Sam O'Riley. Set me up." He sucked both cigarettes and fell asleep. It was hot. He stuck out his tongue to catch the water, the rain washed the sweat from his head. The low bellow of a river barge foghorn awakened him. A guard grabbed him.

His sheets were on fire and the fire extinguisher was making a big mess. The jailer handcuffed and escorted him into a holding cell, "Enough ruckus! Everyone go back to sleep, fire's out."

Trapper returned to sleep. No one could blame him for trying.

▼

The two individual holding cells were for temporary placement and the previous record was two days. That was ten days ago and Kevin still showed no possibility for reunification with the other prisoners. The cells were located next to the dispatch area for ease of access and observation and had been remodeled from two storage closets. A wire glass window provided viewing from the dispatch area and the food door was on the double locked side. The simple room contained a four-inch raised concrete step with a white plastic mattress. Everything was painted gloss white for swift clean up.

At 4:00 A.M. the first night in solitary, Kevin screamed as though he was being murdered. Jill Jenson, dispatch extraordinaire, almost called 911 on herself. The skreak tumbled Jill out of her chair.

▼

Kevin burst through the whitest wall of his mind into a continuum of white. He screamed louder. His emerald orbs wide, his unseeing gaze darting from wall to ceiling, floor to bed. The door was locked. Why couldn't he penetrate the whiteness? He looked frantically for a point of focus – the room held nothing. "Yes!" he shouted, "My sleeves are orange."

"You proud of that, boy," a gruff voice escalated.

Kevin flailed at the jailer, who cuffed his hands to his feet and lay him on his stomach. He could finally see, but now his hands and feet were locked so he screamed non-stop until his throat was raw. He couldn't hurt the room, but he could hurt himself and the pain reminded him that he was still alive. The jailer stood guard wishing he had ear plugs. County staff watched the show through the window. No one was hurting him – at least not anyone you could see. Forty-five minutes later there was sudden silence.

Kevin smiled at the stunned jailer, "Hey, how come I have handcuffs. I will behave. I promise." Released, Kevin curled in a fetal position on his concrete pad. Everyone tried to ignore him since interacting prolonged the ruckus. An afternoon nap repeated the drama for the day crew.

▼

Jill Jenson hadn't complained in twenty-six years. She could tune out Kevin's muffled screams, but his zoo actions and the noise he called 'jukin' was unbearable. The little window near her station was a drum machine he rapped, tapped and slapped. Each time she looked, he gave her a chimpanzee grin and whatever attention she gave him – positive or negative – only increased his behavior. She felt incarcerated.

"If something doesn't change. I quit!" she shouted.

"It's getting tough, Larry," Ali agreed. "Kevin's behavior doesn't make sense. I called a city colleague who recommends a forensic criminal psychologist with a reputation for assessing complex clients."

"Don't like highbrow city professionals that don't know a thing about the problems they're hired to solve," Larry groused.

"Kevin poses a city-style problem, they say Dr. Watkins is the best."

"Might take a city slicker," Larry rubbed his chin, not about to be held accountable for breaking state or federal laws.

There was no room for mistakes. Balancing the budget was a nightmare Larry was glad he wasn't saddled with and though his boys helped out by collecting fines and forfeited bail monies, most of the budget came from property taxes everyone thought were too high. The commissioners ran Harris County lean and mean and took pride in their independence – less government was better government and no one appreciated high fa'looting lawmakers telling them how to run their county. They ran it fine without help for almost 150 years.

Larry was sure he'd hear about this. Kevin was a problem. It was unsafe to keep him in lock-up with the permanents, but it was unbearable to keep him in solitary. His screams set off rumors, and Jill had been warned by concerned citizens visiting jailed loved ones that allegations of improper care of an inmate to the state department were eminent. So Larry asked the sheriff in the county to the west to house Kevin and got laughed at. The county up north also refused.

Then to top it off, even though Kevin's confession made life legally easier, Larry had begun to question the kid's competence to stand trial or even do the crime. Yet, if not Kevin, who? Who else had issues with Doc? It was no accident. Had Doc waved to someone he knew and that someone blew off his hand with the first bullets and then put a hole in his chest with the next to finish him off? Or had someone mistakenly shot Doc in the chest and when he raised his hand for help blew his hand off? Maybe Sam was right, Doc should have had a German shepherd to put down the enemy, and then again, maybe Sam did it, or Gunner. Or Porter Potts. Doc Johnson's place in the community was vacant and hard to replace.

"OK Ali, give the guy a call. Twenty hours. That's it," Larry gave up.
This is driving you crazy. Larry, let it go.
▼

"Dr. Watkins office, may I help you?" an upbeat female answered.
"Dr. Watkins please."
"I will check to see if he is available," a pause too short for access. "I'm sorry, he is busy."
"I really need to speak with him," Ali begged disclosing the details.
"Yes, I understand, Ms. Hunter. I will see what I can do."
Click.
Ali prayed.
▼

Two hours later, Dr. Watkin's administrative assistant called to schedule Dr. Watkins for Friday, next Monday and Thursday. She requested Ali write an email summary of Kevin Abbott and send it immediately.

9
A ROAD LESS TRAVELED

P er usual, Larry rose early to ride his stationary bike, look at his weights and lean on his treadmill. He had never married, and he tried to keep his physique in bachelor form. Perhaps in a few more years he'd become a husband-replacement for a Riverdale widow. Most of the local women were engaged soon after high school and he missed the first marriage-go-round. Larry slicked back his hair and left early, anticipating the arrival of Dr. Watkins.

▼

Dr. LaMar Watkins donned his Italian-cut black suit, polished shoes, and checked his nails and mustache. He flicked off the stereo, picked out a couple CD's for the ride, and grabbed his aviator shades. Twenty hours was minimal, but he was good. The blue bird September day made his vehicle choice easy. He clicked the remote, listening for the retractable soft-top to snap into place, the engine purred waiting for a pleasant autumn ride.

The sounds awakened little Johnny Diaperman who tackled his leg as he began to open the door, "Daddy, Daddy, lub you Daddy. Bye, bye."

The giant father scooped up his little quarterback, feeling the weight of a wet, warm and dirty diaper hidden under footed pilot pajamas.

"You be good for Mama today, I'll be back at dinnertime." With a kiss to the cheek and a mustache nuzzle to his tummy; Johnny flew in the air like a fighter pilot. Up the stairs soaring in his daddy's big arms. The duet rumbled with a mirage of motor noises softly landing in the big bed next to Mama. "Honey, it's early, and little stinky pants is up. I gotta go. See you at dinner. I love you," LaMar gently kissed his beautiful wife.

"Lub you Daddy. Br br br rooom...." Johnny bounced on the bed.

Tamara grimaced hoping that nothing packed in that diaper was leaking on 'her' bed.

▼

Some days begin with a bad smell and just continue that way. LaMar pulled onto the freeway behind an SUV emitting heavy metal bass that shook his car like an electric shaver. Worse yet, he was lodged between a honey-dew truck filled with used port-a-potties, and a foul-smelling roofing truck. The tar truck driver simultaneously chewed tobacco and smoked a cigarette. LaMar tried to maneuver his car out of spitting range as the traffic ground to a halt. The rising sun heated the gaseous green and brown structures tied to the Jiffy Biffy truck and the putrid scent poured into the confined air space occupied by his black BMW Z3 Roadster.

The traffic creeped.

"What kind of person would work for Jiffy Biffy?" LaMar breathed through his mouth, and avoided eye contact with the toothless driver lustfully eyeing his vehicle with puckered lips. The next exit unshackled him from the gridlock of odiferous vehicles and the GPS computer female voice complained that he was off course, go straight .7 miles, follow the freeway entrance to the left. LaMar ignored her and drove on.

"Ahhh," he grinned taking a deep breath. He resettled into the creature comforts of creamy leather and racecar dash admiring the superb engineering and handful of power. If it weren't for a perfect driving record, he would have challenged the speed limit, but that was part of the Roadster Challenge – maintaining the perfect speed – one mile under the maximum radar allowance, without using cruise.

His sixteen-inch cross spoke alloy wheels spun.

He punched in a Wynton Marsalis CD for the two-hour drive and balanced the speakers. Marsalis was the essence of the American equation – greatness, earned through hard work, humble in success. LaMar felt a camaraderie with his impassioned trumpet playing. He could feel the jazz music rooted in the African American culture deep in his bones; the vibrations on his lips. LaMar, duplicated his style with a sophisticated work ethic and respectful persona mixed with a cadenza of creativity and innovation – calculated to attainment. His adoptive parents provided him a middle class opportunity and he took advantage of it. He respected his elders, practiced music three hours a day, and got straight A's. He pushed for a higher standard and fixed any character flaw he uncovered.

He turned up the music.

His adoptive father, Reggae, was a talented coronet player and under his tutoring he played well. Jazz became lucrative. Scholarships led him to the University on a full music ride. Yet despite membership in a number of ensembles, jazz band, orchestra and marching band, his career dream was not music. Three schools of higher education later LaMar became a doctor of criminal forensic psychology. Somehow, his creative musical improvisation led him out of music and into the acoustics of the mind.

He entertained attending med school and a doctorate in psychiatry, but the more he studied psychology, the more he preferred viewing psychological problems as a result of life stress and coping behaviors, rather than a biological or disease process. Even today, he viewed medication as a sometimes necessary, but overused client management tool. He preferred spending time with clients and directing them to discover their own ways to solve problems, and build healthy attainable lifeplans.

Over the years, he worked with both victims and perpetrators, and during the last couple years, he had found himself spending more time in forensic psychology, performing clinical evaluations and providing court reports. The work was lucrative and satisfying.

▼

The countryside flowed from one crescendo to the next and synchronized the Roadster to the topography. A red brick church guarded a hillside among buckskin cornfields ready for harvest. Dark tilled soil waited for spring soybeans butting against bright green sprouting winter wheat. Two-story white farmhouses surrounded by windrows of pines buttressed wooden red barns and metal pole buildings, preparing for blankets of snow. Lazy brown Guernseys and black and white Holsteins greeted the Roadster with loud moos. Blue ponds reflected the cloudless sky between rustic hills.

The composition moved serenely from harmony to discord with a loud backfire. A tangle of vehicles grew out of a mass of unmown grass and three scrawny children in rags rode a curious ATV-lawnmower-tractor jalopy from behind a shack enmeshed in tarpaper and plastic sheathing. They bumped down a rut-ridden road. The youthful driver tactfully swerved to plow gleefully through the darkest puddle. Muddy water sprayed high into the air dousing school backpacks. The children raised their hands in triumph.

Two outbuildings struggled not to crumple.

He neared the drive as the children climbed off to reveal a duct taped seat and random pieces of scrap metal attached with the same adhesive. The tallest child, a long haired boy or a short haired girl, took a large rusted chain and attached it to a weedy sign declaring 'Porter Potts Scrap Metall, Recicling Yer Junk'. Two younger urchins riled about something locked arms in a wrestling match under the crooked mail box. Arms swung under the advertisement 'priseles honney Potts.' A wet backpack hurled by the tallest young one opened and a waterfall of school papers covered the ditch. An angry male shouted, and then a shotgun. Crows scattered in the distance and the children stood regimented.

▼

A green sign read 'Riverdale, population 1,550 and it appeared the small midwestern town was built along the banks of the meandering Dale River. It began as soon as you crossed the narrow concrete bridge lined with red, white and dark purple flowers. The blooms themed the village and were repeated in the huge baskets that hung from two old fashioned green light poles proudly displaying American flags. The first, Old Glory, waved proclamations of freedom to the independent spirit of a hard working people. The second, a flag of mourning, waved "you are not forgotten," a reminder to Riverdale's citizens of men and women who did not return home. It seemed the past was not forgotten in Riverdale.

LaMar slowed, looking for the Harris County Court House and Jail. Shopkeepers rolled down awnings. The barber polished the red and white pole. A yellow school bus passed. A few people walked into Dee's Café. A man with a yellow rain suit walked a small mongrel wearing a bright blue sweater. Everything was extremely quiet. He passed Alma's Wash Depot and Cleaner. Many stopped to stare at the slow moving black convertible. LaMar glanced at his side mirror. He was being followed by a patrol car. He thought to pull over but decided against it.

He scrupulously paid attention to the law, yet even with careful compliance he had twice become suspect. Regardless of professional training in interview and conversation techniques, those experiences severely encouraged him to avoid uniformed encounters. He didn't need conflict with the very people who hired him.

Thoughtgully he ran down an autopilot checklist, insurance in the glove box, seatbelt on, hands on steering wheel, cell phone speaker connected, license in wallet, tabs current, speed under the posted speed limit, music too loud, roof's down so no need to worry about rolling down the window, glass clear, no cracks in windshield and no dingle balls. He had checked his brake and signal lights the week before. He hadn't turned so he didn't worry about signaling. His mother's spirit whispered, "Use kindness. Don't cause a fuss. Smile. Keep your hands on the steering wheel. I want you home, not dead, on the street, or in jail. Use caution. Whites put their faith in police protection, even support their efforts. They overlook our individual differences. Don't let yourself become fodder for a lineup, don't allow opportunity for misidentification of another's crime."

The jazz concert blared. The squad car was so close he felt heat on his back, "I could slam my brakes and let the patrol car kiss my bumper to ask where I am to work today," revenge wasn't his style and there was a possibility of any number of hidden infractions he could unknowingly commit. His dash post-it note said to make a right at the stop sign.

LaMar signaled turning off the main drag.

Larry followed closely.

"At least the cherries aren't flashing."

A large granite stone proclaimed Harris County Court House, 1883, oldest jail in Minnesota. It's Romanesque and Italian architecture surprised him as he pulled into the visitor parking space.

The Sheriff pulled alongside.

LaMar checked his waves. "No wonder people stared, a du-rag in a lily-white town outfitted him as a gangster. Great first impression." He ripped it off and stashed it in his glove compartment, his waves smooth. He grabbed his brief case and walked up the red, white and purple petunia lined walk. Wafts of sweetness rose with the warm morning sun.

He straightened his tie, smoothed his slacks, pulled back his shoulders and walked up the stairs. Boot steps tap tapped behind him. LaMar clicked the remote to put the soft-top back into place. The footsteps stopped. LaMar smiled, he didn't need to look back.

The jail entrance was secured with two entry points, he pressed the intercom and Jill buzzed him in. The second door opened without pushing a button.

Jill greeted him from the front, the sheriff, from the rear.

"Visiting day is Sunday," Jill offered, "Unless, you're Kevin's attorney."

"You here to see someone special?" Larry panted. He was glad he beat Dr. Watkins.

"I am Dr. LaMar Watkins, and, I am here to see, evaluate and assess Mr. Kevin Abbott," LaMar stated.

"You sounded . . ."

LaMar stopped the sheriff in mid-sentence . . . "white on the phone."

"I didn't say that," Larry hedged.

"No, you didn't, I did," LaMar offered, "I figured you didn't want to begin our relationship with an epithet." LaMar's eyes twinkled. "I spent time learning to talk like the six-o-clock news. Don't worry. If you'd be," he paused, "more comfortable, I *can* sound black."

Embarrassed, Ali put out her hand, breaking the ice with a sincere smile, "Dr. Watkins, we spoke on the phone, I am pleased to meet you. I'm Ali Hunter and we'll be sharing office space."

LaMar obliged his hand to a plump, graying woman with a ponytail.

"And I'm Jill Jenson, 911 Dispatch," another matron of ample size.

"It's nice to meet you," LaMar scanned the dispatch area. Monitors flipped through jail cells. A muffled scream came from behind a window above the bottled-water. LaMar went to scan inside. One holding cell was empty. The other contained a small, red haired prisoner standing in the corner, waving his hands next to his ears.

He turned to the Sheriff, "That must be your problem child."

"Yes sir," Larry knew he was small, but this was ridiculous, his head barely reached the top of LaMar's shoulders. "Sheriff Kelly, folks 'round here call me Larry."

"Let's get to work, the budget's too small to waste time," LaMar bent over to shake hands and smirked. Larry felt his bigness.

Jill whispered to Ali, "Seems like a nice black man, very articulate."

LaMar overheard, the air of a stallion blew through his nostrils. Being a black man and being nice was not an oxymoron. He wished the prolixity would end. He rolled his eyes.

Ali escorted Dr. Watkins to her office, chattering with no air between sentences for him to answer. "I cleared a space for you. Sorry we don't have much room. Right now this is the best we've got. I'll be back around noon and we can talk then. Feel free to help yourself to coffee. You're welcome to use my computer. I've got Internet. Bye." She disappeared behind a row of dented metal cabinets.

LaMar compared her body to her desk. It appeared both had had their share of hot dogs, donuts, and farm-cooked meals. LaMar's wire-frames slipped down his nose. "Thank you, Ms. Hunter."

He washed the gray metal desk with a wet wipe from his briefcase. The county was frugal. The chair provided had one wheel that wouldn't turn, was missing an arm and stuffing poked out of the seat. He checked to make sure there was nothing that would snag his suit and sat carefully.

Ali's desk housed a yellowing PC, stacks of dusty folders, dregs of coffee in an old cracked cup, donut crumbs with colored sprinkles, a picture of two young girls, and two inches of pink telephone messages mixed with yellow notepad scribbles skewered with a nail. LaMar tapped her spacebar to activate her screen; she had graciously left Kevin's file open for his perusal. She seemed chaotic, but considerate.

From the report Ms. Hunter provided, Kevin Abbott floated between competence and diminished capacity. His contract was simple: evaluate extenuating circumstances, help Kevin integrate into prison life and provide an adult pre-sentencing evaluation prior to going to trial. He reviewed the daily inmate logs and shift inspections. Kevin had a lot of log entries beginning at intake.

Larry stood behind LaMar. "Expect an expert assessment with the kind of money you're getting. Twenty hours to wrap this up, no ifs, ands, or buts. I had to fight for that."

"Yes, Larry," his short little self made it perfectly clear. He opened his laptop; his wireless connections were working and his smart phone registered four bars. LaMar keystroked his 'To Do' list —

Friday – 6 hours - Meet
    Kevin – complete testing, evaluations
    Alison Hunter, social service
    Tasha Jones, Kevin's girlfriend
    Sam O'Riley, Kevin's employer
Saturday/Weekend – 2 hours
    Find, contact, interview Kevin's parents
    Process testing results
    Review findings, determine course of action
    Outline court report
Monday – 6 hours
    Complete interviews
    Begin write up of court report
Thursday – 3 hours (if fly)
    Deliver completed report

3 Hours Travel Time (minimum each way)
Goal: 20 Hours
Total (o: impossible)

He typed the period with flourish. The large, round, white-faced clock with black hands ticked. It was time to meet Kevin.

▼

Dr. Watkins opened the cell door without Kevin noticing. The young man's hands anxiously butterfly flapped. He shivered in the corner. His voice tormented, "I hate white. White is cracker walls, white is ice floors, white is white. I hate white." The paradox, Kevin's skin was white as snow.

"Mr. Kevin Abbott?"

Kevin jumped kneehigh in a turn.

LaMar stepped back.

Hateful haunting eyes. Familiar. Caged eyes that bounced against the good doctor's soul. It was not his place to judge or feel, he was trained in transference reflection. He sucked back air he held in his lungs releasing slowly. He checked his reaction as unclinical.

"What's up nigga!" Kevin cocked his head to the right, put up an open palm, and then closed it into a fist; thumbs up.

LaMar nodded silently; the verbal generation gap hit him between the eyes. The word felt like a closed fist. Kevin may think the n-word is trendy, with his homeboy body language and transposition of 'er' to 'a', but coming from a family who fought for civil rights, no white man has the right to call me that. This kid was no brother.

He knew intrinsically that white people used the n-word derogatorily so long as there were no black people around; whereas, black people used the word as an endearment within a closed culture most whites never entered nor understood. It really didn't matter on which side of the color line you stood. Light or dark, LaMar equated the feeling he got when overhearing it, to how he felt when he came home to find the babysitter smoking in his smoke-free, air purified home. It betrayed his integrity and lessened the value of the person saying it.

Call it a legacy he was born to carry in his bones, the anger against the word was deep in his cellular memory. It was an insult he refused to use or oblige in any form. The cousin word 'nigga' festered the infection begun when he was tailed into Riverdale and then assumed he was white because of his title, profession and intonation. This was not a good start.

This day of music and sunshine held landmines that burst into a fire ant farm. His personal feelings were moot. His contract of twenty hours was evaporating. This was no place to ponder. He promised Harris County a pre-sentencing report with ideas to help Kevin acclimate to prison life regardless of personal feelings.

"Hello, I am Dr. Watkins. I am here to help you, Mr. Abbott. Today we will be using the courthouse library to talk and do testing," he pushed his glasses up the bridge of his nose.

Kevin cocked his jaw, jutted out his bottom teeth and lowered his head. His shoulders sagged. He moved forward with a personal rendition of the 'Sea Walk', tapped his chest five times with his fist and raised his hand. "I ain't no, Mr. Abbott. Call me Kevin, or call me Ghost, but don't call me that. I ain't no white cracker or old geezer." He flared his left nostril like an ornery dog revealing a set of well cared for teeth.

Dr. Watkins recognized the gang welcome and ignored it. He also noted the teeth. "Why do you act black, Kevin?"

"I am black. My real mom was light skinned and I have a picture of my black brotha."

"Where is the picture Kevin?"

"They stole it when I came in. They put it in a grey box. Can you get it for me?" Kevin pouted like a toddler.

Choosing the minority road made no sense and Kevin's very white freckled features didn't project afro-centricity. LaMar failed to realize the accepting nature of his African American culture. Afro-mixed children chided and disbanded from their Asian or White culture were embraced in African Ethnicity and tended to gravitate to the culture on the darker side where skin color was acknowledged. Kevin, who spent years of teasing in whiteness, found solace in whatever black heritage he thought he could claim.

"How long have you been a Ranger?" LaMar avoided the question.

"Promise you'll get my photo? I won't talk unless you promise."

"I'll see what I can do."

Kevin grinned, "Claiming now fo' fo' years."

"You got any stars?" LaMar crossed his arms across his chest, biting his bottom lip and lowering an urban glare towards Kevin.

"Two, fo' sho'," green eyes speared LaMar's heart in a violent betrayal. A cauldron of death and defecation stirred with the cock of Kevin's head. His body movements unlatched something. He had always scoffed at spiritual demons by taking the high road of logic and science. Shake this off. Stay professional. Focus.

"How'd you get the star, Kevin?" Dr. Watkins lifted his chin, tilted his head left, put out his fist, cocking his jaw.

Kevin connected his fist smiling. "You got rank, doc? You an ol' g?"

LaMar raised his brow, put out his lips, shook his head and forwarded his shoulders. He purposely sent mixed signals to make Kevin determine his own answer. Being raised as a teen of black affluence never taught LaMar the ropes of the street, but being a Sunday school teacher at North Baptist did. His church boyz honed his skills in the underground vernacular of limited words, body language and appropriate eye contact.

"Why ya here?" Kevin asked.

LaMar motioned for Kevin to take a seat next to him in the library, a small room filled with paperbacks and law books, a folding table and metal chairs. A high placed window streamed sunlight.

Kevin suspiciously fondled the back of the metal chair.

LaMar looked down, "Have a seat Kevin."

Kevin winced before sitting in the black metal chair.

"I am here to help you and I need to ask you some questions."

"OK," Kevin sat on the very edge of the chair. Whenever someone offered help, it never seemed good.

"Why don't you have an attorney?"

Kevin looked at him like he was from Mars.

"There is no name in your file. No lawyer has visited you."

"Don't worry Doc, I have a lawyer. I met him. They said if I couldn't afford one, they'd get me one and they did. I need a free one cuz Sam don't pay much. The paper says attorney. I like him."

"Kevin, I have a copy of that paper and that attorney is prosecution and representing the county." It wasn't the first time LaMar had run into this misunderstanding. He tried to explain. Kevin refused to understand.

"Don't worry Doc, I'm lawyered up!"

"Do you know why you are here?"

"Because you asked me to come."

"No, I mean do you know why you are in jail?"

Kevin was silent, his eyes rolled back and forth, and up and down like a gambling machine, finally landing on a winner. "The guys didn't like me?"

"Is that why you're in solitary?"

"I dunno."

"Do you know why the other prisoners don't like you?"

"I dunno."

"Do you always answer 'I dunno'?"

Kevin's smiled like he had just gotten caught with his hand in a cookie jar, "It's easier if I dunno, then it doesn't count if I answer wrong. I just dunno. People talk too fast, they put words on top of words. They ask questions like why, I don't answer why questions. Makes my mind feel like I'm in the mirror house at the carnival." Kevin rolled his emerald green eyes in a familiar way. "Can we turn the lights off, Doc? I can think better when the lights are off. Then I don't jiggle."

LaMar took notes and accommodated Kevin's request, the late morning sun filtered through the windows.

"That's better. I'm allergic to crazy lights. I like you, Doc," relief spread across his face.

"Kevin, tell me about your family." LaMar was compelled to smile. What was it about Kevin that revolted and enchanted him at the same time?

"Margie is nice, she understands me. Q is fun. I love Tasha."

"No, not that family, your other family."

"Oh," Kevin looked startled, "You know about them?"

"Yes."

"Chief is one rad dude, he might even be a diplomat one day. He looks out for me. Stayed wit' him in the city. He gets women. He set me up in business, kept me safe by getting me a frontin' job. Then I screwed him . . ." Kevin paused and rubbed the curliest red, nappy hair LaMar had ever seen. "That's why I came here. I'm safe with Tasha. Chief was going to kill me. He'd really do it. He's got two tears! I saw them!"

"Kevin, tell me about the family you lived with as a little boy."

"Oh, you mean Mom and Dad. They're crazy? They ran away from me," Kevin's statement was matter-of-fact. "Their phone quit working. Margie's my mom now." Kevin paused, then continued sadly in a little boy style voice, "How come you think they ran away? They used to visit and bring cookies."

"Tell me more," LaMar avoided using why.

"Well, like Mom would tell me she didn't want me to be with this girl or kiss her or make out, so I just went over to her house and saw her instead. And then she'd get all mad because she said I disobeyed. She never told me not to go to her house."

"Explain," LaMar motioned to encourage Kevin to continue.

"Well she didn't tell me I couldn't see her, did she?" LaMar noted the conversation, he expected Kevin to bust a smile.

"How did you get that scar, Kevin?" LaMar ran his finger down his own indented cheek and pointed to Kevin's hand.

"Oh man, that's cool isn't it? Mom said don't hit people, so I punched a window. It sounded cool. There was blood all over. Mom took me to the doctor to get sewed up. It didn't hurt."

It seemed Kevin preferred to be a cool criminal rather than a dumb boy. "How come you hit the window?"

Kevin's eyes glared at LaMar, his voice filled with anger, "He stole my money." His facials switched to a pride "but I didn't hit him. He went home when Mom brought me to the doctor." The anger returned. "Took my seventy dollars and I never got it back." Kevin smiled, "he bought some cool shoes!" The anger resurfaced, "I hate those shoes! He's still my friend."

It was like watching a televised baseball game when his father controlled the remote. He removed booklets from his briefcase, "Kevin we will be doing a significant amount of paperwork today. I need you to cooperate if you want me to help you."

"To get my picture," Kevin winked at LaMar. "I don't do tests with mostlies, sometimes, and maybe's. I only do true and false."

LaMar waited to hear what more Kevin had to say.

"I can't answer mostlies, it either is or it isn't, yes or no, true or false. I don't have mostlies. Do you hear me?"

Dr. Watkins spent the remainder of the day paper testing Kevin. While performing concentration tasks, there seemed to be marked suppression of the executive functions. Kevin stabbed his pencil through the paper, broke it in half, turned it into a projectile. He verbally let Dr. Watkins know explicitly how highly he thought of the value of his testing. LaMar wished for a SPECT scan to see brain functionality, he expected decreased activity in the left prefrontal cortex and the left temporal lobe areas but not enough to determine incompetence.

By the end of the day, LaMar was as drained as Kevin and felt like he'd been through a war zone.

Kevin took no blame for his behaviors, "The test made him!" Dr. Watkins noted Kevin's reactions and responses.

"Kevin, we're through. You can head back to your quarters."

"I don't have quarters, they put mine in a grey box with my pictures." Kevin was serious, his mouth remained open, as it had all day.

"You promised my pictures," he seemed sad, floating away. "Will you find my Mom and Dad? Mom makes good cookies." Lost.

LaMar felt lost, too.

Quintell Lawrence Jones, usually referred to as Q, son and protector of Margie Jones, pressed his nose to the school bus window to check out Hans Hardware. The desiderate knife glimmered just as a shiny black convertible drove slowly into town. The familiar swirl in the pit of his stomach he had felt so often as a child returned.

He worried about Mama. Why now? Why here? He didn't like what, or whom he saw. Q grabbed Tasha as she entered the high school front doors. "Mama's got a man coming today. Saw the 'dubs' from the bus."

Tasha hurried to class nauseated. She pressed her hands tightly together under her desk and rubbed hard back and forth. This couldn't be happening. Slowly with her head hanging she shuffled, "Miss Anderson, I'm not feeling well. May I please visit the nurse?"

"My, Tasha, your hands feel warm. Here's a pass. I hope you feel better." Tasha pocketed the coveted paper and continued rubbing her hands. She held her breathe to gain color. Luckily Nurse Johnson was not used to dealing with a hot, flushed black female.

Tasha called Mama from the office, their emergency safety plan was fail proof, "Mama are you all right?"

"Of course child, why you asking?"

"Q saw a man."

"I ain't got no man, got enough to do with working and Dee's Pie Booth at the Riverdale Apple Festival, that's Sunday afternoon. Saturday Ms. Ali invited us to a canning," Mama laughed. "Get me a hot sauce recipe."

Tasha heavily rolled her shoulders, held her mouth open purposely to look lethargic, "Mama says I should make the best of it. She thinks I'll feel better soon." She returned to class with no faculty the wiser of the ruse. Q must be imagining things.

▼

For the rest of the school day time stood still. Each second a minute, each hour an eternity. He appeared hebetudinous as he gazed out the window in a worry. Q liked that word, heb·e·tu·di·nous, and he rolled the syllables on his tongue, appearing to be chewing. Worry is a strange animal and it fearlessly crept up the back of his neck with rotten memories that stole his present and confused his mind mixing fact with fantasy and working its way into the crevices of his . . . mathematics . . . "What, what? I'm sorry. What did you say Mrs. Leibert?" Shocked into the present, Q was captured in a fret about the impending after school trouble.

"I said, what is the common denominator of these fractions?" She raised her voice glaring at Q, who appeared lost in the ozone, motioned to her mouth and then the trash with a scowl as if he was deaf and dumb.

He wasn't hard of hearing. The hand signals were unneeded.

She waved her hand toward the fractions.

"Huh?" He didn't know where to begin even though he knew all the answers. He hated being accused of something he didn't do. Teachers behaved nicer if they feared setting him off. So, usually he blew things out of proportion and played defense with such finesse no one guessed his game. He was notorious in causing a commotion by saying or doing the wrong thing at the wrong time. He held back, there was trouble enough.

Mrs. Leibert pointed, forcing him to walk like a dead man to a front room hanging. The back of his neck burned as he recited multiplication by the dozens. A spectacle. He obliged by spitting out fantasy gum.

"Never mind. Mr. Jones. Sara can you answer this simple question?" Mrs. Leibert emphasized the word simple, as though she too had given up on his intelligence. The teachers in Riverdale hadn't exactly figured out what to do with him yet. They didn't know if he could or couldn't, would or wouldn't, yet they seemed to think he was a professor when it came to black history and culture. Did some unwritten law exist that endorsed him in his fourteen-year-old self as a scholar and an expert? It was a new front street twist he didn't think much of.

He was perfectly capable of rising to any academic challenge but he

learned long ago it was easier to take advantage of ignorance. Dumbness
was expected and it didn't cause unnecessary attention. His 'smart mouth'
gained him notoriety and changing schools two or three times in one year
pretty much made teachers throw up their arms in despair and placate him
by complimenting him for getting C's. They were surprised he could perform that well, as if that was good enough. He silently played the dozens,
snapin' and cappin' while they tried to teach him things he already knew.

They didn't know Q was a laureate. Alone in bed he sharpened his
mind on the worn and tattered pages of a Webster's dictionary, preparing
for his next verbal victim. In a war against wits, Q was king and considered himself a royal pugilist. He'd gotten beat up at age ten with oral mortar, and he vowed never again. He had knockout linguistics and personal
poetry. He conquered the best, painting sound bite pictures against oppo-
nents with verbal boxing. He mixed words in checkmate strategy. Once he
got wound up, he spit game faster than a speeding bullet. It took guileful
craftiness, strategic facial expression, perfect body positioning, and darting eyes that were quick to sense the next blow. He had the mind and the
rhythm to cock the hammer and then fire a series of verbal H-bomb snaps.
He could bring down a whole crowd in mad respect of laughter about his
opponent's mother, sister, brother, body, style and gear. Unbeknownst to
Mama, it was his verbal skills that earned him scout status without a jump.
No one could say he was pusillanimous, pyoo-suh-LAN-uh-mus. He rolled
the larger word for timid enjoying the multiple mouth movements.

He had acclimated to being placed in classes with lower functioning
students being taught at the lowest level where he had plenty of time to
think about things other than schoolwork. His lessons and worksheets
were so easy it took hard work to slow down. He was a doodler with
finese. Too bad Riverdale was beginning to feel similar to the schools he'd
previously attended. In his heart, Q wanted someone to push him to reach
his real potential, but no one except Tasha ever challenged him and though
Mama was mighty streetwise she was no book learner.

The day droned on. Q zoned out. Zoning out was useful when Mama
had men in and he didn't want to hear or when she striped his arms with
the extension cord. Zoning was different from indifference. It happened
because he cared too much and worked well whenever life got out of
hand. Q hadn't quite figured out the new almost all white student body.
He had tried a game of snaps only to discover that the person he targeted

grew even whiter, called him 'rude' and walked away. He wasn't rude at all compared to the about-face he got when he tried to be a little friendly. So far the only language skill he'd been allowed to show was translating rap lyrics in the halls after a "hey man, wad duz 'ride it ma pony' mean to you."

▼

Mama was a survivor, but she didn't always do the best thinking. She was barely fourteen, his age, when Tasha was born to a cracker daddy who died walking into a stray gang fight bullet. She was sixteen when Q arrived. Neither father ever paid child support. One dead. One beat.

His Daddy, wow, that was an old lost thought. He was four-years-old when Daddy went away. He watched the whole sorry mess listening to his little boy heart exploding hiding under the sofa while Daddy talked to brown-shoe man who came to get the white 'don't touch, it's not sugar baby' package BadOne left. BadOne had tyrannosaurus rex eyes and he was real real bad. Brown shoe was happy because he found the little package. He asked Daddy to heat it and Daddy's black working boots walked into the kitchen while Q rested his head on his forearm to make a pillow. The microwave door opened and closed. The bell dinged.

The last school bell tripped Q into reality; he grabbed his backpack and ran, stopping for a blink in the gym. Bat in hand he slid it down his wide right pant leg and held it through his pocket. Then he boarded the school bus as a wooden soldier. His leg rested across the cracked green vinyl. He snarled at the Potts' boy who asked for a seat. He morphed from vigil to vigilante, sitting near the front of the bus. His Mama would never be hurt again.

He'd been the man of the family for ten years, and now that 'BadOne' was gone, he held top dog position.

Brown shoes faced Daddy's boots. He sounded like a cop on TV. Brown shoe said, "You're under arrest."

Then Daddy said a naughty word. Slap. Clap. Skin hitting skin. From under brown shoes long shirt came a long black handle. He hit Daddy so hard it would have been a homerun, but it was his good, good daddy. Daddy crumbled to the floor.

Q started to crawl from hiding, but Daddy's eyes caught him and he mouthed. "Stay there baby. Hide!" Then Daddy's eyes closed and Q locked his feet around the leg in the back of the sofa so he wouldn't get up. He had the best daddy in the whole wide world. "Jesus don't let my Daddy die," he repeated, and repeated, and repeated. Before he came in from playing he'd seen brown shoe man laughing with BadOne playing low-low, a game of fool your friends. To this day, Q refused to know BadOne's name. He was a nightcrawler worm and his Daddy was a stallion! Daddy said nothing good happens after midnight, BadOne said nothing happens until midnight. BadOne was slick with English so fine he sounded like a teacher, and words so foul he should have been chewing lava soap. Brown-shoe man called the real police to kidnap Daddy. And Q was left alone while Mama was in church singing 'hallelujahs' and 'Praise Jesus' with Tasha. Q told Mama he wanted to kill brown shoe.

Years later Mama explained, "Yer Daddy never did drugs. He never had a record. BadOne wanted me so he set him up with a sweetener size packet of cocaine. That was a misdemeanor until it was heated and turned into a federal felony. Never happen in my house again!" she shouted and then threw their microwave off the balcony. "BadOne claimed to be Daddy's 'dawg.' The '5-O' watch you when you are friends with gangster. It's a loser life. Drama, drugs, and death is all your get."

"Possession. Guilty! The public defender didn't do squat. It would have taken over two hundred pounds of weed to get the same mandatory sentence. Lucky I was in church or you'd be in foster care and I'd be in jail too. I would have hit that undercover with my frypan," Mama sneered. "You telling me for one punch yer Daddy got beat and rapped with assaultin' an officer."

"Yes'm," was all he could answer and he still wasn't sure if Mama was exaggerating felonies and Federal Prison, but he did know Mama was serious. He'd felt the buckle side of her belt impacting his seat of learning. Somehow Mama figured it took a good swat on the butt to reach his hard head. He was still angry that the innocense of his childhood was taken away the day that Daddy joined the statistics of a hundred black men arrested for every black college graduate.

"He was saving his money to marry me and move us to the 'burbs." Mama often said sadly, she was bound and determined to keep Q flying the straight and narrow. "Your Daddy is a good man. He had real schooling and worked a real job. He expects that of you too." He hadn't seen Daddy in ten years. There were no buses stopping at the prison and it took ten months to save for the taxi.

And Mama was right. BadOne showed up right after the police

telling her how pretty she was, and how much he loved her in his fancy car. BadOne never let Mama, Tasha or him even sit in that car!

Q was an insider. He knew if you ate BadOne's candy, you became his slave. Good boys changed under BadOne's spell and pseudo 'scout' program meetings. He was a gang leader, not a troop master and children sold their virtues for tokens and C's. By middle school most of his old friends floated through reality. Send aways, he scoffed at while he ingratiated whiggers, like Kevin, to do his dirty work with pellet pistols while he carried a 45 in his sock. They were his expendable front line.

BadOne kept a burner up his sleeve and pretended to target practice TV divas with the same crudeness he forced on Mama in the middle of the night before handing out early morning delivery orders to smiling children honored to do his dirty work.

Police liked him. He spoke of community pride. He held a dozen roses like a proper man and bragged about buying pretty Mama's finely braided hair and a new dress. Truth be told Mama was holed up inside the apartment, with her eyes swollen shut and a cigarette burn on her thigh.

And she forgave BadOne because of roses! It infuriated Q. The cost was far too high for finely braided hair that frizzed by the time she was presentable enough to leave the house. Q hated rose stench. It reminded him of all the times his Mama's pretty mahogany skin turned ashy as the unwatered roses drooped into brown petals on the table. Thank God, Mama got sick and tired of all that. The neighbors told her she souled out her race, but he was proud of her and their new beginning. It was brave of Mama to stand up for herself and her kids. She told that skinny-lipped white faced social worker in the city her truth and that truth sent them to the rural white people of Riverdale, with a promised freedom.

Q was not about to risk losing all they had worked for to some phony sugar daddy. If this fancy man in the fancy racecar was a drug dealer, he was not about to wait the six seconds to think in a crisis that his stupid high school counselor tried to plow into his head. Too often, Mama said she'd never go back and later cuddled in BadOne's arms.

Today, he was the man, Mama's protector! Q held the bat tightly sure the 'nigger vulture' had returned. He was no dumbbell. His feet may have been transplanted into the country but the root was all street. The man was a 'nigger vulture' not even deserving of the 'nigga' term of endearment. Q watched out the bus window for the flashy black BMW.

▼ MIKE

Mike passionately slammed the locker door echoing a rifle shot. Once again he had charged ahead without thinking and killing was easier than he imagined. Its memories now lodged quietly next to the first accident with Shawn. He should never have covered Shaun's eyes with his hands and then shouted rabbit, but there was no turning back. He would have to live with it. Since Shaun's death, it had taken years to find solace, but then came tweeking. Honey sure flowed from the Potts. No one suspected the truth. It was his secret and a small secret compared to his grandfather's, his murdered grandfather. Maybe he served under a generational curse of operating under orders. The discovery of true heritage blindsided him. Was he a madman too? He was just looking for change in his father's desk drawer and there was the picture of the grandfather he never knew wearing . . . standing next to . . . Blindsided, he shot at a flushing grouse. A heart shot. The next three shots were instinct learned from high scores on video games and years of beer can pistol practice. Too bad his 'old man' suspected the truth about the Potts.

He arrived amped to keep his mind crystal clear. He flexed his shoulders and pulled on his football pads. He had a game to win, college plans and a life. Kevin was a loser anyway.

▼ ALI

Ali was the whole social service team of Harris County and all 550 square miles of landscape held only 17,000 people. Riverdale was the county seat and seven other small villages sprinkled out farms and single family homes. Management of her department relied on the rural knowing of everyone's business and her new conduit was Margie. For access to knowledge she laid down professional boundaries and gained a new friend.

"Hi Love, want a cup of joe?" Margie's shift was over and she was heading home. Dee's high school crew was aproned and ready to serve.

"Oh Margie that's okay, just wanted to make sure you are planning to come out to the farm on Saturday." She looked forward to canning with Margie and sharing the abundance of her kitchen garden. Ali's little jars of sauces and jams were her calling card when she made home visits.

"Wouldn't miss it for the world. Never did a canning before. Have a seat," Margie joined Ali at a café table, pouring herself a cup.

"Been one of those days Margie," Ali yawned. "Somethings just aren't the way they seem, are they?"

"Never been, never are," Margie shared, "Some think it's what you see, what you get." She laughed, her good nature was contagious.

"What do ya mean?" Ali paused to let her friend think. Margie's ideas were usually a process and given time and space she saw the world in brilliant color. Ali patiently stirred her coffee.

"My man was a looker, slick to police and services. It was all show. He promised protection. He was strong and big. Drove a fine car he never let me sit in. Promised me support, food for my children. I learn street fast, not book fast. Learned to keep my kids quiet while he slept, stay low when he worked deals, beg for church donations to feed him. In Riverdale, I become me without a dark shadow. I'm free here of name calling. Free of the back of his hand. The knuckles of his fist. "

"Given a snapshot anyone can look good," Ali offered.

"My Margie was shredded into bits and pieces. I quit believing in me. His protection turned me into his property. He kept my keys, medical card and ID. Said I'd lose them. He said sorry. I forgave him, kept my mouth shut about his side girl." Margie had refused despair and clung to her children. "He'd open the window and wiggle out snake fast when social services came, listening for me to say the wrong thing. Said government people'd take my kids. I feared social services more than him. He offered me drugs."

"Did they help?"

"Ali, I never did no drugs. It's hard enough to keep my brain working. I need all I got to help my kids. He wore me to a frazzle, called me his special lady. I'm no special nothing, special ed, special services, I've had it all. All that talk means pull out, set aside, not good enough."

"Margie, I've never yet taken away someone's children. I don't judge a lifestyle; I was trailer trash. Child protection will always be a part of my job, but I have a team of community behind me." For twenty years, Ali's families had a voice, her phone number was public.

"You've been in my skin, girlfriend, as an other? " It was ridiculous. This white lady was now her best friend.

"I don't understand?"

"Come on, 'others' is simple. You hear it. Let's help the others or do you think the others want a ride? Should we invite the others? I wonder what the others are doing? Sometimes I've been a big other. Here I'm a little other."

"Others," Ali smirked, "Other's know how to give a hand up and walk the fine line between keeping children safe and families together. I find it better to use churches and civic club members to answer prayers than increase county taxes. An untimely visit to my childhood home would have placed me and my sisters in foster care. Alcohol abuse can suck a whole family into a tornado. I would have sabotaged the placement and probably gotten sent up. My spirited father would have tried some crazy thing to get us back and been sent to jail. I listen to my childhood. "

"How come, you'd have gone to foster care?"

"What you see, isn't always what is. My father stayed sober when he worked and unemployment melted our family into seasons of poverty. Work was the glue that stuck us back together."

"I got that work glue Ali. It sets my day into a rhythm. I got two good jobs, here and Smitty's. You never do for me, you do with me. You know when you don't need to be there. You don't talk about me, just to me."

"Thanks Margie."

"You hang out with me instead of pull me out into a service or a therapy I don't think I need. Talk is cheap and talking with someone about who I am or what I need to be never got me nothing but confused. You get me started doing. Doing instead of just being, started me garage sale shopping, started me sewing those new curtains, now canning."

Ali smiled sipping her coffee.

"I got a roof over my head here Ali," Margie nodded. "Three bikes, food stamps and paid utilities. I'm good enough Margie here, not marginal Margie. You look at what's good about me and make that grow. You say what I don't want to hear, but I know it's the truth. You don't tell me what I want to hear and then push me down on my face."

"You're a good mom, Margie."

Margie radiated, "I've got real smart kids. I was scared coming to a little white town, but you said every family started here with a someone. And you said I was a someone. No one had ever called me a someone, so I emigrated in a fat white lady's minivan to dirt roads and spring manure with everything we owned in Q's backpack."

"You testing our friendship?" Ali challenged.

"That's how you looked in the beginning to me Ali. You was a fat old white lady. But then once I gots to know you my heart changed and I don't see your fat no more. You're just my friend.

Ouch. Truth.

The new immigrant population of single mother families collided with the established traditions of third generation immigrants. The equal opportunity game of misunderstanding recycled through Riverdale for another lap. The Irish forgot what happened when they came after the Scandinavians who forgot about the Germans and a recent wave of town folk behavior emerged. Local mothers called their children to stand by them, ladies clutched their purses at the checkouts, and clerks followed the new shoppers. As far as Ali knew none of the newcomers had attended a birthday party outside of their small neighborhood. No one from Eden Valley played on a sport team. Prejudice was unintentional; it happened by unknowing and overlooking with the busyness of life. Once again perseverance would build community, just as it had 150, 100 and 50 years before. Margie provided Ali with wisdom she needed to prevent disaster. She broke down the whitest walls in Riverdale and let the color shine in.

"Tell me about Kevin," Ali questioned.

"That's a problem I had nothing to do with," her lips sealed.

"You want a ride home Margie?"

"Naw, I like my bike. Fills my brain with air to think. See ya' Saturday girlfriend. You're my real friend Ali," Margie gave her a quick hug.

"I'll get extra jars at the hardware," Ali waltzed down the sidewalk to Hans Hardware kicking up leaves in a trail of confetti behind her.

Calves as big as branches with sturdy shoes, LaMar noticed, clicked the remote in his pocket and waited for his soft top to open. His entry was down to a science. He placed his left hand on the door and jumped, avoiding contact with the leather seat, landing two feet on the floor.

"Touchdown!"

Ali turned back and smiled, "Good afternoon, Dr. Watkins."

"Good afternoon, Ms. Hunter. I'm heading up to Ms. Margie Jones' home. Can you send me in the right direction?"

"Straight out, over the bridge, make a right at Jared's cornfield."

How would he know which cornfield? Ethanol production encouraged almost every field to grow corn. LaMar dialed in his GPS assuming global positioning was far more accurate than any social worker.

▼

A big sign surrounded by cornfields announced Eden Valley and under the huge letters, Hope for a Future. By all accounts it was a multi-housing development. In the midst of golden cornfields a mini-urban-polis was emerging. Jump ropes lay on the sidewalk on top of tilted hopscotch lines. Sheets hung half attached to windows. A Hispanic teen flexed his muscles as two dark haired girls preened and strutted their newly formed chests. Red bewitching puckered lips elevating testosterone.

Townhouse 248 was unusually well kept. Blue sheets were carefully tied back as curtains, a stained-glass bird swung from the windowsill; the sidewalk was swept clean and sportballs filled a basket on the steps. A handpainted welcome neighbor sign greeted him, along with untrampled marigolds. The curtains move slightly as he rang the doorbell. A woman about his age opened the door.

"Ms. Jones?"

"Yes," she hesitantly answered.

"I am Dr. L.R. Watkins. May I speak with you?"

Margie opened the door, "I guess."

The home was nicely organized and cleanly . . .

Blind with anger Q swung the bat with the momentum of pent up refrain. This 'nigger vulture' would never hurt Mama. He would protect the safety they had finally achieved.

LaMar collapsed.

Margie frisked Mr. Handsome lying in her entry. Q posted over the black vulture as Mama ran her coarse hands under the smooth vest and shirt looking for heat.

Margie knew it took only seconds to wake up. She had life proof to mistrust men. His well-formed chest felt like a soft nail cleaning brush. She smiled and moved down to his shoes, checking his socks for a hand-gun. Muscular legs lead to his pockets and she picked the wallet from a firm booty, referred to as derriere among the polite folk of Riverdale.

"Q, I don't know this man," she stepped back. The black leather wallet was not a dollar store knock-off. She opened it to a classy photo of a smiling Lamar, Tamara, Shayna and Johnny. Then another happy photo of an older black man and woman embracing a young man in a cap and college gown. A driver's license. LaMar Reginald Watkins, 1862 Shaker Heights Road, Mapledale, the fancy place she'd heard talk. A pilot's license. Six platinum credit cards. Margie's street smarts hit her go button. She grabbed a piece of paper and copied the digits from the platinum credit card, remembering to copy the little three numbers on the backside.

"Neva' know when they'll come in handy. Looks like we just got numbas off a sugar daddy, Q. What cha say?" Margie winked at her son.

She slipped fifty dollars away from the almost four hundred dollar stack. "There's a mess of 'em, probably won't even miss it." Call it desperation, call it locked in the old cycle, call it whatever you want to. She found the money. She needed it. It wasn't really stealing. She only took one.

She balled the bill and put it into her pocket.

"This ain't no playa, Q. This is a real baby's daddy. He's a real man," she was jealous of the beautiful woman with two small children. "Why do some people get everything?" She longed for a man she wouldn't have to dump. She had spent a lifetime trying to make men love her. She dreamed of a man to mean 'I love you' and fill her heart's emptiness with 'sugar' and 'honey'. She hated being laughed at in front of another brotha. She hated that all the men in her life that tried to up their manhood by bringing her down. No black knight in shining armor ever rode into her life. Margie felt daddy hunger. She had tried so hard to find a lovin' that she missed the boat on finding a man. Sex became a price she paid to prove she was good enough to be loved. Even Kevin, who asked for nothing, was in jail and the extra $250 a month he paid in rent had evaporated like morning dew.

Hard working and hard partying Margie's mama raised her as best she could. People said it was mama's hard partying that made it so tough on Margie. Folks called her simple. Margie never understood why, life was never simple. Kids in school called her retard. She hated that word.

▼

At Hans Hardware a 1950 potato ricer lived in a back nook next to the manual apple parers and both were built to last your lifetime and your grandkids too. Ali always found something she needed at the store even if it was only a refreshing outlook on life. The Palmquist family had owned the building almost since the inception of Riverdale. Hans had taken it over from his father, who had taken it over from his father and now his daughter-in-law Annie, who was also Ali's sister-in-law worked there along with Eddie Shultz. Eddie, born with Downs Syndrome, spent his day straightening shelves, sweeping the shiny linoleum, and keeping the place in order. Hans let Eddie bring his dog Blue, who slept the whole day under the cash register, behind the ammo counter, on top of his doggie blue sweater and Eddie's yellow slicker with pants worn everyday just in case of rain.

Hans, otherwise known as Bobpy P, spent his day fixing appliances and small engines for the town folk, while Annie ran the store. Four-year-old Kissy spent her day standing on an old stool with her arms up to her elbows in icy minnow water until her little girl fingers resembled a wrinkly old woman. When she was so cold her ears hurt, she'd wave her wrinkled digits in front of her Santa Claus grandfather, Bobpy P. It was always a perfect pickup nestled under his white beard while he warmed her frosty fingers in his age spotted mitts. She was the only girl in Sunday School with a really live Santa Claus for a grandpa. She knew for sure because he 'was' the firebarn Santa at Christmas who passed out tiny stockings filled with candy canes and gumdrops.

It was fun to work with Mommy and Bobpy P. When it was a quiet day, she and Eddie ran turtle speed trials in the back room. On boring days Bobpy P let her play Blue's Airplane on his computer and when everyone was busy she'd curled up with Blue and her puppy Lucy behind the Ammo Counter. It was warm and toasty. Bobpy P said it was because the register was there. There were four registers and only that one made warm blowy air. It was also the safe place where big people talked about things no one was supposed to know and Kissy liked knowing.

She liked pretending to sleep in the puppy pile on Lucy's big dog pillow and Eddie's blue raincoat. She was glad Daddy saved Blue when he was a puppy. They had found him tied in a burlap bag in the Dale River, all the other puppies had died, but Daddy did mouth-to-mouth like a doctor and Blue sputtered and choked and then his eyes opened while she cheered and prayed for Jesus to save him. Then Mommy kept Blue at the Hardware Store until they decided to give him to Eddie, who lived all alone. Kissy loved Eddie who let her undo screws and unpack boxes. He was her grownup favorite playmate, besides Kevin who bought her gumballs from Uncle Sam's candy machine. Eddie and Kevin smiled and laughed bestest.

Except for Sunday School, Kissy's relationships revolved around adults. Her two grandfathers — Bobpy P and Bumpa, spoiled her with hugs and tickles, and a big yellow bi-plane named Yellow Lady. Uncle Sam took her to the gun range to watch and cheer and Daddy . . . she didn't want to think about him. She missed him too much.

When Kissy grew up she was going to fly Yellow Lady and run Bobpy P's store after she became a fighter pilot. She was good at figuring things out and finding missing stuff. She already planned lots of adult things to do

and she couldn't wait til' she got big. She was going to go to war to find
Uncle Russ who Bobpy P said was missing in action. When she grew up
real big she was going to be the first ever girl Blue Angel. Bumpa said she
could.

Kissy liked listening and smelling things. Daddy taught her how to
sense change and she played Daddy's listening game behind the ammo
counter. She discovered Bumpa sounded like Bum...pa when he walked
with his farm boots and Bobpy sounded like Bob...pee when he walked in
the store. Daddy said they were good nicknames. The best person's sound
was Sam. His feet went slap, tap, tap, but Daddy told her you had to be
careful with nicknames and Sam wouldn't like slap-tap-tap. Daddy gave
her, 'it's for me to know and someday you'll find out' look, that she knew
not to challenge.

Kissy liked guessing before peeking. She was almost always right!
Everyone smelled and sounded special just like animals. Mike sounded like
Doc, but he smelled different. He had a new smokey sweet scent. When
Daddy came home she would ask him about it. Bumpa smelled like wood
shavings and earth. Bobpy P smelled like the hardware store. Sam smelled
like grease and cars and Ali . . . smelled like butterflies! The inside of her
nose wiggled and she sneezed. Daddy called her 'Eagle Beagle' when she
discovered something new. Kissy peeked as Ali entered Hans Hardware.

"Ali, Ali!" Kissy jumped into Ali's arms. Blue toddled behind.

"Where's your grandpa, Kissy?"

"In the back."

"Thanks sweetie," Ali set Kissy down to pet Blue and wiggly Lucy.

"Hi Ali," Hans was built like Santa and wonderful to hug.

"Sam needs dad-help, and you and Gunner are nominated."

Kissy couldn't hear what else Ali said, but Bobpy P looked concerned
and nodded like he did when he had something important to do.

"Don't worry, Ali. It's in our hands. Sam's coming Sunday to watch
football at Gunner's," he picked up a box of mason jars. "You better buy
two more Ali, I got the prices so cheap, so you can save more!"

"I think I've saved enough Hans," she chuckled.

"Can I come to the canning Auntie Ali?"

"Not this year honey, but we'll put up enough to share with you." Ali
loaded her car with four cases of canning jars. "See you later alligator."

"After while crocodile," the little girl skipped back into the store.

Ali looked forward to Saturday, the farmhouse would be empty of men except for her eighty-year-old father-in-law Gunner and he knew better than to interfere. He'd leave canning to women folk and disappear into his tool shed. The line of farm responsibilities had been drawn a century ago and even retirement didn't bring men into the kitchen unless they were eating, debating or planning. Gunner cared for the lawn with his new bright green lawn tractor, Jared tended 200 acres of crops on a monsterous John Deere and Ali and MaLu kept the house. The farmstead had quieted. Ali and Jared's daughters had graduated high school and moved on for medical studies in Fargo.

Ali's organic garden was a meeting point knitting her to the farm men. Gunner tended window seedlings, shared weedings and watered throughout the summer. Jerad tossed out the clean kitchen wastes to the compost on the way to the barn. Gunner fed the compost to the tomatoes and peppers, now hanging heavy for picking. Gunner was a man of few words, but loud actions who wordlessly proclaimed 'I love you'. He showed his love turning beautiful garden stakes on his lathe, carefully painting them in Ali's favorite color and placing tiny brass hooks at the end of each row to help her remember what heirloom tomato she had planted. Ali loved sitting in the garden with Gunner at harvest time and pouring salt on a warm sun ripened tomato. Together they watched the main field harvest as Gunner shared Jared's boyhood with devilish glee. Warm tomato juice cascaded down their chins and they laughed so hard tears ran down their cheeks and their bellies hurt. Ali loved that Jared remained rooted in the farm and she was now Hunter family.

Gunner and Lucille Hunter raised three children, Joe, Jared and Annie, on the farmstead built by Gunner's father's father Daniel Aaron. He was a massive German-speaking man who had emigrated from the Ukraine in the mid eighteen hundreds and very little was known about family history beyond that time. The Hunter's had become pillars in the community and they attended Lutheran Church of Peace, or so it seemed. The townsfolk believed they were dyed-in-the-wool Lutherans. A few months back, Ma Lu shared life secrets she wanted to keep out of her grave. The disclosure freed MaLu and from then on the couple publicly honored the Sabbath at Friday sundown and during that day they refrained from all creative work.

Oddly, since Doc's death Gunner became almost jovial in sharing family history and his comment "some people should just never have been born" regarding Doc, didn't set right. Doc had been entertained at their farmhouse for years; he was on Gunner's shooting team and one of her husband's good friends. Her father-in-law's action after his statement perplexed her further. He smiled coyly and almost skipped to the shed. How could you live with someone for so long and not know all the secrets?

▼

Ali walked up Margie's steps and rang the doorbell. In a community of frugality and care, it was sad to see new development in disrepair. A broken bicycle lay in pieces on the front garden alongside a rusty screwdriver and wrench. Cigarette butts lay half hidden in the shrubbery. Margie's perfectly planted flower bed was still standing. It didn't surprise her. No one was about to trample Margie's turf.

Margie pulled back the blue twin bed sheet curtains she bought for fifty cents at Mrs. Johnson's garage sale and saw Ali. She glanced at the man lying on the floor, motioned to Q to stay armed, pocketed her token treasures, and opened the door. "Ali, we gots ourself a little problem."

"What's wrong Margie? Are you all right? I was just stopping by to let you know when I'll pick you up tomorrow to do the tomatoes. You can have half my canning, if you help." Ali stepped in the door, her feet nearly tripping over LaMar. "What happened, Margie?" Ali shouted.

Q stood armed with the red wooden bat.

"What did you do Q?" Ali was not playing.

"Ah thought he was gonna hurt Mama, so I hit him before he could hit her. Am I going to jail like Kevin?" Q asked and lowered the bat.

"Oh my God, Dr. Watkins, are you alright? Do I need to call 911?" she prepared to dial on her cell phone. Ali bent over LaMar to check his pulse. He opened his eyes. He was pleasantly surprised to see Ali.

Margie's heart dropped. Obviously, her friend Ali knew this man. Her hand sunk deep into her pocket, her fingers felt hot as they closed around the balled up money. LaMar felt his forehead for blood.

"I think I'm fine. I caught the bat as that kid swung," his hand tingled. "I don't remember what happened next. I came to speak with Tasha."

"You can find her at the library," Margie directed sheepishly. She held out his wallet. "Think you've been living in the white world too long Doc, ya gotta watch your back." Margie didn't apologize.

Dr. Watkins tucked in his white shirt, smoothed his trousers and jacket, and took back his wallet. There was no elixir to fix the chasm of life experiences between Margie and LaMar, illiteracy and education, generational poverty and success, even though they were the same age and the same color.

The bat only psychologicly hit LaMar, but it felt like it had knocked him upside the head. He was now sure something deep lay buried as a death knell waiting for illumination. His adopted father shut the door on his youthful questions; he knew he must pry them open. What preceded his adoption? Why was he so seldom angry? Had he shut out the emotion of anger that Q batted around? It was a common male issue. Was this also his issue? Did he deny his emotions because one day they were unsafe?

▼

Kevin was a worry and something nagged at her. Ali was drawn to his innocent world view and she hoped Dr. Watkins had answers.

11
ANGELS & RED NECKS

Kevin sat on the white concrete in the all white cell wishing he could pretend he was in the library holding Tasha and listening to her read. Pretending wasn't happening. When Tasha read to him life changed. Tasha's voice danced through words and sentences making the words alive and he could picture the story. He missed hiding in the books away from the jungle of expectations.

▼ TASHA

Ipods and laptops, GPS and jump drives, cell phones and Internet were a very real part of the Riverdale teen life Tasha was too poor to own. Thankfully the library filled the gap of lacking, offered a future and filled whatever emptiness she felt when she entered the red wooden doors. Friendly book pages clothed in a garden of colorful spines offered wisdom. She loved the sounds, the tip tap of the librarian's high-heeled shoes on a shiny wooden floor, the shushed laughter of a little child, and the murmur of turning papers. Ink, and paper, and dusty shelf smells were a constant in her life.

No one bothered her in the library except Kevin and they enjoyed entwined reading, his head resting on her shoulder. In public nothing extracurricular was expected – no kissing, no fondling and no sex. It was the kissing part that messed with her brain and led to further advances. As long as she could avoid the kiss, she could avoid the rest. She fondled the worn dictionary, her back leaning against a bookshelf – Influence – noun 1. power exerted over the minds or behavior of others . . . Related Words: command, domination, dominion, mastery; ascendancy, dominance, eminence, predominance; consequence, importance, moment . . . She smiled.

Webster's Dictionary and *Britannica* transported her to exotic places. In Timbuktu she became African royalty. Word adventures tumbled her head over heels into the New York Times and self-expression of writing free verse on scraps of paper. On rainy days she daydreamed managing money she didn't have. Today, Mama ordered her to find hot sauce – preferably Louisiana. She had already researched the cookbooks and found no such recipe. The shelves of this library are a desert. "God, can't you please put some color in this place and send me an angel to help Kevin."

She found no books by Richard Wright or Toni Morrison, not even poetry by Maya Angelou. She did, however; find stories of Black authors such as Booker T. Washington, Sojourner Truth, and Phyllis Wheatley written by white authors, which was exasperating. Regardless if it lacked color, the library held mind adventures and when midterms were posted her name stood out at the top usurping the academic leader which initiated surprise that a black kid could get good grades.

LaMar found Tasha sitting on the library floor in the cooking section looking for hot sauce recipes. "Tasha Jones, I presume, I need your help," a bright, pretty, light-skinned teen looked up and smiled.

The Lord must have listened. Unbelievably, a black man as tall as an angel was seeking her out asking for help? "Who are you?"

"I'm Dr. Watkins," his eyes twinkled.

"You need my help?" she stammered.

"Yes. Do you need my help?" he questioned.

"As a matter of fact I do. In Riverdale I go by default to all white movies, watch all white television, listen to white country music, eat plain white rice without black-eyed peas, eat spinach instead of collard greens, use baby oil for my hair, sit in church on a pew with my hands in my lap and sing dirges. No catfish fries, no real barbeques and a library full of books and novels by only white authors," she paused to take a breath. "And, if you think there is a book in the cooking section with a hot sauce recipe, you're sadly mistaken."

He asked and she purged unexpected floodgates. He tried again, "What white author are you reading the words of now?"

"Besides Noah Webster's 1828 dictionary, I'm reading *Pride and Prejudice* by Jane Austin. I thought perhaps the study of manner and the relationships of classes would serve me well here in Riverdale. Perhaps like Elizabeth, all my former prejudices can be removed and I can learn to forgive pride."

"That's admirable. I'm here to help Kevin. I heard he is your friend."

Tasha showed off a smitten Juliet to Romeo smile, but answered cautiously, "Yes, he is my friend."

"I need to ask you a few questions. May I sit down?"

Tasha motioned to the angel to sit beside her by moving her pile of books covered in bits of paper.

LaMar felt tightness in his lower back and wished for a chair. He accepted Tasha's offer and settled unnaturally down next to her, scattering her pile of writing. "Do you write Tasha?" he hoped to open further conversation.

Tasha held her tongue.

"This seems like a nice library."

Tasha remained silent and glared.

"Well, let's get started. Does Kevin have a bad temper?"

Tasha weighed her answer.

LaMar watched her protect her thoughts.

"Kevin may get angry easily, but he doesn't mean anything by it. When he's mad about something, nothing he says counts. Mostly he gets snarly when he's tired or hungry, when he's stressed, when plans change, or when things don't go the way he expects." Her eyes danced, "I feel the same way when a computer program is revised and I know that I know how to do something, but I can't find the right button. When keystrokes I already memorized give me the wrong data. Empty. Frustrated. Confused. He's a lot like Mama."

"Can you explain?"

"Well, like let's say he's supposed to get to Sam's early. That's where he works. And the alarm clock doesn't ring because he trips over the cord on the way to the toilet in the middle of the night. Why is it in the middle of the floor, you ask? It's his solution so he does not annilate it when it rings at 6:00 A.M. Then in the morning he cusses the poor thing out for not working. He caused the problem. It isn't the clock's fault. Like Mama, he doesn't understand cause and effect very well. Q and I have been laughing at Mama since we were little. Now there are two of them," Tasha paused introspectively and smiled, "We laugh with love, of course." She gestured with her thumbs shooting up and flying away. "Q and I have this special 'thar she blows' signal, when Mama's running off the pier."

"If you tell him why something went wrong, does he get it?"

"Oh no, we never use the word 'why,' that sends both of them straight to the loony bin. You have to state your sentences with how, where, who, when and what."

"Explain"

"Well everything has to be matter of fact. Let's say he throws the ball through a window, he'd never admit breaking it because the ball broke it, not him. Or if you accused him of taking your soda, he'd say he didn't take it, he drank it. Do you get it?"

"Ok, I think so. Do you have another example?"

"Let's says the light switch won't turn on because the bulb is burned out. I think, oh 'maybe the light bulb is burned out.' Mama might flick the switch over and over and then punch it. Now there's a hole in the wall and the light still doesn't work. The problem is when it is off you can't see it is burned out and because it is broken it won't turn on. It's a simple circle of abstraction; you see with both of them you must be very concrete." Tasha batted her long curly eyelashes. "It's okay though, Q and I are used to picking up the details and keeping care of Mama. I don't mind watching out for Kevin. I think he's cute, sometimes he just needs an external brain and I don't mind brain coaching. Have you met him?" LaMar noted her conversation switch to a lower level.

"Yes, I've met him," comforting her with his smile "Thanks, you've been a big help. I must be going to another meeting" The woman was wise and by initial appearances more adult than either her mother or Kevin.

"Dr. Watkins?" Tasha folded a yellow post it note and smiled. "Yes I do write poetry. Keep it for later."

LaMar pocketed the note in his trousers, and rose to meet with Sam O'Riley at Smitty's Poolhall.

The angel departed. Could her short conversation help Kevin? She hoped the doctor liked her poem.

▼

Smitty's Pool Hall smelled of workingmen — sweat, spilled beer, old tobacco, and agricultural dirt. Cleaning and polishing didn't remove the odor. The well-worn linoleum floor was sparkle clean and the bar freshly wiped. The smell was ground in.

Since Doc died and Kevin was sent to jail, Sam closed the garage early for a drink at Smitty's leaving his credit card eating machines to do his work. He needed a drink. At 4:30 P.M. Smitty's was quiet, just he and Smitty until work crews arrived at five for a brew. In thirty minutes Sam pounded down a few brandies and chatted with his friend Smitty before he walked home to Deb.

Sam, Doc and Smitty had played football together at the Lion's Stadium, hockey at the ice rink, and baseball at the ballpark. Together they sponsored the local youth summer softball teams with shirts and registration fees. They had a truce; Doc and Smitty didn't hold it against Sam for not joining the Lion's Club and Smitty and Sam didn't hold it against Doc for being Lutheran. And Sam and Doc. Well, Doc wasn't holding anything anymore.

Sam, sitting at the end of the wooden bar, lifted his brandy to Smitty, "Cheers." Lately a few had increased by quite a bit.

The initial odor of the pool hall slapped LaMar in the face.

Sam saw the black stranger enter, his eyes squinted judgingly.

According to the sheriff, Sam was a man of community prestige and responsible for the upkeep of local vehicles regardless of the make, model or year. He fixed Jared Hunter's tractor in no time, took care of all the patrol cars and just finished a brake job on Mike Johnson's truck for the local parade.

The praise of competency resounding in the courthouse did not reflect brains or power off the old man sitting on the barstool. Greasy jeans rode up one of his hairy legs and left a bare band between a graying sock and a mud caked cowboy boot. The other bootleg was covered with a pant leg stretched tight, as if something was holding it back from riding up. His flannel shirt sported more greasy spots and was opened halfway down his pooch of a beer belly. His red hat was grimy and the tag of his dingy t-shirt waved like a surrender flag against his sunburned neck.

LaMar stared back at Sam, struggling to formulate a plan for conversation. This was the very type of person he tried to avoid. He hoped there were no unwritten rules of Riverdale bar etiquette, "What's on tap?"

"The usual."

"OK," whatever that was LaMar accepted it. He nodded to the wizened bartender busily washing beer glasses.

"Fine," Sam sneered, his lip rose like a dog barring his teeth, flashing traces of chewing tobacco, a breath of brandy fire blazed toward LaMar.

"Name's Dr. L.R. Watkins. I'm working down at the Sheriff's office,"

LaMar put out his hand.

Sam looked straight through LaMar as if he didn't even exist. He said nothing. His hand remained on his glass, "Yeah, I heard." Sam sucked the tobacco off his teeth to resume chewing.

LaMar absorbed the icy stare. He remembered the feeling he'd received as a teen standing in a line of smiling white folk exchanging business currencies hand-to-hand waiting for his turn as the change was placed on the counter for him to pick up, an unspoken body language of unworthiness. He had wondered, as a child, if white people worried his color would rub of . . . old, old tapes.

Sam frowned, still staring.

"Can I buy you a drink?" LaMar offered.

"Another brandy, Smitty, on this gentleman here," Sam sarcastically emphasized gentle.

"Can we talk?"

"Guess we are. Whether I like it or not."

The red neon bar sign caught a silver edge of a pin on Sam's ball cap – the blue and gold pin of the III Corp. The same pin LaMar's Dad sported on his fishing cap. "You serve in 'Nam?"

"Why's that your business."

"My dad was in III Corp and I saw your pin."

"So," LaMar felt Sam soundly shut that conversation door.

"Look, I'm here to talk about Kevin Abbott. I need some information. I was hoping you could help me."

"Can it help him, if I talk to you?"

"Do you want it to?"

"Maybe, maybe not. Don't rightly know."

This was going nowhere fast, "Kevin is having some trouble in jail and it's my job to help integrate him with the population and to determine his competency to stand trial."

"Bet you know a lot about that integration stuff, don't you."

LaMar wasn't sure if Sam just threw a racial slur or was talking about the jail situation. He avoided the bait. "Thought you might know how best to work with Kevin, since Kevin worked for you for three months. Heard up until the murder he was well liked in Riverdale."

"That what you heard?"

"Also heard he really thinks highly of you. Kevin likes working for you and was proud of the work he did. He said you had nice customers. He told me you are a good man."

"Did he?" Sam's eyes connected with LaMar's.

"Look, here's my card. Let me know if you can think of anything to help make jail life better for him."

"Wha'd ya say your name was again, Doc?" Sam paused to chew, "You remind me of Miss Margie Jones. You meet her yet? You'd like her."

"Dr. L. R. Watkins," putting out his hand. "Thank you for your help Mr. O'Riley."

Compared to Margie? Why would red neck Sam compare him to Margie — because of their skin color?

Sam's hand remained unoffered, gripping his glass of brandy.

LaMar swallowed to hold further words hostage. Riverdale was getting the best of him and bite-by-bite it was devouring his spirit and exposing his heart. Sealed agony soulfully tried to cover all joy with darkness. So far, he had been escorted into town by the Sheriff; attacked by a thug, and placated by a drunk. He choked back, attributing it to small town inexperience with the African American culture.

"Dr. LaMar Watkins," Sam shouted. "Yeah, yeah. Thought you said that. Used to know a black Sergeant Watkins, son of a bitch kept me alive. Wouldn't be here in this god-forsaken land without him and his damn pressure. He kept me from bleedin' to death. You might know him. They called him Reg."

"Thanks for your time Mr. O'Riley." LaMar left his money on the bar, refusing to wait for another insult. Just because he was black didn't mean he knew every person of African American heritage. He turned his face to the door; the smell of cheap brandy and tobacco remained oddly familiar and nauseating. He had no time for a drunk.

Sam watched the stranger depart. He hadn't meant to be rude. He just didn't feel like talking.

TOUCHDOWN

Maybe dead was better than jail? Since he could remember, he lived life in absolutes - alive or dead, black or white, hot or cold. The single cell was lonely, he missed the Jones family and Margie was the first adult who dialed into his station. She didn't expect anything other than him to be himself. He was glad he called Tasha when all hell broke loose in the city or he would be dead. Margie tuned into him without radio static. He felt confused, "Hey guard, I need more milk! Chocolate, please."

"Only got white here and more of that will make you constipated."

"I don't give a crap," Kevin yelled.

"If you drink more milk you won't do that either," the guard laughed the way people did when Kevin didn't understand the joke and had become a part of it.

"Quit laughing, all I want is milk!" He threw his dinner tray. Even the food didn't break through the whiteness – it was white chicken, cauliflower, and rice on a dirty white tray. "Mom says, think of one thing good. I like doctor what's his name. Maybe he can get me out of this box." He picked up the two-inch thick mattress and threw it too. "Unbelievable!"

▼

LaMar left Smitty's, taking a moment to draw in his thoughts and relax before leaving Riverdale. He adjusted his stereo, checked his seat and finally shifted into gear to leave town, moving from first to second quietly and then pushing the shifter into third. The car rode low, and smooth. The highway was empty as he accelerated to fourth. He liked feeling one with machinery, controlling the movement, power, and rhythm. He was movin' out. Whatever was left in Riverdale needed to stay in Riverdale. He drove like a racer.

Though he had control of the Roadster, the clarity of the dangerous weapon available at his fingertips suddenly surprised him. Like food poisoning waiting to exit his anger bubbled and his jaw trembled as he fought to catch his breath. He had studied rage and counseled patients who dealt with excessive anger responses, but he was a man of patience, self-control, and education. As far back as he could remember, he had never felt his soul ripping. Or had he?

Were Kevin's eyes a key to unlock the gargoyle? He had felt the rattlings. On the empty two-lane highway a guttural darkness overtook him and he screamed primally. He pulled to the side of the road to assess his cognitive failure. He had to stop before he crashed.

"This is nonsense. I am not imprisoned like Kevin, I have no disparity of mind." LaMar silently self-talked back to sanity, reminding himself that anger can actually create an automatic prejudice where none existed, almost as if it appeared out of thin air. He was not a man of prejudgment, yet Riverdale ignited a prejudicial attitude over the trivial.

He let himself get angry, and for a blink of time it captured his logic and made him less than he thought he was. How many times had he told someone else, you react to something because of what it means to you. He resigned himself to self-analysis. Sheriff Larry and his little patrol car were no threat, and he most certainly didn't deserve the emotional expense expended. Ali had been kind enough to share her desk, it was all she had to give and she gave willingly. Kevin was his patient and though he represented many of the very issues LaMar despised, it was his professional obligation to serve Harris County. Margie was simply a single mother trying to do the best she could with the life experiences and tools she had on hand, while her son Q acted defensively possibly due to historic trauma. Tasha captured his heart in that library, like she felt captured in Riverdale. He wanted to reach out and offer her the depths of beauty of the African American culture. He wished he could present her with a key to access her dreams. Sam, well Sam was a character of a complex life experience. Doc's friendship and his murder set a significant grief cycle in place that was taking on a life of its own. Sam's inebriation was not necessarily a good indication of who he was.

Face it LaMar, you didn't do too well yourself today. Where was your balance between rage and capitulation? What something in your past is affecting your present?

LaMar accepted some blame; his arrogance had defeated him. Not one of these people were part of his inner circle. He was the outsider. He'd go home, regroup and work through his issues to be ready for Monday morning.

His hands felt numb as he pulled back onto the highway, flipping his sound system from a jazz CD to FM urban hip-hop, temporarily recouping in street beats and ebonic radio jargon. The computerized drum machine beats and monotonous looping rhythm soothed his thumping heart. The violent lyrics voiced his angst without him having to own them. He rapped along. His hands tingled. How hard had he gripped the steering wheel? His logical side kicked in, and the feeling retreated, but its remains slithered under his skin. In two days, he had to return to Riverdale and he better figure this out or let it go.

▼

Hearing the garage door rise, Johnny and Shayna jumped up to greet Daddy. Mama's rules said, 'no stepping past the porch steps when cars were coming'. Shayna held Johnny's hand as she bounced next to the jogging stroller. The American flag blew in the breeze above tiny heads as the setting sunlight transformed the children's shadows into nine-foot puppets against the stucco wall. The sight of his children's love evicted his anxiety. He was home safe and out of Riverdale, at least until Monday. "Let it go, LaMar. Let it go. Perhaps I've grown my anger into a shadow puppet."

He turned off the car and did a one-hand over the door. The sound of the dying engine triggered little feet with permission to run to Daddy and he picked up each child in an arm. He spun them around as he hugged them before setting them down.

Johnny ran to get the basketball almost as big as him and stood under the toddler hoop. "Slam dunk it, boy!" If only life could be so simple?

"Two points!" Johnny dropped the ball into the net. "Two points me!"

"Me too, me too," Shayna squealed clapping her hands.

He scooped up his daughter. It wouldn't be long before she was too big, and he relished the fact that she still considered him Superman. Shayna deserved to be treated well. He loved nuzzling and wrapping his strong arms around her. He never wanted her to feel rejected. He wanted her future choice of a mate to be someone with integrity, someone he respected. He was the standard by which she would judge all men.

"Mama took us running and we went really fast, Daddy," she giggled.

Johnny baby-tackled his leg and LaMar wrestled his children into a pile of freshly fallen leaves while Harry, the poodle, bowed and pranced.

The children threw leaves as fast as he could wipe off his Italian suit. "Come on kids, help Daddy get these off."

LaMar looked at Tamara, "Hey pretty bride." She was the most beautiful woman on earth, and she deserved every thread of her white bridal gown and veil when her daddy gave her away. She challenged his chivalry for three long years and she was his virgin. Her sleek figure was well toned despite giving birth to their two children. He loved her and only her, forever, especially in running gear.

Tamara drew delight in the moment of her husband's frolic tugging his tie as he swooped in for a sweet kiss. His body language busted him out. It had been a hard day. She knew him well and he was not smooth enough to hide it. The after business hours relief look from racial stress blinked like fizzling neon. The world didn't always understand.

"Damn, I gotta get these off." LaMar rolled his shoulders wincing. He'd tried to repress his identity to avoid distancing himself from his new colleagues. He hated the 'push me-pull you' of cultural misunderstanding. He felt 'whiteness' up to his ears.

"Mama! Daddy said a bad word!" his little girl held her hand to her mouth waving a pink fairy wand.

Johnny parroted, "Bad word, Daddy. No! No! No!" little brown eyes squinted and he scrunched up his nose. His baby nostrils flared like LaMar's did when he was angry. He shook his tiny finger.

"Sorry guys. You're right, no bad words in the Watkins's house." LaMar carried his children across the threshold.

▼

"Wad'da day!" LaMar stripped off his querulous mask of whiteness and changed into urban flava' gear. His vernacular embraced casual Ebonics, his too big shirt knee-grazing ova' his low ridin' pants showed off the Snicker Bar boxer shorts Shayna and Mommy bought him. He put a small diamond stud in his left ear. Normally, LaMar felt color comfortable. Tonight he needed to feel his blackness. What was he going to do with the sleeping volcano ready to erupt? He flipped on his computer, clicked onto Flight Simulator to shoot a few IFR approaches to clear his mind.

"How about a pizza and movie?" Tamara handed him his favorite beer.

He smiled. They had been together long enough to pass love and commitment between each other silently.

"I'll take the kids to get videos and pizza," Tamara offered.

"Me stay Daddy!" Johnny demanded.

"It's okay honey, you can leave him with me."

Johnny ran to LaMar and scaled into his lap, "I fly airplane!" Holding Johnny put LaMar into a safe and simple world. "Blue's airplane. Fly Blue!"

LaMar switched from adult reality to a blue cartoon dog piloting a biplane to produce loops of letters.

▼

Sunlight cascaded through bedroom lace curtains, catching the Swavorski Austrian Crystal snowflakes in rainbow patterns and Sally watched the blues and yellow hues dance upon the white fluffy down comforter. The bed linens had remained unwashed for three weeks and she, who was normally very particular about bedding, remained very particular about keeping the sheets where they were. Lying on Doc's side of the bed she felt his presence, and reached over to grab Doc's essence filled pillow. It had replaced holding Doc. She moved over to sleep on his side of the bed and held on tightly. Happy curled at her feet as a sentry alerted to every movement with a guttural dog growl even when it was Mike.

She had traveled beyond denial of Doc's death. It was real, too real. Doc wasn't coming back and no amount of praying, or grace, or mercy, or medicine was going to allow him to return to her unless she went to him. Oh, she thought about it – suicide would be so simple, but Mike deserved better, he still needed a mother and she hadn't been much of any kind of parent lately. Ali had invited her to share in the canning, but she had declined. Deb had stopped by with a hot dish and came every other day to see how she was doing.

Doing? She wasn't doing. Her grief ebbed and flowed. She had become ghastly with new wrinkles. Her cheeks burned red from a million tears that were nobody's business. Doc's death hit so hard. Death was part of her profession, but death in the emergency room wasn't personal, it was professional and by being professional it isolated her. She went home at the end of her day. Doc's death destroyed her dream, their home, and their life together. It was more than a murder of a body. The murderer killed her soul driving a wedge between her and her beloved son Mike.

Today she would try to inch her way into a new life.

She cuddled Doc's pillow and dozed. She had tried returning to work, but the sight of the injured and dying was so raw it peeled the thin layer of normalcy she had begun to grow. Two days ago she left a patient in tears and Dr. Samuelson wrote a prescription to help her sleep. He cautioned her unnecessarily about the dangers of overdose and she fumed at his condescension. She knew the dangers of overuse so last night she broke the tiny pill in half to sleep. Then unfairly, she was startled by Happy who paced around her bed, barked loudly and planted wet nose prints on her just cleaned bedroom window. Mike had returned home. The clock said 11:00 P.M.. It was a school night. She took the other half tablet to return to sleep and felt strangely exhausted, her arms heavy with emptiness. That was yesterday, it was now 11:00 A.M. and she had slept 12 hours.

Sally dressed in comfy clothes thinking of the day's possibilities. Her mind had cleared a bit. She hadn't thought of the future for a long time and Happy had lived solely on dog food for over three weeks. She decided to make some toast. Peanut butter would be good for the two of them. She was pleasantly surprised by a pot of fresh coffee and a note.

Dear Mom,

I'm playing quarterback tonight, and I know you will worry, but it will be okay. I will stay safe. I made you a pot of coffee.
Hope you feel better.

Please come,
Love Mike

▼

The lighted Riverdale High football field offered the illusion of warmth for freezing fans huddled under fleece blankets on cold aluminum bleachers. Football was the leading fall Friday night event and the concessions provided hotdogs decorated with red, white, yellow and green condiments for dinner while the band offered music improving with each game. Grandfathers and fathers held hot chocolates and coffees cheering on sons and grandsons. They relived past games of long ago, feeling their feet lift as they vicariously caught the ball and ran like the wind alongside. The old men stood together in support while the cheerleaders chanted in short skirts to encourage young males to battle. Grandmothers and mothers rooted for their precious young men, almost knocking their significant others off the bleachers when a son or grandson was tackled. They bit the ends of woolen mittens awaiting the results, saying prayers of protection and claimed yardage.

For over thirty-seven years John Nelson had coached the Lion's High football team. Both Doc Johnson and his son Mike played on his team. He had considered pulling Mike from Friday's game, but Mike begged to honor his father. Who could deny a grieving son?

The cold wind blew between the metal cracks and up the back of Tasha's sweatshirt. She tensed, shivering to stay warm. Not much missed her, she was street. Tasha watched Amber sport cheerleading facials wondering if the heart behind the beautiful face knew the pain she caused when she taunted her in school. She overheard Mike make a comment at the lockers to Amber saying he was thankful about Kevin and it was only an accident. She noted their dark secret fear when they thought she heard and covered it up with a pathetic wave.

Mike called the quarterback draw. He faked the handoff and then ran, weaving and dodging like his life depended on this score. The river of players parted, the crowd wildly stamped feet and clapped hands.

The speakers broadcast, "A Lion's touchdown by Michael Johnson in honor of the beloved Dr. Emmett Johnson." Both bands exploded with bass drums and symbols as puffed cheeks blew into tubas, trumpets or trombones while both audiences screamed non-competitive hurrahs.

▼

Wind lifted cleated feet and miraculously Mike's mind was clear and he ran fearlessly. He flashed on Happy who avoided him since his father's death and closely guarded his grieving mother.

"Run! Mike! Run!" he self-talked. Think of nothing else! The goal is seconds away. The defensive backfield closed in. Thunderous roars, bass drums, symbols, the gun, his father. No more.

"Touchdown!" He felt his father watching. Thankfully, his father knew the truth. He hoped his mother was in the stands. He raised his arms in triumph. Whatever it took, he would win.

▼

Q missed the touchdown; he hiked up his pants and tightened his belt at the opposite hundred-yard line embroiled in a loud discussion with another student about comments yelled after halftime. The shouting turned into pushing, and the pushing into shoving, and who knew who threw the first punch. It didn't matter. The larger white boy raised his hand like a starting flag. That was enough of a rally to rev up his steaming hot engine, Q didn't wait for the punch and he fought like a Kilkenny cat.

He relished the adrenaline rush of a fight. It was easier getting into fist-t-cuffs than getting out. Blood and bruises were inevitable. He moved to avoid getting hit and wrapped his legs around the kid to get another swing. He wouldn't quit until he was stopped.

Innocence was a hazard to your health in the hood and Q had lost his naiveté at age four under the sofa when the police took Daddy. The remaining leftovers were trashed each time he tried to fight 'BadOne' for Mama. He lost his innocence at six, and eight, and ten, and twelve trying to protect her. Innocence was gone for good when Kevin got him blessed into the Rangers as a 'lil bro.' He'd spent a mess of nights, just sittin' chillin' on a wooden telephone reel stolen from a construction site. He'd felt all grown up, smoking Newport cigarettes and watching his gang homies grope their gurlz. Some nights they'd even pass a blunt.

The crowd continued cheering for Mike.

Q, impassioned with righteousness, swung hard. The white boy, a varsity wrestler, was used to fair fighting until each fighter's energy was expended. He was clueless to street fighting and he fought for his life. Q had no clue of wrestling rules and he fought because he didn't have anything to lose. They fought in two languages as fists and legs flew.

Tasha looked upfield. Her heart fell, a crowd encircled her brother.

Q felt his body rise above earth and his feet solidly hit the ground. Sheriff Larry didn't put up with fighting students.

"Take your brother home. Now! I'll see he is banned from games for the rest of the season," Larry pushed Q toward Tasha.

Police were pushy like that, messin' with their game. It was like you grow taller and all of a sudden they see you different. Long ago a cop put out his finger for him to hold when he was scared, not that he was ever scared anymore at fourteen. The same cop gave him a teddy bear and blanket while Mama and 'BadOne' worked things out. Another cop drove them to a shelter and took 'BadOne' away. There was a time cops put their hats on his head or let him wear a jacket to stay warm. But those were the old days before cops changed. Growing up meant a police about face — soothing voices of understanding transposed into loud arrogant voices of demanding. Q hated cops ever since he turned a teen, a black teen, a black boy teen.

LaMar snuggled with his family under warm blankets to enjoy a Cinderella video night and before the horses turned back into little mice, Shayna and Johnny were asleep in their parent's bed. LaMar clicked the remote to an action flick as Tamara whispered sweet nothings in his ear, taunting him with delicacies and caressing his lower parts. He tried to concentrate, but she made it impossible and the drama was at a crucial point he didn't want to miss. Diverted to a higher agenda he picked up the sleeping children and put them to bed. Upon return, Tamara slept soundly. Her steady breathing rose and fell between action film explosions in light fluttery snores.

He flicked off the TV, exhausted.

▼

His dreams broke down his guard. Twice he sat upright drenched in sweat. The events of the day exploded in jumbled Technicolor as his life merged into a nightmare. His hippocampus collided with his amygdale paralyzing him. A wicked red-haired man swung a wooden bat and knocked him down. Beloved eyes glowed green and hovered above his body. He bled. The sickening smell of brandy blazed his face as a dragon turned into a witch. Then his gloriously brown-hair mother screamed his name. Her hands were covered in his blood. She sat on his stomach. The roundness of her belly was at the breaking point with a child. He was a little boy. Then, like a watermelon hitting the concrete on a hot summer day, the dragon's head exploded with the sound of a bat cracking for a home run. Pieces of the head rained and the soft brown curls straightened. The dragon fell. Dead. The white man ran.

LaMar screamed.

"Wake up, LaMar! Wake Up!"

LaMar fought to keep the rainstorm of dragon pieces away.

"Jesus help me!" Tamara, put her strong hands upon her husband's cheeks and climbed over his chest, sitting on his belly as the nightmare dragon. She lightly stroked his face and massaged his neck and shoulders. Her breasts lightly touched his chest hairs. She kissed his brow. "Come on Baby, it's me, Tamara." She tasted his salty wet skin.

LaMar fought.

Tamara held on lovingly and did the only thing she knew to do. She sang, at first softly, and then in powerful worship.

LaMar fought the bloody dragon so he could kill the red-haired man.

Tamara's worship moved to warrior singing as she called on the angels of heaven to release her husband from his torment. She had never seen him act this way and she wasn't about to let go. LaMar was her knight in shining armor and she watched her strong, stable husband struggle to the safety she coaxed him toward.

LaMar yelped, his breath short. Soft hands held his wet skin, shook him, pulling him into the world's hardness — the world of an incomprehensible war initiated in Riverdale.

"Lord in heaven, Jesus, awake this man!"

The voice was his lover and LaMar opened his eyes to Tamara. The dragon was gone, but his energy spent in the deadly battle. Tamara's ebony skin shone in the moonlight and her dark, almost jet-black eyes sent signals of love that dove deep into his masculinity.

Tamara nuzzled his cheek and wrapped her arms tightly around him. She kissed him ever so gently, moving her tongue softly along his shoulder, lightly touching his ear with her finger nail circling the small diamond stud. Each kiss filled him. Each touch gave him strength.

"LaMar what's with you?"

"Nothing," LaMar answered evasively, "It was just a bad dream . . ."

"Lord in heaven help us. Jesus, bring peace to my loving husband's sleep. Protect him. Guard him from whatever demons he is facing. Bring him wisdom. In Jesus name, I rebuke whatever is attacking my husband. In Jesus name, I ask for truth, and release, and peace. Amen."

If Tamara was shaken, LaMar couldn't see it. She prayed solidly and wore her ancestral gifting well. He had listened carefully when the prayer mantle passed to Tamara on Grandmother's deathbed. The wizened woman had recited a warrior lineage of hundreds of years. His wife solemnly accepted her heaven sent disposition and maintained her responsibility. LaMar's savvy was too strong to choose a prayer route, yet he felt immediate release when Tamara offered up words of petition. She seemed to have a face-to-face relationship with God he didn't understand, still he honored her valor and boldness even if he didn't completely agree. While he played church, Tamara was church. The only comment Tamara made since the gift was she wished she could have sat under Granny's training umbrella instead of starting a new work. Tamara was invincibly strong, fearlessly independent, and passionately determined. She boldly went before The Father and was blessed, unafraid of man or demon and LaMar loved her more than life itself.

He imagined her on the African plain as the honor of her people. Her noble ancestry preserved through 300 years of intermixing, separated by an ocean and continent. He had admired her from the first time he saw her royal face under the giant oak at the University of Maryland Campus. She carried herself like a queen, her skin dark, her voice secure and confident. Her glorious jet-black hair crowning her head in the purest of African form so kinky it could start a motor. He inhaled its coconut aroma, lightly pulling on a curl and watching it rewind as tightly as it began. He marveled at her darkness and ran his hand gently across her cheek and over the plateau on her nose. He kissed her neck admiring the ridges and valleys of her body. Someday they would test their DNA – perhaps she was a long lost princess of Timbuktu? He nuzzled her. DNA testing would place him all over the map. He knew his heritage. He was a mutt.

He wrapped his arms around her soft skin kissing her full lips. His manhood rose as he gently touched his bride. She mounted him and made love passionately, saving face for the scared little boy hiding inside. Satisfied, they wrapped safely in love and LaMar fell asleep. Tomorrow he would talk with his earthly father, Reginolt 'Reggae' Watkins.

▼

Kevin threw his mattress against the wall. "Thank you Jesus. You're rough and black, and black and rough, and now I can sleep! Why didn't I throw you sooner?" It was a miracle; Kevin curled into a fetal position and slept soundly. He no longer feared the white demon; he had a point of focus, besides orange.

▼

"Woof, woof, woof," Johnny crawled over the crib rail.

Harry roused to lick 'his' boy's face.

"Woof, woof, woof," Johnny toddled past the baby gate.

"Bang, bang, bang," on Daddy and Mommy's door.

Awakened, LaMar opened the door to two knee-high chocolate drops. Johnny held his blanket in one hand and Harry's ear in the other.

"Good dog. Thank you for escorting Johnny, Harry" LaMar talked with the family pet like he was Dr. Doolittle. "Do you want to come in?"

Harry jumped upon the bed, sported a couple dog circles and curled into a ball on LaMar's pillow. LaMar pushed the dog to the foot of the bed, planted Johnny between he and Tamara and struggled to gain a corner of the down comforter and flannel sheets. His feet remained uncovered. Johnny fell back to sleep surrounded by love.

"I asked God for a fortress," Tamara whispered.

LaMar felt comforted as Harry placed his furry head on his ankle and gently licked his toes. Four years ago, LaMar spent months searching the Internet, calling breeders and filling out puppy questionnaires. He wanted a dog kind and gentle enough for his children, yet protective for his family when he traveled. He'd settled on a giant standard chocolate poodle and hoped the dog would join him as a therapy dog. That was two babies ago. He simply didn't have the time for proper training.

LaMar set appropriate dog rules for him – no sleeping on the bed, no eating human food and no riding in the BMW. Harry lovingly challenged every rule and won. He didn't believe he was a dog, he was just another chocolate baby and every curly haired member of the family knew LaMar was a sucker for puppy eyes. Tamara had christened the wooly booger, Harry, after her favorite Harrods' Chocolates. The rambunctious royal standard scoundrel now stood thirty inches at the shoulders and weighed almost ninety-five pounds.

▼

Sally filled a travel coffee mug and opened the kitchen door facing the ravine trail. She took a deep breath. She would step out.

Happy bounded out the door to the trail head, wagging her tail.

"Okay, let's give it a go," she smiled at her courage to join Happy walking old beloved twisted trails. Death's hand painted new strokes on her life canvas and unfortunately, at each turn Doc's memories whispered.

The yellow jackets hovered on pink asters with the chain saw buzzing of cutting 'dead' wood, fireplace wood Doc planned to cut. The purple hostas danced while honeybees gathered honey for Porter Potts' bee hives. Honey that she and Doc bought at the Apple Festival. Doc always tipped each child extra dollars to see them smile. Doc called it 'smile honey', the most expensive this side of the Mississippi.

She avoided the trail where Doc . . . taking the left fork home. Porter Potts and Doc argued on the porch a while back. They had been neighbors for years. She hadn't heard her husband so angry. He sounded like a sergeant as he banished Porter from their property. The right fork led to the Potts' home that Doc referred to as a junkyard.

Her running shoe kicked up a rock startling a grouse that flushed out of twisted bittersweet vines Doc cultivated. Orange berries burst into a brilliant red of scattered memories. She gingerly picked a floweret. Forget the peanut butter! She ran home. Mike's game! Since the accident with Shaun, Mike's academics had developed into a point of contention between the father and son. She grabbed a box of light bulbs to fix the porch lamp, the box held a lonely bulb. Maybe she'd forgotten them too.

Life was easier with a sleeping pill and she laid down. Would there ever be another painting?

▼

LaMar felt the morning rustle of his children and pretended to sleep. Johnny prepared for a baby shark attack, mouth open wide.

Pre-attack, LaMar scooped up his baby boy and snuggled him under the down comforter. "Come on Johnny, you can hide with me under the covers," LaMar pulled the blankets over his head to whisper man-to-boy, "Do you want go to fishing with Bups and Daddy?"

Two chubby dimples indented, "Kitty fish!"

"Wake up Daddy. It's the weekend, Baby!" Shayna mimicked a radio announcer.

"The weekend baby!" Johnny clapped and fell into a pile of blankets. Shayna jumped on the bed. Lamar rolled over to grab Johnny to save him from his big sister dancing with her fairy wand.

"You will become a scary-fairy-merry-horse Harry. You will become Prince Charming, Johnny." She pointed the soft tube stick and twirled in her princess pajamas. "And you are my forever Daddy!"

"Careful Shayna," he warned.

"This is my trampoline! Daddy, I can go high, like an airplane. All by myself!" She giggled as she jumped from the foot of the bed to land in the softness. "Bups said, I can fly his airplane! I can be a Blue Angel! Bups said, I can be the president of the United States!"

LaMar held Johnny above his head and made airplane and bebop noises. Johnny flew through loops and dives gurgling and chuckling.

"Guess what Daddy! It's hair day. I'm gonna get my hair did."

"Yes, you are going to get your hair done with Mommy and Granny T," LaMar corrected, snuggling both children. "You smell coconut good Shayna."

"Johnny smells like Mr. Stink," she giggled.

LaMar challenged her with tickle fingers and she rolled quickly away to jump off the bed and soon return with a shoebox of bobbles and hair things.

"Granny does Mommy's hair, Mommy does my hair and I do Harry's hair. Harry has hairy hair," she giggled at her word play.

Hearing his name Harry wagged his tail. Seeing the shoebox, he covered his nose with his paw.

"I, Mr. Stink!" Johnny's eyes sparkled. "I, Mr. Biggie Stinkman!"

LaMar laughed pulling on a pair of basketball shorts and a beater before he carried the children into the kitchen. Thank God, Tamara woke early. The smell of fresh ground coffee wafted into their bedroom.

"You smell good too, Daddy. Just like Mr. Stinkman!" Shayna's carnival ride ground to a stop on the kitchen chair. She grabbed LaMar's du-rag off his head, the du-rag he slept with to train his frizzing head. "I got it Daddy. Now you need to get your hair did too!"

LaMar poured a coffee noticing the pancake batter Tamara mixed up for him. "Who wants pancakes?" he playfully waved the carefully seasoned cast iron fry pan he'd declared off limits to Tamara.

"Teddy Bears, Daddy. Teddy bear faces!" Shayna ordered.

"Turtle, Johnny Cakemans," Johnny made a pleading pout.

"You leave your lip like that little man, a birdie just might fly over and poop on it!" LaMar put chocolate chip eyes in front of each child, "Don't you dare eat them until I give you your pancakes."

Six puppy eyes impatiently followed every action and LaMar's heart melted like chocolate chips spreading on fresh hot pancakes. Raggae, his robust adoptive father, stood laughing at the kitchen door.

Saturday morning was a great time to be a grandfather and Granddaddy Reggae, otherwise known as Bups, had already shared a quiet cup of Kenyan coffee with his wife Tina, read the newspaper and driven across town to begin hair day and a guy's day of catfishing. The smell of griddlecakes, maple syrup and smoked bacon greeted him as he entered the warm Watkins's kitchen.

"Hi Pops, grab a cup of joe, want me to flip you a flapjack?"

"No thanks," He was proud of his doctor son who had come so far and lived through so much. Strict parenting and playing music each Sunday in church had paid off in gorgeous grandbabies with golden sticky fingers. Reggae laughed at the half eaten turtle pancake swimming in an amber sea of maple syrup with rivulets of butter. He loved spoiling grandchildren with fringe benefits and limited responsibility.

"Bups! Bups! Bups!" Goo slid down Johnny's face.

"Hi kids," Granddaddy radiated.

"I'm five Bups!" Johnny, held up ten gooey fingers ready to be licked by a syrupy face. The baby boy now wore a size five shirt and in infantile logic a number was a number, ages and sizes were the same. He had aged four years overnight? "I big Shayna!" She was four.

He showed his numbers on his hand. "One, two, three, four. One, two, three, four, five!" Johnny was definitely five masquerading as a precocious two. Johnny was built for football – strong, agile, and massive. "Five adds Pinky!" Tiny bright baby teeth gleamed.

Overhearing the conversation between his son and his father blazed open a door into LaMar's thinking. Did Kevin live in Johnny's worldview? Kevin's answers lacked abstraction though his language seemed adequate. Idioms were taken literally. The nuances of English flew through the air in snippets and bits. Metaphors boomeranged. Did Johnny's language skills give him clues to Kevin? Could Kevin carry on two-way conversations? Was his communcation the way LaMar felt when he tried to speak Spanish with Maria his cleaning lady? As long as he was doing the talking, he did fine, but when answering questions he missed the subtleties. He had thought Kevin was uncooperatively word playing, now he wasn't sure.

Reggae unstuck Johnny from his bib and wiped him with a warm washcloth before scooping him up. The chubby Sumo wrestler wrapped tightly around Bups neck. "You're one strong player Johnny." He chucked Johnny under the chin and winked at LaMar, "you could have one ready for offense." Both men understood the statement's racial insinuation.

"I, a big playa." Johnny parroted.

Reggae rubbed Johnny's soft wooly head, "Yeah boy, you're a playa alright. Play on Bup's heart strings you do." Reggae swung Johnny up on his shoulders and deferred to LaMar, "Our little horseman has potential, Johnny is a fine steed and the soil is ready. The excavation the Civil Rights soldiers died for, I toiled for, and you stand on LaMar is ready to sprout a new generation. Integrated not intersected, free to grow unfettered in the 21st century."

Granddaddy continued with Johnny, "Let's get dressed strong man, we need to get these ooey, gooey, sticky, icky jammies off you, boy."

"Ooey gooey, sticky, icky, Johnny Mr. Stinkman," Johnny chortled and plopped on his diapered bottom. "I dressed. I five!"

"You're one,' Granddaddy corrected.

Johnny broke into tears shouting, "I five! I five! I five!"

"OK Johnny, today you can be five." Granddaddy acquiesced. "That little boy is a bright one. Let's get outta here before the women decide to do our hair. Don't feel like Tina messin' with my locks, today. That woman knows how to twist this old man's fro and right now I don't feel like being twisted. I got the feelin' in m' bones for some cat fishin' I can hear 'em yowlin'. "

"Cat fishshshs" Johnny blew lip bubbles. "Meow! Meow!"

"Pops, can you keep an eye on Johnny? I have to make phone call."

"Always at your service," Reggae bowed and rolled his hands like a genie. He hoisted Johnny upon his shoulders and nickered out the door. The proud little rider galloped on a graying stallion.

"My children are so blessed to have Pops," thought LaMae.

The weight of yesterday nudged his heart, "And so am I."

▼

Saturday hair day was serious business for Tamara, Shayna, and Granny Tina, other wise known as Granny T. LaMar was surrounded in a hair toy store, albeit ultra clean, thanks to Maria Sanchez who scrubbed the Watkin's home every Friday. The pristine periwinkle Corian counter was filled with hair curlers, jars of fine smelling Afro hair products and Granny T's ruby red enamel Golden Supreme Elite Thermal Stove with ten different irons. There was a rainbow stack of bandannas and scarves, a crockery jar of pics and combs, and Shayna's clear plastic box of bobbles and beads. Undoubtedly new treasures were being purchased, in addition to the extra large jar of African Royale he requested. Ma had teased him about where in the limited amount of hair he was he going to put that and he flashed his 'I'm your son and you don't need to know' smile and poured a cup of Colombian Supreme. The women departed for their jaunt to the Holy Yokes African Hair store.

LaMar entered Kevin's parent's names into his smart phone yellow pages. Blink. It was right there. They lived in the same area Kevin went to school. Why did he say they moved?

LaMar sipped his joe watching Johnny, Harry, and Pops shoot baskets in the tiny tot hoop. It was uncanny what Pops could get a dog to do. Johnny put the ball into the hoop and Harry pushed the ball back to him with his nose.

He reviewed notes from a foot of reference data in Kevin's file.

> Infant: Failure-to-thrive and sucking issues
> Baby: Failure to sleep, did not like to be held, attachment issues?
> Toddler: Easily over stimulated
> Preschooler: Highly social, No stranger danger
> School: initially social, happy and liked school
> Reading and math difficulty – grade 1-12
> Behavior problems escalated – grade 4
> Diagnosed ADHD, ODD – IQ 90 – age 10
> Middle school / high school
> Diagnosed EBD – IQ 84 – age 13
> Abundance of tardiness, In school suspension,
> Classroom disruption
> Caught shoplifting
> Experimenting with drugs/alcohol 6th grade
> Failed anger management classes 7th grade
> Expelled from school for fighting 9th grade
> Involved in gangsta rap underground music
> Black Stone symbols on his notebook
> Four tries with accommodation to pass state basic standard testing
> Special Ed classes 40-60% day schedule
> Individualized bus transportation
> Has not seen parents in two years
> Court Issues
> Accused father for physical abuse – age 17
> Stabbed a ten-year-old girl in the park, 90 days juvenile detention
> Ran away summer of 17th year, unseen by parents since age 19.
> Functional Assessment – IQ 74, GAF 45
> (Why the IQ decrease – attitude, teen rebellion, chemical use?)

According to police records, Mr. and Mrs. John Abbott adopted
Kevin at six months. Early medical records indicated he was a failure-to-
thrive infant with sucking issues but otherwise normal. "Hasn't changed
much, now he's a failure-to-thrive adult with behaviors that suck. Seems
like not thriving and sucking are a theme for him." He activated the phone
number hoping to reach Kevin's parents. The telephone prefix located
them in an upper income part of the city, conflicting with his first impression of Kevin. From Kevin's behavior he would have expected struggling
white or lower working class.

"Hello, Abbott residence," greeted a professional woman's voice.

"May I please speak to Mr. or Mrs. Abbott?"

"This is Mrs. Abbott, how may I help you?"

The woman was obviously trained in etiquette, perhaps he had a
wrong number. The language syntax was unlike Kevin's.

"Do you have a son named Kevin Justin Abbott?"

"Yes," her voice changed from friendly professionalism to a worried
mother. "Do you know where he is? Is he all right? Is he hurt? Is he alive?"

"Your son is alive and well Mrs. Abbott. I am a doctor trying to help
him. I need some information to help me. My name is Dr. L.R. Watkins."

"Is he in the hospital? Is he hurt, Dr. Watkins?" Lydia pleaded.

"No. I'm a psychologist for Kevin and I need to ask a few questions."

Kevin's mother was no longer listening and she shouted to her husband, "John, John, Kevin's alive, he's not hurt. There's a doctor on the
phone who wants some information to help him."

"Mrs. Abbott, I would appreciate it if you could tell me a little about
Kevin and your family? Could you begin with his birth?"

Mrs. Abbott seemed out of breath, "You can call me Lydia, we never
got birth information. Kevin seemed like an answer to our prayers. We
adopted him at six-months-old. His mother was a homicide, and the county had him in five foster homes before he came to live with us. The social
worker told us he was a normal Caucasian baby needing love. We figured
we had enough love for any baby, but pouring love into him was filling a
sive. Nothing we tried worked. We parented him the best we could, sent
him to special schools, and got him an expensive tutor. When he was fifteen he used the transit with his friends like the other kids. That's when
life got stormy. The school called him EBD for Emotional Behavior
Disordered. He hobbled through high school between in-school suspen-

sion and Special Ed, but he graduated. We were so proud."

"Kevin didn't like our rules. Called us preppy, whatever that is. Never liked our extended family or our friends and we didn't like the kids he associated, boys wearing pantihose on their heads looking like hoodlums"

LaMar spun the black knot of his du-rag on the counter.

Lydia continued, "The boys used extensive profanity. I couldn't believe it. They could use the f-word as a noun, verb, adverb and adjective in the same sentence. Their girlfriends wore clown makeup and hooker clothing." Lydia huffed.

"Scared me to death." She softened her voice. "We were afraid of being robbed. They were black boys. I'd run my purse off to my bedroom as soon as I saw Kevin's cronies. I always hoped I'd see one of them trip on their pant legs. They wore pants so big they'd fall off my husband and he's got the belly to hold them up." She laughed carefully.

LaMar rubbed the indented space along his cheek listening without reproach; he'd recently been down this road.

"I kept telling Kevin it wasn't a proper way to dress and he'd tell me I didn't know squat. Then Kevin started rolling up one of his pant legs and tying a red bandanna around his head. He's always had a quick temper, but the last year he lived with us his temper was fierce. He hit me."

The energy was clearly departing from this woman, "After that I stayed away. I didn't discipline him. I'd find knives behind his door and under his bed after he left for school on the little yellow bus he called the retard racer. I prayed he'd move away and disappear. And then he did. I believed love transcended everything, but the last months he lived with us, we hardly talked. I didn't care. I was exhausted. He scared me screaming that I denied him his culture. Somehow he got a picture of a woman he called his 'real' mother from some social worker. It proved he was Black. We were told he was white, why did he want to be Black?"

LaMar sidestepped to reroute her, "Can you tell me about when he first came to your home?" He closed his eyes thinking if she only knew.

"Kevin was a tough little guy. I tried hard to be a good mother to him. He was cute and at first we loved him like the dickens, but our love couldn't fix him. He didn't like to be held or cuddled and preferred to be left alone. We couldn't play with him like my friends' kids."

"Did he have any eating problems?"

"Well, let me think. First he didn't suck and then he didn't chew. He was a projectile vomiter and spit four feet in the air. You had to watch yourself."

"Did he have any sleeping problems?"

"He slept about four hours a day his whole life. We quit encouraging him to sleep because when he awoke he screamed and you'd think we were killing him. Doctors said not to worry and called them nightterrors. Kid had them day or night, he'd wake up from a nap and scream. I tried everything. Even thought of going to the Catholic Church for exorcism and we're Lutherans. Weirdest thing though," Lydia paused, "all of a sudden he'd stop screaming. It was the only time as a youngster he acted like he was glad to see me and was sweeter than honey. His body relaxed and his face burst into the most joyous smile. Then and only then for a moment he cuddled. He'd jump off my lap like nothing strange happened and start to play. I was dish rag weary. Doctor, are you sure he is safe?"

"Yes, he's safe. Mrs. Abbott, could I speak with your husband?" LaMar twisted his diamond stud and jotted case notes.

"John, they found Kevin, a nice doctor wants to talk to you."

"Hell-O. This is John Abbott," Mr. Abbott sucked in his belly, pushed out his barrel chest and pulled up his pants. "May I help you?"

"Could you tell me about raising your son?" LaMar twirled his durag between his index finger and simple gold wedding ring. The Abbott's were none the wiser to his ethnicity, but he was pretty sure about theirs. LaMar's mind wandered as he mentally retaliated. The voice is a master of disguise. Funny the perception you have when all you have is sound. LaMar tried to picture these two very white adoptive parents in his mind. A front office gum smacking receptionist and an over-the-road trucker.

"Always wanted a son. We gave him the world and he didn't want it. Kevin didn't like rough housing until he was a late teen. I couldn't throw him up in the air or tickle him as a tyke. That set him off. He stood on the sidelines to watch kids play. He never joined in. It took me months to teach him to ride a bike, but he finally did it."

LaMar felt the pride in John's voice.

"Once he learned I couldn't get him off. He'd fixate. Did the same thing with roller blades and video games. He'd played those beeping buzzing games alone for hours and we let him sit there. He cheered when he reached a new game level, but if I taught him something new, he yelled at me. I quit helping with his homework."

"He flunked classes after fourth grade and teachers thought he was lazy. Told me church kids were jerks. I think they got sick of putting up with him. He made friends with the rough kids from the seedy side of the city. He'd sneak out the windows after we fell asleep, steal food and blankets. I fixed him," John's laugh was almost evil. "I screwed the windows shut. When he walked out the door I changed the locks and didn't give him a key. I didn't want him around if I couldn't trust him. Locked him out unless we were home. I even installed a motion detector, but his hoodlum friends were sneaky. He walked and talked like them, put a quarter inch cubic zirconium in his ear and told me it was real. Yeah, real pressurized plastic. Talking to him was like spittin' in the wind. I told him, he was going no where hanging with a crowd like that. He was raised better. He needed to buck up and become a real man," John Abbott paused and took a deep breath.

LaMar twirled his small quarter carat diamond stud. The conversation stopped. John's breathing labored.

"Kevin never liked being touched until he got teen girls interested in fondling him. I watched him like a hawk—even listened in on a few phone calls, confiscated and read school notes. He got picked up for standing in front of the lingerie store staring at women through the window. He never moved for three hours. Is he in woman trouble? Voyeurism?"

"No sir, not voyeurism. Murder. I can schedule you to meet with me on Monday and see Kevin. Would you like that?" LaMar offered

"Lydia, Kevin's in the slammer. Do you want to see him?" John yelled. "He's in for murder and if I get hold of him I'll kill him myself."

LaMar explained the details and Kevin's parents agreed to arrive on Monday afternoon. "Part of me hopes he finally learns from this. I won't pander to his manipulation. We got him graduated from high school, but the last year he lived with us was pure hell. It's taken us years to recover from trying to parent and we're still pretty shell shocked. He can't expect us to bail him out, but we will see him. He is our son. Jail might be a good place for him, keep everyone safe."

John paused, "What kind of parent is glad their child is in jail? Dr. Watkins, Kevin talks big, I don't think he'd kill someone. Good bye."

LaMar hung up the phone, like father, like son, either this was one 'bad kid' or his parents were in denial. Something was out of sync. LaMar pictured Harry Potter's stepfamily and added a check to his 'to do' list; it was time for cat fishing and he went to find Pops.

Pops had given Johnny a cane pole with a weighted red bobber and was teaching him to cast by hitting the basketball. Harry and Pop's dog Chorus sat obediently watching from the sidelines. Harry was sitting, just sitting and even his tail was still. He seemed happy. He had a dog smile on his face and his tongue hung down. How did Pop do that?

14
CAT FISH

To some people, catfishing remains the butt of jokes perpetuating the myth of a sluggish and primitive fish that finds its habitat in dark murky waters. To others it permeates memories of lazy summer days along the banks of a rippling river. And to a select few, it draws upon the wisdom that only comes with tried and true experiences of trophy hunting one of the world's most intelligent fish – the channel cat. Reggae enjoyed challenging this fish species in a game of cat and mouse. He liked introducing the sport to his son and grandson using lazy afternoons to catch up on each other's lives. He relished checking local cat haunts and prowl status. His favorite was exploring out of the way river snags and cat holes with his boys in a game of catch and release of the largest whiskered fish a water offered.

Reggae selected a private site for Saturday's retreat where the banks of the river sloped about thirty degrees on the outside bend of a side channel near a significant old logjam. The large tangled mass offered a warm snag or sanctuary for young channel cats. It was perfect as some of his holes were already empty as the cats schooled up and migrated in cooling weather. Behind the snag was an eddy where water slowed to offer an ambush for darting catfish. Off a rock downstream was an ideal place to catch blue gills on a bobbered cane pole for Johnny alongside a sugarsand beach to play when he tired of fishing.

LaMar was incredulous at the conglomerate of things Pops packed for a single afternoon. In addition to a selection of black, white-tipped rods and reels, he had a cooler, two picnic baskets, a tackle box, a grocery bag of food, and two dark green backpacks that converted to fishing chairs. He remained silent. Long ago he learned not to interfere with his father's catfishing process and on each adventure he learned something new. Johnny darted down the slope toward the water followed by Chorus, Reggae's German shepherd. To a respectable German shepherd a playful poodle and a toddler were trouble. If Harry got too far away, Chorus nipped at his heels sending him tail-down yelping to lie at LaMar's feet. K9 work was demanding.

When Johnny toddled near the water, he gently tugged his shirt. When Johnny intentionally ignored him, he wrapped his big white teeth around the little arm and guided the toddler back to his daddy. A look of disdain and a loud 'harhumph' informed LaMar that 'this one is yours'.

Reggae unloaded the shopping bag containing two boxes of macaroni and cheese, a jar of minced garlic, strawberry Kool-Aid, a mason jar of flour, a jar of his wife's barbeque sauce, two tins of fishy cat food, an old salt shaker, a can of parmesan cheese, a bottle of lemon juice, and a jug of pure maple syrup.

Out from the cooler came graying hamburger, half-frozen chicken livers, a mason jar of murky water and a container of night crawlers. He positioned it neatly on his portable camp table with built in seats.

"LaMar fetch me one of my catfish kits in the picnic basket," Reggae surveyed the spread, pumped his fists and winked.

"Sure Pops," the basket contained sandwiches, apples, and cookies.

"No, the other one," Reggae whispered, "Shush your voice. Cats'll hear ya'll coming. They're not stupid. Cats are the most advanced game-fish in the world, inhabit every continent except Antarctica and make up over 10% of the fish species known to man. They pick up sound waves in their skin, that's why we're making the stink bait up here before we head down to the river. They passed the Farabee Intelligence test beating out trout and walleyes."

LaMar quietly opened the second basket harboring his father's home-made catfish kits — twelve one-gallon zip lock bags each containing two black thirty gallon trash bags, three large zip lock baggies, two pair of plas-tic disposable gloves, nylon stockings, a small package with ten straight shank hooks, a variety of weights of bell sinkers, and special line his father swore by. Pops honed and studied cat fishing like other men practice golf. He handed one kit to his father.

"Get me that stainless bowl," Reggae opened the macaroni box and poured the cheese into a plastic bag and threw away the pasta. "Show Johnny how to dip the night crawlers in the cheese for Blue Gills. He might even pick up a small cat on the cane pole."

He repeated the process. "Do these up too," this time adding the strawberry drink mix to the cheese and shaking it. He set it next to the chicken liver container.

"Tie me some leaders while I make the stink bait," Reggae rubbed his hands admiring the mad scientist buffet. Into the silver bowl went the hamburger, stinky cat food, garlic, a couple shakes of salt, a glob of BBQ sauce, a whole lot of parmesan cheese, jiggers of syrup and a douse of muddy water. Johnny watched intensely as Bups donned blue plastic gloves to avoid touching the mixture. He dumped the flour and began mixing the gooey mess. Johnny reached in, but LaMar diverted disaster by showing him how to dip wiggling night crawlers and chicken livers.

"These blue gloves save my marriage," Reggae wiggled icky fingers. "If I want lovin' when I get home, I best be stink-free."

Johnny stuck out his tongue and scrunched up his nose, "I no Mr. Stink. Bups Mr. Stink, Biggee Mr. Old . . ." Johnny held the word, his lips looking like a baby bird awaiting a wiggly night crawler, and then he shouted, "Stinkman!" His baby joke meant no disrespect.

"If we're going to catch cats boy, we better not smell human."

"You man stink!" Johnny giggled.

Reggae laughed, "A good knot is the difference between landing a fish of a lifetime or telling the fish story."

LaMar tied Hook Snell knots while Reggae kneaded the sticky stinky into ten balls and placed them into nylon netting that connected to the hooks on LaMar's leaders. He set up two poles with stink bait of different weights for varying depths making a fine meal presentation for underwater kittens.

LaMar baited Johnny's cane pole with a breaded night crawler. The remaining stink leaders were zip lock sealed for immediate use without having to handle it again. He poured the chicken livers into the drink cheese mix and shook them. Harry salivated and begged for leftovers disgusting Chorus laying at Reggae's feet knowing there were never scraps. Reggae poured the remaining muddy water into the bowl and added sand to scrub the goo off the edges. He dumped the mixture into the bushes and then repeated the process. He finished by dousing the bowl with lemon juice and wiping it clean with a dry paper towel, putting the gloves and the towel into the garbage, and the bowl immediately back into the basket. The area was clean of the dough ball enterprise and not even Tina or Tamara, who shared no kindness toward stink baits would notice.

Reggae sanded his hands, "Johnny, my little man. When it's time to fish. It's time to fish."

▼

Downstream LaMar helped Johnny cast the bobber into the river. The diapered fisherman popped his line so often the cheese coated night crawler spent most of its time midair finally entangling in a tree. The stuck mess triggered a tired Johnny meltdown as LaMar cut the line to add a new leader. Recovered from the tantrum he chased Harry who delighted in water pouncing, rolling on a dead fish and digging a flying sandhole.

LaMar watched the little red bobber ripple the water just past the curly hair of his son. He didn't hear the footsteps of his father.

"Something's bothering you LaMar. I know that look."

Pop's concern was genuine and the question stung. He held his breath, biting the bottom of his lower lip. Freeze frame images rippled past. He tried to relax his emotions through he felt like he needed his own check up from the neck up.

He dodged the question, "Got any plans for the week Pops?"

"I'm on call for Military Honors on Tuesday. Monday and Wednesday I have studio bookings and Thursday, if weather permits, I'm flying the Cirrus one last time before it gets too cold."

"Maybe I'll join you Thursday if I wrap up the court report. I promised Shayna another airplane ride this year. I was thinking of flying to deliver the report instead of driving. I'd like to see the fields and rivers from the air. The trees look beautiful." LaMar masked his emotions, remaining silent.

Johnny caught a clear teardrop off his father's cheek and tasted it as he climbed onto Bup's lap. Reggae wrapped his arm around his son's broad shoulders and hugged in tight. No one spoke; the silence belonged to LaMar's imprisoned boyhood. Granddaddy Reggae prayed silently, he had waited a long time for this day.

▼

Huddled together on the banks of a river great enough to divide a country it seemed fitting to discuss issues great enough to divide a man. Torrents of ancient glacial melt creviced through landscape that now soaked up water from raindrops, underground streams and storm sewers. Beginning with a wilderness trickle the mighty water grew with flood-plain runoff to soulfully pass into the bayous of the south and the great salty gulf. It had been a journey point for many and appropriately the river continued to provide a place to reroute, rearrange, and revise a life. The river, like their souls, had refused to be mastered even though both were dredged and dammed. Both had braved cold so dry it burned life into stone. On the banks of the mighty Mississippi, the time had come to unbind a child held hostage for twenty years so that the child held in his granddaddy's arms was free. The gulf held harbor a sea of truth rich in nutrients to feed growth ploughed soil. Knowing this, the men dared to toil for beloved Johnny whose roots deserved to grow deep and unburdened by the curses of past generations.

LaMar initially questioned his youth at thirteen but was silenced by Raggae, his new father, who believed the truth was too painful for a young adolescent. LaMar feared losing a man he had grown to love and obeyed. Pop's words rose up invisibly, but loudly each time he thought of questioning, "Going back in your past will do you no good son. What's done is done, no sense in talking about it. I closed pieces of my past for a better life and I can tell you it did me no harm. You need to do the same. Tina and I are your forever parents and we'll help you make something of yourself. You got a new chance at life son, embrace it." Those words were the ice dam that held him back until today and LaMar's questions cascaded as quickly as the song of the breakup of spring ice crystals. It was easier to ask his questions all at once than wait for an answer. "What do you know about me, Pops? Why was I in the hospital? Who were my birth parents? What really happened to them? Do you know what they looked like? How did my birth mama really die?"

"What do you remember?" Reggae coaxed. It was time to defrost the frozen truth. His son had a right to know why that long scar ran along the side of his face.

"I remember the smell of brandy and cigarettes. No, it was chewing tobacco. I remember soft brown curls on a mocha colored woman, red hair and a baseball bat, then startling green dragon eyes sending fearful messages. I cannot put the pieces together."

"And, " his father encouraged.

"A fourteen-year-old boy thought I was his mother's abusive boyfriend. He swung a baseball bat at me yesterday. I caught the bat before it hit me, but a strong memory flashed as though I was hit. I collapsed on the floor. It was a post traumatic memory."

"I'm listening son," Reg handed warm and sleeping Johnny to LaMar.

"Last night the dreams came like a roaring fire. One flame ate up the next to expose a new flame with a new scene. Each scene increased in violence. I saw my beautiful mother with soft brown hair and mocha skin. She was light skinned, Pops. Black, of course, but racially mixed, perhaps also Hispanic or Mediterranean."

"Go on."

Their professional roles had reversed and his musician father played LaMar's heartstrings and mind symphony as professionally as any qualified therapist. LaMar shared the litany of yesterday's experiences – his humiliating escort into town by the Sheriff; his mistrust and dislike of Margie; his emptiness for Q; his sadness for the isolated Tasha locked in a white community; and his meeting with the curmudgeon Sam O'Riley."

And last he shared Kevin, "I'm working with a young man whose intense eyes are a feature in every dream, like a key to the Pandora's box of my childhood. His eyes become my eyes, then one eye, then we separate. We spin and fall." LaMar's voice trailed off. "Over and over we fall. Usually my dreams relive a day's experience, solve a complex problem, or practice something I am learning. These dreams disorient me. How do they fit in my life? They are my life, my very being." LaMar watched a backwater current spinning like the eyes in his dreams.

"Do you know what my mother looked like? Can you tell me what happened? I need to face my childhood and wake up. I've been sleeping for twenty years." LaMar's eyes pleaded with his father, Johnny rustled, his hot breath heating the area on LaMar's chest over his hurting heart.

"Do you remember anything else?" Reggae tightened his embrace on LaMar's shoulder.

"Mama was sleeping when a heavy old church woman with a big red hat swooped into my house. She was a feisty old bird who pecked at Mama and clucked and fluttered like an old hen protecting her little chick. She yelled at Mama. Then she took me under the wing of her dark green coat to a house that smelled of apple pie and lavender. I called her Granny

Henny, from the nursery rhyme Henny Penny my Black Hen. Her cluck-
ing felt safe," LaMar paused.

"I remember Mama sitting with a big man. They were arguing before
she came into my room to kiss me goodnight. She smelled of cheap
brandy. I didn't want to kiss her so I turned away. She slapped me for refusing her affection. I cried to sleep. Those smells still nauseate me. Sam
O'Riley drank that same brandy, chewed that same tobacco, old red hair
was hid under his cap." LaMar closed his eyes. "It's just bits of information
I can't put into any order."

"Mama bent over and her big belly bumped my chin. I don't remember her being fat. In most of the freeze frames she is lustfully formed
attracting many men. I think she was well along with a child." LaMar
paused, gently rubbing sleeping Johnny's arm. "That's all."

"I can't help you much with the details, we never got a picture of
your mother, so I can't tell you what she looked like. Your kin had all died
and the neighbors were silent. Seemed like your family moved around.
Her boyfriend split town and the police never got a description. Your
father was unknown."

LaMar felt sick and swallowed hard.

"It was 1974. I don't think they figured she was worth continuing a
case on. Your mother was poor and colored. You didn't remember anything
and they didn't want to traumatize you more than you already were. Mom
and I agreed to let sleeping dogs lie once you joined our family."

LaMar felt as though he was carrying heavy puzzle pieces in a maze
of fragmentation. "I woke up in a hospital not knowing why I was there.
My legs were in casts. The nurse told me they were broken at the shins but
I could walk again. My head hurt. I touched my face and counted fifteen
nylon strings along my cheek. The top of my head was covered in bandag-
es. The nurse told me I slept for ten days, and it was time to remove the
stitches from my face. I told her 'Musta been some fight I was in' and she
said 'Sweetie, you beat death in that fight. Your mama didn't make it'." And
then I knew Mama died, but I didn't remember. I didn't even know my
own name or where I lived."

"I listened to the clip of the stitch and felt the tug of the thread and
the friction as it passed through my cheek. I tried to remember but I
couldn't. I wanted my daddy and I didn't know if I even had one, so I asked,
'Where's my Daddy?' and the nurse answered, 'I don't know, sweetie.

We've got some really nice people looking for him.' "

"I was so scared. I was all alone and hurting when the nurse pulled out my stitches. I closed my eyes and prayed, 'Lord, please find my Daddy; I know you know where he is. Please send him to get me.' That's all, that's the ending. I think I fell asleep. When I woke up you were my father."

Reggae built a fire to warm the cooling day and it soon crackled and burned nicely. He watched LaMar hold Johnny as the flames reflected a glow on similar colored skins. "Sometimes, you have to have a mess to have a message. By the time you joined us, Tina and I had been married eleven years and still no children. We moved out of state away from friends and built a reputable business. We owned a home in a quiet mixed community and were active in the local music and civil rights scene. My music had a small national following and a large local following. Our infertility made way for our future and our inability to conceive was an answer to your prayer LaMar. We've never been rich by any means, but we had enough to adopt you. "

LaMar relaxed and leaned forward. Reggae felt the change in ambiance, "I was sitting on the porch reading the news – Thursday's Variety Section, March 27, page seven." Reggae laughed, "I remember the exact page that changed my life and the picture of a skinny boy named LaMar with no last name who needed an African American father. I knew who his father was. It was one of those 'you know what you know' moments."

"The eleven-year-old staring at me from the newsprint was my son, perhaps not biological, but in every other aspect. Your picture stared at me and the paragraph read you loved music and sports. My heart pumped loudly as I dialed the numbers for the Waiting Children Line. I felt like I had when I snuck behind Mama's back trying to make adult choices too big for my britches, hyperalert like I might have to pee. Then you push aside the feeling for the rush of going for it." Reggae stirred the fire.

"I did it without telling Tina, but I was sure she would approve. I noticed her looking at the little Thursday Child every week. Some weeks she commented what fun it would be to take in a foster child or adopt. I wouldn't have even paid any attention to those cute little photos if Tina hadn't shown interest."

"Your picture captured my heart. The phone call with the social worker pierced a safety bubble of old scars I had suffered as a child. My wounds rose from the ashes of my mind into my present. I understood innocence lost in the wasteland of the desolate urban culture. There's no death to memories even if you bury them," Reggae noticed LaMar's twenty-year-old scar deepened in the shadow of the fire, running down the side of his face. An old sharp pain jabbed his side triggering old experiences. Reggae pondered sharing, perhaps his mess could build a bridge for LaMar's.

"When I saw you in the hospital, it mirrored my eleven-year-old life. I knew you needed a father, because I needed a father. I felt abandoned when my brotha' Lance went to college. College was a big deal. Without Lance it was just Mama and me. We were dirt poor. Mama rose early each day to care for a wealthy family's kids and while Mama watched rich white kids my brotha' had watched out for me since I was a nappy little fro. He'd been my daddy since day one, my real daddy served with General Patton's 761st Battalion in World War II. Mama got pregnant before he'd been shipped out. He was one of the fifty percent who didn't come home. He never met me. He returned in a wooden box and Mama got his Purple Heart. She kept his American flag on her bedroom dresser, near the side of the bed where she slept. She never remarried, she didn't want or need another man. She told me Daddy left her the 'best present ever' – me. Mama gave me Daddy's bugle, it was really the only thing I ever shared with my Daddy except my genes."

"I grew up loved and protected by Mama and Lance. They rode me hard to keep me on the straight and narrow, until that day . . ." Reggae drew in a deep breath and looked past the catfish snag, toward the other side of the river, " . . . that, that pivotal day."

"It was Lance's first year out of the hood and it was unheard of, but Lance had gotten himself a college basketball scholarship at a white college. Coach Wilson pretty much sat on Lance to behave through his three years in high school and that sitting paid off. He was goin' somewhere special and Mama was real proud. To me, Lance was a role model. He was my hero, besides brother, daddy and friend."

"It was my eleventh birthday and Mama needed eggs from the corner store to bake my cake. Her employer gave her a handful of hardly used little blue car candles they were going to throw out and I was excited to see them all lit up. I hurried to Eddie's Market a block away. The problem with Eddie's . . . well it was where the gang boys hung out with the

gonnabees and the wannabees. Somehow Lance had kept from gettin' a
rag. He was tough and valiant heading for NBA. He wore size fifteen shoes.
I couldn't fill Lance's shoes; I was going to try to fill Duke Ellington's. I
always missed in hoops."

"Lance held status in the hood outa' respect for his skills. He also had
Mama and she was no woman to mess with. Not even the Chicago gang
members played games with Mama. When Mama said go, you went."

"Lance had left his watch on the little table where Mama kept her
umbrella. The watch was a gift at graduation from Coach Wilson. I
remember how proud Lance looked wearing it and how he stood up
straight and looked the coach in the eye, telling him, "I'll make you proud
coach. I'll be on time, for time and score time. This is a wonderful gift.
Thank you."

"No one in all the generations of the Watkins family had graduated
from high school and Lance held his diploma like he was wearing Daddy's
Purple Heart. I remembered looking up at all 6'7" of him; he was a true
hero and going to college to boot! He was a pioneer into the world of
advanced education, breaking the color barrier. I planned to at least fill
one of Lance's big shoes. Mama sure made her boys big, so the neighbors
said. It made me feel proud watchin' Lance. It made me feel even better
when I saw Mama. She was crying and Mama never cried. I planned on
making Mama proud too, someday in the future."

"I felt grown wearing that watch and marching to the corner store.
The watch represented hundreds of hours Lance and Coach Wilson invested in hard won scholarship success. It glittered in the sunlight and under
the shiny hands it said Timex. I planned on only being gone a second and
no one would ever miss Lance's watch."

"Eddie's Market was a simple convenience store lined with everyday
things people in the hood used daily. Eddie doubled his prices from the
stores in the shopping areas. Mama said it was due to all the five-finger
discounts when folks didn't have enough. Everyone pays when one steals,
Mama would say and shake her head."

"Inside the store it felt safe with yumlicious penny candy. Eddie
always let me sample when he was at the checkout. Eddie was big and
tough. He'd been a professional boxer before he injured his head. No one
messed with him including the strapping young men hugging his lightpole.
Everyone showed respect to Eddie in a big way. I wasn't afraid of the store

or Eddie. I didn't have reason to be. He liked me and up until that day I was Mama's boy, a good boy. But," Reggae pointed to LaMar, "I was afraid of Eddie's corner and there was no place else to walk to get Mama her eggs." Reggae watched LaMar who was listening intently. "Things didn't work out like I planned. I got the eggs like Mama said and Eddie gave me some pocket change. Mama told me I could use what was left to buy some candy for my birthday. Nineteen cents left would buy me a heap of candy. I lazily picked out Laffy Taffy and Bazooka, checking the window to see if the boys left. They hadn't. I picked out a couple Tootsie Rolls and a jaw-breaker. They was still there. Then another jawbreaker. They weren't leav-ing so I picked out another one. I got the very best colors — blues and two hues of green. Eddie took the rest of my money and I filled my pockets with my treasured stash. I put my hand in my pocket fisting my goodies tightly."

"Happy Birthday Reggae," Eddie smiled and added another jawbreak-er, "Say hi to yo' mama."

I hurried out the door. "Dark shadows hugged the light pole. The biggest shouted, 'Hey, church boy! Watch'a, wat' cha doin? Why yo get-ting' eggs for yo mama?' His words made my ears feel fuzzy as I walked faster. I saw the flicker of light on a long silver screwdriver and I walked faster. A sharp pain pierced my right side, a loud thruck sounded in my head. Lance's watch, Lance's beautiful and precious watch was being ripped from my wrist. 'Keep yo mouth shut boy. Yo' ain't hurt. Yer' lucky we got no knife. Run home to mama. Run home to yo mama. Run. Run. Church Boy!'"

"Fear empowered me as I raised myself off the sidewalk to run. I moved as fast as my feet could carry me as the world became slower and slower. I felt as though my feet were running on warm Laffy Taffy. Everything became slow motion, like when you flick those animation book pages, to make the cartoon character run at different speeds. The gate was just . . . just . . . and then I collapsed on the shattered egg carton. I pulled my hand from my pocket to try and catch myself falling and I saw yellow yokes, mixed with my blood trickle down into the dirty sidewalk cracks. My bright blue and green jawbreakers rolled into the gutter too far away for me to reach."

"Mama saw me fall, and I heard her scream . . . someone shouted 'police' . . . and then there were police cars and flashing lights . . . the ambulance and flashing lights and nurses and doctors and brightness and darkness and shouting and nothing for what seemed like a very long time. I could hear Mama crying and praying with aunties at the edge of my hospital bed. I couldn't wake up, no matter how hard I tried. Finally, when I awoke Mama's crying turned to wailing with singing praise to Jesus, and Hallelujahs to the Lamb of God, the Lord on High. And I went home."

"But life was never the same. Darkness froze my boyhood joy and I felt dirty. Lance disappeared and I never saw him again. I heard on the streets that the boyz who attacked me came to shoot hoops by our flat. Lance shot twice. He never missed. Vengeance was bittersweet. The police had no evidence. The gun was never found. People scattered. The rule of the hood 'an eye for an eye' was completed. Another card was laid down. You could feel it. You could cut the silent tension with a knife. The best chance Lance had to live was to lay low. The attack on me put the freight train in motion. A freight train, which, at that moment, I didn't even know I had jumped on. Justice was served, and a hero fell. Once more a black-against-black crime, brotha' against brotha' - senseless."

Reggae shuddered, "Always senseless."

"At first, I didn't realize that the 'accident' as Mama called it, initiated me into the very gang that attacked me. Somehow my survival and Lance's disappearance proved me worthy. The times were a mix of the good and bad, every season of change is like that. I am proud to be part of some of it. Then again, I also did things I that could have landed me in jail. It was the pack law, all for one and one for all. We had a sense of community — national community. We set out to break structural oppression and we did it, at least on the surface. The public rally cry was civil rights, power to the people, and I jumped on the bandwagon alongside my homeboys. Mama never jumped on the Black Power movement; she was hardly participating in life except for praying for my soul. The movement was where I met Tina."

"Luckily I never got messed up with the police and when the Vietnam War needed more soldiers I signed up, following in the footsteps of my great granddaddy and father. There was nothing left for me in the hood. Mama died of a broken heart — the death certificate said heart attack. But I knew the truth. I'd killed her by taking the stupid watch. I saw the light go out of Mama's eyes after the accident. She'd come home from cleaning and caring for that rich white family and stare out the window as if her staring would bring Lance back, put him back in college, and keep me from running with the gang. She never saw Lance again; he never knew she died. Someone said he ran a tire shop in Detroit." Reggae's words softened as if their very speaking floated upon clouds. "I wonder about him and tried to find him. I think he's under an assumed name."

Reggae changed the subject. "Tina came from a suburban family where they sat down to soul food Sunday dinners and talked about politics, civil rights and the Vietnam War after church before we listened to the baseball game on the radio with her Granddaddy. Both her Daddy and Granddaddy encouraged her to be independent and rise up for what she believed in regardless if she was a girl. She was an American citizen and as far as they were concerned it was time for the people, of the people and by the people to represent 'all' the people. So blessed and prayed for Tina made and carried banners in Black Power marches and joined park sit-ins.

I caught a glimpse of her at a rally. She was a looker filled with an aire of determination to peacefully change the world – the black world. Youthful and loud speaking she edified a multitude on warm green grass. I had the urge to merge with that woman, but there no girling Tina. She had firm no trespassing zones. My gentleman's wily ways of courting didn't fool her and neither did white people. Her DNA carried a legacy of underground railroad workers, Union soldiers and financial investors in the abolishment of slavery. Tina walked alongside white folk without trying to be like white folk. Her charisma, personality, and smile crossed more racial barriers than I can count. She's herself and I admire that.

I offered to join her at church and help with her studies. She never settled for poverty and neither did her family. They knew I was from the other side of the tracks and I was the kind of people they helped in their church offering plate. Tina's male folk piqued my interest, especially since I'd never known my daddy. Eddie didn't count and Lance was long gone. I listened and I grew. I worked hard to make a good impression on her Daddy. Tina was his baby girl and I wanted him to look at me like he looked at her, with the fire of respect in his eyes. As northern blacks they had a sense of freedom for education, employment, and business ownership new to me. I wanted the integrity they held in their manhood, I lost interest in being sneaky and jonesing their lives, instead I stole pieces of their character to become my own. They lit my roaring fire for independence, freedom, and entrepreneurship. I spent time with the men folk so I could spend time with Tina. Luckily they liked me and thought I had a head on my shoulders. I told them I was planning on being someone that made a difference. And pretty soon I became the man they saw in their own mirrors. There was always plenty of uncles and granddaddies hanging out."

"Eventually we became secret lovers. We were lucky that each month passed without pregnancy, but I wanted to be Tina's baby's Daddy. I was jealous of the boys who already had babies and sported trophy children on their shoulders. For my gang friends a baby proved manhood, a ticket to leave the gang life if you chose to and become an ol' G. It was the one card a gang member could flash to leave honorably without an exit jump. A baby was a treasured prize of womanhood. The baby proved that there was a future and that dreams could come true."

"When all you have to look forward to is a career no one else wanted, working for some white family or being a janitor, trapped in an endless cycle of low-paying jobs, the opportunity to be creative was overwhelming. The chasm between the haves and have-nots was deep. While Tina's girlfriends talked of scholarships and colleges, my friends' girls sported rotund bellies like a fashion statement before they worked themselves to death to remain in poverty. A baby allowed you to focus on something pure and innocent."

"For us, pregnancy never happened. She graduated high school and demanded a racially mixed college. She came to Minnesota on a scholarship and her Grand Pop and Daddy's savings. I was so poor, I'd never even heard of savings accounts. I joined the Army for expense paid tours of Vietnam."

Sleeping Johnny's breath made a wet circle on LaMar's Chicago Bears jersey. His baby snores reassured the men that life continued. His father had never shared his past. LaMar felt the heat of the glowing embers sear cracks into truth. He was glad he had a Daddy.

LaMar admired this mighty man of strength, gray hair deftly braided, brown eyes reflecting the fire's flame. He was a man of passion. The music he performed bellowed it and the lyrics he wrote struck the secret places of all people. His inner furnace roared equality. He could imagine long ago a well traveled elder sitting outdoors in Africa, a man of honor and power, soul and spirit. Reggae was a man's man, and LaMar was honored to call him Pops. His decorated fishing cap lay upon the earth as a tribute to the his life. The firelight transformed his pins into surreal fireworks, the gold and blue III Corps pin lit up like a sparkler.

"After three tours in 'Nam I came home, married Tina, and moved to the Twin Cities for a fresh start. My little ol' six block hood stifled me and while my friends settled for poverty I couldn't. The only thing we had in common was childhood. For them, there was safety in 'same-o same-o'. Tina and I needed to be Civil Rights. We were the front lines of the new Black, just as equal as whites. We didn't try to be white. We didn't need to. Tina and I feel good in our skins. We wanted careers not jobs; investment abilities not bill paying. We wanted to grow and advance and be successful because of our merit. We weren't the kind of folk to be window dressing. We were proud of our skills. We proved we were not tokens. We were worth every penny you paid us and we came through on our promises though we never gave up our 'soul' for profit."

"We succeeded because we believed in the impossible. And it became reality. I've been called a Buppie by more than just Shayna and Johnny and it's been said with disdain. I've been called a 'house nigger' because of my success," Reggae laughed, "Those of our race light-enough to pass for white, scored points and became the house servants of the white massa', fact is Tina might have made the first cut. LaMar my skin is so dark they wouldn't have let me near the house." Reggae switched to early rhythmic slave vernacular smiling. "M' kin . . . deys wuz in dem fields . . . in dem fields, doz darkies, like me . . . .were sorted out young and put outside to be darkened up more. It wuz in dem fields da seeds wuz planted dat birthed m' soul."

His voice trailed only to return with steam power, Reggae created his story with vocal melody, creating ambiance so real you touched his words. He continued proudly, "It was in them fields my oppressed forefathers used their imaginations to maintain their intelligence and humanity through rhythm, and music, and story song. It was the fields that birthed the passion in my bones. It was them fields that put music in my heart and raised up my spirit. My soul. Those cotton pickin' fields created the rhythm that flows through my blood as unstoppable energy. It was them fields, and then the underground railroad, and then the other side of the tracks in Chicago that created the generational legacy of freedom I stand for today. It was losing my daddy, my brother, and Mama . . . so many losses . . . since the beginning."

He paused, "Being born and raised in the 50's, and an adolescent in the early 60's I held tight fisted to Black Equality and wasn't about to be anyone's servant. I started my own business with Tina. We weren't rich. We weren't status quo. We scraped and saved enough for a home and took ownership in a white neighborhood. We built community. We believed our life and our music could make a statement. It has. It did. We didn't try to be someone we weren't and it felt good. "

"I refused to enter business debt. Tina didn't want fancy clothes and I didn't need car payments. Glamour and glitz strip away success and money was too hard to come by. It made no sense to let something that hard to get flow through bedecked fingers. We invested every dime to make more money. I didn't want to be an indentured servant to man or bank. Growing up, I'd witnessed first hand what happens when one can't repay. I was not about to be wakened in the middle of the night with a masked man and a crow bar. Hard times were easy to come by."

Reggae smiled youthfully, "We dreamed of owning a recording studio where people of all races could share their talents on our label. We weren't afraid to work hard and we survived on little. Our meager savings purchased used soundboards and put a down payment on a condemned building. Everyone laughed at our fleabag structure, but room-by-room, window-by-window, Tina and I remodeled it. It felt like play"

"Sixteen-hour days flew by while we did odd jobs to make ends meet. I was a janitor, a busboy, I even washed puked on hospital dishes. Tina worked second and third jobs in waitressing, retail and cashier work. As time went on she took more college classes in law and became the head legal assistant for the largest law firm in the financial district of Minneapolis. Tina moved up the ladder not because of affirmative action but because she is talented, her knowledge proved beneficial to build In '10' City Records. And that brings me to where I met you."

Reggae turned toward LaMar and spoke deliberately, as if each word was a gourmet treat left on the banquet table of their lives carefully prepared for LaMar to savor, "And I vowed to Jesus, something I had only done on my wedding day to Tina as I stood at the foot of your hospital bed that the scrawny little kid with a bandaged head and two plastered legs held high in the air was my son. Yes, you were my son and I looked at you. Eleven-years-old, at the crossroads between man and boy, success or failure, education or gang, unlimited opportunities or an open door to self-annihilation. I wished for you a boyhood that the streets had taken from me. I vowed that, for you, I'd defrost my frozen truth. I'd stand proud as an honorable man to be a good father. I kept my vow. You are a man that I am proud to call son, LaMar."

Reggae placed his musician hand on LaMar and Johnny. "Son, I've got a new mission. Been thinking about it for a long time. It's time for me to share and ask for your blessing." Reggae appeared to be lining up with something he was trying to sell; LaMar had seen him hunker down for business before. Something was on his father's horizon that was serious.

"The flap of a butterfly wing in South America can cause a hurricane in Florida, I don't know if that's true but I'm gonna flap until the day I die. In the 50's and 60's we pushed to change our roles and status in this country. We rewrote the rulebook on relationships between colored people and uncolored, we called ourselves Black and them in the dominant culture white. From a yoked freedom we struggled to be noticed, and then to be included, and then to be equal. Now we ask to be equal and unnoticed, unyoked unless we self-determine a yoking, selected by our own free will."

"Son, what began as the Civil Rights Movement became the diversity movement. Some believe this is watering down what we started. I don't think so. I think it is making America more American. Our culture needs to stand up with self-respect. People is people and we don't need to blend. We need to mix. Mix into business, mix into the community, mix into traveling to new and different places."

"We have moved away from the 'melting pot' theory, realizing we're more like a big national salad 'each flavor enhancing the whole taste' without sacrificing our unique differences. It is the buffet of differences . . . the mixture of us hot dishes and cold dishes that has made America the great experiment and though everything is not right for everyone, this experiment has slowly made progress. It takes a very few to begin a movement. America's been good to me – and it's been worth fighting for.

"America is conflicts. It happens even in a good marriage of similar cultures. Why would we be so ignorant to believe it would not happen when we mixed ethnicity and color, gender and sexual orientation, religion and socioeconomic class, age and ability, and geography and occupation?" Reggae took a deep breath placing an artistic pause within his passionate rhythm. "Cultural competence means we learn to use our heads and our hearts, so that we can reach toward cooperation, respect and true integration. It's taken me a long time to learn that self-determination and my music is what I want to share with others at the end my life. There are still some deep-seated fears and misunderstandings between cultures and unless we create dialogue and step out of our comfort zones we're not going to address the real issues of difference to move forward."

"Ma and I have been role models for the movement. We've stepped out in front, been tripped up, shot at and arrested for our cause, but neither of us would give one iota of those experiences back." Reggae paused gazing at Johnny, "For him and his seed everything we done did was worth it . . ."

Reggae was momentarily silent peering at LaMar.

"We've been thinking about retiring and we're considering giving back. The continent of Africa needs strong men and women with wisdom to help save it. We may go, son. I got that pioneering spirit in my bones. We're going back on ship from New York to Spain, and then we're finishing our life on a Safari. 'Safari,'" the way Reggae said it sounded almost like song, "is the Swahili word for adventure. We've been planning it for two years now and we'll continue to study, and prepare, and search where we best fit, where God leads us. We are sure our place has already been chosen. We believe we have been prepared for such a time as this."

LaMar was speechless, Reggae didn't notice.

"The Continent of Africa mystifies. South Africa captivates us with stunning nature reserves, seaside playgrounds and verdant wine producing valleys, a native people in poverty, pain, and alcoholism. Kenya and Tanzania feature spectacular game reserves, where stealthy carnivores stalk herds of grazing prey, while observers wish they had brought more film and poachers take the life of more and more of God's special creatures. The ancient history of Egypt and Ethiopia, and the more recent intellectual history of Timbuktu enthrall Ma, she wants to see the magnificent places. She has a heart for the refugee camps where hundreds of thousands of our people are barely living. She sends money each month hoping that education and food is provided to ten children by our efforts. Nigerian gospel strikes my soul."

LaMar knew his black history; he'd heard it all before. He also knew his father well enough to know he would not be reiterating it unless he had a purpose, and so he listened intently for the clues.

"LaMar, we passed by death's door as survivors. The African people

are survivors. The hardiness and strength of those who survived their journey to America amazes me, some were held by chains and shackles in slave
pits for months before being loaded like cattle on ships sailing unwelcome
seas for a duration I cannot imagine," Reggae winked. "We're booking a
transatlantic cruise to sail back in style. Sleep on feather beds with our
head on goosedown pillows. I plan to stand on our balcony and watch the
sunset over my beloved America and sunrise over my homeland."

"Losses upon losses . . . your homeland . . . your tribe, your brotha's
and sista's. I hear the tears of my heritage locked in the stones on the
African soil. Slavery tore our families apart, it made friends into trader
traitors to save their own skins and secure profits. It wasn't a white against
black racial problem, it was a bad business problem. Sailors didn't just get
off ships and collect tribal people and stuff them into shipholds."

"Slave traders picked the best of a continent, the strongest, the
heartiest . . . vying for salability. They carried nearly 12 million people out
of Africa. Without the cooperation of a smooth network of African rulers
and merchants it wouldn't have happened. It took underhanded relationships to shackle brother against brother and throw them into a stench of
vomit and feces for months in dark holds of trading ships. The end prize;
slavery. "

"It was in shipholds where chains of slave trade bound the black race
together. African people began as strangers who spoke different languages,
came from different tribes, and shared different customs. It was an unfath-
omable journey that lasted centuries. And though our African brothers
came from vastly different backgrounds we became a group, more from
our experiences than the colors of our skins. Ask any war veteran, they'll
tell you brotherhood isn't skin color, it's life experience."

"It won't be just us. We're taking a team rich in African DNA mixed
and sifted with European, Native American, Asian and Hispanic descent.
We want to make a difference."

A difference that didn't make LaMar feel better.

"One difference being - we'll have open ended tickets to return
home. I'm going back to build a business in honorable trade to empower
a new African generation," Reggae smiled wryly. "LaMar, I want to walk
into that dark slave holding chamber and through the Door of No Return
and then Ma and me are going to turn around and walk right back into
Africa. We're going to walk back in the footsteps of my forefather's exit.

We're going to return with the knowledge and wisdom we have gained in this Negro journey. We're going to make one last Civil Rights march against enslavement; we're going to walk back home. Our final home will be in Africa. Son, we've been feeling the calling. We know we're needed."

"We will share the legacy handed down from our roots, forced through the fires of slavery and refined in the heat of Civil Rights. I will use what I learned as a teen embattled in the jungles of Chicago and as a young adult sweltered in the heat of Vietnam. My walk has softened, but I am bolder with the wisdom I achieved living life as a successful American, walking out from a past that held me down, standing tall and straight and strong. I made my mark in business and music and Ma made her mark in law and justice to change the lives of African Americans. Africa needs honest, smart and caring business people who will keep their boots on, roll up their sleeves and give back. Son, me and Ma plan on coming full circle in this life, and in Africa we will accomplish just that. We plan to be in Africa to leave our old bones."

Johnny slept soundly and Harry snuggled his warm, wooly brown body against LaMar's legs inches from Chorus who was off duty dreaming. LaMar watched his father continue speaking in the firelight. The old man relished his idea and his son saw only the movement of his lips. Lamar no longer listened because his own thoughts had become too loud. A chill ran through him and he no longer knew what to think. The fire no longer blazed and the embers were dying. It was time to go home. The women had fish to fry. Reggae had purged a part of his past to his son and offered up his secret future. LaMar was grateful for the sharing, but unready to bless the journey.

Reggae stood, folded his hands and stretched, "Well what do you say? When it's time to go home, it's time to go home."

▼

Saturday welcome home smells announced no fish to fry. Somehow between braiding and talking, straightening and curling, the women fixed a fine meal. Tamara's secret ribs were roasting in the oven, while a jar of Reggae's red sauce sat on the counter alongside a plate of colorful appetizers. Two bottles of fine Merlot Tamara had chosen from the small, but elite selection of African American vintners were breathing on the counter.

How they managed all the doos the men never knew, but they did know better than to mess up the women's hospitality. Gnawing on blackened grilled and greasy ribs seemed a fitting way to end a blessed day. LaMar ignited the stainless gas grill, while Reggae iced down the fish. It was time to take notice of the doos on the heads of their ladies and hopefully avoid the one question a woman asks that turns a man's blood ice cold.

With a good offense Reggae and LaMar could run a side pass and a dash around "Do you like my new hair?" A senseless question no man ever answered correctly. Both men knew the drill.

Granddaddy Reggae gave Johnny his first lesson in manhood, "Hey little man, notice the smell of the ribs. Notice the smell of the greens. Notice the smell of the cornbread. And pay no attention to any nasty salon smells," he chucked Johnny under the chin.

"Then before they can say anything, kiss 'em and hug em with an 'ooo eee' and notice their beautification. You tell Shayna how pretty she is Johnny."

"Buuueeeecatun," Johnny tried his new word. "Shayna pretty girl!"

"Yeah, boy, just like that."

Shayna's tightly braided hair, decorated with pink sparkly pony beads, danced as she jumped into her daddy's arms. Mommy's straight hair surprised LaMar who was turned on by her kinks. Tina had an intricate ancient African designed braid that must have taken Tamara most of the day. LaMar no longer wore braids. Being a professional and family man, he'd discover short, waved, and organically oiled was his new style and required only a nightly du-rag. It simplified life unless he forgot to remove it and a fade crossed his mind.

Reggae secretly planned to put in a quiet, sexy request for Tina to braid his hair later in the week. And once the affection and wonder was completed, Reggae offered the fish to LaMar for Sunday's football game with the boys. This Sunday it was LaMar's turn to host his frat brotha's at the Watkin's home and he had just purchased a 60" flat panel plasma HDTV – Vikings vs. the Chicago Bears.

15

DRIVE ON

The yellow light glowed from the kitchen window of the old white farmhouse silhouetting a man and a woman. The red tailed rooster announced the sunrise and the radio predicted a warm, dry autumn weekend. The corn was ready to be brought in and the hired men would arrive shortly. The couple sat at the table. It's construction using hand-cut mortise and pegged tenon joinery had made it a strong and safe place for many Hunter family conversations. The rooster crowed again, followed by the cackling of the hens.

"Going to be a nice day to bring the corn in," Jared lay down his Internet crop report printouts and reached across the table touching his wife's hand. He saw past the added pounds to the woman he wooed, married, and brought back to the family farm twenty-five years earlier.

"Going to be a nice day to put up the tomatoes," Ali replied.

She had given birth to his two beautiful daughters, been active in school activities, shared in the farm work and still maintained a career. As the only social worker in the county she cared deeply for those in the community whose lives tipped out of control. She was the rock of Gibraltar for many, a woman of integrity.

"We'll be working well after sunset," Jared sipped his dark roasted coffee. He was glad he had chosen her as his life partner. He watched her turn the pages of the weathered recipe book written in Russian, German, and English, the first page dated 1864. Jared liked watching her plan their life and he wondered what family gem she uncovered – births and deaths, calamities and celebrations. Recipes mixed with concoctions of day-today, transcribing farm life of Hunter women – from clearing land and hand held horse ploughs to crop planting with computers and GPS.

"Think I'll use the tomato recipe from 1946, it's in German," Ali smiled turning a treasured page, "but MaLu translated it on this old card."

"I like that one, it was her grandmother's. Why don't you ask Ma to join you today, she won't work, but I bet she'd like to fellowship," Jared kissed her neck.

"And when is it you will decide not to work through observances?"

"Or you?" Jared laughed, "Have a good day, honey."

Ali cherished their empty nest morning moments.

▼

The sun had skimmed the treeline when Ali arrived to pick up Margie, Tasha, and Q for a day of canning. Q wasn't exactly sure what canning was, and he wasn't interested in getting up at dark on a perfectly good Saturday morning, but Mama had gotten the day off at Dee's Café and she was determined to keep him close with all the ruckus he'd caused.

He'd argued and even offered to pick apples for Mama's boss, but Mama wasn't having none of that. Except for making money to pick apples Q avoided Dee's Café filled with old white people who always turned their heads and gave him the once over. Mama told him it was down home hospitality that went along with the homecooked food that Dee and Mama made each day – homemade bread, homemade soups, and homemade apple pie. He had thought the apple picking idea might work. It didn't.

Q grumbled as he climbed into Ali's mini-van and feigned sleep. There was nothing in this agenda that qualified as fun. The Hunter's weren't kin and they weren't friends to hang out with. Being it was a day of all women, he was sure there would be no informal play.

He opened one eye passing by a gray mailbox covered with vines bearing small green pinecones. Ali turned into a long straight dirt drive, an old fashioned bright green ancient tractor was parked alongside. Q had never seen something 'that old' looking 'that new' except in a museum.

"I'll just park here at the turn-around," Ali said to no one in particular, she smiled and waved at a very old bent man sitting quietly on a park bench next to a tall pole with a triangular box.

Q was curious but apprehensive about men, especially old men, and more especially about old white men. He looked a century old. Why on earth would he be up so early, it was too early to be awake. Maybe he had fallen back to sleep. Maybe he was already dead.

"Here ya go, Q," Ali handed him a box of jars and he followed her into an old farmhouse kitchen. The entry smelled of hay, earth, and animal dung. Blue coveralls hung on hooks, leather and tall brown rubber work boots were lined up underneath, a basket of work gloves was set next to an old wooden bench. He placed the box on the table. "Fetch me up the rest of the boxes Q," she ordered.

Outside a younger man with gray hair joined the white haired man and together they quickly hoisted a worn flag up the flagpole. The old man put his arm around the middle-aged man. They seemed to like each other. Then the old man threw his head back and laughed as he walked with his little box down a stone path, to a small house, set away from the two-story white farmhouse. The younger man entered the big red metal shed and Q recognized him as Jared Hunter.

"Ain't no slave boy," Q muttered as he carried another box of empty jars up the sidewalk. "Slave boy to women folk. Think all a boy is made for is fetching, fixing and fronting." He refocused pretending to be a weight lifter.

All the men folk had disappeared and he could hear deep sounding voices with laughter coming from the red metal building. He was curious to join them, but they were all white, and except for teachers, he hadn't spent much time around white men. Actually he hadn't spent much time around men at all. Mama's boyfriends didn't count. He didn't like them. They didn't know jack. The closest he'd come to man-to-man time was with Kevin and the Rangers. He was lucky; Kevin had gotten him 'blessed' in when he was almost twelve. They needed a scout and Q enjoyed being a lookout. He took pride in keeping his Ranger homies safe, but there were no Rangers in Riverdale except for Kevin, and Kevin was in jail.

Eventually Ali's van was empty and Q figured he could turn on the tube and watch cartoons, but no sooner had he dropped off the last box than Ali handed him two empty bushel baskets and sent him out to the garden to pick the remaining peppers and tomatoes. The old man drove off in an old rusty brown pick up with Jared Hunter as little puffs of dust kicked up behind the tires and floated across the drive. Q wished he could join them. He was shocked anyone that old still drove.

"I ain't no slave boy," Q threw the baskets into the garden, "on no white folk plantation." He filled another basket and carried it to the house.

"Good job Q. How much is left out there?" Ali smiled.

"You mean I have to fill more baskets?"

Ali and Mama both gave him the mother look, translated into 'shush and drop off the attitude.'

He lodged the upcoming words in the back of his throat. "Yssm'," he offered in good boy polite and returned to the garden surprised that a basket was partially filled. Someone had secretly offered help.

Q looked around. "Bugs!" he huffed, slapping a mosquito in disgust. "Mama don't put up with dawdling, and until every veggie is picked I ain't gonna be free."

The old truck had returned and the old man walked slowly to the mailbox holding a can of bug spray.

Q wished he'd share. "Take that! You old rotten tomato!" Q threw the fruit hard splattering the white wooden fence post now dripping anger.

"What you think you're doing little man?" the old man scowled.

Q ignored him and hoisted the brimming basket onto his shoulder to deliver to the women. He felt as hot as the boiling jars in one pot, and as steamed as the tomatoes in another. The windows were white with the cool September day. Anxiety jiggles rose in his arms and legs.

"Hey Q, look what I can do," Tasha sat at an old wooden table covered with towels, bottles and two huge stainless steel bowls, one filled with split skin tomatoes and the other filled with peeled tomatoes. "Look, Mama boils 'em and the skin slides off. Bobe Lu told me how."

Q didn't care, he had scouted the property for things to do while he was picking produce and was looking forward after one more basket to checking out the tree house he had spotted a ways down in the woods. He rolled his eyes and bent over to set down the basket. As he bent over, the loudest, gas passing noise he had ever heard erupted somewhere near him.

All four women glared. Mama's brows furrowed, "You get that little black bootie to the bathroom and take care of your business."

The whitest woman he had ever seen laughed at him, summer sky blue eyes glittered under a cloud of white hair. Her skin was so light you could see blue veins rising like mountains on her hands. The room was hot, why did she wear a long sweater?

"Oy Vey, Gunner. You get in here! This is not a day for you to be pushing buttons." Her voice was accented, mixed with sternness and Tasha style flirting.

Why would an old woman flirt with such an old man?

Sheepishly the old man came from behind the door holding a tiny black box with a big red button.

The old woman pointed a gnarled finger at him, "You tell this nice young man what you did Gunner Hunter, and apologize."

The old man crossed his arms smirking.

"What's your name, son?" the old woman asked.

"Quintell Samuel Jones, everyone calls me Q, miss, miss, ah Miss Hunter," Q gave it his best shot.

"Gunner, I haven't been called 'Miss' for sixty years. You show him what you have in your hands. I was Miss Katz ages ago. My name is Lucille Hunter, folks 'round here call me MaLu, my grandkids call me Bobe Lu."

"Thanks, Miss Bobe Lu," Q stammered.

"Gunnert Aaron Hunter, you should be ashamed of yourself," her voice was sharp like Mama's. This little wrinkled lady was going to ride that old man until he fessed up to what he messed up.

"Son, you want to see my remote fart machine? I can set you off fifty feet away," Gunner chuckled like Santa, and held out the remote. "See, you push this little old button here. It works swell and gets 'em every time. My great granddaughter Kissy gave it to me."

Q was beginning to like the old man who seemed to have a sense of humor like his. Q pressed the button, "Bet those are the only farting tomatoes in the county, Mr. Hunter. Hope the women can do something about that." He tried not to smile, but the corners of his lips and eyes moved upward in reflex. Miss Bobe Lu shook her head in disbelief.

"Oh, I think they'll be in hot water any minute. Hey, you ever driven a lawn tractor? I got one last mowing before winter and could use help. You carry my stool and I'll carry the basket. I'll trade ya. I'll help pick the rest of the tomatoes. Then you mow my grass. You ever drive a riding lawn mower?" he repeated.

Margie looked apprehensive.

"Oh, dearie, never mind them. Q is in good hands. I'm sure he and Gunner will have a wonderful day. You just leave them be. You three have a lot of work left to do and I'm getting tired of watching."

Tasha peeled the hot tomatoes and wondered why the old woman didn't help. Ali had told her folks in Riverdale don't take kindly to slacking. It didn't make sense, Ma Lu was a slacker.

▼

Q felt awkward with Gunner.

"Don't trust me, do you?" Gunner offered a warm ripe tomato reading Q's mind.

"Ah, yah, I mean, no."

"Well, I don't trust you either, but I honor your no and I thank you for being truthful. Truth is truth, you can't fight it," Gunner held out a tomato and looked stern. "Best part of summer is a vine ripened tomato, nothing beats' em right off the vine. Good fruit is good fruit." He pulled out a tiny saltshaker, sprinkled his tomato and stared at the brilliant gloosh radiating against pristine white. "Values is values and principles is principles. Here, you want some salt?" Gunner nursed the tomato savoring each tiny piece, staring at the fence. "And I'm not trusting you until you clean off my post. There's a rag inside my stool."

Q had wondered why Gunner's stool was so heavy. It was no wonder when he opened the lid to find a blue extension cord, hammer, screwdriver, bottle of aspirin, extra batteries, bandaids, grey duct tape, bailing twine, WD40, pliers, tweezers, can of green spray paint . . ."

"What cha' thinkin' boy! Quit rummaging through my stuff. Get me the rag," Gunner's voice boomed and startled Q, he wasn't expecting such a full sound from a frail old man.

"Ah, my bad, Mr. Hunter. Here's the rag."

"No son, you're not bad, you are sorry. Here's your rag and take these. It's your tomato. Go!" A twisted finger pointed to the speckled red and white fence post. "Water's in the pig pen. You'll need it."

Gunner sat down on his tool stool and began silently picking tomatoes. Q knew from being raised by Mama not to argue; off to the pigpen he went.

The water spigot lay on the other side of the mud filled pigpen containing a giant pig, and a litter of frolicking piglets. Q looked down at his new white Nike's and then back towards the withered man picking tomatoes. Perhaps he could tip toe.

"Schnarck" the gigantic pig gained tonage.

Gunner glared.

The red straps called 'these' became a solution to his pants problem. Earlier he had poked fun, 'never be caught dead in pants so high you might choke.' He looked back.

Gunner smiled.

Q connected the red ugly suspenders transforming as a perfect tool to save his favorite jeans. He hiked his pants up past his ankles. Surprisingly, the huge pig didn't pay him no mind and the little pigs scampered grabbing the rag. Q turned on the spigot and little pig snouts clamored into the water. He filled a bucket with water and added it to the nearby pig trough to shoo away the pigs. The giant mother followed to get a drink while he climbed the fence.

Gunner smiled and waved him on. "Hey, Q, you're a smart young man. I saw how you deterred the pigs to accomplish that job. Bet you're pretty good in school." Q went to work removing his tomato splat from the post, forgetting his mistrust of the old white man and his red suspenders.

"I do okay,"

"You know, I'm too old to help in the fields. Jared's relegated me to mow the yard. He's afraid I'll do something stupid without thinking. You ever have that problem?" Gunner spoke deliberately.

Q sat silently near Gunner as they finished picking.

"This farm was my grandfather's, then my father's, then mine, and now it is Jared and Ali's. Lu and me live in the cozy cottage down the hill. You play pranks son?"

Q picked.

"Bet you figured I like pranks. I got a bunch of swell ones, you better watch out." Gunner's blue eye set deep in a withered face winked at him; his old yellowed teeth broke into an open laugh smile. Q had never worked alongside another man before. He could smell the oldness and wondered if all old white men smelled the same.

"They retired me from the fields. Fired I call it, say I'm 'too old'. They'd tell you, you're 'too young'. Don't know everything, do they?" Gunner looked down at Q, but didn't wait for an answer. "They let me drive my riding lawn tractor around the yard to appease me and my old truck into the fields on sandwich and coffee hauls. Made me promise to stay off county roads." Sadly he stared past the old wooden barn, his eyes focused on two small green tractors moving slowly at the top of the distant hill, "I've been driving longer than they are old!" he shouted. Then he was silent.

Q kept picking, he didn't know what to say.

"Q!" Gunner roared, "Haul the basket up to the kitchen and I'll start the mower. You game to drive it?"

Q had only ridden a bike. He never had a chance to sit on his daddy's lap and pretend, his daddy never owned a car. Was he game? Of course he was. "That would be nice, Mr. Hunter. I think I can."

"Call me Gunner and I know you can."

▼

Q left the tomatoes in the kitchen and returned the stool to the shed as the old man made lawn mower circles around the flagpole.

"You getting dizzy yet?" Q shouted.

"Jump on boy!" Gunner hollered back.

Q stepped back, not wanting to put himself out to the world wearing snugged jeans with red suspenders on the back of a riding law mower.

"What you afraid of? Gee willakers, you got the heebie geebies? Think I'll bite? I said, step on the hitch!"

Q stepped onto the 2" ball trying to balance just as Gunner shifted into high gear to cut a long strip up the drive. The jerk of the engine catapulted him onto the old man's shoulders and he clung tightly as Gunner mumbled driving instructions that were more than get on and drive. It seemed like the old man kept his voice barely audible so he was forced to hunker down. There was a lot more to grass mowing than Q had figured.

"This here is the brake," the old man shouted and suddenly stopped.

The red suspendered boy flew.

"Looks like it still works good," the old man laughed.

Q looked up. From grassview Gunner appeared huge.

"Paying attention means paying attention. Get up and get on. It's my turn to ride back," Gunner stood on the hitch barking orders like a drill sergeant. Q tried hard not to do something wrong. He liked tractor driving and didn't want to hurt the old man by making him fall off.

"Pull over and shut it down!" Gunner yelled.

Q did as he was told wondering what he had done wrong now.

"Boy, I got work to do and you're ready to handle this Deere alone," Gunner stepped cautiously down and headed to the shed, "finish it up, Q."

It was a responsibility driving alone, but Q soon felt secure. He carefully finished the acre of grass, drove up to the shed and shut down the mower with a smile that collided with Gunner's. Their eyes met in approval. Gunner's summer-tanned face no longer looked withered.

The old man turned silently away and entered the shed and Q followed into a magical smelling place of wood, metal, and oil. Strange and curious equipment filled the room. Tools hung from the rafters, jars filled with metal pieces sparkled on the shelves and an orange tabby cat named Katz slept on a pile of sawdust in a ray of sun slightly shadowed by a spider webbed window. An an old border collie named Klutz lifted one eyelid as Q approached and then went back to sleep at Gunner's feet.

"Hi Q. You done already? Guess I better go inspect what I expect." Gunner turned off a whirring machine, opened his stool and grabbed the can of green paint Q had mistaken for bug spray. "Come on, Klutz, old boy, we got work to do," and he proceeded to spot and spray every missed grassblade. Klutz lifted his leg to mark the ones Gunner didn't. "Run back and finish your job, son, while I fetch the mail."

The old man turned his back, "Klutz, old boy, you been running herds for thirteen years and you're getting a bit crotchety like your old man. You was bred from good German mountain herding stock, actually same initial blood line as Sam's German Shepherd . . ."

Q left Gunner and Klutz speaking dog talk. He wasted no time cutting missed areas and drove up to Gunner squatting by the old tractor with the can of paint. Klutz slept in the shade of the big tire.

"What's the green paint for Gunner?"

"That's not just green paint son, that's agricultural green paint. Be specific. Pay attention to the details. Old Betsy has a rust spot I missed this morning, got to keep her shiny and new," Gunner set his paint can on top of the small pile of mail and waved his arm pointing at parts of the yard Q still missed before his finger landed. "See that boy, that's a serial plate, 1935, they call 'em Brass Tag, I call her Betsy. I was eleven-years-old when Daddy bought her. She was as exciting an addition to Riverdale as Ma O'Riley's flush toilet in 1910. You bet cha, nothing beat either of 'em when you needed to get a job done right." Gunner winked at Q and gave him thumbs up. "I wasn't alive yet for the toilet, but Daddy was. We plowed hundreds of miles of earth with Old Betsy, first only Daddy plowed, but then about your age I got to drive the tractor myself." Gunner smiled down at Q.

For the first time in his life, Q felt like another man accepted and respected him. He had a Grand Daddy.

"I like those big open fields and the smell of fresh turned earth. Old

Betsy and I have fond memories together. I did hours of thinking sitting right here." Gunner patted the old metal seat.

"Can I sit on her?" Why would anyone take care of something for as long as Gunner cared for Old Betsy. Until Riverdale, Q had never even kept a bike for more than a few months because someone always stole it or they had moved.

"Sure, that's why we keep her here at the end of the drive and take care of her. She is a farm icon," crow's feet appeared with his smile. "I take her inside for the winter, don't want the old girl to get cold. After she retired from real work, we let the kids climb on her. I drive her twice a year, once in the Riverdale Parade and once to the tractor pull. She don't pull nothing, but she gets smiles and attention from all the farm boys."

"The more you have to work with something Q, the more attached you get to it. Old Betsy and I became 'one unit working as a team' to get those fields turned. Make some new fangled thing that's automatic to replace something tried and true; don't mean I'm going to like it. I like what I know. Machines you have to work with are machines you love . . . bolt action rifles, stick and rudder airplanes, trucks with clutches and gears, and women with spit 'n vinegar like Ma Lu," Gunner winked at him.

Q wondered about Gunner's intimate relationship with Old Betsy. Someday perhaps he would care enough about something or someone. "Do you love Miss Lucy, more than Old Betsy?" Q asked.

"Ma Lu and I go back to war time. Loved her the first time I saw her. She was hauntingly beautiful, survived the unspeakable, she did. My heart said, that is my bride," Gunner's memories of love for Miss Lucy erased his age. "I had to finish my duty in the European Theater. Then I sent for her with every penny I had. We've been married fifty-six years this spring. Never looked at another woman, only needed one. Didn't even really touch her until Josef was born, the boy became my son. One woman's enough for any man, providing you're willing to be a man. Tough thing to do Q, but I expect you're man enough to tackle it. Man's got two heads Q – a big head and a little head. It's your big head's job to keep your little head out of trouble."

Q tried not to laugh. He'd never thought about having only one woman. The boys in the Rangers traded girls like baseball cards. If he had stayed in the city he would have lost his virginity by now. It was an expected rite of passage. Mama had many men in her life; Q's Daddy was gone and Tasha didn't remember hers. They were different men.

"You only had sex with Miss Lucy?" Q queried.

"Yep, never needed to lessen my manhood. Made a commitment and I kept it. I don't go back on my word. Your life philosophy will determine your destiny more than your circumstances," Gunner began walking to the house whistling, stopped then turned, "Think about it Q. What is harder - working an honest job or taking what you need when you need it; going with the flock or being courageous enough to stand-alone; having sex because it's available or restraining to wait to make love to that one very special woman? In life you'll find the harder the path, the stronger you become. The more self-discipline you gain, the more you increase your manhood. Chivalry only dies if you kill it. Are you gallant enough to remain a gentleman?" Gunner turned his back to Q, "Come on, Klutz."

It was the end of the discussion, Q started the lawnmower.

"Hey, Gunner, you want a ride, hop on."

"Don't mind if I do, thank you. Like how you pay attention to others, I hear ya listening to my riddles, some are very subtle."

Q carefully stopped in the turn around by the red shed.

▼

Ali had readied two picnic baskets filled with food, two large thermoses of coffee, and a heavy cooler filled with cold drinks and fruit. Ma Lu told her what to pack and Q didn't think much of bossy Miss Bobe Lu. She seemed to be full of words but didn't lift a finger to help. On the other hand, the old man was knitting into his heart. Gunner's eyes told Q to pick up the cooler and head to the truck; it was a silent offer between two men to ride along to the field to feed the crew. Q was comfortable with Gunner, and while he wasn't a homie, he was possibly better.

Gunner drove the back way to the field to avoid the county road; along the ravine and treehouse.

"Nice treehouse," Q whistled.

"Deerstand," Gunner mumbled and continued driving past a twisted apple grove, and up a rutted path. Q laughed hitting his head on the truck cab ceiling when Gunner floored the gas to run over a fallen log, climb a ledge and pop out of the Halloween woods in front of two huge tractors that had looked toysize.

Gunner shut down the truck, "Over ten tons each, 660 horsepower and six cylinders; they're a lot different from Old Betsy, but she still swoons me." Then he jumped out of the truck like a youngster as he grabbed the thermos. Q piled both picnic baskets on top the cooler, while the men dropped the tailgate for lunch.

"Guys, meet Q. He finished mowing the whole acre at the house. Think you're looking at a promising farm hand. Should have seen him handle the pigs, jumped in the pen to fetch me some water and diverted them by taking care of their needs first. Might want to consider hiring this one on, seems to be able to think and pay attention."

Q felt empowered. Respect was new. He had always felt less than and never able to measure up. Jared Hunter and the three migrant workers smiled approvingly. For once in his life he was welcomed with warmth for his integrity and not his badness. The group of men wrapped him into their fold. "You know Pa; I do need more help. Q, you interested in coming out and spending next weekend here with me and Ali?"

Q was speechless, he nodded and listened. He longed to know what they knew. What did it mean to be a man? Jared handed his father a small metal piece from the wagon and asked him to fix it for the morning. Q jumped in the passenger side of the truck, "Get behind the wheel, I'm going to let you drive home, Q."

"Do we have to go back the way we came?" Q didn't want to let on he was a wee bit scared.

"Naw, we're going straight across the fresh-cut field; we've got a clutch," Gunner smiled. The men laughed remembering their first driving experiences. They continued laughing as the old brown rusty truck lurched like a wild bronco toward home.

Humbled, Q pulled into the turn-around, narrowly missing the lawn tractor and handed the keys to Gunner.

"Great job, young'un, never had a ride quite like that. Reminded me of the roller coaster at the Minnesota State Fair. Need to let you know though, only person I let hit Deere is Ma Lu, that woman could back into a Deere and nail it, left green paint all over my trucks. You interested in deer? I recommend you learn to shoot my Ruger 44, good woods gun. But there will be no Deere hitting with my truck you hear me?" Gunner patted him soundly on the back of the shoulders. "Come out to the shed, I got a project for you, while I ready my rifle."

In the shed, Gunner handed Q a piece of twisted firewood, "Know what kind of wood that is, son?"

"No."

"It's gnarled and twisted with life experience, a real beauty of a piece of apple," Gunner pulled out a pen from his shirt pocket, "You want to make one for yourself?" Gunner's hand knotted from years of farming, gently passed the pen and pencil to Q.

Q stared at the old man's hand.

"My hands are a treasure," Gunner's eyes drove into Q's soul. "They have safely held newborn babies just as this branch has and weathered storms you have yet to see. We've been bent and twisted and shaped by life. This old piece of firewood you see as worthless is priceless. You will see it become your pen."

"No way, I couldn't do that, not with this."

"Couldn't has no place in your vocabulary. By the time dinner comes, you will have a pen. If you believe, you will find a way to succeed. So, do you want to take this old hunk of firewood and turn it into this?"

Gunner transformed from infirmed to informative as he taught Q to use equipment that whirred and spun. Together they cut the firewood into a small three quarter inch square by six inches long block. Then Q cut the little piece of wood in half on the band saw. Gunner helped him bore the center with the drill press and glue the brass tubes inside. Then Gunner set up the lathe and gently held Q's hands as he began turning the pen. Like he had done with the lawn mower and then the truck, he let go and Q proved to himself he was capable while Gunner took a rifle from the back room and began cleaning it.

"Wow, Gunner, you sure have a lot of guns. What for?"

"Every gun I own is a tool, serving a different purpose. You can't use that lathe you're working on to cut a log."

Q was puzzled. It never occurred to him that guns were tools.

"Take this Model 1903 Springfield rifle, it was built by the Smith Corona Typewriter Company during World War II. I carried one just like it in Germany, now I use it for Military Honors. Hans and I drive to the cities and spend the day shooting, then we check out the city hardware and sporting goods stores. Hans looks at the displays and I scout out the clearance bins." Gunner winked, "Not a day better on earth, than to do that with your best friend." Gunner ran his hand down the wood stock, polishing it to a shine.

"Why do you like guns, Gunner?" Q wasn't sure what kind of shooting old men did in the cities.

"Like protection? Like responsibility? Like self-control?" Gunner rid-
dled, "You answer me."

"I dunno."

"That's ignorance and you're not ignorant. If you don't know something ask someone. Most people will help you learn if you're interested."

"What if I don't care."

"Well, that's apathetic and that's a sorry state. Everything you will be
required to do as a man matters," Gunner smiled at Q. "With a gun you
have the power over life and death. You can cripple or maim, you can
injure or kill," Gunner x-rayed Q. "When I hold a gun I am not helpless
in front of an aggressor, the playing field changes control. Do you think
that's power?"

"Sure," Q answered knowing he was right.

"Wrong!" Gunner sounded ballistic, "The power comes in the act of
shooting. If I pull the trigger, I am responsible for where the bullet goes.
This gun is far more accurate than I am. If the bullet doesn't go where I
want it to, it's my fault. A gun is the ultimate in self-control; it is constant
practice towards perfection. Every time I shoot I have to practice self-control. I have to sync my mind with my body – my ears, my eyes, every
breath, and muscle – right down to pulling that trigger. It's all self-control. It is mastery in the face of nervousness and the ability to adjust the
smallest variable to remain in control. It is the awareness of every detail of
what you are doing and what happens. A lot of people think that its just
pointing the thing and pulling the trigger. The skill of shooting transcends
into many other parts of my life Q. I don't take it lightly. I choose to pull
that trigger."

"I've shot for over seventy years and there aren't many days I reach
perfection. It is a challenge to my mind, to my body and to my emotions.
Q, you will be given a lifetime of opportunities for power – fast cars, fast
women, hot guns – only you can decide how much self-control you will
use. You choose each and every time. No one chooses your behavior except
you." Gunner held up his trigger finger, practicing pushups.

Q stopped the lathe and watched Gunner work on the rifle. He
caressed the wood stock, like Q had dreamed of touching a girl, massag-
ing in scented oil with strength and gentleness. Readying seemed a labor
of love.

"A man's going to be a man Q, it's built into us whether we like it or not. And even though this sissy modern culture tells us it's not so, the founders of our country knew better. When push comes to shove, a man will defend himself," Gunner checked Q's reaction. Q was busy reminiscing last night's fight at the football game and rubbed his shoulder where the other boy had connected hard with a fist. "The most basic male instinct after sex is defending one's family. I don't know one man in Harris County who wouldn't put his life on the line to defend his children and the Second Amendment makes this our civic duty. A well-regulated militia, being necessary for the security of a free state, the right of the people to keep and bear arms, shall not be infringed," Gunner recited the line from memory. "Been that way since the beginning of this country. If we accept that right, then we accept the responsibility to go along with it – to protect family and country. Each man over seventeen-years-old is a part of our Militia. Go to school and read the code yourself, Title 10, Chapter 13, Section 311 written in 1956. It includes each of us – you and me. So when you reach seventeen and until you're forty-five you're in, unless you're like Hans and me, we committed our lives."

"Your generation must decide. Will you be trustworthy and productive citizens and accept this responsibility or will you be a part of an unruly crowd who needs to be ruled over? This is a country of the people, by the people and for the people. Your generation will have to decide what kind of people you want to be. Believe it son; this rifle is a symbol of Democracy. When I was discharged from the Military, I didn't lay down my defense position for this country, I can't fight air combat anymore, but any man on the ground is in trouble thinking they can invade my land. Some traditions have deep meanings." Gunner patted the gun as an old friend, slipped it into a buckskin colored gun case and mumbled, "Seven men shooting three volleys, the sum of the numbers of the year 1776." Another riddle?

"Did you ever shoot anyone?"

"Yesterday I'd say that's none of your business, but when you went into that pigpen I took a likin' to you. I promised myself I'd stand by you with the truth. Yes, I have shot men, and you know what? I ain't proud of it. It was war and the question was them or me. I answered first. I did what I had to do. I only shoot when I have to, and I only kill an animal I'm going to eat."

"Life is a gift you can't give back if you take it. Pieces of that person stay in your heart. Lu lost everyone before she was even seventeen. When you're my age, you know more people dead than alive. Life is hard Q."

Gunner drifted into the past while Q finished the pen trying to listen. The Rangers bragged about shooting in the hood. They even tattooed tears on their skin. Gunner shot an enemy, an enemy ready to shoot him first and he still wasn't bragging. "Yeah son, the military lays a good foundation in life for a man, no matter what the details are."

At sunset Q added the first coat of tung oil to a lighter version of Gunner's pen. He touched it gently. Accomplishment was a new feeling.

Gunner smiled, "Don't worry son, it will darken with age. Being smart is not a sin. Use what you got. Wisdom is wisdom."

Q smiled back. Life was hard, but Gunner was right. Beauty was hard won and he determined in his heart to drive on.

16
OLD GLORY

The shed was crowded but uncluttered. Nooks and crannies were filled with bits and pieces, stacks of rags, tools shining like new and other implements so old they'd grown into Gunner's treasures. A lot of things suddenly looked different. The afternoon had passed swiftly in the aromatic room while Q took his time to oil the pen. His normally snoopy self had abstained from messing. He noticed the sun setting; the golden glow, low in the sky, painted an autumn picture in black trees silhouetted against pastels. It was pretty. How could he be thinking something besides a girl was pretty? What was left of the sun's rays caressed a triangular box, finely oiled. It was the same box Q saw Gunner holding in the morning, but it was empty.

Gunner, bent from working on the rifle, walked slowly towards it. It had been a long day keeping up with a young one. He tenderly picked up the box. "Q, I need your help to take down Old Glory."

"Did you make that box?" Q asked, "It's apple too, isn't it?"

"I noticed you paying attention to detail. You are astute Q. Yes, it is apple from a tree my Grandfather planted. And yes, I made it. It houses one of my life's treasures. Come and meet her, her name is Old Glory. Love always creates treasures," he winked and walked out to the turnaround where the flag waved. He gently placed the box on the bench, his eyes closed.

Q wondered if he was praying. Then Gunner stood straight, his shoulders back, his chest out. He was taller than Q had imagined, and he looked high in the sky and saluted the flag.

Q wasn't sure what to do, so he pulled in his stomach and pushed out his chest and saluted, too. He wasn't sure why.

"Ever taken a flag down son?"

"No, I guess not."

"Well either you have or you haven't. You can't guess. Truth is truth. Did you or didn't you?"

"No, sir."

"The military lowers the flag slowly as the light of the day blends and vanishes into night's darkness. The red and white stripes fold into the blue field of stars to honor American Revolution patriots. They sure were some courageous males and females who initiated and fought for our rights and privileges. They stood on the front line to lay their lives down for Lady Liberty. Thirteen folds represent the original colonies to look like the hat of a patriot and it fits in my father's box."

Enchanted Q watched as Gunner slowly lowered the flag.

"We receive Old Glory into waiting hands. Have you ever done a Flag Folding Ceremony?"

"No, sir."

"Well, now's the time, for the whole megillah." The old cotton flag was at waist height, and Gunner took hold of the outside corners. "Q, unhook the flag. She must never touch the ground. Hold her securely and face me."

Q kept his stomach in and his chest out like a rooster.

"Fold her lengthwise, in half and then half again. The thirteen stripes begin in red and end in red, the bloodshed of our valiant defense of countrymen and women. The equal size red and white stripes represent the thirteen original colonies. The blue field on the outside is important. Got any idea what the colors mean?"

"No, sir."

"Blue field represents vigilance, perseverance, and justice of a people, for a people and by a people in each state. Each star represents a state and man's aspiration to the heavens.

"Do you know what that means?"

"No, sir."

"It means you keep on keepin' on even when you're worn out and don't feel like it. It means you seek the truth in a matter, you tell the truth even when it hurts, and you don't let an innocent fall. If you do we will lose the preciousness of what the white stands for. White stands for liberty that is only kept through purity and innocence. The red stands for the hardiness and valor of bravery. Understand?"

"Yes, sir."

"The flag has gone through twenty-six changes since 1776. I like to think of it as Betsy's design, but there is no proof. Ready?"

"Yes, sir."

"Each triangle fold has a special meaning. Let's see if I can remember them," Gunner closed his eyes for a moment and smiled. "This isn't exactly military. In fact, military probably wouldn't do this, but I like it."

Gunner folded the first triangle. "The 'first fold' of our flag is the symbol of life," Gunner took a deep breath sucking up life prayerfully.

"The 'second fold' is a symbol of our belief in the eternal life." Again Gunner waited, the duration of the silence felt eternal to Q, but he remained paralyzed, as if any wrong move would break the spell.

"The 'third fold' is made in honor and remembrance of the veterans departing our ranks who gave a portion of their lives for the defense of our country to attain peace throughout the world."

Again he paused. Q had no clue why anyone would give up any of his or her life for someone else? Military service made no sense. A tear ran down Gunner's ruddy cheek, but he smiled. Don't cry you old coot.

"The 'fourth fold' represents our weaker nature. As American citizens trusting in God. We turn to Him in times of Peace, as well as wartime. We must ask for His Divine Guidance."

Gunner folded again. "The 'fifth fold' is a tribute to our country. Keep your integrity Q, a group of people can become a mob, a group of peers can make choices a single man would never dare. It is your friends son, who will get you into trouble, not your enemies."

Q thought of the Iraqi prisoners, and the shame he'd felt for his country when the media displayed our mistreatment. Q wondered from how long ago Gunner was remembering all this, or if he were making it up.

"A rotten apple can spoil the whole bunch Q. The actions of a few taint the lives of the whole." Gunner looked straight through Q who suddenly felt naked. How could one old G pierce his heart so deeply?

Then Gunner winked. Was he telepathic or just old.

"The 'sixth fold' is for our heart. We pledge allegiance to the flag of the United States of America, and to the Republic for which it stands, one

Nation, under God, indivisible, with Liberty and Justice for all."

As a young schoolboy Q had pledged allegiance to the flag like all the others in his first grade class; but later on, he decided he wasn't going to pledge to any stupid colored fabric. He'd pledged to the Rangers though and he begin to wonder why.

He watched while Gunner made another fold.

"The 'seventh fold' is a tribute to our Armed Forces. Through the Armed Forces we protect our country against her enemies, whether they be found within or without the boundaries of our republic."

Q didn't know anyone in the armed forces and the day he'd talked to the recruiter his homeboys jabbed him as a war monger. Then when he told Mama, he wanted to grow up and enlist for education money, she told him it was another way they killed black people.

The flag dance continued and Gunner's voice remained secure and smooth. Q stood stoic, sucking it all in.

"The 'eighth fold' is a tribute to the one who entered into the valley of the shadow of death, that we might see the light of day." Dead like Tasha's Daddy lying in a pool of blood in a dark alley, imprisoned like Daddy in the shadow of death of prison.

Gunner was serious, "The 'ninth fold' is a tribute to womanhood through their faith, love, and devotion in molding the character of the men and women who have made this country great."

Q noticed the light go on in the kitchen window and the shadow of Miss Bobe Lu and Mama as Gunner paused. Even in his most difficult times Mama loved him and she would kick his butt to protect him from himself. She would lay her own life down and not count the cost . . . Mama was a ghetto soul jar.

"The 'tenth fold' is a tribute to Fathers who have given their sons and daughters for the defense of our country." Gunner drew a deep breath in a wince of pain. His eyes closed tightly.

Q also closed his eyes while thoughts raced silently and bitterly in argument between the injustice of fathers. His baby daddy was serving time, black time. The police were wrong in arresting Daddy. BadOne needed the incarceration. Gang friends always played the game 'hit it and run' as street corner daddies chilled, kicked back, and hung with homies, exploited the mamas and abandoned their children. His Mama's cheeks were swollen too often, her arms bruised from being controlled and set in her place. Q opened his eyes to Gunner, a kind of man he had never before met. There were tears on his cheeks, but he was strong, and brave, and valiant. Somehow the old man was adding water to a parched youthful soul longing for a fresh, new beginning.

Gunner carefully handled the flag now rich in thickness, "The 'eleventh fold', represents the lower portion of the seal of King David and King Solomon, and glorifies in the Hebrews' eyes, the God of Abraham, Isaac and Jacob." Visions of Sunday school lessons passed before him, fighting stories of Jacob wrestling with the Angel, and David killing Goliath with his slingshot, and the walls of Jericho coming down.

"The 'twelfth fold', represents an emblem of eternity and glorifies," Gunner held the flag securely, "in the Christians' eyes, God the Father, the Son, and the Holy Spirit. When the flag is completely folded, the stars are uppermost reminding us of our nation's motto, 'In God We Trust', the thirteenth fold," Gunner handed Q the flag.

Q felt humbled. It was a different from the fleeting feeling of guilt he felt when he got his behind whooped or his ears boxed. "Can I ask a question, Gunner?" Q cradled Old Glory. She had become real.

"Sure," but without a pause Gunner placed his hand upon Q's resting on Old Glory. "The thirteenth fold represents liberty. Liberty is no joke son; we have to hold onto her with a tight fist. Democracy is a fleeting thing and if we don't pay attention to it we lose her." Eye to eye, soul to soul, Gunner continued. "Once she is lost, she waits until another oppressed people are ready to fight for her glory."

"Can I . . ." Gunner raised his index finger to silence Q.

"Do you know who Alexander Tyler is son?"

"No, sir."

"He was a historian in the late 1700s when our original thirteen states adopted their new constitution confirming for the freedoms of life, liberty, and the pursuit of happiness. Tyler talked about the fall of the Athenian Government. He believed democracy cannot be a permanent form of government because the voting citizens eventually realize they can vote for gifts from the treasury. They vote for political candidates who promise the most benefits until there is no money left. Eventually the government collapses in fiscal ruin and a dictator gains control. A dictator is no joke. Ask Ma Lu and she'll tell you of empires run on violence and hate. Those times may be short-lived, but feel like eternity. Ma Lu'll tell you, that for a democracy to run we have to be able to make our own way. It's the independent self-supporting philosophy that keeps this country strong. I dare you Q." Gunner winked. "Get MaLu going and you'll know more than you want to hear. She's lived on both sides of freedom, economics, religion and politics. You want a history lesson talk to Ma Lu."

"Liberty is a gift we can't let slip through our fingers. If we do, 400 years of sacrifice could be lost to a UN stratocracy."

Q looked puzzled, he made mental note of 'stratocracy.' History never appealed to him. It was filled with dead people, but Gunner enlivened it.

"In democracy, you have to be responsible for yourself. It means you never take what's not yours to take and gifts of support are a temporary privilege, not a right. Each person has to figure out how to make it on their own honestly with whatever means they can and capabilities they have. Privileges are fleeting if you don't honor them; religion, marriage, driver's licenses, firearms, freedom," Gunner paused, looking toward the harvesting. "You decide, are you going to love God and use things or use God and love things?"

Q held Old Glory protectively pulling her next to his chest, not wanting to lose her, "a people escape from bondage through spiritual faith. With great courage they fight and win Liberty. Through Liberty the country becomes abundant, but its through that abundance that it's children become apathetic – that means they don't care or understand the historic cost. They become dependent on her abundance. They never grow up and take ownership of their responsibility to her. It is that dependence that leads them back into bondage. Without honor, Lady Liberty will let you go. Don't let this happen in your lifetime son, our democracy is already on a path of self-destruction; it is already older than most democracies. In 1976, she had her 200th birthday and that's how long historically a democracy has lasted. I need your vigilance for another lifetime. George Orwell was right when he said 'people sleep peaceable at night only because rough men stand ready to do violence on their part.' " Gunner finally paused allowing Q to ask a burning question.

"What are these metal tags for? They look like dog tags." The tags hung from the brass grommet on the bottom of the flag.

Gunner rubbed the tags in his hand, "They were my father's Army tags in World War I. He served in Germany, as did I. This is his flag; he died in 1959 right after the US got fifty stars. I've been flying her ever since on historic days. Most don't fly a veteran's flag, they keep her on a shelf. With tender care this flag has lasted until mine is ready and my father's fighting spirit flies in the wind on days of significance to freedom, today is Citizenship Day. Old Glory was new when I began flying her. She has served me well. Let's put her to bed son and carry her home."

Q rubbed the circular, Monel metal tag, A. J. Hunter, 12.15.19, 9.15.00, "What does this mean Gunner?"

"Aaron Jacob Hunter enlisted December 15, 1919, born September 15, 1900. Gunner placed his thumb over the tiny six pointed star. "The military is a good source for a solid foundation for young men. Since 1899, dog tags have provided identification when you can't provide your own." Gunner paused. "My son Josef returned from Vietnam in a box. Because of his tags he came home." Gunner's voice trailed off in a vacant stare across the field his other son, Jared, was harvesting. "Hans never got Russell's tags, don't know what happened to him or them."

Gunner cleared his throat. "You won't find wealth in your pocket Q, it lives in your heart and grows when it's given away. You live in a world different than I, don't believe everything. Turn it over. Savor it. Truth is truth."

Q gently set the flag in the apple case, the glass front showed off her white stars and the two dog tags as the lid closed. Gunner ruffled his hair, "Come on, let's go have dinner. The men are coming in from the field, and the ladies will have the canning cleaned up. Dinner will be waiting for us. You ever had cholent? It's a Ma Lu special." Gunner licked his lips.

Q looked confused.

"Don't worry, you can eat it. It's just stew."

▼

Gunner and Lucille Hunter held hands walking the lane to their carriage house. "Lu, I like that kid, I hope Jared takes him on as a hired hand, he could use some man time."

"I watched you through the window. He took a liking to you too." Lu gazed up at her still handsome husband and squeezed his hand. Three stars shone down upon the stone path. "Did you forget your observances?"

Gunner avoided her statement. "I sure still take a liking to you too, Lu. According to law I am permitted to work when I am saving a life." Gunner pressed in close and kissed the top of her head. Lu wrapped her cardigan tighter around her soft, long departed waistline and snuggled into Gunner's warmth.

"I saw you fold that flag with him. What took so long?"

"I was remembering an old flag ceremony. Remembered the whole thing too. Not bad for an eight decade geezer," Gunner winked at his cherished wife, "Made up what I didn't remember. I planted riddles today. Hope he figures 'em all out. "

Lu laughed, "At eighty-two you act twenty-two. I saw you riding on the back of the mower." She shook her head.

"Didn't fall off, did I?" Gunner tightened his hug. "Lu, you worry too much about me, we're in good hands and it's almost the new year."

"Oy vey," she snuggled closer enjoying her husband's scent, compassion and strength. She saw him as she remembered him in his youth, past the wrinkles and rolls into the spirit she vowed to love until death. They had enjoyed a wonderful life dance twirling and spinning, dipping and diving, stepping back and moving forward.

"I love you Lu."

Lu raised her shoulders and cuddled under his arm. Gunner used 'I love you' like he said it everyday. In reality she had heard him say it unechoed less than twenty times in fifty-six years. It wasn't that he didn't love her, he loved her with all his heart; he just wasn't a man who believed in repeating himself unless it was necessary. As long as she knew he loved her, enough said. He told her early on in their marriage, if he changed his mind - he'd let her know.

"If something happens to me, I want you to give the boy my veteran's flag. I think it will have meaning for him. Jared will fly Josef's flag when we retire Dad's." Gunner looked to the heavens, the harvest moon lit the path to their small villa, the handle on the Big Dipper pointed the way, and the North Star shone like a guiding light. The oil lamp on their cottage table transferred blue light through the stained glass Hamsa Hand, blessing those who entered the gate to their home.

"Ya, Lu, I planted living seeds today, harvest time is coming too soon. Make sure Sam gets my Springfield, Jared keeps my 44, Sam's already got one. Take Hans to DC for me, finish your business Lu."

Lu savored the moment. She kissed his warm weathered hand gazing into his eyes.

"Don't worry love, I did what I was meant to do today. You may have thought I was working, I was lifesaving. Might be time to open your sealed chambers too," his eyes repeated the seldom-said four-lettered word in the lamplight and then he said "You know I love you forever, sweet Lu."

She knew his pledge was solid til' death do them part. He was not a man to repeat himself. This must be a special day.

"I love you too, Gu," she echoed.

S unday was a day to free your body, heart, and soul, look your
        best and let your little light of glorious color shine out. Since
        slave times the church had remained pivotal in developing
solidarity, building leadership, provisioning strength, and offering support.
Churches had served as stationhouses for the Underground Railroad and
delivered coded messages through sermons and spirituals.

LaMar winked at his father as they escorted their beautiful ladies up
the steps of the high school, serving today as a place of worship. Tina wore
a red caftan dashiki skirt from Gambia with the top embroidered delicate-
ly in gold. Tamara and Shayna were outfitted in caftans of purple with
golden elephants. Tina, Tamara, and Shayna had begun shopping on the
Internet for traditional clothing direct from Africa, bypassing the middle-
men and supporting a number of small African businesses and Shayna had
discovered the 'elephones' with Mommy surfing the web as Harry the
poodle stealthfully surfed the kitchen for dog treats hidden by Johnny in
a game of 'find the cookies'.

Reggae and Tina's Hope for All Nations church was a strong group of
multi-ethnic believers who worked, grew, and worshiped together.
Reggae, as a church elder, referred to the church as a post-Black church
for the Joshua generation. He and Tina chose to worship as an African
American family within the tapestry of humanity, breaking communion
bread with an Ethiopian couple to their right and an elderly Mexican man
to their left. Listening to a home-run sermon by a talented young Asian

preacher and a solo by an Eastern Indian college student, accompanied by a white pianist. Some Sundays, Reggae brought his Caribbean percussion instruments, and on other Sundays he offered up music from his coronet. The diversity of the congregation was contagious. It was also fraught with the ups and downs of learning to get along and risk understanding differences. The worship at Hope for All Nations exuberantly embraced the brotha'hood and sista'hood of Christ. Hues of holy hands raised heavenward as multicolored banners to the Glory of God the Father, Jesus His Son, and the Holy Spirit from black, grey and beige metal chairs.

Learning to love among diversity was a tough but necessary banner of civil rights to continue marching toward a dream. According to Reggae, it was time to break spiritual dominant culture walls and embrace the individual differences of each person as Christ did. It was why Reggae and Tina worshiped at Hope for All Nations. Their style refrained from judging a culture, ethnicity, livelihood, or education. They looked through the kaliedescope called humanity.

On the other hand, LaMar and Tamara felt called to inner city ministry and worshiped at North Baptist. The tapestry of their congregation was abundant in harmonic and rhythmic spirituals with heart-searching sermons. It was rich in hues from coffee with cream to Tamara's deep ebony. Twice a week Lamar and Tamara reached out to urban youth and returned home before they drowned in street culture pain.

LaMar taught teen males at the park while Tamara yielded to the call of teen mothers. LaMar's team at the hoops sharpened his street wisdom and vernacular, while he tried to plant seeds for futures of success. He no longer thought of these young men as lacking brainpower or talent. He discovered Ebonics and rap was his starting point to cross the bridge to his student's reality, culture, perspective and pain. He had to get down to rise up. It was not his job to judge, he could leave judging to the Big Guy upstairs. He was their teacher and as he got to know each young man his attitude changed. Instead of correcting the dialect, he played with it, offering a dollar reward for ten proper English conjugations and once the price was paid the bar was raised holding each young man accountable.

Reggae talked LaMar into attending his church to celebrate harvest season. Jesus was universally ethnic. He was the minority of minorities.

Reggae sang bass boldly as LaMar harmonized with tenor. Johnny sat high upon LaMar's shoulders accompanying with an off tune repetition of

"Awesome, Awesome God." The only thing anchoring LaMar's restless spirit was his little son's random bold singing as he bounced upon his Daddy's shoulders, clapped his hands and then ran baby fingers through Daddy's hair. LaMar's mind wandered. Thoughts rapidly mixed without making sense. His stomach rumbled and he looked forward to breaking bread after the services at the small 'to die fo' soul food restaurant across the street.

"Amazing Grace how sweet the sound . . ." John Newton's nightmare "that saved a wretch like me . . ." when all of Europe was consumed by a raging fire . . . "I once was lost but now I'm found . . ." And he repented being a captain on a slave ship to become an abolitionist . . . "was blind but now I see." Thoughts of Kevin pestered his mind. How was this mixed up with Kevin? What did Kevin see between sleep and waking? Did something in his brain disconnect from his vision? Could that happen? What was the whitest wall? Why was Kevin pretending to be Black? How did Kevin fit into his nightmares? The worship continued with his thoughts blending lyrics into a medley.

"You raised me up so I can stand on mountains. You raised me up to walk the stormy sea . . ." LaMar's thoughts tumbled. "I am strong when I am on your shoulders . . ." Johnny placed his head upon the softness of LaMar's hair. LaMar wrapped his hand around Johnny's foot, feeling one with his son. "You raised me up to more than I can be . . ." igniting a thought. "I could have died like my Mama, but I lived. I lived!"

Shoulder to shoulder, LaMar reached out his hand and did something he had never done, he put his hand into Pop's palm. Peace and Forgiving of a past coagulated with Thanksgiving for a future.

"Let us rejoice and be glad in Him."

▼

Back in Riverdale, Pastor Wilson had spent all day Saturday writing his sermon and was confident his specially selected words could improve his congregants' lives.

▼

Ali stopped at Eden Valley Center to fetch Margie and her children on her way to Lutheran Church of Peace. It was a battle in the waiting. Q set his feet in concrete determined to sleep in, but Ali held an ace card. Just before she left her farmhouse Gunner offered Q a seat on the couch to watch Sunday football, on one condition – Q attend today's church service and return 'his' suspenders.

Head down, pants sagging, Q strutted reluctantly to the car. Everyone was welcome in the white clapboard church so they said. He felt like a church outcast, a sorry mess. He was too old for Sunday school, never attended confirmation, had never even been a shepherd in a Christmas program or went to Bible Camp.

Built in the beginning of the 1900's, its high steeple was a local monument. It's bells rang out Sunday services, moments of mourning and announced twelve o'clock noon. In the all white stoic church, with the all white hard edge pews, and the all white frozen people, Q and the stained glass windows stood out. Both were dressed in their best, one in multicolor broken pieces of glass and the other in broken down hoodlum attire, bling blinging among the rows of freshly ironed, white shirt, black trouser, superficial polite young men pathetically singing in the choir. Their song was old. Q was fresh, new and used to singing in the spirit.

At Lutheran Church of Peace you were noticed if you raised your hand to cover a sneeze. There was no swaying and definitely no dancing.

▼

Ali, surprised by a sudden heat wave, fanned her body with the church bulletin. Thinking Ali was providing a subtle cue, Tasha raised her hands in the air as she sang "For I'm in the Lord's Army." Pastor Wilson smiled enjoying Tasha's release of the spirit. Cora Anderson, head of the choir, got very wide eyed as her cheeks sunk in and her mouth suddenly dropped at the corners. Her lips pursed in the middle reminding Tasha of an old prune. White puckery ladies made her homesick for Brotha Smith bravado and the dirt poor church of her youth.

Tasha pretended Pastor Wilson was Brotha' Smith of Shiloh Church where she danced in the aisles and clapped her hands in worship. Brotha Smith fed you the Word and then once you were Worded Up fed you a banquet. What little the congregants of Shiloh had, they shared and there was always enough to go around. Those who lacked were given food and if there was nothing in the cupboard on the way to church, there was always blessings for your cupboard to take home. Tasha fantasized Miz Taylor's red-hot chicken wings – they were the bomb with proper hot sauce. Tasha wondered what Riverdale folk knew about banquets.

Brotha' Smith met the Lord in prison and he preached real good shaking the walls of hell to topple out sinners and opening the gates of heaven to shower down blessings. There was no turning back when you walked into one of the Brotha's sermons, he wasn't afraid of the Holy Spirit and he wasn't afraid of tellin' it like it is. Most of the men in Shiloh had served black prison time and once released faced the emptiness of rebuilding a life they barely had a chance to begin. Brotha Smith admonished the men to show off their manhood by getting down on their prayin' knees. He admonished the women to strut the right stuff and stay pure. He shouted admonitions that if you give you give with no strings attached.

Brotha' did warfare in the Name of the Lord, arming the men and women of Shiloh with holy 'Fruit of the Spirit' weapons. He spoke of getting out in front of the pack and not being dogs sniffing each other's booties and neva payin' no mind to real future needs or the needs of your neighbors. He yelled at the top of his voice that if you took loot with strings attached you became a puppet – a puppet of others or the government. He shouted that life wasn't about clothes or money, it was about laying our burdens down and asking forgiveness. It was about building bridges with your brothas and sistas and not burning them.

Brotha Smith was sincere in giving a healthy dose of the Holy Ghost and if you were there you felt the Power. He prayed against poverty so Tasha wouldn't steal out of need, and he prayed against too much wealth so Tasha wouldn't forget her needs in the Lord. Going to Brotha Smith's church was like serving penance, once you got your life straight on Sunday, you had the whole rest of the week to mess it up again. It was about that one moment in your life – at your death when you would come face-to-face with your Savior Jesus. You would be all alone without anyone or anything but your own naked soul. What would you say then?

Tasha knew when to . . . For thine is the Kingdom and the power and the glory. Amen . . . when to wonder why if most American blacks and whites pray to the same God, why they didn't sit together in the same pews. She missed singing, "Lift Every Voice and Sing." At Shiloh, Tasha knew when to say a loud Amen.

▼

Margie climbed aboard the Lord's chariot and rode it like a roller coaster, and her insatiable appetite to be loved often defiled her own temple. Her sins were not an issue of her morality, but of impulsivity and immediate perceived needs. No one could miss Margie's true spirituality; she wore it on her shirtsleeves. Riverdale was a done deal. It was a new start. She longed for the safety of intimacy she saw between Ma Lu and Gunner, between Ali and Jared, between Deb and Sam, Larry . . .

There would be no more negotiable affections . . .

"For thine is the Kingdom and the power and the glory. Amen."

▼

Ali's mind drifted into a childhood grounded in honoring the union, voting Democratic, and avoiding the small town hoity-toity while Pastor Wilson delivered the sermon. Her mother had volunteered religiously and her father ushered the lovely blue haired whispering ladies to self-designated Sunday pews. Well-groomed on the outside these gentle appearing women seemed harmless. But in the pews they gleefully shared the gossip from the other side of the tracks where Ali lived. One day she discovered from the 'nice folk' her family was 'trailer trash' and it amazed Ali that those who appeared to have so much, felt privileged to talk of others. Her family wasn't afraid of hard and dirty work. You did what you had to do to get something done and wore your blue-collar ethic with pride. You played on the team and drove where the jobs were, hoping to God there would be another job after you finished the project you were on.

Ali sang drowning out the righteousness screaming in her head. 'As a deer panteth forth the water, my soul longest after thee . . .' She sang to bury the words of dear whispering ladies, who forgot the parched seasons in their past. Poverty of the heart added a drought to their mouths.

Ali's childhood hadn't always been verbally paraded around the community in such harsh terms. A year of layoffs forced her father to sell their home and move to a trailer park with other people who hit hard times, recently retired or were starting out. Life in a trailer cut expenses enough to pay bills. Then weeks of unemployment took the wind out of her father's sails and he sold the trailer when relatives offered Uncle Joe's cabin that was hardly bigger than an icehouse. Ali understood poverty and the pangs of neglect, but for her family poverty was a season. When jobs opened her father worked overtime to pay back debt and rebuild a meager savings always devoured by lurking unemployment . . . waiting . . . always waiting. Ali knew how to kick herself in the butt, put a smile on her face, and see past glumness. Some days her butt got pretty sore. She never dared hope for an advanced education. But, in tenth grade Ali's English teacher noticed promise in her work and she encouraged her to apply for college scholarships. It was Ali's first bold step of independence.

She understood the importance of second chances.

Her teacher stood in the gap between the deficit and the potential of a future. She traded tutoring Ali in college prep for classroom organizing three times a week. It was during those cleaning times that Ali gained more than academics and dirty hands. She learned about herself, her capabilities, and her beauty. Ali soaked up the lessons of virtue from Mrs. Everson like a dry sponge in a pool of warm water. It was through Mrs. Everson that she determined to help others less fortunate than herself. Mrs. Everson applied for college testing and filled out all Ali's scholarship and college admissions paperwork. Then days after high school graduation Ali began her adult life in the big inner city all because one person believed she was capable of achieving her dreams. Ali set her heart's compass to be that believer for others; she glanced at Tasha and smiled, hoping to be her Mrs. Everson.

▼

Q had a hard time sitting still, thinking about meeting Gunner after church for the game. The hymns were dirges. Q held the heavy hymnal in his hand, paging through hundreds of songs. He balanced the book on finger tips.

Mama gave him her look.

If he could spin a basketball on the tip of his fingers he could certainly balance an old music book.

"Our Father who art in Heaven . . ."

Ali glanced over at Q fidgeting with the hymnal. He had already made two paper airplanes from offering envelopes and he had the visitor card rolled up like a joint . . .

"Hallowed be thy name, thy kingdom come . . ."

Q had carefully adjusted his belt just below his waist and it had been slowly riding down his upper thighs. "Thy will be done, on earth as it is in heaven. Give us this day, our daily bread . . ."

The large wad of gum in his mouth crackled like a hot fire on green wood and an old pair of red suspenders dangled from his back pocket.

"And forgive us our trespasses as we forgive those who trespass against us." Ali kept a watchful eye on him, feeling like a mother hen of a two-year-old. It was not her responsibility, but it was her church.

"Lead us not into temptation."

Q looked around at the white folk with closed eyes and lips moving like fish blowing bubbles. He parroted the rhythm of the woman behind him, wagging his head and coming eye-to-eye with Ali. He broke into a full-lipped smile and quickly shut his eyes.

"But deliver us from Evil. For thine is the Kingdom and the Power and the Glory forever and ever. Amen."

Pastor Wilson added a somber, "We will pause for a moment of silence."

Q heard the words as Pastor Wilson spoke them. The church was pin-drop quiet and as luck would have it, the hymnal with it's hundreds of white pages, hopped off his two fingers and slowly, ever so slowly and spun out of control reminding him of a maple seed on a helicopter falling to earth.

Ali one-eyed Q just as the dark green hymnal slipped from his hands in an aerial dive to the hardwood floor. It hovered before exploding like a shotgun and she was too matronly to prevent it.

Q shouted "Oh Shit!" the solitude of prayer was broken, he grabbed his crotch to haul up his pants. SHHHHH echoed between the stained glass windows of Zaccheus in the tree and Peter in the boat.

Mama grabbed his collar choking off his air.

Two elderly women shrieked.

"In the name of the Father, the Son, and the Holy Ghost, go in Peace." Pastor Wilson raised his hands in blessing to the congregation as he looked at the young man most eager to escape. The black cloaked preacher glared at him, followed by a smirking proper white boy with a candlesnuffer. There was no getting around it; the only way out of the church was to shake Pastor Wilson's hand in the greeting line. The clergyman held his hand tightly and did not let go, "I assume you were making sure no one was sleeping in church today?"

Q smiled politely and ran to Ali's minivan. He didn't say a word when Tasha and Mama were dropped off to work at Dee's Apple Pie booth for the Apple Fest. His lips were sealed and his hands folded. Q silently sat in the back seat and refused Ali's front seat offer. He looked forward to a friendly face who had not seen him in church.

His old friend Gunner stood at the door smiling. "Hey, Q, nice to see you. You hungry? MaLu made a fine pot of venison chili. She thought you'd like to pass a little gas while the game is on. Better chow now before Hans and Sam come. They'll scarf it right up." Happy wrinkles graced his eyes.

"I didn't see you at church today Gunner. You skip or what?"

"Oh, I go alright to weddings and funerals. That's enough church for an old man like me. Fell asleep the last time and rumor has it I was snoring bass during the sermon. Me and Ma celebrate private-like. We're getting old if you hadn't noticed."

"Sure, thanks," Q accepted the hot bowl and joined Gunner at the table. He wasn't sure if he'd like venison chili, he'd never eaten Bambi before, but he trusted Gunner and he felt like he had known him forever. He admired his silky white hair and twinkly blue eyes.

"Son, we need to talk." Gunner looked serious. "Ali told me you got in a fight after the game. I want to hear all about it."

Q figured Gunner would compliment him on his defensive prowess so he began boldly. "This guy put his hand on the ball and the ref called a bad play. He was stupid and pissed me off. We could have lost because of his dumb call. The kid I fought asked for it. He told me to shut up and I met him at the end zone to go upside his head. He pushed, I shoved."

Gunner was silent.

"He pissed me off Gunner! He put his hand on my shoulder and I told him to shut the f** . . ." Q slowed his roll. "Ah, sorry Gunner . . . to shut up. I was sittin' mindin' my business, so we took it to the end zone."

Gunner remained quiet.

"There is no greater dishonor than to get whipped by a white kid. I let him have it good." Q figured Gunner understood honor, wasn't that what yesterday was all about?

Q's description of Friday night was admittedly truthful. Both teams were playing lousy football. He had been sitting smoldering because Mike Johnson was running quarterback and playing a perfect game while the rest of the team was fumbling. He wished he could run defense. If Mike threw the pass to him he'd have caught it and run like his life depended on it. So, when the idiots dropped the ball, he loudly admonished the Riverdale Lions. When the ref made a lousy call, Q let the ref verbally have it too. Except for his mouth, he really was 'just sitting.'

Gunner ate. Silent.

Nervously, Q raced his bread around the beans in his chili.

Gunner ate slowly. Very slowly and silently. Then he cleared his throat, blew his nose and looked piercingly at Q. "Ali says you're a sportsman and you can shoot a basketball better than anyone in Riverdale. She said you wanted to make the cut for football, but your mom didn't have the money, so you didn't even try out."

Why did Miss Ali tell him all that? Talkin' about him reached right under his skin and set him off. His life was nobody's business. Q played with his chili and placed the tip of his tongue between his teeth to make it behave.

"I bet you've played some really tough games in your life, won a few and lost a few. What helps you when you're having trouble with a game?"

"I make the team win."

"I betcha' do son, you're smart, fast and can think on your feet. It's not just your muscles; it's your mind that plays the game. You like being called a 'fucking' idiot when you are trying your best to play and win?" Gunner's f-word sounded uncalled for and nasty. Q wished he could take back the word he so brashly used. That was the problem with words, once they slipped out your mouth there was no way to stuff 'em back in. He wasn't sure if Gunner was heading toward a lecture or a pat on the back.

"I play to win, Gunner," Q offered boldly, but his eyes peered at Gunner like a puppy who had just pooped on the floor and got caught.

"I know you do. You play harder than anyone else. So let's say your team has a bad game and you get the ball. Now it's you, and the ball, and the basket. The other team is all over you. You turn. You dribble, then turn again. You're deciding what to do next - where to go. Do you pass? Do you keep the ball? Do you shoot from where you are? Calculate the risks?"

Q nodded. Gunner made the game real.

"All you can think of is getting the ball in the basket, then suddenly you hear Tasha screaming 'Go Q! You can do it!' What happens next?"

"When I hear Tasha I try harder. I settle myself and calculate the risk. I probably shoot and score, but I think first for Tasha and the team."

"So you gain power when someone cares about you?"

"Yep."

"What happens if you blow a shot? How do you feel then."

"Bad."

"What happens when people call you an idiot when you feel down?"

"I punch their lights out after the game or I smoke."

"Q, you are powerful, one of the most powerful young men I've met in a long time, and I have a lot of time behind me. You are a born leader, brave, strong and capable of honesty. People follow you for the good or for the bad. Your huge voice can be heard across neighborhoods. At the game what do you think the player who was having trouble would do if you said 'Go 16, you can do it. Go! Go! Go!' instead of what I think you said."

Q was silent.

"As a person of power you are required to empower. Disparaging remarks and dishonesty depower others and yourself. You gotta learn to take orders before your give orders." Gunner switched plays, "What do you want to be when you grow up, Q?"

"An attorney to help kids dealing with stuff back in the city." Q was grateful Gunner never questioned his city life.

"Q, right now, today you began to be that attorney."

"Huh? I ain't no attorney. I might not even graduate. I've been kicked out of school for fighting more than once."

"When innocence is betrayed, that's when you fight. Ya, I reckon you'll make one fine attorney. When you get up from this table and walk through that door to watch football, with the men you begin your future. Life is your playing field. It's your game. It's your touchdown, your basket or your homerun. You must play a strong game to win. This is the moment you begin, not tomorrow and not when you are thirty-years-old."

"A fighting spirit is a challenging gift. Use your spirit to stay in school, fight poverty, fight to be an attorney. You want to earn an extra half million dollars cash by the time you're my age Q? That's what a high school diploma gives you in a lifetime."

Q looked shocked.

"You'll make more than that with a college degree, but it's not how much you make Q; it's what you do with it that matters. You'll graduate and you'll go to college. You will be the man you see a glimpse of in your mirror. You're a winner Q."

Gunner stood up to bus his empty bowl to the sink, his smile felt like dry warm air on a cold wet day. Q had been titled loser many times, but never winner. Winner in the game of life?

"You and I start out the same each morning – twenty four fresh hours waiting for us to spend. Those hours are the most expensive thing we own and yet they are given to us freely. Do we manage that precious time by achieving our goals, by helping another, by bettering ourselves? Do we set our values high so we can clearly execute them with our best male integrity? Time is just beginning for you. Time is fleeting for me. The sand in my hourglass is almost sifted through. Let's go get a seat before the guys come in. First come, first seated. I demand the remote and my seat is at the end zone." Gunner pointed to a worn green chair. Q quietly returned the suspenders. Gunner raised his bushy brows and took control of the remote.

Except for Sam O'Riley's word whooping and a few shouts for touchdowns Gunner was quiet. There was no game cussing and Gunner never spoke another word to Q as he sat in Doc's sofa space.

▼

For twenty-two years, Sam had a standing invitation to join the Hunter family for Sunday afternoon football and Ma Lu's chili. When he first returned from in-country and convalescing, Gunner avoided him as he grieved the loss of his son, Joe. As time passed, Gunner took him quietly under his wing and helped him through veteran rough spots realizing he had no one to reach out to for understanding. Sam's dad had died before he left for 'Nam and his mother didn't understand the depths of the conflict he was going through.

Somehow, Hans Palmquist and Gunner Hunter had helped him walk out of the doldrums of despair. They had provided rides to the VA when he couldn't drive and quietly consoled him without judgment. They verbally beat the tar out of him for self-pity.

Sam knew the moment he arrived that Gunner was in a tar-beating mood. He knew their signals and when Hans provided a look of 'go' a strategic military attack was about to begin. These weren't men to mess with. They offered advice mixed with military toughness, albeit layered with life experience and fatherly compassion.

Today's what for, bottom line was that Sam had a lot of life left to live and he could destroy it or enjoy it. As far as Gunner and Hans were concerned, destroying it was pretty darn stupid. Hans's son Russell remained missing in action (MIA) and Gunner's son Joe was a war casualty. They had been silent for thirty years, but today both men spoke about their lost boys and by doing so broke up scar tissue. Their sons had been Sam's best friends throughout childhood, "Sam, me and Hans we understand, but solid relationships last forever, a departed loved one is always just a memory away and the wounds remain open."

Q listened intently, he hadn't realized older men reprimanded other men. They sure did not mince words.

Old Gunner was heated up to refresh Sam's memory and Hans sat opposite nodding uh hmms. They left Sam with no verbal space to change the subject and he expected Gunner to be forthright while letting him have it right between his eyes. He'd heard similar speeches before.

"Sam, life is full of whammies. It's never been fair. We all lose, but you're not a loser Sam! You make the choice on every loss to gain something. You pick your attitude to put on for each experience. Find someone to fill up that loss with. Damn it! Don't fill the hole up with booze. You're half empty Sam, flip it over to half full. Quit being so self-centered and tough, sometimes it's more courageous to be vulnerable. We are all vulnerable. Sam, none of us get out of life alive. By the time you figure it out, it's time to die."

"War stays with ya. Either you control it or it controls you. Life's experiences will continually mess with your head. You think I like secondary inspections every time Lu and I go to the airport; shrapnel in my leg keeps setting off those darn machines. I've learned to make the best of it. Now I ask the cutest girl on the line to wand me because I'm an old injured vet," Gunner winked at Hans, "You going to quit going on cruises with Deb because you don't want somebody wanding your fool foot? You think George Washington established the Purple Heart for the weak hearted? It might not be the medal you wanted, but you came home alive."

"This isn't just about you Sam. It never was. You think my Papa avoided battle fatigue from his time in Germany, or Hans got off Scott free from his tour of the Pacific Theater, or I don't have memories from my time rebuilding bridges or liberating concentration camp detainees? You may have been discharged from the military, but God's not letting you forget the war. Those memories will make you or break you. You think the young men and women from this community coming back from Iraq are going to have different memories than you, or me, or Hans, or Papa, or King David?"

"You think my Papa's shell shock was different from my battle fatigue or your damn post-traumatic whatever the hell it's called. You better be ready, because you are the one left standing for the next generation. Those men and women are coming home. Each soldier's sacrifice falls into obscurity as time erodes the memories of others. In a perfect world there would be no veteran. War is hell. I know it, and you know it and twenty-five million men and women vets who are still living know it. You're not alone.

Over forty-two million people have fought for this country since it started, including me, Hans, and you. And because of all of us, we have freedom and my son Joe and Hans' son Russ, your two highschool best friends,
did not die in vain. I wore my dog tags proudly. I had the freedom to
remove them. Freedom costs plenty. Risking your life to preserve
Freedom is an honor. We need you standing for the men and women coming home and for the families of children who never make it back."

"How long are you going to wallow in your own pigpen? You can
control it, but you can't cure it," Gunner resettled himself in the recliner,
pointing the TV remote like a loaded weapon at Sam. "You better keep
your damn boots on Sam, because you're standing next in line, over a
thousand World War II veterans are dying every day, and what we have
been doing for others you are going to be called to stand on both your feet
and do too!"

Sam didn't argue. He was silent for the rest of the game. He never
said another thing to Gunner who had fallen soundly to sleep. Sam smiled
at him with respect as he left, offering Q his hand and a ride home.

▼

Deb O'Riley had determined to remain strong through the
onslaught of Sam's relapse. Sam did right by her when she struggled with
sobriety. It was her turn to do right by Sam. He was silent when the fighting began overseas and soldiers lost their lives in battle in Bosnia, Rwanda,
Afghanistan and now Iraq. He barely talked when he heard one of the local
Riverdale boys had been injured. She had been out of town when Sam
came home after finding Doc and she knew that the bullets that penetrated Doc's flesh also penetrated Sam's emotional armor. Except at the death
of his son and his mother, Deb had never seen Sam cry. She knew he carried the memories of Vietnam in his shirt pocket, close to his heart. Her
father had worn his battle fatigue in the same pocket on a similar shirt, and
no matter what her mother had said to encourage him to talk, he simply
said, "What's done, is done, leave it be."

Deb had let it be for thirty-years. She loved Sam, and before he
destroyed himself and what family the two of them had left, she had to
help him clean out that wound and prepare it for healing. The trouble was
Sam had always been hard of hearing, now he was hard of listening too.

Deb had spent the day with Margie at Dee's Apple Pie booth chatting
with the local women. It had been a pleasant day and she knew Sam had

chosen to spend the day with Gunner, Hans, and Jared up at the Hunter place. It would do him some good to be with the guys to watch football. She turned off dinner and opened the front door, admiring the maple's canopy. Shaun's old tire swing hung silently from a sturdy branch, tied tightly with a thick sisal rope. She loved that beautiful old tree, lit up like a pumpkin from the streetlight. So many times she had watched Shaun enjoy himself – climbing and playing hide-n-seek. She pulled up a warm woolen blanket, holding a cup of hot tea and gently rocked on the porch swing Gunner had built for her and Sam as a housewarming present.

The rhythm lulled her as she waited. Living in town had its drawbacks, but when Sam fell off the wagon his walking home kept him out of jail. And lucky for Deb, Sam was a compassionate drunk and not abusive.

"Funny how life encircles us," she smiled knowingly. The gentle rocking and cool fall breeze soothed her and she closed her eyes to an earlier time in their lives before their only son, Shaun was born. It was her weakness for alcohol that created a renewed strength in Sam as he struggled to heal wounds inflicted from Vietnam. She was only seventeen, spunky, independent, and beautiful. Sam, five years older had grown up next door. His strong shoulders and sparkling golden red hair made him appear taller than he was. Rumor had it he would soon be home. She had swooned over him since she was a little girl, fantasizing they would one day marry.

Deb knew he had been injured, but the adults kept a hushed silence about the details. She could hardly wait to see her handsome crush walk down the sidewalk. He would be so surprised that the little neighborhood pest had turned into a beautiful woman. That Saturday she had sat in her room peering out her window. Mom had asked why she didn't join the family for breakfast and she had lied about needing to get a big school project done. Her heart broke as she watched her father and little brother Larry lift Sam out of the station wagon and wheel him up the walk looking ever so handsome in his dress blues. She had thought that after months convalescing he would be his same old jovial and prank playing self. He wasn't. Deb, determined as ever, set her mind to fix him.

▼

The jail cell was lonely and Kevin sat on the floor wondering if he awoke on the wrong side of reality. He had always lived his life by anchoring time with activities one process at a time and the activities in solitary were simple — sleep, wait, eat, wait, sleep. Except for the doctor's visit nothing changed. He tried to change it by sleeping. He cracked his knuck-les in each hand and then each toe to stop the itching white nightmare, but each time he fell asleep the whiteness remained. He felt exploding red. The cops stole his stress card! Red made him want to scream and the hot irritation that began in his chest wound down his legs and arms into his fingers and toes. The red packed itself tightly behind his skin and held his body hostage. A dream?

He screamed to release the pressure.

▼

LaMar's front yard at Shaker Heights looked like a BMW collection for Sunday afternoon football. The six men from the frat had reached attainment professionally and though none were rich, all were upper mid-dle class, held prestigious jobs or owned their own enterprises. Andre was a criminal investigator and professor at the law university, Terrence was an optometrist specializing in developmental visual issues, Aaron was a CPA and had recently moved into financial management in a brokerage firm, Tyrone owned a manufacturing business and Ali was a professor in law. They each had beautiful wives and delightful children. They called them-selves the Strategic Six – and together they worked out professional strategies to beat the man.

These six very different young college freshmen developed a cohe-siveness that had lasted eleven years; and yet the only thing that initially brought them together in a prominent multicultural campus was their dark skin. They had different backgrounds, different religions, different interests, and very different personalities. They played fair, obeyed the rules and won the race game. They were fathers who took fatherhood seri-ously, lovers of and providers for the mothers of their children, and hon-orable leaders in their communities and businesses. They had agreed to disagree and were able to discuss anything.

LaMar smiled as Aaron arrived carrying a grocery bag. "I saved Johnny's crappies for you." He handed his friend the plastic bag with the two small fish. Aaron pulled out a finely seasoned frying pan, a spatula, oil, Kosher beer and some good-looking snacks LaMar planned to eat.

The men took their respective positions in front of the new screen feet up, pillows propped and microbrews in hand. It was the Vikings vs. the Bears and the afternoon vacillated between intrigued silence, exuberant shouts and high fives as yardage and scores were achieved.

The Strategic Six followed two unwritten laws of football. One, that words or the void of words had the power to change the plays even if they were silent to the players. Two, that a trip to the bathroom caused you to miss the best play.

Luckily halftime provided bathroom breaks, fried fish and a heavy snack spread as they laughed and compared purchases of SUV's, smart phones and laptops while heavily snacking.

LaMar didn't openly discuss his clients or cases, to do so would have been unethical, but a couple issues regarding Kevin perplexed him and the first was the physical manifestation of the whitest wall.

Was there a connection between sleep, vision and the whiteness? Why did it take screaming to bust through? He'd ask Terrence.

▼

There was no alcohol served at Gunner's. In fact, Gunner provided fresh milk with the chili so Sam was more sober than he'd been in a long time. He dropped Q at Eden Valley and then decided to visit Doc's woods. He felt called to the solitude of the ravine where his best friend was shot. He needed to think alone in the violent fallen place so he parked at the end of the drive to avoid Sally or Mike.

Sam couldn't wait for snowfall as it meant the end of defoliation. Death. He sat upon the leaves. Blood. Some protected from rainfall still held spots of brown. Life. He wept. He wept for the death of his father and for the loss of his childhood when he took the responsibility as the man of the family. He wept for his mother, who worked her fingers to the bone as a widow and now for Sally left with the sole responsibility of raising Michael. He wept for Shaun, for the brain injury he sustained from fetal alcohol, and his young death caused from overreaction unavoidable because of his brain injury. He wept for Michael, now fatherless who would struggle with his own brain injury because of the brain injury of his son Shaun. Sam's poor choices became their poor choices that made more poor choices ripple out life. He wept for his comrades who fell before him in Vietnam and for the father of the son of the man who was injured recently in Iraq. He wept for the son returning home without a leg. And then, he wept for himself. Sam couldn't remember when he had last cried for himself.

In the woodland garden belonging to Doc and Sally, he prayed for salvation, and forgiveness for the unforgivable, against ugliness and for the removal of his pain. When he raised his head, the stars were brilliant. The moon lit the orange leaves of what seemed a hundred red maples blowing in the wind like tiny fires against the universe each filled with unaccountable histories and mysteries. Happy slept at his feet. Sam noted an ominous shadow running across his back and over his head. The shadow held a firearm.

Sam turned to make eye contact with the perpetrator. It was Michael. His eyes were reptilian cold in a blank stare. "Hi Mike."

Mike shook his head to pay attention. "Mom told me she heard something in the woods. I took Dad's 44 off the mantel and came down to check it out. I saw you . . ." he helped Sam up.

"How are you Michael? I think about you often."

"Doing OK, I guess."

"Bet your Mom's worried about you."

"She's sleeping. She took some sleeping pills. She won't wake up until morning when she goes to work."

"I miss your Dad, Mike. I bet you do too," Sam reached out, but the boy backed away. Since the accident Mike had been untouchable.

"Ya, I guess. Come on Happy, we've got school tomorrow," and without another word he walked ahead of Sam on the trail home.

Sam chocked the silence up to grief. Still, Michael had always been his buddy and the whole encounter didn't feel right.

Then again, he wasn't exactly in a frame of mind a teen boy would understand. He didn't exactly understand it himself the burden that had just been lifted, the harness removed. He drove home. For years he hated the street light that lit up the giant maple tree in his front yard like a pumpkin. The irritation had grown in the last year and up until this moment he had planned to take his chainsaw and cut the thing down, but somehow in the last few hours his frame of reference was changing. The orange glow welcomed him home to Deb. He admired her, wrapped in a Hudson Bay blanket on the porch, illuminated by streetlight and shadowed by the maple. Funny, he no longer felt the need to avoid the tree. The forest purging had released the tyranny. Life was too short. He could not destroy the good times left. He would share his truth and allow Deb to join him in his next life season. He loved her more than life itself though he feared sharing his future. They had already lost their only son.

What Doc took to his grave was that Sam was losing a big battle. The bullets that killed his best friend may have saved Doc the misery Sam now faced alone. They had served in different units in III Corps, but showered equally in air raid poison in 1968. Six months ago they were diagnosed with non-Hodgkins and they made a pact to refrain from telling their nursing wives. They pledged to be guinea pigs for science, with ammunition of vitamins, essential oils, herbs, diet, and exercise. They wanted to avoid western medicine regardless if they needed it.

Doc researched the Internet discovering a First Nation's concoction that had been tested successfully in China, but unapproved in the US. Sam bought a gas pump for the airport to funnel money into their project and Doc journeyed to Canada on a pseudo fishing trip to train under a medicine man. It was a grand plan and they felt like little naughty boys. Doc concocted a new fangled regime that neither Deb nor Sally's western medical perspective would endorse because some parts were illegal.

Deb ignored the ruse of mega vitamins, improved diet and chelation treatments three days a week at Docs for, as Sam said, 'to get the lead out from all the years of gas station work," though she called it quackery, she didn't tell Sally and neither women knew Doc did chelation on himself.

▼

The smell of pot roast in the warm kitchen greeted him along with tail wags from Reg III who rubbed hard against Sam's thigh. Normally he would have sidestepped his inebriation with a shout of "what's for dinner?", but tonight his game was not needed. He tip-toed through the house and stood with Reg III in the doorway watching maple leaf moonlight dance on his wife's face. Sleep softened her lifelines and she looked youthful snuggled warm and cozy under the blanket. If they truly were a team, then it was time he stepped up to the plate. He walked to the porch swing, bent down and stroked her cheek.

She rustled.

He ran his fingers through her soft hair.

She hummed dreamingly.

He sat down and held her, his most special of all treasures and he kissed her lightly until she awoke. There was no smell of liquor.

"Deb, we have to talk," he said lovingly and dove right in. "Non-Hodgkins scares me. It could mean surgery and chemotherapy and it does not matter western medicine saved my life once. I don't trust doctors."

Late into the night Sam shared. Deb listened finally understanding

Sam's recent strange behaviors.

"When Doc got the same diagnosis we made a pact over a beer at Smitty's. If we were going to die, we were going to die fighting and not from treatment complications. We wanted to fight the war we never finished. Maybe our spirit of independence was plain stupid?"

"We needed money so Doc and I invested together in chelation equipment using the credit card eating machine lease as a guise. We told you that leaded gasoline was my poison. Then Doc arranged national speaking engagements near chelation training sites. He took specialized classes while Sally basked in the sun. His research discovered a special path of a First Nation's nurse in Canada and we tried it."

Deb had tried to remain composed, but reflexively gasp.

"Don't worry, hon, it wasn't as poisonious as the leaded gas I've laid in or the Agent Orange I've showered in. The tonic has been tested and proven effective for three years in China before we tried it."

Deb held her breath.

"It took the groin swelling down and before Doc died we quit having night sweats and itchy skin. It just doesn't seem fair that we survived bullets and grenades, but poison from my own comrades led a new attack. We were going to beat it, Deb, without you or Sally needing to know. We were going to do it our way."

Sam held Deb tighter, "I'm worried about Jared, the herbicide he's used for years on his fields contains some of the same chemicals."

"Sam, you better mention this to him," Deb finally shared. "And you better promise me you'll visit the VA and explain everything including your harebrained scheme of an idea. I'll come with you."

Sam was quiet.

"A complete physical Sam, honest about all your health and share the details of treatments and the results you and Doc had achieved. I'll stand alongside you. I can get Sally to help me access Doc's research and paper work. He was thorough and in his current condition it won't risk his license or reputation. I'll get on the Internet and make some calls regarding VA benefits. We'll do this together Sam. You're not alone. I'll make sure you get the very best care."

Their conversation was cut short with a phone call.

"It's Pa."

The sun slept behind the hill when Margie Jones mounted her bike to ride to Dee's Café. She enjoyed watching the big yellow ball crest over the hill behind the church steeple, in the purple morning sky. A sharp burst of wind whistled past as she glided down the dip in the road and into a pocket of fog. It hovered silently. She relaxed as the sky awoke until the crisp air stung her bare legs turning them ashy. She wished she had pulled on a pair of sweats before waking the kids with a kiss for school. "Think warm Margie, you can do it girl," she shivered.

The town was quiet as most of the songbirds that greeted her all summer had flown south. The flags silently waved her into town, "America land of the free and home of the brave. I am brave. I was brave when I signed up for the Riverdale Project to start life over. It was brave to have enough of not having enough. I was brave walking with those I thought were the enemy." When she was well rested her mind was clear and she pondered questions, at least momentarily. Was this what it was like to have a complete brain and not work so hard for everything? If only thinking was always so easy.

"How do I stop experiences from splitting into black and white? The reality of another is colored more by life experience. When I look into a face why do I see difference first? The spirit is colorless. The body is simply a paintjob for the soul, it means nothing." The geese honked Margie back to marginal. Her questions unanswered. She swung her bike behind Dee's and set the lock. "Least in Riverdale, I'm not a crockpot in a microwave world. They're all crockpots here," she laughed, she liked herself. She had become the community conduit relaying the scoop from the sun up farmers to shop owners. She listened carefully to share details and compare stories during coffee time, lunch and early senior dining, embellishing each with her street smarts and glorious humor.

Dee kept her prices low to encourage local patrons and paid her $6.50 an hour. It was too little to buy extras. For that she needed the paper tips and not pocket change. Her new tricks improved her results — she now greeted everyone by name, refilled cups with free coffee and added a smiley face with a heart and thank you on each check.

Ali was surprised her mood was fresh with all that had recently transpired. She was at peace with the coming events, but the week would be hard. She expected to do much of the details for Ma Lu, Annie and Jared.

▼

Ali meandered from one side of the sidewalk to the other listening to the crackle of multi-colored leaves under her feet, enjoying the aroma of autumn. She looked forward to the diversion of meeting Dr. Watkins at Dee's Café. She was curious regarding his impressions of Kevin.

"Lucky Sheriff Larry's not following you Ali, he'd think you was already drinking this morning," Margie chuckled.

"Nice to see you this morning, you look nice today," Ali smiled.

"Waitress apron always looks the same here, girl," Margie filled a cup with fresh coffee and placed the napkin rolled flatware next to her. "Sure had fun Saturday. Thanks for the sauce, sure you didn't drink mouthwash this morning?"

Ali loved laughing with Margie and gave her a testing look, "I had fun too. Maybe we should get together and cook more often. I bet you have some great recipes to show me." Ali's cold hands wrapped around the warm beige china mug and she pulled it to her nose. The coffee was too hot to drink, but perfect for warming her cheeks.

Dr. Watkins entered looking sharp in his wool sweater.

"Ali, I suppose you want the regular?" Margie avoided looking at him, the stolen fifty-dollar bill burned her thigh where she had dropped it into her apron pocket to buy groceries after work. "He wants the regular too?" She filled another cup. "Little creamers next to sugar, salt and pepper."

Ali looked up trying to soften the tension. "Breakfast is good here, Dr. Watkins. They make a great plate of roast beef hash and eggs over easy.

I like Dee's hot apple pie with a slice of white cheddar cheese and a scoop of ice cream; it covers almost all the food groups. Got that this morning Margie?"

"Five pies baked fresh this morning. Still got some pieces left."

Ali smiled back knowingly and nodded to LaMar.

"Your husband took two pieces before he headed out to the fields. Packed him a take out. Said they should get a good crop this year. Corn prices are up and the corn is ready. Said this would be a busy week with having to take Tuesday off for his Pa. Used those good Honey Crisp apples from Sam's apple tree. Q picked 'em. Sam said he could sell them to Dee." Margie pointed to LaMar, but fixed her eyes on Ali. "What about him?"

"A piece of Honey Crisp apple pie, please," LaMar looked directly at Margie, a soft, kind smile clowned up under his dark perfectly groomed mustache, shaded under long black lashes. His brown eyes twinkled, his hair waves lay perfect, and he smelled of cologne.

"Yes, sir. I'll get them right away," she hurried to the kitchen.

LaMar shook his head and picked up his coffee mug testing the temperature with his lips before taking a sip.

Ali watched his expression as he swirled the light brown mixture in his mouth and she burst into laughter as he swallowed, "Weak?"

"I think I got the hot water they washed the pot out with. Did Margie do this to me on purpose?"

"Nope, locals say it's the best coffee in town," Ali laughed. "It's a small town tradition. Coffee was expensive when they immigrated from northern Europe. I think they learned to like it one bean at a time. Next time order tea, the water is fine. I've lived here over twenty years. Believe me it's easier to drink it, than change it."

LaMar updated Ali on the testing results, the arrival of Kevin's parents and the outline of twelve hours he had spent. He took the check Margie had laid down on the table up to the cash register and handed Margie a twenty-dollar bill expecting over ten dollars in change. Margie handed him back $14.62. Then she reached in her apron pocket and gave him fifty more.

She smiled, feeling lighter as she went to clear the table.

LaMar nodded, mouthed "thank you," and departed.

"Musta forgotten this," she mumbled and picked up a brown paper bag. Under the bag was $4.62. "Nice," she checked its contents.

A yellow sticky paper said, "for Margie" she could read that much. Then under the note was the fifty-dollar bill folded like an airplane, and under the little plane was a huge jar of royal African hair gel, and under the hair gel was a big bag of black-eyed peas, and under the black eyed peas was a bottle of carrot oil. And the reason that little ol' bag stood up so proper like was because there was this cute little notebook with a pretty black teen girl and another post it said, "Tasha, from Dr. L. Watkins."

"Sweet Jesus, thank you. Now I can do Tasha's hair," her hands entered her apron pocket and grasped the little paper with the digits she had scribbled from LaMar's platinum credit card. She shredded the paper between her fingers purging her soul. A silent tear fell and made a dark stream against the rough brown paper. Margie never cried.

Sam stood next to Dee's coat rack and held out his hand in truce to Lamar, "Dr. Watkins, may I speak with you about Kevin Abbott. I have some information that may help you. Can you please spare a moment?"

LaMar was surprised the man knew how to speak in sentences, used proper grammar and could behave politely.

Ali glanced back, "I gotta head back to the office, see you later."

Sam and Dr. Watkins returned to the booth he had just left.

"Dr. Watkins, you back again?" she seemed coy, "Liked my coffee huh?" Margie's face had relaxed and she poured Sam a coffee he hadn't asked for and prepared a cup for LaMar.

"I'd prefer hot water and a tea bag, please," he refused to get stuck with another cup of Dee's famous beige brew.

"Be right back Doc," Margie winked, "How 'bout a piece of pie for you Sam? Fresh baked ya know. Made with the best apples in the county, some old garage owner's tree."

"Thanks Margie. A piece of pie is perfect. Then me and the doctor have some private business to discuss," Sam half smiled.

"I'll stay out of your hair Sam, what little there's left of it," she chuckled as she entered the kitchen.

"Follicly challenged, Margie, now scoot!" Sam wasted no time, "Kevin arrived in town early last summer with a trucker when the weather was beginning to warm. He stopped into my garage looking for a girl named Tasha. Only kid I knew by that name was Margie's daughter. Told me the girl was mixed, light skinned so I took him down here to Dee's to talk to Margie. It was like her prodigal son had come home. She threw her arms around the boy and told me he'd stayed with her a couple times in the city and helped her around the house."

"Kevin seemed like a nice kid. He reminded me of my son. Shaun was a good kid, but always into trouble and never seemed to know how he got there. Kevin walked like Shaun, slapping his feet to the earth like he was afraid he wouldn't connect. He ate like him too, chewing with his mouth open, picking up food with his fingers, slapping his tongue on his teeth to chew – Deb used to tell Shaun he ate like a Guernsey cow." Sam laughed.

Dr. Watkins took notes.

"Idioms, double meanings, metaphors – Shaun rarely caught on and acted upon the literal meaning. If I told him, 'I'm going to kick the tires and find out.' I'd catch him ten minutes later kicking the police car's tires. If I asked him what he was doing, he'd say 'finding out.' I'd say 'finding out what.' He'd say 'I dunno, you told me to.' "

"He resembled Shaun more than his red hair and freckles; Kevin is small, spontaneous, and doesn't generalize. Just because you think he knows what you're saying, it doesn't mean he understands a thing you said. If Shaun was in Kevin's place he would have answered all the interrogators questions honestly and all his answers could have been dead wrong."

LaMar leaned forward interested in what Sam had to say.

"Shaun, like Kevin was a good kid with a big heart, in need of friends. Shaun's personality, like Kevin's when shaped in a safe environment ingratiated the people of Riverdale, like Eddie at Hans Hardware. Deb and I have a soft spot for these kids."

"When you raise a special kid for twenty-nine years you know the kid inside out. You get to look behind the stage before any of the glitz and cover up gets put on. I caught Kevin reading a little card he carried in his pocket that told him what to do when he got stressed and afraid he'd explode. These kids don't have the emotional resources to cope with life's normal demands. They are vulnerable and easily eaten alive by human predators and police. Deb and I used our Shaun parenting skills with Kevin. Both boys tried so hard to be accepted."

"Kevin filled a gap in our lives with his quick smile, naiveté, and kindness to my customers. Poor kid didn't have anything. I gave him the job. Margie let him have her sofa. I think he paid her a bit to help out."

"Deb and I think Kevin and Shaun were knit together by the bond of alcohol consumed during their mother's pregnancies. They are bootleg brothers. When I met Kevin I was sure he was a clansman. Kevin has so many of the same mannerisms as Shaun did. No one can put back what alcohol stole and no one is exempt if you drink while you're pregnant," Sam sadly continued, "Shaun entered adolescence at age twelve and was still a teenager at twenty-nine. He was impulsive, made choices without thinking and obsessively completed crazy idea missions. Kevin behaves the same way. Their brains circumvent their behavior. They'd run off the end of the pier if frustrated. Shaun never managed that curve with the four-wheeler because he didn't want to hit a rabbit. He never considered hitting the tree. No cause and effect whatsoever. He never drove a car, but we figured a little ol' four-wheeler was okay. Kevin is still alive, in prison. But prison will kill him; just as sure as the tree killed Shaun. Prison will take hunks out of him you can't replace. He's a little boy in a man's body."

"It's the no-seeums of FASD that eat the spirit and I didn't help with my expectations. He's been gone two years and now I finally see through the acting these kids put up for their audience. If I were a betting man, I'd say Kevin has the same brain damage Shaun had, the same brain disorganization Margie does. Kevin took to Margie like a magnet. If Shaun were alive I could see them creating a union. She's one nice lady, her assets were Shaun's deficits."

LaMar noted support of interracial relationships, even for his son. Nothing in life was clear and Sam was emerging as a diamond in the rough.

"I don't think Kevin murdered Doc. I did initially. Then I got to comparing what I knew about Shaun and what I thought I knew about Kevin. Shaun never learned to use a firearm and he was around them his whole life. He didn't like the noise or the recoil. He never joined the Hardware Men at the gun club, even though he enjoyed being in our company. As far as I know Kevin only held a gun two times, once when he found Doc's 44 in Mike's truck and then when Mike took him shooting down at the gravel pit. I had the kid around me for almost four months. He talked tough, but like Shaun he was a pussycat, an engine backfire scared the b'jeebers out of him."

"The day after he went to the gun range with Mike it sounded like he shot all the ammunition out of Hans Hardware. Then in the quiet moments he asked me how come his arm hurt when he only shot twice."

LaMar checked his watch realizing Kevin's parents would be arriving at the jailhouse within moments. "Thanks a lot, Sam. Please excuse me, I have a meeting. If you think of anything more give me a call."

"See you around, Dr. Watkins," Sam held out his hand. There were obviously two sides to the man.

Margie filled Sam's coffee as he sat for a quiet moment before returning to the garage. Two years ago, Shaun swerved and hit a tree to miss a rabbit that ran across the trail. It was like Shaun to protect innocent lives. The rabbit made it to safety. Shaun died instantly. Mike, a sweet, fun-loving and active boy who loved to please people was thrown from the all terrain vehicle hitting his head against a large boulder. He cracked his helmet. Thank God, he was wearing the helmet; he was unconscious for less than twenty minutes and hospitalized overnight. He had some recovery work, headaches and blurry vision, but at least he was alive. Mike remembered the rabbit.

Since the accident Mike had been seeking conflict, especially with his father. His anger had escalated and Doc spoke to Sam about his concern for Mike the night before the murder. They discounted the behavior as typical wing spreading, though Sam felt Doc held back something. He'd commented on Mike stopping his meds and self-medicating with a bit of weed, some beer, cigarettes and some of Pott's homemade secret brew. Mike had come to his father because he wanted to sleep again. Doc refilled his medication and Sally had mentioned she caught Mike staring and shaking his head to regain composure. His hand trembled. She wasn't sure if this was repercussion from the accident or if Mike was grieving as they were both depressed. At least his appetite was ravenous, but she'd set an appointment with his neurologist. Meanwhile Mike was busy applying for city college scholarships hoping to study private investigation and criminology. Sally seemed proud of Mike. He was one kernel of life she had left.

▼

Dr. Watkins observed Kevin from the small window of the solitary cell. Upon waking he had begun pacing, but not screaming. Back and forth. Back and forth. One trip around. Back and forth.

"He's sleeping like a baby under that mattress," a guard commented.

"Some piece of work." LaMar closed Kevin's thick file.

Kevin didn't understand why everyone thought he shot Doc Johnson, but there were times his mind played tricks on him. He used the gun with Mike, but Doc wasn't there and the last time he had seen Doc was at Sam's. Maybe he saw him when he was drunk. Sometimes he forgot things, but killing someone was big. He should remember that.

"I'd like to meet with Kevin and his parrents in the courthouse library. I need to obeserve in a more normal setting to gain behavioral insight. The wire glass window will not be condusive to this meeting."

"Leg irons and two guards, you got a deal, there's a little button under the table if you get into trouble. I'll clear it with the jailer."

▼

Dr. Watkins waited preparing the outline of his court report on his laptop. Hearing the door open, he looked up surprised. John Abbott wore an expensive golf shirt and fresh starched black trousers. He was in good physical shape with lightly graying hair, his arms were tanned and muscular and even though he appeared nearing fifty, his stomach was trim. Lydia was dressed in a fashionable skirt and color coordinated blouse, her jewelry was tasteful, not overly done, but from the reflection of the sunlight, real gold with small gems. From their body posture and stance of entry they projected professional positions. From their tasteful but classic clothing, he guessed they were educated.

LaMar rose to greet them. They seemed startled he was an African American and scanned him as closely as he profiled them. "Thank you for coming, Mr. and Mrs. Abbott."

"Thank you for allowing us the privilege. Please call us Lydia and John," he extended his hand and his wife offered hers.

"Shall we begin," LaMar motioned they be seated and noted the couple holding hands under the table, their subtle smiles toward each other and intimate eye contact. Their marriage seemed more intact than he expected.

"When you adopt a child you believe love heals, but we couldn't love away Kevin's genetic or complex preverbal memories. He had the best environment we could offer, I quit my career as a dental assistant and stayed home to keep him safe. How can you try to do everything right and still get such bad results?" tears fell down Lydia's cheek, "We tried so hard. At three-years-old he'd already been kicked out of three daycares."

With the precision of a baton passed off in a track meet, Mr. Abbott continued. "How can I convey in an hour what we failed to understand in twenty years? What do you do with a diagnosis that your child may have brain damage seventeen years after you should have noticed it? When he demands independence and you discover you did everything wrong because of one piece of information – missed by doctors, missed by schools, missed by the community. We knew there was something very wrong. We were told it was our parenting and if we did this or that then he wouldn't act up. Eventually you start to believe you are incompetent. Then you find out it wasn't your or your child's fault."

LaMar remembered Sam's warning, "Did his mother drink?"

"No one ever said. Does it matter?"

"Perhaps."

"We tried all kinds of 'out of the box' ideas. We gave him a pager because he'd forget to come home. He never did learn to tie his shoes. We thought he was being stubborn. Eventually we bought shoes with Velcro. As a teen he pulled out his laces and flopped around saying it was cool. He never learned from his mistakes. Two days after burning down our garage with all my shop tools, gardening gear, and Lydia's car, we caught him playing with matches. We did everything we could, but no matter what we tried – therapists, summer camps, love, discipline – he slid down to the underclass," John lowered his eyes hoping not to have stepped inadvertently on racial toes.

Lydia took the lead, "A lifetime of misunderstanding led to trouble with the law, substance abuse, anger, homelessness. Lord knows we did our best with Kevin. As an infant we used massage and all the enrichment programs we could afford. He received Title One in second grade, but it took him until grade six before the school felt he was behind enough for special education. They asked if we ever helped him after school, poor kid went to school and then sat and did homework for two or three more hours every night from grade three on."

John added, "He's a smooth talker. People thought he was lazy and so did we. Kevin overwhelmed us. He never saw past his immediate desires. His lack of impulse control, poor judgment and limited memory caused us all frustration. We thought he was willful. The university doctor explained his repetitive misbehaviors were increased due to possible brain damage. We didn't have information about his birth mother. There was no proof of oxygen deprivation, fetal alcohol or early infant stroke. We didn't remember any big bump on the head, though there were times I would have liked to have hit him there myself. I never did. The doctor questioned fetal alcohol because of Kevin's behaviors, life experiences and school records There was no follow up. They provided names of professionals, but Kevin was uncooperative. We'd thrown enough money to the wind."

"We worked hard to keep him out of the morgue during his teens, but he'd sneak away as fast as a dog with a pork chop. He hung with real shady characters, defiant and outspoken. He was determined to get his way. We prayed he didn't end up in prison, but he was a walking time bomb with no sense of conscience or consequence," John paused. "At least now that he's in jail we know where he is and he can't get into trouble."

LaMar smiled thinking about why he had been called to Riverdale in the first place. After meeting his parents, it was clearer now why Kevin was so articulate and if brain injury was correct, superficially competent. But the results of Friday's testing did not indicate mental incompetence. Kevin's GAMA IQ was low normal at 86. His MMPI-2 had K elevations that indicated defensiveness and control issues, not unusual for a recently incarcerated person and there were other pieces of the results that LaMar still needed to question. The PCL-R results showed the lack of affective ability – empathy – to feel concern for others and limited ability to understand or appreciate another's point of view.

The scientific practice of psychology through assessment was fighting the human relationship factor. Even with mitigating factors, LaMar still believed Kevin had sufficient cognitive ability to understand the nature of charges against him and was competent to enter a plea or stand trial for his crime. John had stated that no proven indicator for prenatal or postnatal brain injury existed.

The jailer knocked before entering with Kevin.

Seeing Dr. Watkins, Kevin's smile almost reached the tips of his ears. LaMar felt the warmth and noticed for the first time his flared nostrils on a wide nose with a depressed bridge and no tip. The nose was the same shape he would expect Johnny's to be as an adult – it was Afro-centric, compared to the Euro-Caucasian straight, narrow bridge with refined nostrils and a well-defined projecting nasal tip of his adoptive parents. He noticed the texture of Kevin's hair, the red mop was as kinky as his black locks when they were not in a fade.

Kevin put out his closed fist.

LaMar validated it with a complete street shake. He kept his eye on the response of Kevin's parents.

Kevin turned, "Mom! Dad! Where have you been?" He raced into their arms the way little Johnny raced into LaMar's arms after work. "I tried to find you. You shut off your phone. Did you bring cookies?"

Lydia cupped her hands around Kevin's face and looked him straight in the eyes, "Oh Kevin, are they treating you alright?"

John embraced the pair and Kevin looked thirteen as he buried his head into his mother's shoulder.

"Can I go home now?" he sounded much younger.

"No!" silenced his father.

"But you came to get me. Take me home now!" Kevin sounded more like little Johnny than a man of twenty-one years.

"I don't like it here. I don't like the people. I don't like the food. Take me home now!" Kevin badgered.

Lydia held Kevin tighter, "We can visit you and see if we can get you transferred closer to home."

"Where did you move to?" Kevin asked.

"What?"

"Where did you move? I went to the house, but it looked different."

"What address did you go to Kevin?"

"8246 Pleasant Ave."

"We live south, you probably went to Pleasant Avenue North, honey."

"They printed the stupid bus schedules wrong," Kevin ignored the correction and continued.

"You could have called us."

"I did, I kept trying the number and I kept getting the stupid lady." Kevin mimicked the female computer voice, "The number you are calling is unavailable in this area code. Please hang up and try again."

"Oh Kevin! They changed our area code from 612 to 952."

"I tried again and again. I ripped the phones out of the booths and threw them across the park. They all said the same thing. I ripped ten phones out. The dumb lady wouldn't talk to me. She ripped me off so I ripped her off," Kevin laughed toddler style and then whined. "I don't know where you moved." He quickly switched into control and then out of control. "What did you do with all my stuff? You threw it out. My new tennis shoes! I need them now, I hate these slippers. What did you do with them?" Kevin's voice was antagonistic.

LaMar had not previously seen this behavior and was stunned as the parents swerved in and out of Kevin's confusing conversation.

"Your things are all in your room. We did not move anything out,"

Lydia accentuated the next statement, "I cleaned it up."

"Yes you did! You moved. I lost you." The brick wall of miscommunication grew as the family tried breaking through. Kevin backed off, spat on the carpeted floor and ground the spit in with his chained slipper.

"Kevin! You can't do that!" Lydia utilized mothering 101.

"I'm a grown man and I can do what I want. I don't need you or Dad. I am doing just fine!" he stomped his wet slipper.

His mother reached out to gently touch Kevin's shoulder, he recoiled. Her extended hand pulled back quickly and stabilized in her suit pocket, "I love you Kevin. I do love you."

His father checked his wristwatch and cocked his head in salutation, "See you later son." Then they were gone; the time allotted for their visitation was up.

"I hope they bring cookies next time," Kevin withered.

Predicting the weather was about as plausible as predicting Kevin's actions, but from testing, background history, and general observation LaMar believed Kevin was capable of future violence and could be dangerous. The initial computer generated results of the MMPI-2 showed a definite proclivity to appear unrealistically virtuous and signaled a red flag.

Kevin remained lost his thoughts. He had spent a lifetime being demeaned and it made him tough except when he felt like crying. "For crying out loud. The gang had been family. It was fun in the beginning, but it wasn't real family, then it caught me. I love the hustle. Pocketed a thousand dollars over lunch hour hustling the green. Better after football games. White people aren't afraid of me, no siree." His homeboys liked how he could talk to strangers, and he became a natural outlet with regular clients. "Weren't Mom and Dad great! They found me after two years! I was hiding good too, even the gang boyz can't find me. How come I bought those stupid new clothes? Had money from weed market sales in my pocket, it was raining so I just came in from the cold. I wanted to look fly. Last time I was wet they called me a white soppy dog."

Then he was quiet. Since moving into jail he had begun to hear voices, the jailer told him he was listening to himself which was better than making everyone crazy. If he wanted people to like him he had to shut up. He was getting good practice at thinking with his mouth closed, he was learning to think by himself.

Kevin sat still for the first time in LaMar's memory. His arms crossed against his chest, breathing shallowly through his mouth. Looking little — very little. He remained silent as LaMar entered data feeling a hint of compassion and briefly questioned his testing results. "Do you ever wonder about your birthmother? What she looked like?"

The question went out into the short expanse of air as small talk. LaMar did not have the budget nor energy to put additional services into this young man. The county contract was up and he was ready to refine and type it for the court to deliver later in the week.

Kevin alerted, "I know what she looks like! I have a picture. Social services gave it to me when I was in juvie. You wanna see it?"

"Yes, I would like that Kevin."

"Could you let me keep my pictures in my cell with all my families so I won't be alone."

"I can't promise that, Kevin," LaMar didn't know why he cared.

"Can you let me see the pictures?"

"Yes, Kevin, I promise to make arrangements for you to see your pictures." LaMar walked Kevin with a jail guard back to his cell and removed the green fleece blanket he had folded in his brief case. He had secured approval as a comfort item for Kevin to hopefully stop the screaming that drove Dispatcher Jill Jenkins up a tree.

▼

LaMar watched Kevin wrap in his new blanket. Life was getting better. Mom and Dad found him. Jail wasn't so bad — breakfast, then quiet, then lunch, then quiet, then dinner, then quiet, then sleep. The schedule anchored him in time and now maybe he could have his pictures. Then he wouldn't be alone. His brain didn't make pictures. Exhausted Kevin curled up under the new soft green blanket on top of the thin upside down mattress on the concrete white shiny floor.

"Hey Doc, thanks for the blanket," his impish smile was childlike. "Now I can stop the whiteness."

LaMar looked back through the small window as Kevin put the blanket over his head, "I have darkness and in the darkness I can come out. I can be anybody or nobody, but I don't have to be somebody."

He smiled and waved. Whatever planet this kid came from, he still deserved a special place in the universe. There was such an uncanny innocence about Kevin, even if he was presumed guilty.

"Dear God, tell Mom to send more cookies. Amen."

19
BURIED TREASURE

Q lay in bed in the wee hours of the morning thinking of Gunner and his last two life-changing days. The old man had challenged him to be responsible and he could use the research for his school report to find answers to Gunner's riddles. He decided to write on the historic significance of dog tags and release his repertoire of collegiate words to the unsuspecting faculty. For the first time in his academic history he'd risk sharing his capabilities. The report he avoided last week on World War II now took on a new meaning and captured his full attention. He was not going to waste a minute.

As soon as he heard Mama leave for Dee's he was out of bed and ready for school. He hopped on his bike to arrive as soon as the school media center opened so he could access the Internet.

He raced into the media center, smirking as he saluted the teacher, "Can I use the Internet to finish my report?"

"Oh course Q," her eyes narrowed. Though he had never been in the media center the whole faculty knew of him.

Hans' statement about his missing son rolled over in his mind, "no one ever found the dog tags." He casually typed 'found lost dog tags' in the Internet search and hit www.founddogtags.com and with a click he was into a page that popped up the names from dog tags of over 400 Vietnam Vets. He typed P for Palmquist. What did he say his son's name was? Russ, perhaps Russell, Q scrolled down the list, his heart beat so loudly he worried the media lady would kick him out for noisemaking. What if he found the missing tags? Palmer. . . Palmer. . . Palmquist! And near the bottom of the list was Russell, Russell Palmquist! There was no guarantee it was Hans' son, but he clicked the name and printed the page that included known contact information. He hoped the printout would serve as a ticket to hold the coveted hunting knife. Q carefully folded the paper, pocketed it and for the first time looked forward to visiting Hans Hardware. Hans was no longer a grumpy old man who peeked around the corner with a yellow Labrador puppy.

This is fun. It was like finding buried treasure. What were Gunner's riddles? Gunner was yelling at Sam. He challenged him to keep his boots on for the wounded warriors returning from Iraq. Q typed 'wounded warrior' and found www.woundedwarriorproject.org, an opportunity Sam might be interested in. Sam didn't look disabled, but Gunner had definitely alluded to it, perhaps his injury was hidden. The guys in the Wounded Warrior program seemed to be having fun in spite of their injuries. Sam needs some fun. Q printed out the program and put it in his pocket.

Gunner had said a slew of words Q hadn't heard before. He'd told Sam he'd been getting 'fluffy' and he'd better put a stop to it. Q didn't know what fluffy meant except for marshmallows and clouds. He searched on fluffy and K9, and that sent him to www.k9fluffy.com where he came face-to-face with Fluffy a military K9 who resembled Sam's dog Reg... a soldier in Iraq found an abandoned mongrel. He wanted to keep reading but it would be pretty stupid to arrive at school ninety minutes early and be late for first class. Q printed the project to help military K9 teams.

Somehow one report multiplied into four new ideas that were going to involve Gunner, Hans and Sam and perhaps his whole history class. For the first time he was excited about a school project. The first bell rang and once again he watched the clock, excited to share with Hans and Sam.

▼

Riverdale was a funny place where you could leave your bike for twenty minutes without worry. Behind the window display holding the knife, Hans and a little girl were unloading hunting gear. Hans reached out and grabbed Q's collar as he rounded the corner by the canning jars, "Whoa, buddy, what's the hurry?"

Two days ago, Q would have been mad as a hornet that any old white man grabbed him by the shirt collar and admonished him. But today, he smiled because he had something bigger than his own ego in his pocket. Out of breath he handed over crumbled paper. "Hans, Hans, I found it!

Remember you said you never got Russell's dog tags. Guess what?"

The small blonde haired girl stood behind the boxes, tilted her head like a puppy and smiled at him. She wore tall green boots with big yellow eyes bumping out at the toes.

"Whoa, son, what are you saying?"

Q pointed to the name Russell Palmquist he had circled with his turned apple pen, "Right there, that might be your son. The story says some vets went back to Vietnam on a vacation and they bought a whole bunch of the dog tags at a back alley kiosk in Ho Chi Ming city. It says they are looking for the owners. See, some of them say 'alive.'"

"Well, I'll be, I've got to call Gun ——," Hans stopped mid-sentence as if someone had just pinned his happy bubble.

"Bobpy P, you can't call Bumpa. You have to use prayers," the little girl placed her two small hands together.

Q was silent, did something happen to Gunner? He was afraid to ask. "Thanks son, I'll give them a call and see about it. It was really nice of you to think of me. Come by anytime."

The meeting hadn't quite been what he expected, Q turned to walk out, stopping in front of the hunting knife. He looked back at Hans who smiled and nodded his permission to pick it up. Q had never held such a fine knife before. He stroked it gently. It would take a lot of apple picking and he wasn't sure if the tree had enough apples. He carefully laid the knife back in the display and waved to Hans. The little girl waved shyly with an impish smile, her shoulders pressed up to her ears. He crossed the street to the O'Riley Garage. His heart pumping, perhaps Sam would tell him if Gunner was all right.

▼

Sam was busy inside the hood of an old maroon Buick and Q didn't want to startle him so he sat quietly watching him work. At least he had something personal in common with Sam. Both he and Sam had gotten a verbal whooping from Gunner yesterday. He wondered if Sam's ears still burned with the power of each word Gunner had said to him.

Sam looked up, "Hi kid, what can I do for you?"

"Remember when Gunner said keep your boots on for the men and women coming back from Iraq? Well I found this Wounded Warrior program," Q handed Sam the paper, dropping a second sheet that hovered in the air before it landed in front of Reg III, who, seeing the paper as a game retrieved it, and delivered it to Sam.

"What you got old boy? Operation Military Care, the United States War Dog Association: Help Needed," Sam read the paper; his German Shepherd sat at attention, head high as if he had delivered personal orders to his commanding officer.

"K9 and Soldiers In Need of Care. . . Please send chips in containers, no bags; hot cocoa, hand lotion, instant soup, beef jerky, writing materials," Sam looked at Q and smiled. "You want to run an operation son, I think we can do it. Bet the whole community might pull together for this one, we got the Lions and the churches. We could advertise in the local paper and package it here in my shop. I'll call Gun —." Then Sam did exactly what Hans did. He shut up and stared.

Q looked sternly at Sam, "What's wrong with Gunner? Hans did the same thing you just did."

"Yesterday after the game son, Gunner died."

"No, he can't die! He can't leave me! I just became his friend!"

"He lived a good life son. It was his time to go. The last thing he did was tell me off," Sam stared at the paper in his hand.

"The second last thing he did, was tell me off," Q wanted to run out of O'Riley garage and never come back. He wanted to run all the way to Gunner's farm, and Gunner's woodshed, and Gunner's cottage, and find out if it were true. Why, when he finally decided to put his trust in another man, did he go? Just like Daddy.

He turned to run, but Sam pulled him close. No man had held Q since he was a four-year-old. "Life goes on Q. Life always goes on. Now it's me and you to carry on," Q was surprised by the gift of strength given in the embrace. Both men were silent.

Miss Ali shattered the silence, "Sam, I came by to let you in on the details of tomorrow's funeral."

"So soon?" Sam asked.

"We're honoring Ma Lu's wishes. She wants you to do honors at Gunner's internment at Fort Snelling."

"I'll ask Father Flanagan if he'll loan us his fifteen-passenger van, then we can get by with just Gleason's hearse and one vehicle."

"Can I come?" Q asked.

"Ask your Mama, " Miss Ali said.

To his surprise Mama said yes.

It didn't seem right that he felt this much grief over an old man he hardly knew. In life Gunner gave Q the treasure of his time; in his death Q understood the value. Gunner's death was like an exclamation point in his life. A loud command to get up, do something, and be somebody.

LaMar pulled into O'Riley's Garage to top off his tank. He could have used his credit card, but Sam's overture earlier in the day had made him think this was a man with knowledge he may need, "Sam, heard you have a pretty yellow bi-plane at the airport, someday, I'd like to see her."

"Yep."

"If it's a nice day Thursday, I'm thinking of flying my Cirrus to deliver the court report. Is there a way to get from the airport back into town?"

"You can use the airport station wagon behind the blue hanger. The keys are under the rear right tire in a little black box."

LaMar looked surprised.

"But, I'll pick you up if you want." Sam reached out his hand and their eyes met and the distance narrowed further.

24
LAST RITES

The day was as drizzly and grey as Q felt. Mama insisted she be a part of paying her respects to a man she hardly knew because he had meant a lot to Q. "That man he did something to you Q. He lit a spark I haven't seen since you was a little boy." She stayed home from Dee's to accompany him to Gleason's Mortuary for what Ali referred to as the local 'short 'n sweet', before Military Honors at Fort Snelling.

Q remained quiet. There were no words to explain how he felt. He was too big to cry in public, so he shut up. He cried enough in his room.

Ma Lu had requested that no one splurge on flowers and no one listened. The arrays of golden sunflowers, purple asters, white daisies, and Black-eyed Susan's filled the room and as Q entered the sun broke through the clouds and it's rays directly pointed upon a simple closed pine box drilled with small holes. Eight six-foot potted hardwood trees surrounded the box symbolizing each decade of Gunner's life. They created a backdrop of a woodland scene; the small green pinecones hung from the potted trees nestled between ivy and a variety of ground covers. Ma Lu and the Hardware Men would plant them in the open area by her cottage.

Finally Q knew what those funny little green things were, he overheard Jared explaining to another person that one of Gunner's favorite hobbies was making fine home-brewed German beer. Jared seemed excited to try a new brew with the new hops variety after next year's harvest and name it Gunner's Brew. Smitty volunteered to hold a tasting.

The early morning mood was more festive than sad as people told

stories and laughed about Gunner. Pastor Wilson and Father Flanagan
cajoled that Gunner finally settled his spiritual self and that they were
proud of Ma Lu risking to step out. Two pretty college girls sat silently in
the back of the room looking as if their world had spun out of control.
They looked like Q felt. He spent his knife's savings for a a white shirt and
black tie. He had carefully selected his tightest pair of pants and snugged
up his belt.

Most everyone had dressed nicely and Q's fashion choice fit in. Jared
wore a black tailored suit; his green John Deere baseball cap was replaced
with a small round embroidered baby cap. Tiny Ma Lu nuzzled into his big
body and smiled proudly. Jared wrapped his strong arms around her, and
Q overheard her say, "You are now the patriarch, it's about time you pro-
fess your faith." Jared said some word Q didn't understand and John
Gleason passed out black ribbons of cloth. Q watched as the family tore
each strip down the middle. Slowly, ever so slowly, Q tore his too. It was
time to go.

▼

Mama told Q that a funeral was a time to give and receive heart care.
So why would a little girl bring a present for a dead person?

Kissy carried a huge cardboard box, sealed with duct tape, knot-tied
with pink and purple ribbons, decorated with stickers, magic markers, and
at least a dozen scattered holes used as flower centers. She struggled to
bring it to the white fifteen-passenger van. The box, like Gunner's casket
had more holes. Another perplexity Q had not yet figured out.

"Can I help you?" Q bent down.

"You be careful, they are my and Bumpa's treasures," she was very
determined. "Daddy and me found them and we share them. Bobpy P
paints the numbers on with finger polish. Then Daddy and I take them
home, only Daddy couldn't go so Bumpa said he'd go, and now Bumpa
can't go. I'm gonna' do it myself."

"Kissy, your box can ride in the back of the van," Jared intercepted.

Something or some things were making hurried little scraping
sounds. Q put the box down, next to two rifle cases under the last seat and
then climbed up to sit in an empty row. He was surrounded in strange circumstances. Holey boxes, rifles, a van as big as a bus filled with all white
people? Q hated buses and he really hated buses filled with only white
folk. Ever since he had changed from a cute little nap haired brown boy to

a young black teen male he had felt like the loser in the pickings for Red Rover. The seat next to him always remained empty, like an invisible wall had risen stating tainted. He noticed it also happened to other black boys his age, and to avoid the loneliness he'd made it a habit to 'ride deep' on city busses by traveling with a crew of friends. Then they could laugh, joke and goof off, but more importantly avoid the one empty seat next to them if they rode alone. Didn't people realize that being ignored because you were feared felt violent? That in their unknowing ignorance of what to do, they made him feel demeaned and that the very act of ignorance made him uneasy and when he was uneasy he got angry. Those scared people with their solemn unfriendly faces could have broken through his anger with a simple smile, hello, or "how ya doing?" Once judged Q refused to smile first. Wasn't that what Rosa Parks was all about?

Q sat alone as everyone talked and laughed outside the van. Chatter, chatter, chatter, white folk chatter. Q zoned out. People would rather stand than sit next to him. He was there first, it wasn't right to stand up and let two seats go, just so one white person could sit down.

He had made sure he was clean, didn't have cooties and except for Friday had been a perfectly nice person in Riverdale. He would test these people and see if they thought he was an untouchable by sitting on the outside of a bench seat. He watched the small white child freely walking between adults, she seemed to belong to everyone. No one judged her.

▼

Kissy Palmquist was born into the Riverdale community and had always been surrounded by adults. She was born when her grandfather Hans' wife Betty was battling breast cancer and Kissy became the gentle diversion of love and hope for a future. Hans was consumed in caring for his beloved wife so Annie and her infant daughter took over the day-to-day operation of Hans Hardware. When Betty died, Kissy had bolted herself into the store and downtown Riverdale. She took on an adult persona you didn't often see in a young child. Her precocious behavior irritated some who expected childlike responses, however most people found her endearing. Q longed for the freedom the little girl had in the security of her belonging. Kissy belonged to everyone.

"Mommy, I'm going to sit next to the brown boy who wants the hunting knife at Bobpy P's," Kissy smiled and hopped up next to Q and began buckling her seatbelt. She had wanted to get to know Q since she first saw him and she was glad he came.

"We call that black, honey, not brown."

Kissy looked confused.

Q had heard such conversations before and he always felt uncomfortable, not because of the color of his skin, he liked his brown skin color. What he didn't like was the unspoken awkwardness of those not knowing what to say or how to act. It was as if civil rights had created color blindness instead of color acceptance. Who should care if he was black or green or pink? Wasn't he human, undeserving of being singled out?

Kissy had never seen a 'real' brown boy and the ones on television or storybooks didn't count.

"God's pretty smart," she whispered to Q, "He made brown and gold and pink people. He should have made purple people. Sometimes I get a boo boo and I turn a little purple. Mommy calls it black and blue. I don't see any black, and I only sometimes see a little bit of blue." Kissy motioned her finger for Q to come closer and she whispered, "Mommy's wrong, you're not black and neither am I." Then she raised her voice loudly, eyes smiling, "Brown boy, do you turn black and blue when you get a boo boo?"

The chatter stopped. Every person froze, as if a little child acknowledging the different color of his skin was a verbal transgression. Q thought the question was funny. She was a cute little kid and little kids asked honest questions. They weren't riveted in stretched politeness like the twelve adults now giving him their rapt attention.

He smiled, obviously they didn't know he had compared his skin color with his Black brothers and sisters for years making up luscious names for hues of brown and golden tones – flavors of ice cream and candies and nuts, the goldens of honey and butterscotch and caramel, browns of earth, and herbs, and woodlands. They obviously didn't know that brown was yummy and scrumptious and as a child he felt superbly special being Mama's little chocolate kiss. He watched Annie clamor into the van and whisper in her child's ear, "Kissy, we don't talk about color," as if it was bad or something to be ashamed of.

Pastor Wilson broke the deadly silence when he delivered a cooler from the Riverdale Lutheran Church of Peace Ladies Altar Guild filled with tuna salad sandwiches; fruit, cookies and sodas for the afternoon trek north. There was a sudden urgency to get on with it and the van quickly filled with Annie and Hans; Ali, Jared, Ma Lu, the two very pretty girls,

Sam and Deb O'Riley, two of the Hispanic men Jared was working with on Saturday and another man wearing a tiny little hat like Jared. There was one empty seat, Sally Johnson had declined the invitation and sent a card, saying it was too soon for her to attend another funeral. Trapper sat in jail.

That empty seat was where Q had expected it to be, next to him. Kissy appeared to be delighting in it's emptiness and had quickly filled it with a scrubby brown teddy bear, a dirty old blanket, and a scuffed up backpack stuffed to the bursting with who knows what.

Sheriff Larry dressed in a black suit and tie seemed more like a real person when he looked like everyone else. Ma Lu requested Larry drive the slow way up the meandering Mississippi River. She wanted to enjoy the vibrant colors and the cloud reflections, "sharing a final road trip with Gunner." Larry obliged and climbed into the driver's seat. The van started hard, whining and sputtering. Larry scrunched up his face as if those actions could help turn over the engine. It seemed to work as he commanded "Come on Betsy."

Q smiled, remembering Gunner's beloved old green tractor.

While the adults chatted and laughed, Kissy wiggled and lightly touched Q's brown hand with her little pink finger making a figure eight. She didn't want Mommy to hear so she whispered, "Do you use Bumpa's black soap or his white soap? One time I used his black soap and it turned me all black. Is that why they call you black? Bumpa always plays jokes and he got it for the workmen so they looked like they couldn't get the grease off, only it made me look like I got in the grease."

"They just call me black, like they call you white," Q answered. Kissy looked confused, she had never been called white before, she had been called Kissy by most everyone, Monkeyshine by Daddy, and Bumpa called her a purple people eater. Sometimes Mommy called her April when she was naughty, but no one had ever called her white. Besides, she was more pinky-yellow.

Kissy pulled her well-used gold cigar box of 120 crayons out of her backpack. It was the biggest box of crayons Q had ever seen. She busied herself removing all the brown, and pinks, and goldens. Q remembered doing the same as a small child with his small package of twenty-four.

She found a color and handed it to him, "Read it," she ordered.

"Burnt Sienna," Q read.

Kissy smooshed up her pug nose and shook her head, "No, you're not burnt." She handed Q two more brown hues.

"Mahogany, and this one is Brown," Q smiled.

Kissy laid both crayons on the back of Q's hand, "Nope." Then she took out a little stubby well-used crayon, the words barely visible with most of the paper torn away. She handed it carefully to Q, her blue eyes sparkled. "Do you know what color this is? Be careful. It's my favorite. It's almost gone."

"Fuzzy, that's all I can read, the paper's ripped," Q looked at the white smooth haired little girl who was gently rubbing his hand.

"It's your color. It's Fuzzy Wuzzy Brown. I think you are fuzzy wuzzy, that's what I use to color teddy bears and doggies. See here is black and here is fuzzy wuzzy. You only get fuzzy wuzzy brown in the giantest box. You are my favorite color besides purple. Do you turn purple too?"

Q liked Kissy's freedom in her innocence; her questions made him smile. He had wondered as a little boy, why he didn't get to become a rainbow like his lighter skinned brothas' when he got hurt.

"What's your name?" Kissy asked.

"Q."

"Ha, that's a letter! You can't be called a letter. I'm calling you Q Bear. You can be my fuzzy wuzzy Q Bear. My name is Kissy," Kissy wrapped her tiny arm around his forearm, grabbed her worn brown teddy and blanket, and laid her soft blonde hair on his fuzzy wuzzy brown arm. Her little tongue gently licked his skin and she looked up quizzicly.

"You think I'm a chocolate Easter bunny, Kissy? I probably taste just like you," Q whispered.

Kissy giggled lickings the back of her hand.

Q liked her; she was a nice little kid, who soon fell asleep with warm drool spilling down the side of his arm and he admired the small sleeping child. He had wanted to touch that kind of shiny smooth hair since he was a small boy, but he never felt he had permission. Carefully he raised his hand to her head and gently stroked the tiny head. It felt like a kitten.

Kissy cuddled closer, purring with little snorting sounds, snuggled on the lap of her very own giant, real live teddy bear.

Q gazed out the window as the fall tree colors and the quiet Mississippi River moved by. If he half closed his eyes he could make the colors blur like a Monet painting. Annie looked back and smiled approvingly. He felt good.

Larry pulled off the road into a rest stop. The green sign publicized Lake Pepin. It was a place where the mighty Mississippi River appeared more like a large lake than a river. The weather had cleared and the scene was striking. Sailboats caught the wind and floated quietly in the foreground of majestic orange, yellow, and red hills. Kissy rustled and looked up smiling at Q "This is where I give my present to Bumpa, do you want to help me Q Bear? You carry my box."

Q helped Kissy fetch her box, "Where are we going Kissy?"

She removed her black patent leather shoes and replaced them with her green rubber froggy boots with the yellow eyes that wiggled as she walked. "Down to the river beach, at the bottom of this hill. Come on!" Kissy shouted.

Q looked back. Hans alias Bobpy P waved him on with an okay.

"Do you have a Daddy, Q Bear?"

"I guess so."

"I have a Daddy. His name is Trapper. He's in Uncle Larry's Jail. They wouldn't let him out today, he's supposed to help me with the box, and then Bumpa said he would help. Neither Bumpa or Daddy could help me, they're both gone. Put the box down Q Bear," Kissy ordered, her little hands placed solidly on her hips, her small mouth in a solid pout.

"You must learn to accept orders before you can give orders," Gunner's words replayed in his head. Q set the box on the white sugar-sand beach by a line of riverweeds and he began untying the ribbons Kissy had looped and snarled.

"Bumpa said I'm knot challenged, you'll have trouble."

Q continued working, keeping an eye on Kissy busily picking up rocks too big for her to carry and dropping them with a large plop at the water's edge of the mighty Mississippi River. "I'm making an eddy so my friends will be safe when I let them go. Daddy and I take Eddie with us, he wears his yellow rain suit in case it rains, but it never does. Daddy says we make the eddy, and the arms of the eddy are safe. I think we forgot Eddie today; he should have come, too." Kissy's bottom lip pouted over her top lip, her big blue eyes looked down sadly as she shrugged her tiny shoulders, "Oh well."

"Don't open that box, Q Bear!" Kissy bossed.

"You must learn to accept orders before you can give orders," Gunner's words replayed in his head, realizing Gunner was never going to really

leave him. Q looked down at Kissy's rock pile. She was right; behind the rocks the water was quiet and smooth. She ran to her box and began removing the grey tape. "Hi, Fatso! Hi Slow Ball!, Hi Speedy! Time to go home. It's almost winter. It's time for your 'hide or nation.' "

"You mean hibernation?" Q questioned.

Kissy ignored him and reached down to pick up a four inch painted turtle with a purple number five on the back of its shell. She gently carried the little critter to the still water, singing lullebyes as she walked. Q picked up two turtles and brought them to Kissy who addressed each one by name, kissed the wiggly thing on the lips and sent the reptile on its merry way with a good luck wish in baby making and a sleep tight for 'hide or nation.'

"Has your daddy been to jail? My daddy gets out in time to carve pumpkins. He promised he wasn't going back never ever. He's been there a long time. It was hot summertime when he went. I like it better when he sleeps at my house. My daddy is nice. He likes boys. I'm a tomboy, that's almost a boy. My daddy drank 'al co hall.' It was bad behavior and Daddy got a time out like I do when I'm naughty, only Daddy sits in a 'sale' and I just sit on my little chair."

Q's mind drifted as Kissy chattered. He didn't want a conversation about daddies and jail. He was about her age hiding under the bed when he lost his daddy and he knew more than anyone, how she felt. Kissy's daddy was lucky serving 'white time.' She would still be a little girl when he came home. His father was in the Federal Prison and Q would be almost full grown if he ever met him again.

His daddy was a good man too and he loved him just like Kissy loved Trapper. His daddy zoomed him on his feet while he pretended to be an airplane. Every time he thought of Daddy he heard Mama, ferocious about no drugs, no malls, no hanging out. Her voice rang loud and clear in his brain, "You get your black butt past twenty-one. You stay away from drugs and gangs! I don't want to meet you some night in the morgue! Black boys get killed fifteen to one white boy!"

Q closed his eyes visualizing Mama's spatula waving at him in a tirade. "At fourteen, you ain't got a lick of sense. Too easy to join the ranks of jail and underemployment. You be nowhere fast!" Mama started the lecture when he was twelve and seemed to repeat it at least once a month whenever he did something dumb. Perhaps she felt if she said it enough, by the time he was fifteen he'd have it memorized. Mama burned her words into his mind like tar on pavement. She expected him to walk the straight and narrow. Unknown to him so did his Daddy, who prayed for him daily on his knees in his 7x10 foot cell while he still hoped for a letter from Mama. It had been ten years.

Q handed Kissy turtle number seven. Her cheeks were wet. "Daddy told me to be a big girl and not cry until he came home, but, but," her tiny pink lip quivered. "I love my Daddy. Bumpa went to heaven. I, I, I have to give away Skeezicks too. He's my favorite. I love you Skeezicks, go make beautiful turtle babies for next year." Her tears flowed freely.

Q wiped the warm liquid from her cheeks and felt his own eyes moistening. He was Mama's protector. At four when daddy left he declared himself the man. Why was this little tiny girl chokin' him up? He promised himself he would never cry. Q picked up Kissy and held her, "It's OK sweetie, Bumpa's our guardian angel. I think he's sitting on that big fluffy cloud watching you right now," Q pointed skyward. "He's watching me too. The two of us need our own big 'ol angel to watch over us."

Kissy sniffled, "A big Bumpa angel with his boots on!"

Advising Kissy made Q feel better. He picked up the tattered box and carried it and the child up the hill.

"Will you keep your boots on for me Q-Bear?"

Two days ago he didn't even know what 'keep your boots on' meant, he figured Kissy's understanding today was what his was then. Q smiled and nodded as Kissy buried her head in the crook of his neck. He had never held a little white child before and in holding her he realized how little difference there was between him and her at the same age. He looked forward to someday being a good father.

The river road merged into a freeway. Q smelled the city's closeness. He missed shoulder bumping and streets with houses nestled together. He longed for greeting a brotha' with a knowing head nod.

▼

Fort Snelling Cemetery appeared in a wide expanse of rows of white headstones. Q tried counting them. He used multipliers, but it was mind-boggling. Gunner told him to count the cost of Liberty. He never realized how high priced it was. There were thousands of people who died.

Sam told Hans, "over 150,000 internments last count."

Q figured 'internment' was a fancy word for dead people, he'd look it up when he got home.

In a distance down a narrow road lined with gravestones Q saw Gleason's hearse. John Gleason stood under the canopy speaking with a uniformed guard. Larry, Sam, Hans, Jared, one of the Hispanic men and the other man with the little hat carried the simple pine box to the canopy. Placed on top of the casket was an American Flag, and under the blue honor field with white stars was Gunner. The honor stars covered his head, the red stripes ran down along his legs, Gunner would like that he was blanketed by Old Glory. Q stroked his pen. It wasn't fair. How could one old man change his world so quickly?

Q followed the group; shuffling one foot slowly against his other, kicking up little stones and leaves still carrying the black cloth he had been given. The others seemed to be at peace with this loss, but he was bitter. For Q, Gunner's life was but a day. He roasted in this bitterness hearing only Jared say, "representing a broken heart," Q ripped the black cloth in anger. Flashes of the tomato on the fence post, and the mud in the pigpen, and Gunner sitting on that old tool stool singing behind his back spun him around. The thoughts were so alive he could almost touch them, but they were only thoughts and Gunner was gone.

Forever.

His heart stopped as he remembered the care Gunner took with his old tractor, and his old dog, and his old tools, and his old gun, and his old flag, and his old wife . . .

Slowly, a tour group of men from an old people's home disembarked from a small bus. The last man off the bus struck Q's soul, he carried a trumpet, and the hair under his VFW hat was graying to white. He noticed the fine braiding intertwined in the back of his head. His skin was black. What would the trumpeter play?

The air was silent. Q watched as Hans lifted his rifle to his shoulder and walk with Sam to a line of five nursing home men standing in a row for the final salute. The riddle began to fall into place . . . seven men with seven rifles, three men with three flags, a black man with a bugle and two men standing at the end of Gunner's casket.

"Present arms!" Seven men with seven rifles fired three volleys. Each shot exploded inside Q's body and his hand jumped off his heart as it pounded. He had heard gunshots in the hood; they had created fear in his heart. This feeling was new. It was honor and recognition. It was a feeling of Thanksgiving for Freedom, and Democracy, and Liberty. Gunner's riddle was the Military Salute. It added up to the numbers in 1776.

Q replayed Saturday – the pigpen and lawnmower, the bouncing truck ride and the quiet time turning the pen as Gunner cleaned his rifle, the rifle his son, Jared, gave Sam to shoot volleys over his casket. Gunner's words echoed between his ears, words that were taking root and growing like a beanstalk into a life of their own.

The bugler lifted the legendary silver field trumpet pursing with bravado and humility as had his forefathers. The shining metal instrument had been carried through the American Frontier on the back of a horse ridden by a bugler in the "A" unit of the Tenth Calvary, a Buffalo Soldier, and played by a decorated soldier of the 761st tank battalion in the Second World War – the buglers great-grandfather and father. The same instrument the musician had carried through the sweltering heat of Vietnam.

Q scanned his eyes between the bugler and Sam. *Taps* powerfully filled the air. Honor. Tears. Q sucked down as hard as he could. He couldn't. His tears watered growth in his heart, mind, and soul congealing into a new spirit of male integrity.

▼

Sam watched intently. Angled from the firing parties the bugler raised his field trumpet; the bell of his instrument faced the casket. It was a fluid motion of a master player and Sam had seen few mighty men perform as well. Sam stood at attention with Gunner's 1903 Springfield rifle – a Model 1903A3. The white gravestone dashes stood as stoic banners among the green grass and gold leaves representing thousands of brave soldiers. Twenty-four haunting yet eloquent notes written by General Butterfield were a tender, quiet ending of a day's battle, and a fit finale of a life passing on. Facing Gunner's casket, shooting Gunner's rifle, *Taps* played slowly and expressively with conviction. Every note vibrated ungluing sealed chambers.

The words rolled through Sam's mind, "Day is done, gone the sun, from the lakes, from the hills, from the skies. All is well, safely rest, God is nigh," tapping open the invisible wall Sam raised thirty years earlier. This sounding called Sam back to duty - 1,800 veterans were dying each day – Gunner had given him marching orders.

The bugler rendered a hand salute and brought the trumpet to his side. Sam held the Springfield.

"Order arms," the voice cracked through the echo of *Taps* rebounding between tombstones.

Sam and Hans rendered a hand salute and lowered their rifles.

▼

Q watched as the two men who belted out orders of color and guard folded the flag with the same folds that Gunner had shown him, and Gunner's words replayed the meaning of each fold. He watched as the flag was handed over to Ma Lu, who looked heavenly with her cloudlike hair. Her black dress drew a line of mourning between Gunner's death and life. She looked straight through the flag bearer bringing her the colors.

Lucille Hunter saw her sweetheart in all his glory dressed in his World War II dress blues, saluting her to carry on. Gunner was all of twenty-two and so handsome. Lu yearned to join him. Their earth waltz together was complete. They had danced well, she stepping back as he moved forward, he swaying with her desire for change, twirling together, enjoying the ride. It was the ending of their memory making on earth and Lu wondered what memories she was required to make alone.

The flag weighed heavy in her arms and Lucille 'Rachel Katz' Hunter closed her eyes. Gunner carried her to freedom and taken her son Josef as his own. Gunner had fathered two of her children. Gunner and his family had welcomed her with opened arms into a new land, regardless of her past. Gunner with his smile and twinkling eyes would wait on the other side for her homecoming. Meanwhile she would partake in life on earth opposite the mirror of Gunner's now whitest wall. It was time to make the next move. Ma Lu turned and walked toward Q.

Q watched the tiny old woman walking slowly toward him. He could see Gunner standing behind her smiling. It had to be a mirage.

"Q, I promised Gunner I would give you his flag. He said you would understand." The mirage remained as Ma Lu passed Q the flag.

Gunner saluted. Saluted him!

Q stood tall, and returned the salute. His old friend, Gunner vaporized leaving the dark skinned man with the trumpet smiling. Q felt the eyes of people upon him, he could not move.

"Take it son. It is yours to care for," Ma Lu looked like an angel.

"Huh?"

"Q, come with me," the angel offered.

Q held the flag and followed Ma Lu to the hole where the men had interred the box. Ma Lu reached into the dirt and sprinkled earth upon her husband muttering something in a language he did not recognize.

She turned towards him and Q's eyes grew wet. He gripped the cherished flag. He refused to add dirt on the man he loved. He felt abandoned by the man who was now wrapped in a muslin shroud and tallis within his coffin. A plain pine box for a fine woodworker seemed unfair. It wasn't right that Gunner could fit perfectly into a simple box that fit into a hole to decompose. Ma Lu placed her hand upon the flag and her sky blue eyes penetrated his soul, "It only takes one man to plant a seed, son. There are others who are charged to water and tend to the new planting. Someday you'll understand."

Ma Lu motioned him to follow and trancelike he stepped forward walking past row upon row of memorial markers. She stopped at a tapered marble shaft headstone inscribed with the name Josef A. Hunter. She ran her finger through the lines of the Star of David, then knelt down and rubbed her fingers in the crevices of Josef's name. Gunner's death renewed pangs of long ago loss.

Behind a blue raised vein, Q noticed a tatoo and he held Gunner's flag, speechless.

"Gunner was the only father Josef ever knew," Ma Lu, said quietly, "You don't need to be born from the loins of a man to have that man as your father." Ma Lu kissed the stone inscribed with her first son's name."

Q feared he'd drop the flag. The arms of a strong man reached out to hold his shoulders.

"Perhaps Emit was not such a bad person, but a good person caught up in evil times," she whispered. "They were all just kids, German kids, Japanese kids, Jewish kids, American . . ." her voice trailed.

Jared offered his hand to help her stand and escorted them back to the basin for the ceremonial washing of hands.

Q remained silent.

"I need you this weekend for harvest, Q. Dad said you made a pen with the lathe. I'll help you make the matching pencil. It looks like we have to build Old Glory a home and set up a pole in your front yard."

Q looked up into a set of eyes the same shape and twinkle as Gunner's. Gunner did not leave him alone, he left him his son.

▼

Kissy was waiting in the van holding her coloring books. One for her and one for Q. Surprisingly Q enjoyed the ride home with the little girl and a huge box of color crayons coloring wildlife and butterflies. As a young child he'd never had much chance to color except in school. Mama had struggled to provide soap for clean used clothes. There was nothing left over for the extras like crayons or markers, so he'd never thought of coloring just for fun. Kissy was right, the wilderness held oodles of fuzzy wuzzy brown.

"Just color the animals. I am saving my butterflies for Daddy. He takes me to the flowers to watch my-gray-sun. You can come to see the tigers and monarchs. We have a special place with big purple flowers and peed on spots." At the thought of Daddy, Kissy switched subjects; "You can use my fuzzy wuzzy brown color if you want, after I'm done."

He looked at her and smiled watching her color a muskrat. Her little pink tongue stuck out of the front of her mouth between her teeth as she tried to stay in the lines. "Q, can I tell you a big secret?" Kissy whispered, "Kevin didn't kill . . ." She put her hand to her mouth. "Doc," her voice was barely audible.

Q tried to get Kissy to explain, but she refused.

"Hey son, I heard you've got your heart set on that hunting knife in my window." Hans turned in his seat to Q, "With hunting season and holidays coming up I could use someone in the store on Wednesday's after school. By Christmas that knife could be yours." Q beamed a smile of acceptance as Larry stopped the van outside of Eden Valley Center.

"Hey Q, I thought you might like to go out to the gun range after dinner tonight with Kissy and I. She could use help to cheer on the Hardware Men," Sam offered.

Jared and Hans nodded in agreement, Kissy scrunched her shoulders up to her ears and clapped her hands. She did looked like a monkeyshine.

"Fine, I'll pick you up at seven."

"Thanks. Wow. Thanks." Q walked up the sidewalk whistling. The seeds Gunner carefully planted were already sprouting and taking root in this fertile farming community and four very different men were now watering and tending his tiny shoots. For once in his life he was excited about growing up to be a strong and intelligent man. The new growth stretched him to care about himself, his thoughts and appreciate his African American heritage.

Q reached for his door. What did Kissy know? Could it save Kevin?

CLOUDS OF JOY

Kissy hoped Q-Bear would show up since it was really boring sitting on the fence by herself, especially when she had too much to think about. She always joined Daddy at the gun range, but now she came with Mommy who shot in Daddy's place on the team with Bobpy P. She wished she could shoot. She would shoot for Bumpa, but Bobe Lu asked Auntie Ali to do it because she said Kissy was too little. First Auntie Ali said no, but then Bobe Lu said shoot to honor Bumpa and there was plenty of time to begin mourning in the morning. Kissy had wondered if the double morning was like a double rainbow. All this heaven stuff was new and one thing she was sure, heaven had problems. No one came back once they left. It was not like when Bumpa went on vacation or Bobpy P went to the cities or Daddy got to come back from jail. Bumpa wasn't bringing her back any souvenirs or t-shirts. It wouldn't be the same with just Bobpy P.

Mommy said she'd have to wait eighty years to see him again and that was more numbers than she could count.

In the trap and skeet competition, Mike's Ruffian's tied with the Hardware Men and this would be an exciting shoot-out between the old men and the young bucks. The Hardware Men had all Kissy's favorite people, Uncle Sam and Uncle Jared, 'Silly Billy Jelly Bean' Doc, Bumpa, Bobpy P and Daddy. Life had been hard on the Hardware Men. Doc and Bumpa went to heaven to see Shaun, and Daddy went to jail.

Kissy sat on the gray split rail fence with her red ear 'muffers' to protect her ears and root for the Hardware Men and the new Hardware Ladies, Mommy and Auntie Ali. She used to like watching the Ruffian's do cowboy shooting with their pistols, but she didn't like those big boys anymore. They made fun of Kevin who worked at Uncle Sam's garage.

A while back when she was petting Blue behind the ammo counter she overheard the Ruffian's laugh about how stupid Kevin was. She was hidden under the blanket listening carefully.

Mike and that Potts boy smelled smokey sweet. They didn't used to smell like that. They joked about how funny he looked shooting the 44 with his arm flying off in all directions. They laughed that he could barely shoot the second bullet. They laughed about him shaking like a scared little rabbit after two shots. Kissy felt that naughty hot feeling she got in the middle of her chest when the boys talked about Kevin. Kevin made her laugh. He was nice to her. He told her he liked Mike and the Ruffians, but they sure didn't really like him because Kevin knew about the light bulbs.

Mommy said Kevin was special like Eddy. He helped her crank gumballs and he ate the ugly green ones for her. Then he'd buy her new gumballs until she got pinks, or blues, or purples. All the dogs liked Kevin, too. Daddy said doggies sniffed out the good from bad in people. The Ruffians were calling Kevin stupid. Mommy told her 'never ever' call anyone stupid, not even dogs like Reg, or Blue, or Lucy and especially not people. Never, ever, ever Eddie! Mommy said, 'God never made stupid'. The boys laughed about his moppy hair and called him Carrot Top. Kissy liked carrots. She liked red hair and it was not a mop. She knew they were not talking nice. Mommy would have tapped her bottom for talking like that.

The boys bought more light bulbs because they needed strong glass that could take the heat. The ice was coming and would have to be shipped out on the highway. If he got in the way he'd have to go. Something weird was happening with light bulbs. Kissy felt it. What the boys said didn't make sense. The ice came about Turkey Day for ice skating.

Kissy decided they were talking in secret like she and Bumpa used to before he died. Kissy liked jokes and riddles. She knew the words could mean different things like four and for you, and two and to do. Daddy knew more than anyone in the whole world. Kissy would ask him about what the boys said when he came home from jail at pumpkin time.

After the boys left, Kissy heard Uncle Larry ask Bobpy P to step to the back. That meant go to the ammo counter where she was hiding. And that meant if she didn't scat quick she would be shooed away. She was on a mission. She had to hear what Uncle Larry had to say. Kissy scooted on her knees around the camping display and hunkered down with Lucky Lucy behind the minnow tank still within earshot.

Bobpy P was surprised how accurate a shot Kevin was. Uncle Larry said they found the gun and it had Kevin's prints. Bobpy had said he didn't think Kevin could do it. Uncle Larry told him there were no other prints. Uncle Larry asked to see the copies of the Federal Forms of who had purchased 44's. Federal Forms sounded important. Two shots wasn't the same as four bullets, even an almost five-year-old knew that!

At least Kevin was in jail with her nice Daddy.

"Pull" Bopby P's voice startled Kissy from her figuring out world. Kissy gave the Ruffians a mean face. She hoped they lost the shoot-out. Next year maybe Daddy and Kevin and Q-Bear could shoot too. Daddy was a good teacher. He could teach Kevin and Q. Daddy believed in the possi – billy – a – tees of everybody. It would not be fair if the naughty people won a big prize. She stuck her tongue out at the Ruffians when their backs turned.

"Hi, Kissy. Can I join you?" Q smiled and climbed the fence. Kissy wrapped her arms around him in a bear hug as he pulled her unto his lap.

"Do you miss Bumpa, Q?" Kissy asked.

"Yes."

"Me, too! Mommy said. . . ." Kissy bit her bottom lip trying to remember. "Mommy said, 'Thou art dust, and unto dust shalt thou return'. That's why there were holes in the box. I put holes in my box to keep my turtles alive. Bumpa died."

"Pull!" Auntie Ali shouted.

Bang, stopped Kissy's thoughts.

Q shouted for both teams and Kissy tightened her red shooting muffs with her little hands to protect her ears. She shouted with all her might for the Hardware Men, Mommy and Auntie Ali. When Q shouted for the Ruffian's, Kissy elbowed him as hard as she could and gave him her meanest naughty face.

Riverdale Gun Club wasn't like the hood. Racks of rifles and shotguns were lined up with no worry of theft. Q thought of Gunner and the woodshed with the metal cabinet arsenal, and the woman friendly pleasant smell of Hoppe's No. 9 mixed with the scent of fresh wood shavings

"Pull!" Bang. "Pull!" Bang. "Pull!" Bang, bang. Jerad's off station seven clean, breaking the high house bird, the low house bird and scattering the clay pigeon's pieces into the field. Ma Lu had encouraged him to shoot in celebration of his father's life and he did.

Kissy bounced on the fence post and flashes of Fort Snelling and the vollies exploded in Q's mind.

"Pull!" Bang. Another bird burst in all directions. Kissy put her finger to her lips to silence him. There was no need. Q was already silenced in thoughts of a man who changed his life.

"Pull!" Bang. "Pull!" Bang. The low house eights flew and Uncle Jared nailed a fifty straight.

"Smithereens!" Kissy yelled, hopped up and grabbed Q-Bear around the neck kissing his cheeks. "They won! They won for Bumpa, and Silly Billy, and Daddy and me! I love you Q-Bear. I think they're all sitting on that cloud and smiling. All we gotta do is get us an airplane that can fly us to heaven." She rubbed the top of his free growing dark brown wooly locks and then waved skyward.

"Smithereens?" What kind of word is that?

▼

LaMar struggled sorting through holes and pieces and finally decided to ignore them. The testing results had proven Kevin competent. Sam's comments on Monday and those of his parents provided conflicting information. His optometrist friend Terrence had never heard of white blindness, except in an old college English fictional literature class. There was no historical medical evidence of brain injury, and school reports simply stated mild learning disabilities. He questioned if Kevin's screaming wasn't a ruse of distraction in an attempt to be set free. Kevin's imprisonment seemed more of an imprisonment of the mind that he made up himself. LaMar could come to only one conclusion by adding up the scores and rereading the notes he had taken. By all counts Kevin was competent to stand trial. He was already over budget. To save time and money Kevin would most likely plea-bargain for a jail term that could last his lifetime. All the t's had been crossed and the i's dotted on the court report. The report stated that Kevin was competent to stand trial, the public defender supported his position.

LaMar rang Sam to tell him his Riverdale ETA (estimated time of arrival) was 11:00 A.M.

Three years ago, LaMar and Reggae formed an airplane partnership with a brand new Cirrus SR22. The sleek white airplane with black and red trim, grey leather interior and fancy electronic flight instruments was named November 5385 Charlie commemorating the company Reggae served with three tours of duty in Vietnam.

Shayna packed her little pink backpack the night before adding her favorite flower fairy-coloring book and her celebration box of crayons. She stuffed in her ratty old blankie, her special dolly, a small pillow, and a plastic zipper bag of multi-color fishy crackers. She promised both Daddy and Bups she wouldn't leave any crumbs in their airplane. LaMar packed his own bag. He planned three Riverdale full stops. Reggae picked up LaMar and his granddaughter for the airplane ride to Riverdale.

▼

Kissy joined Bobpy P and Sam at Dee's Café to eat a piece of apple pie and drink a mug of hot chocolate. Nice brown Margie always gave her extra marshmallows and Kissy made it a game to make Margie laugh so she could see the silver dot on her tongue. Mommy had silver cavities, but no one she knew of had a cavity on her tongue. As she picked at her apples, she overheard Sam say he needed to pick up Dr. Watkins at the airport and that Dr. Watkins was flying a fancy new airplane.

In the countryside of Riverdale, Kissy had a rule with the Riverdale Daddies. If they were going to the airport or the sports club, and it was her day to work at the store with Mommy, then she got to ride 'shotgun' on the adventure. Kissy adored flying. Someday she would fly an F/A-18 Hornet and someday she would become the first girl Blue Angel. She loved the jiggled feeling she got in her tummy when Sam and Bumpa flew over air bumps. She liked the whispery feeling she felt when she flew through cottony clouds searching for angels. She especially liked flying at night to see all the house twinkles. And someday she would fly her own loops and rolls and spinaroos with full control of the stick!

Sam turned up the radio and rolled down the windows. The fresh fall air blew Kissy's hair straight up as she opened her mouth trying to catch the breeze and sing along with Sam. She filled in words she knew and made up those she didn't as they pulled into the grassy airport parking area to wait for the fancy new fangled airplane called an SR22. Sam gave Kissy a picture from an airport magazine to help her spot the plane. She clutched the crinkled picture in her tiny hands looking skyward. It was heaven sent to help her see Bumpa, "There it is! There it is!"

Sam saw nothing.

"Riverdale Unicom, November Five Three Eight Five Charlie, five miles north, landing. Request airport information."

"It's them! Sam, it's coming! Get your radio!" Kissy climbed out the window and stood on the truck bed ledge. She rested her elbows on the top of the cab with her hands holding her chin. "Maybe the big brown man has a little brown girl just my size. That would be a real happy deal."

Sam picked up his hand held radio, "November 5385 Charlie Riverdale Unicom, winds 329er at 7, gusts 15, no reported traffic, recommend runway 31."

It was like old times, the past was not forgotten.

"Riverdale, 85 Charilie, do you have fuel on the field?"

"Affirmative 85 Charlie," Sam was pleased with himself. The self-service fuel pump he added on the airport when he leased the new pumps at the garage encouraged airport traffic. Their small town airport now hosted three major annual events – the spring Lion's Smelt Fry, the summer Minnesota Cloud Dancer Aerobatic Contest and the fall Lion's Pancake Fly-in Breakfast. Onfield service made life easier for the local pilots, Yellow Lady, the Hardware Mens' Cessna 182 and Sam's Bellanca Decathlon.

"Riverdale traffic, Cirrus 85 Charlie, one mile north landing Riverdale, crossing midfield for a left downwind, Runway 31. Riverdale." Sam looked up at Kissy now on the roof of his cab stomping her boots and waving her arms. Lucky he didn't care about a few foot dents on his old truck.

"Riverdale traffic, Cirrus 85 Charlie turning left base, Runway 31, full stop, Riverdale." The sleek airplane danced in the sky.

"Cirrus 85 Charlie no other reported traffic," Sam listened closely, there was something familiar about the radio operator, only one other voice said Charlie like that. "Cirrus 85 Charlie, current winds are 330 at 11, no other reported traffic."

The fine airplane flew just off the runway, powering up in a fly-by just off the field. Kissy went wild. It sounded as though a horse was galloping on the cab roof. The plane pulled up and climbed off in a steep ascent, turned crosswind and waved its wings friend-to-friend. Kissy was sure she had seen a little brown faced girl wave to her and she wildly waved back. LaMar looked questioning. Reggae's boyish up-your-sleeves smile surprised him.

"Riverdale traffic, Cirrus 85 Charlie full stop." Reggae had an inkling on Saturday and a few questions on Wednesday, but now he was sure. He made a squeaked landing and taxied to the rust speckled tow truck. Sam held Kissy back as they waited for the engine to shut down.

Shayna applauded and cheered, "Yeah, Bups, you're perfect!"

LaMar gathered his things and helped Shayna clean up.

Reggae hopped out of the Cirrus like a twenty-year-old and saluted, "Corporal O'Riley, get your ass out here! On the double!"

Shayna pursed her lips and put her hand to her mouth, her eyes grew wide. She whispered to LaMar, "Daddy, Bups is a potty mouth."

Corporal Samuel O'Riley couldn't believe his eyes. The well-preserved grandfather deplaning the Cirrus was Sergeant Reg. The thirty years of life experiences they had lost collided into renewed friendship in instant and mutual recognition, "Hey, Corporal you want to go for a ride?"

Sam's eyebrows gave the acknowledgment.

Kissy screamed a resounding, "Yes!" The little brown girl, with the whitest teeth she had ever seen, smiled at her from the open door of the super duper airplane.

Sam threw the truck keys to LaMar, "Take the truck into town yourself. Straight out the gate, make a left and keep going. I got more important things to do than give you a ride, Doc."

"Two hours," LaMar caught the flying truck keys and noticed neither Sam nor his father heard him.

He watched his little daughter reach her hand down to lift up the little blonde girl, and overheard her saying "Hi, my name's Shayna. What's your name? Do you want to be my best friend?" LaMar cherished the moment as his father backslapped and embraced Sam.

LaMar climbed into Sam's truck to finish his work in town. The old Ford was a simple machine with manual gear shift, winch and hoist switches and a button for flashing warning lights. The step up was worn and dirty, a can of chewing tobacco sat on the dash, and upon start up, a twanging country station woke up the gophers at the end of the taxi way. The torn seat was covered with a dark green blanket, a lavender air freshener hung from the rearview mirror and the truck smelled of apples. The unusual mixture of lavender and apple was strangely familiar. Not one to mess with other people's belongings LaMar left the radio station and the volume alone. He placed his briefcase on the seat; glad he dressed casually to deliver the court report. His black slacks and argyle sweater were still overstated for Riverdale, but then so was he.

LaMar settled in to listen to country lyrics of broken down trucks, women that stray, horses that get sick and dogs that disappear. He was pleasantly surprised to discover his prejudiced opinion wrong. Between local community events were relationship and human-interest songs pertinent even to a professional black man. The lyrics spoke of caring and hope in times of sadness, real get-down feelings. True, the melody and rhythm weren't his style, but neither was the urban sound of youth evoking emotion without discipline. It was interesting that both genre's belted out honest forthright anger, though country still provisioned hope.

LaMar, a man of self-discipline drifted off into private thoughts. Hadn't Socrates once said; 'let me write the music of a nation, I care not for who writes the laws. For I will control its people.' The country was being divided, rural against city, races against each other, poor against rich, religions rubbing opposite direction, separating . . . separating . . . not meeting. Perhaps his father was right when he said, 'the music of the youth speaks its heart. It needs strong producers and artists to understand their responsibility in guidance.' In a run down truck, among many he misjudged, LaMar discovered country music was a far cry from the misnomer he had concocted through peers. Neither urban nor country were to be laughed at. They were America. They are America. Rich, poor, all races, all religions, all music – a conglomerate of individuality.

The radio faded into LaMar's consciousness, blasting into his memory . . . Sheena Easton, Kenny Rogers, 1983 singing . . . I know it's late, I know you're weary . . . memories flooding back . . . Granny Henny smelled of lavender and baked fresh apple pie . . . Granny Henny loved him and his Mama . . . Granny Henny whose soft supple arms fixed every hurt and whose prayers shook you to your knees . . . Granny Henny who made your heart feel good and you feel safe.

LaMar hadn't thought of Granny Henny for years and he welcomed these thoughts. She had been buried in the attack that left him without memory of his life before being adopted. He honored the moment by pulling off the road to listen and think. Sometimes treasures are found in unlikely places, Sam's ratty old truck was a gift to his past.

How else would he have combined country music with lavender and apples all in one small space? . . . Granny Henny yelling at Mama for drinking and carrying on with a white man . . . it wasn't right . . . she should think more of herself . . . now she done got herself pregnant and into a mess . . . what will people think?

LaMar directed his mind's eye into his past. His Mama had been one fine woman who had refused like Granny Henny to drink . . . until Mama met red neck . . . Granny prayed in the spirit like Tamara . . . She prayed them through . . . but this day she was gone. Dead . . . already died . . . She could not save him . . . We've got tonight. Who needs tomorrow? . . . and his beautiful Mama with those big green eyes laughed and teased . . . she was drinking . . . he was angry . . . the red hair standing up straight like exclamation points of fury . . . the radio played in the background . . . Let's make it last. Let's find a way . . . Then red neck came at Mama with a bat. LaMar was just a little boy and he ran to tackle him and save Mama . . . the man swung the bat and LaMar fell . . . and then Mama came to him and sat on top of him and she was very pregnant . . . and he could smell the brandy . . . Turn out the light, come take my hand now. We've got tonight, babe, why don't we stay? . . . and the man swung the bat and Mama was gone, blood . . . blood all over everywhere . . . The man screamed in horror at what he did . . . then he ran and all was dark . . . he had no face. Yes, he had a face. A familiar face, but not all of the face just pieces of the face . . . not the eyes, not the nose, not the texture of the hair . . . We've got tonight, babe, why don't we stay. Yeah folks, that's Kenny Rogers and Sheena Easton, Top 10 of 1983. Let's get back after this one-minute break. Corn growers are you . . .?

▼

"This is one swell airplane Reg. It's sure nice to see you again. I never thought I'd see the day Sarge and me would be back in the air." Sam drank in the experience of the moving map display. Kissy and Shayna chit-chattered about daddies, and grand daddies, and mommies, and grand mommies. Sam and Reg smiled as they caught ear-bits of conversation from the little girls who busily introduced and compared doggie differences as casually as they talked about airplanes, skin and hair. Reggae proudly showed off the airplane's details and then offered the control to Sam to pilot the plane.

Shayna had the same crayon box as Kissy, but her favorite color was pink, the same color as the red marks on Kissy's cheeks and Hello Kitty. Her well-used crayon was a paperless stub like Kissy's fuzzy wuzzy brown. Kissy dug in Shayna's box and found Fuzzy Wuzzy Brown, "This is Q-Bear's color. It's my favorite! It's the color on your cheeks too!"

"Do you want to color my fairy or airplane pictures?"

"Airplanes." Shayna handed Kissy her airplane-coloring book filled with old warbirds. "Look there's Yellow Lady. It's a Stearman."

"It is not. It's a PT 17!" Shayna countered.

"Stearman!" Kissy's voiced raised. "Ask Sam. It's his airplane with Bumpa and Daddy."

Reggae turned to offer junior pilot advice that they were both right. "You really got a PT 17 Sam?"

"I reckon I do," Sam smiled. Reggae contemplated getting his hands on its stick. The two little girls colored as the men took off and flew over autumn colored fields, curvy dirt roads and squiggly blue water, a bird's eye view of the troubles of the world.

"Wanna know a magic trick? If you close your eyes when you go up and say 'abracadabra' everything turns into toys and then close your eyes when you go down and say the magic word everything gets big again," Shayna shared.

"I know. Have you seen an angel on the clouds?" Kissy asked. "I'm looking for clouds of joy to find my Bumpa. He died."

Shayna nodded, patting her new friend's hand, "I can look too."

Reg and Sam smiled eavesdropping on the children. "What are you going to be when you grow up?" Kissy asked.

"President of the United States after I'm a Blue Angel."

"Cool, I'm going to be a fighter pilot before I'm a Blue Angel. Then I'm gonna run Bobpy P's store." Kissy put her hand on Shayna. "And marry Q-Bear," she added in a tiny whisper.

The two little girls soon fell asleep together under a very dirty beloved blankie. One dark hand held a favorite pink crayon and a little pink hand held Fuzzy Wuzzy brown. A silky blonde head nestled into a neatly ponyed, bobbled, and braided dark head. Two little hands joined together in a new friendship, backing up two old hands clasped as long lost comrades.

▼

This time when he pulled over to purge locked memories, LaMar was grateful in remembering the beauty of his mother. He savored the goodness of his grandmother. For a moment he simply closed his eyes breathing gently, opening the perfume of his past before he pulled back onto the road.

LaMar promised Sam he would complete his work in two hours. He expected his father and daughter, and Sam and Kissy to wait at the airport and talk after a short ride. He had no idea both his father and Sam were pilots and that just as there was a lot of years to catch up on there were a lot of miles of harvesting fields and exciting things to see from the air.

The concrete bridge with the red, white and purple blooms now felt familiar and welcoming. The county squad car outside of Dee's was non-threatening. And Sam, who he originally pegged as a red neck, had materialized as an old friend of his father and actually provided information that almost swayed into an alternative direction for Kevin regardless of his test scores. Still, he was concerned for Margie and her children, could they retain a piece of their Afro-Centricity amidst rural whiteness? Could they mix in without bleaching out?

LaMar slowly opened the dark heavy red doors of the historic Riverdale Library and a rush of coolness and the smell of aging paper departed into the autumn afternoon. The brightness of the day entered in rays of sunlight dancing on the floor. The old darkened librarian's counter was piled with colorful bound books. He placed his briefcase upon the counter and removed the classics he loved and gained wisdom from, old cherished books deserving a placement in every library, *Black Boy* by Richard Wright, *The Color Line* by Frederick Douglas, *Heroes in Black Skins* by Booker T. Washington and *Letter from Birmingham Jail* by Martin Luther King, Jr. He also added poetry books, one by Phillis Wheatley called, *Poems on Various Subjects* and one by Maya Angelou, *On the Pulse of the Morning* and two novels by Toni Morrison, *Love* and an older favorite titled, *Beloved*. There were so many other African American books deserving shelf placement, but this was a start.

"There's a young woman who will enjoy these. Please place them on the shelves to surprise her."

"Would you like a receipt?" the librarian asked.

"It's unnecessary," and LaMar departed for his final task of the day at the Harris County Courthouse. Besides turning in the report, LaMar had promised Kevin one last visit. Right or wrong LaMar had bribed Kevin to secure the last of the testing data and he would not recant a promise, even for a prisoner. He was a man of honor. He meandered down the sidewalk, gazing in the windows of the shops. People smiled, some waved. Obviously in the six days since he had first set foot in Riverdale word had gotten around about who he was and that he was friend not foe.

▼

Kevin anxiously awaited the kind doctor's arrival. He had a special secret to tell him and for once he could prove he was telling the truth. He had real evidence from a city social worker. He pushed the old lady social worker for a picture of his real mom who got murdered. He needed the picture to know who he was, that he had a real family. He begged and asked so many times she finally gave in and with a mean face handed him the old picture Doctor Watkins promised to help him get back.

▼

LaMar delivered his court report to Sheriff Larry. The decision was final. The testing had proved competency and, except for Sam's comments, merged with some of the things Kevin's parents said, nothing indicated otherwise. Terrence, his developmental ophthalmologist friend, had only heard of white blindness in the historic rhetoric of a fictional book written years ago. Kevin would be sentenced and tried as an adult. Larry was pleased with the findings, and satisfied with the invoice – twenty hours as contracted. He hoped for a quick plea bargain and then prison.

▼

Larry had Kevin waiting in the processing center for he and LaMar to view Kevin's personal belongings. The metal grey box held treasure and Kevin was as excited as Shayna getting to ride in an airplane. He picked up his wallet and held it under his chin in prayer, then biting his lip he gently opened it and pulled out a dog-eared tattered photo.

He handed the picture to Dr. Watkins. "That's my mother and my brother. You asked me, why I act black? I am black. It's in my blood just like you. My mother was real pretty, wasn't she? She died before I was born. My dad killed her."

Dr. Watkins peered into Kevin's hauntingly beautiful eyes that perfectly matched the eyes of the woman in the photo. Her cascading long soft brown hair framed a beautiful café mocha face. There was no mistake. Kevin had his mother's nose. Kevin's nose was the nose of his son Johnny.

"That's my big brother. No one knows what happened to him. The social worker who gave it to me thought he might still be alive. Someone might have adopted him if he lived through the attack. My Dad hit him upside the head to kill him."

The horror and the demon were one and the same; he could no longer walk away. "Oh, I am sure he is still alive Kevin." LaMar held down the top of his bottom lip with his teeth, expressionless.

"Can you help me find him, like you found Mom and Dad? He might know who the real murderer is. I want my big brother."

LaMar paused, "Perhaps Kevin, perhaps." He was unprepared to disclose the facts. This could never be goodbye. The woman in the photo was also his mother, and he, LaMar was the big brother.

"Sheriff, can you copy these photos for Kevin to have in his cell?"

"I suppose Doc."

"Kevin, could I have a second copy of this woman and her son?"

"No problemo Doc, you go find m' Mama's gangsta killa!" Kevin held out his little finger, "Pinky promise? Okay?"

LaMar hooked his pinky, "I'll try Kevin. I will most certainly try."

"See you later, alligator," Kevin beamed his glorious child smile.

"Later it is," LaMar smiled.

"No, it's after while crocodile," the kid's laugh was contagious.

"I must go, Kevin."

His contract ended. His confidence was shaken and his report now chained him to his bootleg brother.

22
RIPPLES

The ripples of one life crash into another like the waves of a tsunami. It begins with a cataclysmic event and washes over the surrounding area with devastation, yet out of the devastation the surviving human spirit heals and continues growth. It is that strength of human spirit that keeps us going and LaMar would not undo his professional findings because his later finding became his brother. He and Kevin shared DNA and blood. Kevin had been right; one piece of paper could make a difference. Kevin's haunting green eyes were duplicates of LaMar's mother's, Kevin's nose a duplicate of his son Johnny's.

One tiny photo held too much information. Stunned, he still did not comprehend or understand the depth of damage his birth mother's drinking caused to his little brother's intelligence, metabolic structure, or the way he viewed the world. In meeting Kevin, LaMar came face-to-face with one of the Western's world's largest white elephants, an invisible disability so vast that few grasp it's magnitude of societal destruction. LaMar faced years of pondering and research to grapple with its enormity. Someday he could step out as a change agent. Today, his first important step was recognizing the disability. Someone he should care about – his little brother – had a fetal alcohol spectrum disorder (FASD).

LaMar feared going forward while Kevin faced years in jail—our current segregated, supportive, and controlled living environment for our adult male population with FASD, a projection of 65% of our inmates, another statistic swept under the carpet. This stealth serial killer remained loose while another of it's victims was captured.

▼

Mike looked forward to graduation and leaving Riverdale. He spent most of his weekends visiting city colleges and when he was home he avoided his mother to focus on Amber.

▼

Restless, Sally transferred to the prenatal unit of Riverdale Hospital, hoping to replace death with life. Her sister lived in Pensacola, Florida and perhaps she could encourage Mike to attend college there. She was proud of him, he was thinking of pursuing a criminal investigation career and had asked Larry for a letter of referral.

▼

Though their adult lives took different paths, Ali and Margie's early growing up experiences knit them together with a tapestry of poverty, alcohol and understanding of abuse. Ali, however was given three gifts at birth that Margie would never acquire, she was born white in a dominant white culture, she was born without prenatal brain injury and she had a high school teacher, Mrs. Everson, who mentored her and empowered her to believe in higher education and finding the right man. Furthermore, Ali's poverty was situational and not generational and though there were seasons of lacking, there were also seasons of catching up that instilled hope even in the direst of conditions. Hope maintained pride that fueled a spirit of independence and self-determination.

Held financial hostage in a professional welfare relationship, Margie and Ali had broken the bonds of professionalism and developed a friendship that shook up the community. Like ebony and ivory on a piano keyboard they used all their keys, sharps, flats, minors and majors, to orchestrate change and to build awareness. Neither kowtowed to political correctness or tried to be someone they were not. Both women were straight shooters of truth and neither embraced the 'isms of age, race, sex, mental capacity, professional, or favorite in the modern world. They interwove their differences harmonically in a melody of friendship. Margie and Ali walked sister pieces of a puzzle, in a new Riverdale symphony.

Margie's street knowledge and simple clarity of thought proved valuable to Ali as more poor city immigrant families like Margie's joined her community. On the other hand, Ali's wisdom, her quick mind and nonjudgmental support nurtured Margie to belong and gain confidence in being a mother, employee, woman and 'true' friend. No one needed to be threatened by Margie or her children. She added texture and color to the tapestry of Riverdale, her cornbread - now on Dee's menu - was a welcome addition to MaLu's sour cream crescent rolls and Dee's Honey Crisp Apple Pie.

Sheriff Larry kept his eye on Margie; he liked her sparkling brown eyes with long curly lashes and her matter of factness. She was a fine lady and he considered asking her out on a date.

▼

Kissy had her very own soft cuddly Q-Bear. He was city. She was country. At almost five, Kissy already knew she had a big job — Q had a lot to learn. Fall was a time of monarch migration; catching woolly bear caterpillars and helping Daddy get ready for trapping. Daddy was soon out of jail. They had pumpkins to carve. Mommy was going to have a baby.

The only time in her life Kissy had her bottom tapped by Mommy or Daddy was when she talked naughty about someone she heard someone else talk naughty about. So she shared it. Mommy called it gos-spit and it was bad, so she promised herself she wouldn't be spitting or gossing ever again. When Kissy made up her mind she became a tin soldier. Steadfast. And soldiers kept their mouths shut and their boots on. They didn't tell secrets!

She figured she knew who killed Doc. She had used her noggin' to figure it all out by herself, just like she'd taught herself to write all her ABCs and 123s to surprise Daddy to come home. Yesterday she wrote all the way up to a hundred!

Kissy was far to little to comprehend the detail or understand she was legally bound to tell. An almost five-year-old was too young to understand guilty to misprision of a felony. She planned to grow up and get smarter, and stronger, and bigger. She would keep watching and listening and asking questions until she was sure. Then, when she was a Blue Angel and a real soldier she would set Kevin free. Daddy always said not to worry about him and that Larry took good care of him. She expected Larry to take good care of Kevin too.

▼

Together, Q, Kissy, and Eddie in his yellow rain coat 'just in case it rained' walked Blue, Sam's dog Reg, and Kissy's dog Lucy around the streets of Riverdale. They were a motley parade and drew smiles of attention without judgement. Unknowingly Q had penetrated the whitest wall

of desegregation. In child innocence, Kissy supported the effort by nick-
naming him Q-Bear. No longer was his dark skin untouchable. When he
did something well, Jared or Bobpy P patted him on the back or wrapped
an arm around his shoulder with a little tug, sometimes they tussled his
hair. When he met Sam at O'Riley's garage they pounded fists and smiled.
Q began confirmation classes at Pastor Wilson's church so under Kissy's
guidance was meeting the 'real' nice boys and not the fakers. Somehow
Kissy had an inside line. She never told him who killed Doc, and Q wasn't
sure if she even knew. Whenever he pressed she pretended to zipper her
lips. He believed in Kevin's innocence, but after attacking Dr. Watkins and
being manhandled by Sheriff Larry at the football game, the law of the
street forbade him to speak.

Q set his sails to carry on. He would become that attorney Gunner
had already declared him to be, and once licensed he would fight to prove
Kevin's innocense. His friend may live in the world differently than others,
but he was not quisquilian. Someday, his ability to spit game would open
doors for the innocent, the present problem he was only fourteen.

▼

Tamara innocently picked up LaMar's trousers, wondering how he
had ever gotten them so filthy. She and the children could drop them off
at the cleaners on their way to the child development center. A handwrit-
ten post-it note fell onto the floor. It was not LaMar's handwriting and it
was female penmanship.

It read —

*I dreamed of finding someone to share my life, a good provider, and a lifelong
friend. Not a dark stranger and one-night stand. I desire more of a man. I desire
more of myself. I desire more of your love. Yours forever. T.*

▼

Tasha found comfort in the library, filling her mind for a future.
When she graduated she would return to the city. It was hard to let go of
Kevin, but she was sure he would remain behind bars to serve black-style
time. She was also sure he was innocent. Kevin was not a perpetrator, but
the victim of another's perpetration. If only she could prove who.

Smuggly, Q waltzed through town with his silly parade and it didn't
seem right one of his best friends was a four-year-old. Kissy was really
irritating, filled with unanswerable questions and she never shut up.

Luckily, Tasha's friendship circle had begun to broaden and Mike and

Amber had invited her to a Friday night river campfire. She hoped she was feeling better. For the last three days she had felt sick.

▼

Ma Lu was peaceful, knowing Gunner was in good hands. He had bestowed upon her a lifetime of memories. Each day she recited Kaddish . . . May His great Name grow exalted and sanctified in the world that He created as He willed. May He give reign to His kingship in your lifetimes and in your days . . .

As Gunner requested she gave Sam the Springfield rifle that he used to shoot volleys. Jared kept his father's 44. She retired his father's flag and now Jared hoisted his brother Josef's Old Glory just as his father and his grandfather had honored other beloved's valor. Gunner's flag carried on at Eden Valley Center, waving proudly on the pole Jared and Q hoisted.

Ma Lu lovingly wrapped the Jones family into her heart and welcomed them into her hearth. She worried for Tasha, there was more than a worry brewing in that child's eyes. She smelled a fear of separation and self-imposed segregation. This talented young woman reminded Ma Lu of a butterfly – a Tiger Butterfly – the most beautiful of all. Perhaps one of her final life acts was to reach out to her. The end of life placed a sensing of order in your path and her time was running short.

She focused on the making of new final memories. Annie announced a soon to be grandbaby and Ali rumored a future son-in-law. She invited Hans to join her to visit Washington DC. He promised to walk the walk of a vet on the Washington Mall from the Vietnam Wall Memorial to the World War II Memorial in honor of Gunner, Josef and Russell. Hans was a dear family friend and with Gunner's passing he'd taken special care to stop by. He understood the loneliness of losing a spouse and a son. He understood the cost of war. But, Washington was not only for Gunner, as promised she would face her own sealed business.

▼

In the world of invisible disabilities, brain injuries and mental illness, only the knowing understand the cries of the innocent. It is a simple oversight to misunderstand neurodiversity when you possess the intellectual power.

It becomes deadly when we are unwilling to face the truth. In the world of race we recognize immediate difference and the values of our creeds are demonstrated in our daily living. Both become visible.

The whitest wall Kevin feared WAS real when his brain refused to connect his vision to the world and somehow his screams flipped the switch of his visual processing into consciousness. His nightmare was only one of many results of a processing disconnect that killed miniscule developing cells and changed his life before he was born. The serial killer, alcohol, joined him to the brotherhood of bootleg – hidden brain damage with symptoms of skewed behaviors – like Margie and Shaun. He was but one of the many babies born each year in the United States, 40,000*, or one in one hundred live births.

It was the invisibilties of damage that murdered his free spirit. His day-to-day world separated him much like the darkest of the whitest walls in our society that most believe is race or creed expressed in tones of skin or adornment. A place of being where prejudice enters when we fear difference instead of embrace commonalities.

The world of incarceration was a secured structured living place and he always did well when his life was ordered. He would serve time. That was pretty funny because he had never lived in time and he had only served Sam's customers. He lived in the present and everyday God gave him a new day decorated in weather of clouds and sunshine.

The jail cell would lock him away from a sociey he never belonged to. He was born locked in an 'other' world of cells uncompleted and disconnected before birth. His greatest fear had always been change and the unknown. Unknown to anyone, in the spring he would have a son, a new member to Kevin's caste.

▼

The past was not forgotten in Riverdale.

To be continued in Tiger Butterfly

*Source: www.nofas.org - National Organization on Fetal Alcohol Syndome

BOOTLEG BROTHERS TRILOGY
BOOKS TWO AND THREE

TIGER BUTTERFLY

While Kevin remains incarcerated, LaMar tries to reconcile his new understanding of his bootleg brother. MaLu works to restore lost beliefs before it's too late and Tasha meets up with Lisa, her blood sister. All is not as it seems as the young women expose the realities of the female transition into adulthood for a person with fetal alcohol spectrum disorder (FASD).

Publication September 2009.

DIFFERENT BEATS

In the conclusion of *The Bootleg Brothers Trilogy*, an unplanned baby surprises the Watkins' household and LaMar and Tamara learn that normal parenting techniques are not effective when raising this child.

Publication September 2010.

SUPPORTING THE CAST

KEVIN
ADULT MALE WITH FASD
ROB WRYBRECHT, LIFE EXPERT WITH FASD

- Realize learning something new can be frustrating and teaching in small steps is the most efficient.
- Seek understanding of a situation before leaping to conclusions or judging.
- If something seems unclear, ask the person to draw, roleplay or say it another way for you.
- Don't forget the cookies!

MARGIE
SINGLE MOTHER WITH FASD
LOIS BICKFORD, FASD LIFE COACH

- Engage persons as an active member in your community — church, social clubs, employment, volunteer services.
- Share community resources. Some things may be difficult — banking and money management, transportation, helping her children with homework, medical and medication needs.
- Find ways to utilize strengths to overcome challenges.

SCREAMS (YOURS NOT THEIRS)
ADOPTIVE MOTHER OF AN ADULT MALE WITH FASD
TERESA KELLERMAN, FASD RESOURCE CENTER
WWW.COME-OVER.TO/FAS/AdultFASDResources.htm

- **S**tructure with daily routine and simple concrete rules.
- **C**ues (many times), verbal, audio, visual, whatever works.
- **R**ole models (family & TV) to show proper way to act.
- **E**nvironment with low sensory stimulation, not too much clutter.
- **A**ttitude of others, understanding that behavior is neurological, not willful misconduct.
- **M**edications, vitamin supplements and healthy diet are quite helpful.
- **S**upervision - lack of impulse control and poor judgment.

S U P P O R T I N G
FASD WEBSITES

To learn more about Fetal Alcohol Spectrum Disorders google –
Fetal Alcohol, FASD, Fetal Alcohol Syndrome, or visit:

- www.nofas.org – National Organization on Fetal Alcohol Syndrome.
- www.fasstar.com – Teresa Kellerman's site for parents and the community.
- www.betterendings.org – Supportive ideas for families and professionals.
- www.cdc.gov/ncbddd/fas – US National Center for Disease Control.

S U P P O R T I N G
MEN & WOMEN IN UNIFORM

- Adopt a person in the military - www.mysoldier.com

By enrolling in the My Soldier program, participants agree to adopt a soldier as a pen pal. They receive a "starter kit" with guidelines for writing letters to their deployed soldier in the United States Armed Forces and a red My Soldier bracelet to publicly show their support for American troops.

S U P P O R T I N G
MEN & WOMEN RETURNING HOME

- Your time together is what is most important. Be a concerned listener.
- Include the veteran in normal activites and events – (fishing, biking, picnics, birthdays, sporting events) – give space for declining some invitations.
- Realize not all injuries are visible and all wounds take time to heal.
- If the veteran has experienced major combat episodes realize there may be hearing loss or traumatic brain injury.

DISCUSSION TOPICS FOR BOOK CLUBS
THE WHITEST WALL

1. Discuss the significance of the whitest wall? Do you have a whitest wall?

2. Which characters had brain injuries and how did they occur? How do you think it affected their lives?

3. Do you believe Doc's murder was accidental? What do you think really happened?

4. How did the author illustrate the realities of common visible prejudice in comparison of an invisible disability?

5. Do you believe the whitest wall Kevin experienced was made up? Why?

6. Do you believe Kevin will be incarcerated or released? When?

7. Discuss how life experiences in the past can cloud the reality of the present?

8. How does Gunner influence Q's life? Do you believe this is possible?

9. How do you believe LaMar will handle his new reality?

10. What do you believe is Ma Lu's mission in Washington DC? What secret has she been hiding?

11. What insights have you gained by reading *The Whitest Wall*? Has it changed your life or perception in any way?

12. *The Whitest Wall* contains parallel characters, who are they and how are they similar? Different?

13. What are the metaphors the author uses in *The Whitest Wall*?

14. Gunner left Q with unanswered riddles? Did he figure them all out?

15. What is the symbolism of the cover?

16. What is the definition of Bootleg?

Note to teaching professionals:

Mrs. Kulp speaks to colleges and high school classes, adoption and foster parents, civic groups and police departments on Fetal Alcohol Spectrum Disorders. For information about incorporating *The Whitest Wall* into class curriculum or lesson plans visit: www.betterendings.org.

ABOUT THE AUTHOR

JODEE KULP

Jodee Kulp is an international award winning speaker and advocate for families and persons with Fetal Alcohol Spectrum Disorders (FASD). She has presented in United States, Australia, Canada, and Sweden. She served on the Board of Directors of the Minnesota Organization of Fetal Alcohol Spectrum Disorders (www.mofas.org) for ten years. Mrs. Kulp is the author or co-author of eight books supporting healthy and creative approaches to living with FASD.

Together, Karl and Jodee help professionals and families utilize strategies to support young people and adults with this often hidden disability. They currently live in the Midwest with a camaraderie of canines, felines and avians.

BETTER ENDINGS NEW BEGINNINGS

Giving ordinary people, extraordinary voices to show that better endings are possible and new beginnings can be achieved with powerful stories to inspire, build hope and provide wisdom to change the world one person at a time.

JOIN LIBERTY VOICES BOOKCLUB
VISIT WWW.BETTERENDINGS.ORG

QUANTITY BOOK PURCHASE AVAILABLE
FOR CLASSROOM USE